THE JUDGING EYE

PRAISE FOR R. SCOTT BAKKER

"[R. Scott Bakker is a] class act like George R. R. Martin, or his fellow Canadians Steven Erikson and Guy Gavriel Kay. He gets right away from the 'downtrodden youth becoming king' aspect of epic fantasy in his very impressive first novel – *The Darkness That Comes Before* . . . Odd, fascinating characters in a world full of trouble and sorcery" "10 Authors to Watch", *SFX Magazine*

"*The Warrior Prophet* . . . leaves most of the competition trailing" *Guardian*

"Bakker's challenging debut, the first in a new trilogy in the Tolkien tradition, gratifies those weary of formulaic epic fantasy" *Publishers Weekly*

"*The Darkness That Comes Before* is a strikingly original work, the start of a series to watch" *SF Site*

"Exquisitely intelligent and beautifully written, R. Scott Bakker's first novel in The Prince of Nothing series inspires both confidence and anticipation – this is fantasy with muscle and brains, rife with intrigue and admirable depth of charact
history and detail. Take nc
has begun here . . ." Steven

By R. Scott Bakker

The Prince of Nothing Series
The Darkness That Comes Before
The Warrior-Prophet
The Thousandfold Thought

The Aspect-Emperor Series
The Judging Eye

Neuropath (writing as Scott Bakker)

R·SCOTT BAKKER

THE JUDGING EYE

Book One of
The Aspect-Emperor Series

www.orbitbooks.net

ORBIT

First published in Great Britain in 2009 by Orbit
Reprinted 2009 (twice), 2010

A CIP catalogue record for this book is available from the British Library.

ISBN 978-1-84149-538-5

Typeset in Goudy by Palimpsest Book Production Limited, Grangemouth, Stirlingshire

Printed in the UK by CPI Mackays, Chatham ME5 8TD

Papers used by Orbit are natural, renewable and recyclable products sourced from well-managed forests and certified in accordance with the rules of the Forest Stewardship Council.

Orbit
An imprint of
Little, Brown Book Group
100 Victoria Embankment
London EC4Y 0DY

An Hachette UK Company
www.hachette.co.uk

www.orbitbooks.net

To Ricky—friend and brother

But who are you, man, to answer God thus? Will what is made say to him who made it—Why have you made me this way? Does the potter not have power over his clay, to make, from the same mass, one vessel for honour, and another for dishonour?

ROMANS 9:20–21

Contents

Prologue 3

Chapter 1: Sakarpus 19
Chapter 2: Hûnoreal 46
Chapter 3: Momemn 66
Chapter 4: Hûnoreal 100
Chapter 5: Momemn 125
Chapter 6: Marrow 152
Chapter 7: Sakarpus 190
Chapter 8: The River Rohil 219
Chapter 9: Momemn 244
Chapter 10: Condia 270
Chapter 11: The Osthwai Mountains 295
Chapter 12: The Andiamine Heights 309
Chapter 13: Condia 325
Chapter 14: Cil-Aujas 348
Chapter 15: Condia 406
Chapter 16: Cil-Aujas 428

Interlude: Momemn 495

Appendices

Character and Faction Glossary 498
What Has Come Before . . . 503

Acknowledgments 511

Map of the Kellian Empire in
4132 Year-of-the-Tusk 512-513

Exalt-Minister, most glorious, many be your days.

For the sin of apostasy, they were buried up to their necks in the ancient way, and stones were cast into their faces until their breathing was stopped. Three men and two women. The child recanted, even cursed his parents in the name of our glorious Aspect-Emperor. The World has lost five souls, but the Heavens have gained one, praise be the God of Gods.

As for the text, I fear that your prohibition has come too late. It was, as you suspected, an account of the First Holy War as witnessed by the exiled Schoolman, Drusas Achamian. Verily, my hand trembles at the prospect of reproducing his vile and abhorrent claims, but as the original text has already been committed to the flames, I see no other way to satisfy your request. You are quite correct: Heresy is rarely singular in its essence or its effects. As with diseases, deviations must be studied, curatives prepared, lest they erupt in more virulent form.

For the sake of brevity, I will limit my review to those particulars that either directly or indirectly contradict Doctrine and Scripture. In this text, Drusas Achamian claims:

I) To have had sexual congress with our Holy Empress on the eve of the First Holy War's triumph over the heathen Fanim at Shimeh.

II) To have learned certain secrets regarding our Holy Aspect-Emperor, to whit: That He is not the incarnation of the

God of Gods but rather a son of the Dûnyain, a secret sect devoted to the mastery of all things, body and spirit. That He transcends us not as gods transcend men, but as adults transcend children. That His Zaudunyani interpretation of Inrithism is nothing more than a tool, a means for the manipulation of nations. That ignorance has rendered us His slaves.

(I admit to finding this most unnerving, for though I have always known that words and events, no matter how holy, always admit wicked interpretations, I have never before considered the way beliefs command our actions. For as this Achamian asks, if all men lay claim to righteousness, and they do, who is to say which man claims true? The conviction, the belief unto death, of those I send from the world now troubles me, such is the treachery of the idle intellect.)

III) That our Holy Aspect-Emperor's war to prevent the resurrection of the No-God is false. Granted, this is merely implied, since the text was plainly written before the Great Ordeal. But the fact that Drusus Achamian was once a Mandate Schoolman, and so cursed with dreams of the First Apocalypse, renders his suspicions extraordinary. Should not such a man hail the coming of Anasûrimbor Kellhus and his war to prevent the Second Apocalypse?

This is the sum of what I remember.

Having suffered this blasphemy, I understand the profundity of your concern. To hear that everything we have endured and cherished these past twenty years of war and revelation has been a lie is outrage enough. But to hear such from a man who not only walked with our Master in the beginning, but taught him as well? I have already ordered the execution of my body-slave, though I mourn him, for he only read the text at my behest. As for myself, I await your summary judgment. I neither beg nor expect your pardon: It is our doom to suffer the consequences of our acts, regardless of the piety of our intentions.

Some pollution begs not the cloth, but the knife; this I accept and understand.

Sin is sin.

Prologue

When a man possesses the innocence of a child, we call him a fool.
When a child possesses the cunning of a man, we call him an abomination. As with love, knowledge has its season.

—AJENCIS, *THE THIRD ANALYTIC OF MEN*

Autumn, 19 New Imperial Year (4131 Year-of-the-Tusk), the "Long Side"

A horn pealed long and lonely beneath the forest canopies. A human horn.

For a moment all was quiet. Limbs arched across the imperious heights, and great trunks bullied the hollows beneath. Shorn saplings thatched the intervening spaces. A squirrel screeched warning from the gloom of interlocking branches. Starlings burst into the squinting sky.

They came, flickering across bands of sunlight and shadow.

Running with rutting fury, howling with rutting fury, through the lashing undergrowth, into the tabernacle deep. They swarmed over pitched slopes, kicking up leaves and humus. They parted about the trunks, chopping at the bark with rust-pitted blades. They sniffed the sky with slender noses. When they grimaced, their blank and beautiful faces were clenched like crumpled silk, becoming the expressions of ancient and inbred men.

Sranc. Bearing shields of lacquered human leather. Wearing corselets scaled with human fingernails and necklaces of human teeth.

The distant horn sounded again, and they paused, a vicious milling rabble. Words were barked among them. A number melted into the undergrowth, loping with the swiftness of wolves. The others jerked at their groins in anticipation. Blood. They could smell mannish blood.

Seed jetted black across the forest floor. They stamped it into the muck. They exulted in the stink of it.

The scouts returned, and at their jabbering the others shuddered and convulsed. It had been so long since they had last glutted their rapacious hunger. So long since they knelt at the altar of jerking limbs and mewling flesh. They could see the panicked faces. They could see the gushing blood, the knife-made orifices.

They ran, weeping for joy.

Cresting a low ridge, they found their prey hastening along the base of a back-broken cliff, trying to make their way to the far side of a gorge that opened as though by miracle several hundred paces away. The Sranc howled and chattered their teeth, raced in wild files down the slope, skidding across leaves, their legs kicking in long leaps. They hit the ground where it flattened, scrambling, running, burning hard in their rotten breeches, watching the soft Men turning mere paces before them, their faces as enticing as thighs, coming closer and closer, almost within the circle of wild-swinging swords—

But the ground! The ground! Collapsing beneath them, like leaves thrown across sky!

Dozens of them were sucked shrieking into the black. The others clutched and jostled, tried to stop, only to be bumped screeching by their crazed kin. Their screams trailed as they plummeted into the concealed gorge, popped into silence one by one. Suddenly all was uncertain, all was threat. The war-party yammered in fear and frustration. None dared move. Eyes rolling, they stared in lust and apprehension . . .

Men.

A hard-bitten handful, running as though by magic across the false forest floor. They lunged into the Sranc's midst, their heavy swords high and pitching. Shields cracked. Mouldered iron was bent and broken. Limbs and heads were thrown on arcs of glittering blood.

The Men roared and bellowed, hammered them to earth, hacked them to twitching ruin.

"Scalper!" the lone traveller cried out. His voice possessed the gravel of an old officer's bawl. It boomed through the gorge, easily audible over the white roar of water. As one, the men upriver stood and stared in his direction.

Just like animals, he thought.

Indifferent to their gaze, he continued picking his way along the treacherous stones, sloshing through water every several steps. He passed a Sranc, white as a drowned fish, floating face down in a pool of translucent red.

The traveller glanced up to where the gorge walls pinched the sky into a wandering slot. Trees had been felled across the opening, forming the rafters for an improvised ceiling of saplings and sticks, covered over with leaves. The sky glared bright through numerous holes. Leaves still twittered down in a steady cascade. If the numbers of inert forms scattered and heaped about the rocks were any indication, it had been a very effective trap. In places, the river's foam spouted pink and violet.

Most of the men had returned to their work, but three

continued to watch him warily. He had no doubt that the one he sought was among them.

The traveller tramped into their midst. The smell of burst entrails soured that of water and scoured stone. Most of the party sorted through the dead Sranc. Bodies were kicked off bodies. Broken heads were pulled from the water. Knives flashed. It was the same each time: pinch, saw, swipe, then on to the next one. Pinch, saw, swipe—again and again. A flap of skin cut from the crown of every one.

Nearby, a young Galeoth swordsman washed a small hoard of scalps. He rinsed them, then laid them out, glistening and fatty white across dry stone. He handled each swatch with ludicrous care, the way a halfwit might handle gold—which scalps had pretty much become in the High Middle-North. Though the Aspect-Emperor had lowered the Hallow Bounty, a scalp still fetched a full silver kellic from honest brokers.

They were all extremely conscious of his arrival, the traveller knew. They simply pretended to be indifferent. Usually, they encountered outsiders only when they trekked south to the brokers, flush with hundreds of tanned scalps, bound and dangling from lengths of leather string. This work, the work of collecting and counting, was the least manly portion of their trade. It was their menial secret.

It was also the point.

Nearly eleven years had passed since the Aspect-Emperor had declared his bounty on Sranc scalps, before the last of the Unification Wars had ended. He placed the bounty on Sranc because of their vast numbers. He placed the bounty on scalps because their hairlessness made them distinctive to Sranc. Men such as these, the traveller supposed, would be far happier poaching something less inclined to kill back—like women and children.

So began the Scalping Years. Over that time, countless

thousands had trudged into the northern wilderness, expedition after expedition, come to make their fortune as Scalpoi. Most died in a matter of weeks. But those who learned, who were wily and every bit as ruthless as their foe, prospered.

And some—a few—became legendary.

The man the traveller sought stood upon a rounded stone, watching the others work. He knew him from his dogged devotion to the traditional costume of his caste and race: the pleated war-skirt, stained grey and black and shot through with holes; the corselet with rusty scales stitched into rotting leather; the conical helm, bent back like a single ram's horn. He looked a wraith from another age. A second man, his face concealed by a black cowl, sat three paces behind him, leaning forward as though straining to hear something in the water's ambient rush. The traveller peered at him for a moment, as though trying to judge some peculiarity, then returned his gaze to the first man.

"I'm looking for the Ainoni," he said. "The one they call Ironsoul."

"That would be me," the standing man replied. His face had been tattooed with the cosmetics favoured by his countrymen. Black lines about his eyes. Purpled lips. His look neither accused nor questioned but remained mild in the manner of bored assassins. Incurious.

"Veteran," the traveller said, bowing his head in due respect. Failing to properly acknowledge and venerate a survivor of the First Holy War was no small offence.

"How did you find us?" the man asked in his native tongue. From the cadence of his voice, it was obvious that he despised speaking, that he was as jealous of his voice as he was of his women or his blood.

The traveller did not care. Men prized what they would.

"We find everyone."

A barely perceptible nod. "What do you want?"

"You, Scalper. We want you."

The Ainoni glanced back toward his cowled companion. No words were exchanged, only an inscrutable look.

***

Late Autumn, 19 New Imperial Year (4131 Year-of-the-Tusk), Momemn

Ever do Men seek to hide what is base and mean in their natures. This is why they talked of wolves or lions or even dragons when they likened themselves to animals. But it was the lowly beetle, the young boy decided, whom they most resembled. Belly to the ground. Back hunched against the world. Eyes blind to everything save the small circle before them.

His Whelming complete, Anasûrimbor Kelmomas crouched in the granite shadows, leaning between his knees to better watch the insect scuttle across the ancient floor. One of the great iron candle-wheels hung soundless between the pillars above, but its light was little more than a dull gleam across the beetle's wagging back. Holding his knees, Kelmomas shuffled forward, absorbed by the insect's tiny terrestrial struggles. Despite the gloomy forest of columns behind him, the choral voices sounded as close as his many shadows, singing hymns to frame the more fulsome reverberations of the Temple Prayer.

Sweet God of Gods
Who walk among us
Innumerable are your holy names . . .

"Show me," Kelmomas whispered to the beetle. "Lead . . ."

Together they wandered into the deeper recesses of the Allosium, to where only the floating pinpricks of the godhouse votives illuminated the gloom. The beetle clambered about a column's graven base, left tracks that resembled sutures across a swatch of dust—tracks that Kelmomas obliterated with his small sandalled foot. Soon they reached the Forum's outermost aisle, where the idols of the Hundred Gods resided in their adorned recesses.

"Where are you going?" he murmured, smiling. He glimpsed the gauze of his exhalation on the chill air, puffed two breaths just to consider his breathing—spectral proof of material life. He laid his cheek to the cool tile and stared out across the vast plain of the aisle. The glazing soothed his skin. Quite oblivious to his scrutiny, the beetle continued its trek, tipping in and out of the joints between the cerulean tiles. Kelmomas watched it toil toward the leering mountain that was the idol of Ajokli, the Four-Horned Brother.

"The *Thief?*"

Compared to that of his brothers and sisters, the godhouse of Ajokli was as poor as a crippled fuller. The floor tiles stopped at the threshold. The stonework rimming the recess was bare, save for a series of notches scratched into the right post. The idol—a horned little fat man crouching as though over a chamberpot—was not much more than a play of shadow and gleam emerging from the velvet darkness. It was carved of black diorite, but without the jewelled eyes or silver fingernails that even Yatwer boasted. Rigid with the sensibilities of some long-dead artisan, its expression struck Kelmomas as improbable, if not outright inhuman. Grinning like a monkey. Snarling like a dog. Staring like a dew-eyed virgin.

It also watched the beetle as it scurried into its gloomy bower.

The young Prince-Imperial skipped into the cramped recess, ducking even though the decorative vaults reached far above his head. The air smelled of tallow, dusty stone and something coppery. He smiled at the graven God, nodded more than bowed, then assumed much the same posture, crouching over his witless subject. Moved by some unaccountable whim, he pinned the beetle to the gritty floor with his index finger. It writhed like a little automaton beneath his fingertip. He held it for a moment, savouring its impotence, the knowledge that he could, at any moment, crush it like a rotted seed. Then, with his other hand, he pinched off two of its legs.

"Watch," he whispered to the laughing idol. Its eyes gazed down, blank and bulbous.

He raised his hand, fingers outstretched in a dramatic flourish. The beetle scrambled in shining panic, but the arrow of its course had been bent, so that it chipped around and around, sketching little ovals at the idol's stump-toed feet. Around and around.

"*See?*" he exclaimed to Ajokli. They laughed together, child and idol, loud enough to blot out the chorus of chanting voices.

"They're *all* like that," he explained. "All you have to do is *pinch*."

"Pinch what, Kelmomas?" a rich, feminine voice asked from behind him. Mother.

Another boy would have been startled, even ashamed, to be surprised by his mother after doing such a thing, but not Kelmomas. Despite the obscuring pillars and voices, he had known where she was all along, following her prim footsteps (though he knew not how) in a corner of his soul.

"Are you *done?*" he exclaimed, whirling. Her body-slaves had painted her white, so that she looked like statuary beneath the folds of her crimson gown. A girdle etched with Kyranean motifs cinched her waist. A headdress of jade serpents framed her cheeks and pressed order on her luxurious black hair. But even disguised like this she seemed the world's most beautiful thing.

"Quite done," the Empress replied. She smiled and secretly

rolled her eyes, letting him know that she would much rather dote on her precocious son than languish in the company of priests and ministers. So much of what she did, Kelmomas knew, she did for the sake of appearances.

Just like him—only not nearly so well.

"You prefer *my company*, don't you, Mommy?"

He spoke this as a question even though he knew the answer; it troubled her when he read aloud the movements of her soul.

Smiling, she bent and held out her arms. He fell into her myrrh-scented embrace, breathed deep her encompassing warmth. Her fingers combed through his unkempt hair, and he looked up into her smiling gaze. Even so far from the candle-wheels she seemed to shine. He pressed his cheek against the golden-plates of her girdle, held her so tight that tears were squeezed from his eyes. Never was there such a beacon, it seemed. Never was there such a sanctuary.

Mommy . . .

"Come," she said, drawing him by the hand back through the pillared gallery. He followed, more out of devotion than obedience. He glanced back for one last look at Ajokli, saw with satisfaction that he still laughed at the little beetle scuttling in circles at his feet.

Hand in hand, they walked toward the slots of white light. The singing had trailed into a gaggle of hushed voices, and a deeper, more forbidding resonance had risen to take its place—one that shivered through the very floor. Kelmomas paused, suddenly loath to leave the Allosium's dust-and-stone quiet. His mother's arm was drawn out like a rope behind her; their interlocked fingers broke apart.

She turned. "Kel? What's wrong, sweetling?"

From where he stood a bar of white sky framed her, reaching as high as any tree. She seemed little more than smoke beneath it, something any draft could dissolve and carry away. "Nothing," he lied.

Mommy! Mommy!

Kneeling before him, she licked the pads of her fingers, which were palm-pink against the white painted across the backs of her hands, and began fussing with his hair. Light twittered across the filigree of her rings, flashing like some kind of code. *Such a mess!* her grin said.

"It's proper that you be anxious," she said, distracted by her ministrations. She looked him square in the eye, and he stared into the pith of her, past the paint and skin, past the sheath of interlocking muscles, down to the radiant truth of her love.

She would die for you, the secret voice—the voice that had been within him always—whispered.

"Your father," she continued, "says that we need fear only when we lose our fear." She ran her hand from his temple to his chin. "When we become too accustomed to power and luxury."

Father was forever saying things.

He smiled, looked down in embarrassment, in the way that never failed to slow her pulse and quicken her eyes. An adorable little son on the surface, even as he sneered beneath.

Father.

Hate him, the secret voice said, *but fear him more.*

Yes, the Strength. He must never forget that the Strength burned brightest in Father.

"Was ever a mother so blessed?" The Empress beamed, clutching his shoulders. She hugged him once more, then stood with his hands cupped in her own. He allowed her, reluctantly, to tow him out to the towering eaves of the Allosium, then beyond, into the sunless brilliance.

Flanked by scarlet formations of Eöthic Guardsmen, they stood blinking upon the crest of the monumental steps that fanned down to the expanse of the Scuari Campus. The long-weathered temples and tenements of Momemn crowded the horizon, growing indistinct the deeper they plumbed the humid distance. The great domes of the Temple Xothei rose chill and dark, a hazy, hulking presence in the heart of mud-brick warrens. The adjacent Kamposea Agora was little more than a gap in the rotted teeth of interposing streetscapes.

On and on it went, the vast and mottled vista of the Home City, the great capital of all the Three Seas. For his entire life it had encircled him, hedged him with its teeming intricacies. And for his entire life it had frightened him, so much so that he often refused to look when Samarmas, his idiot twin, pointed to something unnoticed in its nebulous weave.

But today it seemed the only safe thing.

"Look!" his mother cried through the roar. "Look, Kel!"

There were thousands of them packed throughout the Imperial Precincts: women, children, slaves, the healthy and the infirm, Momemnites and pilgrims from afar—uncounted thousands of them. Churning like floodwaters about the base of the Xatantian Arch. Crushed against the lower compounds of the Andiamine Heights. Perched like crows along the low walls of the Garrison. All of them crying out, two fingers raised to touch his image.

"Think of how far they have come!" his mother cried through the tumult. "From across all the New Empire, Kelmomas, come to witness your divinity!"

Though he nodded with the bewildered gratitude he knew she expected from him, the young Prince-Imperial felt nothing save brittle revulsion. Only fools, he decided, travelled in circles. Part of him wished he could drag the Grinning God out of his shrine to show him . . .

People were bugs.

They weathered the adulation for what seemed ages,

standing side by side in their proscribed places, Esmenet, Empress of the Three Seas, and the youngest of her exalted children. Kelmomas looked up as he was taught, idly followed the course of pinprick pigeons against the smoke rising from the city. He watched sunlight gather distant rooftops in the wake of a retreating cloud. He decided he would ask for a model of the city when his mother was weak and eager to indulge. Something made of wood.

Something that would burn.

Thopsis, their Shigeki Master of Protocol, raised his massive eunuch arms, and the Imperial Apparati arrayed on the steps below turned as one toward them. The gold-ribbed Prayer Horns sounded, resonating through the roaring chorus. They had been fixed at intervals in the shadow of the Allosium's facade, fashioned of jet and ivory and so long they nearly reached to the second landing.

Kelmomas looked down across his father's Exalt-Ministers, saw everything from lust and tenderness to hatred and avarice in their blank faces. There was lumbering Ngarau, the Grand Seneschal from the Ikurei days. Phinersa, the Holy Master of Spies, a plain yet devious man of Kianene stock. The blue-tattooed Imhailas, the statuesque Exalt-Captain of the Eöthic Guard, whose beauty sometimes turned his mother's eye. The ever-cantankerous Werjau, the Prime Nascenti and ruler of the powerful Ministrate, whose far-flung agents ensured none went astray. The emaciated Vem-Mithriti, Grandmaster of Imperial Saik and Vizier-in-Proxy, which made him the temporary master of all things arcane in the Three Seas . . .

On and on, all sixty-seven of them, arranged in order of precedence along the monumental stair, gathered to witness the Whelming of Anasûrimbor Kelmomas, the youngest son of their Most Holy Aspect-Emperor. Only the face of his Uncle Maithanet, the Shriah of the Thousand Temples, defeated his momentary scrutiny. For an instant, his uncle's shining look caught his own, and though Kelmomas smiled with a daft candour appropriate to his age, he did not at all like the flat consistency of the Shriah's gaze.

He suspects, the secret voice whispered.

Suspects what?

That you are make-believe.

The last of the cacophony faded, until only the oceanic call of the Horns remained, thrumming so deep that Kelmomas's tunic seemed to tingle against his skin. Then they too trailed into nothing.

Ear-ringing silence. With a cry from Thopsis, the whole world seemed to kneel, including the Exalt-Ministers. The peoples of the New Empire fell to the ground, fields of them, then slowly lowered their foreheads to the hot marble—every soul crowded into the Imperial Precincts. Only the Shriah, who knelt before no man save the Aspect-Emperor, remained standing. Only Uncle Maithanet. When the sun broke across the stair, his vestments flared with light: A hundred tiny Tusks kindled like fingers of flame. Kelmomas blinked at their brilliance, averted his eyes.

His mother led him down the steps by the hand. He clapped after her with his sandalled feet, giggled at her frown. They passed down the aisle opened between the Exalt-Ministers, and he laughed some more, struck by the absurdity of them, all shapes and ages and sizes, grovelling in the costumes of kings.

"They honour you, Kel," his mother said. "Why would you laugh at them?"

Had he meant to laugh? Sometimes it was hard to keep count.

"Sorry," he said with a glum sigh. *Sorry*. It was one of many words that confused him, but it never failed to spark compassion in his mother's look.

At the base of the monumental stair, a company of green-and-gold-dressed soldiers awaited them: some twenty men of his father's hallowed bodyguard, the Hundred Pillars. They fell into formation about the Empress and her child, then, their shields bright and their looks fierce with concentration, they began leading them through the masses and across the Scuari Campus toward the Andiamine Heights.

As a Prince-Imperial, Kelmomas often found himself overshadowed by armed men, but the walk unnerved him for some reason. The smell was comforting at first: the perfumed muslin of their surcoats, the oils they used to quicken their blades and soften the leather straps of their harness. But with every step, the bitter-sweet bitumen of unwashed bodies came more and more to the fore, punctuated by the reek of the truly wretched. Murmurs rose like a haze about them. "*Bless-bless-bless*," over and over, in a tone poised between asking and giving. Kelmomas found himself staring past the towering guards, out across the landscape of kneelers. He saw an old beggar, more husked than clothed, weeping, grinding his face against the cobbles as though trying to blot himself out. He saw a girl only slightly younger than himself, her head turned in sacrilege, so that she could stare up at their monstrous passage. On and on the prostrate figures went, out to distant foundations.

He walked across a living ground.

And then he was among them, *in them*, watching his own steps, little more than a jewelled shadow behind a screen of merciless, chain-armoured men. A name. A rumour and a hope. A god-child, suckled at the breast of Empire, anointed by the palm of Fate. A son of the Aspect-Emperor.

They did not know him, he realized. They saw, they worshipped, they *trusted* what they could not fathom.

No one knows you, the secret voice said.

No one knows anyone.

He glanced at his mother, saw the blank stare that always accompanied her more painful reveries.

"Are you thinking of her, Mommy?" he asked. Between the two of them, "her" always meant Mimara, her first daughter, the one she loved with the most desperation—and hated.

The one the secret voice had told him to drive away.

The Empress smiled with a kind of sad relief. "I worry for your father and your brothers too."

This, Kelmomas could plainly see, was a lie. She fretted for Mimara—even still, after all he had done.

Perhaps, the voice said, *you should have killed the bitch.*

"When will Father return?"

He knew the answer at least as well as she did, but at some level he understood that as much as mothers love their sons, they loved *being mothers* as well—and being a mother meant answering childish questions. They travelled several yards before she replied, passing through a fog of pleas and whispers. Kelmomas found himself comparing her to the countless cameos he had seen depicting her in her youth—back in the days of the First Holy War. Her hips were wider, perhaps, and her skin not so smooth beneath the veneer of white paint, but her beauty was legendary still. The seven-year-old could scarce imagine anyone more beautiful.

"Not for some time, Kel," she said. "Not until the Great Ordeal is completed."

He nearly clutched his breast, such was the ache, the joy.

If he fails, the secret voice said, *he will die*.

Anasûrimbor Kelmomas smiled what seemed his first true smile of the day.

Kneelers all around, their backs broken by awe. A plain of abject humanity. "*Bless-bless-bless*," rising like whispers in a sick-house. Then a single, savage cry: "Curse! *Curse!*"

Somehow a madman managed to plunge past the shields and blades, to reach out, punctured and failing, with a knife that reflected shining sky. The Pillarian Guardsmen traded shouts. The crowds heaved and screamed. The young boy glimpsed battling shadows.

Assassins.

Chapter One

Sakarpus

upon the high wall the husbands slept,
while 'round the hearth their women wept,
and fugitives murmured tales of woe,
of greater cities lost to Mog-Pharau . . .

—"THE REFUGEE'S SONG," *THE SAGAS*

Early Spring, 19 New Imperial Year (4132 Year-of-the-Tusk), the Kathol Passes

The tracks between whim and brutality are many and inscrutable in Men, and though they often seem to cut across the impassable terrain of reason, in truth, it is reason that paves their way. Ever do Men argue from want to need and from need to fortuitous warrant. Ever do they think their cause the just cause. Like cats chasing sunlight thrown from a mirror, they never tire of their own delusions.

At the behest of their Holy Aspect-Emperor, the priests of the Thousand Temples harangued their congregations, and the Judges of the Ministrate scoured the land, seeking out and destroying all those who would either dispute the Truth or choose avarice over the mortal demands of the darkness to come. Everyone, whether caste-slave or caste-noble, was taught the Great Chain of Missions, how the words and works of each made possible the words and works of the other. They learned how Men, all Men, warred all the time, whether tilling fields or loving their kin. All lives, no matter how humble, were links that either fortified the Great Chain or impaired it, leading to the First Ring, the link from which the world itself hung: the Holy War against the apocalyptic designs of the Consult . . .

Or as it came to be called, the Great Ordeal.

Never, not even in the days of Far Antiquity, had the world seen the assembly of such a host. *Ten years* were devoted to its preparation. To prevent the resurrection of the No-God, they had to destroy his foul slaves, the Consult, and to destroy them, they had to march the length of Eärwa, from the northern frontiers of the New Empire, across the Srancinfested Wilds of the Ancient North, all the way to their stronghold, Golgotterath, which the Nonmen had called Min-Uroikas in days long dead, the Pit of Obscenities.

It was a mad endeavour. Only children and fools, who confused tales of war with war itself, could think the task simple. For them, war was battle, and they always squinted in surprise when veterans spoke of latrines and cannibalism and gangrenous feet and so on. Even the most illustrious knights required food, as did the horses they rode, as did the pack mules that carried the food, as did the slaves who served it. Food was required to transport food—the problem was as simple as this. Without some intensive system of supply—relays, depots, and the like—the amount consumed would quickly exceed the amount carried. This was why the most arduous battle waged by the Great Ordeal would not be against the Consult legions, but against Eärwa's own wild heart. The host would have to survive the *distance* to Golgotterath before it could be tested on the field.

For years, the New Empire groaned beneath the demands of their holy sovereign's prophecy. Tithes of food were exacted from all the provinces. Vast granaries were constructed above the third cataract of the Vindauga River. Herds of sheep and cattle were driven northward, along coastal trails that soon became favourite topics for court minstrels. In the Home City, mathematicians scribbled indentures, summons, requisitions, and Kings and Judges seized what was needed in faraway lands. The records were stored in great mud-brick warehouses and cared for with the fastidiousness of religious ritual. Everything was numbered.

The call to arms did not come till the last.

Across the Three Seas the Zaudunyani took up the Circumfix, the holy symbol of their Aspect-Emperor: the knights of Conriya, masked and long-skirted, the disciplined columnaries of Nansur, the axmen of Thunyerus, wild-haired and ferocious, the peerless horsemen of Kian, and on and on. The sons of a dozen nations converged on Oswenta, the hoary old capital of Galeoth, bearing rough-painted or finely wrought representations of the Tusk and Circumfix. The sorcerous Schools sent their contingents as well: the haughty magi of the Scarlet Spires, borne in their silk-panelled litters, the dour witches of the Swayal Compact, the robed processions of the Imperial Saik, and, of course, the Gnostic sorcerers of the Mandate, who had been raised from fools to priests by the coming of the Warrior-Prophet.

The children of Oswenta marvelled. In streets choked with newcomers, they saw Nilnameshi princes in their palanquins, Ainoni Count-Palatines with their white-painted retinues, religious madmen of every description, and once, even a towering mastodon that sent horses bolting like dogs. They saw all the ornament, all the pomp and demonstration of ancient and faraway customs, thrown together and made a carnival. The bowl of each nation had spilled, and now their distinct and heady flavours swirled together, continually surprising the palette with some unheard-of combination. Long-bearded Tydonni throwing the number-sticks with wire-limbed Khirgwi. Kutnarmi monkeys climbing the gowns of Shigeki witches.

A summer and an autumn passed organizing the host. Though a generation had come and gone, the Aspect-Emperor and his advisers remembered well the lessons of the First Holy War. The Unification Wars, with their setbacks and victories and butchered cities, had produced a corps of shrewd and ruthless Zaudunyani officers, all of whom were made Judges and granted the power of life and death over the faithful. Trespasses were not forgiven—too much hung in the balance for the Shortest Path not to be taken. Mercy required a certain future, and for Men, there was none. Two Consult skin-spies were discovered, thanks to the divine insight of the Aspect-Emperor and his children. They were flayed before booming, riotous masses.

The Great Ordeal wintered at the headwaters of the Vindauga River, in the city of Harwash, which had been an entrepôt for the Twelve-Pelt Road, the famed caravan route connecting Galeoth to the ancient and isolate cities of Sakarpus and Atrithau, but was now little more than a vast barracks and supply depot. The season was hard. Despite all the precautions, dread Akkeägni, Disease, fondled the host with his Many Hands, and some twenty thousand souls were lost to a version of lung-plague common to the humid rice plains of Nilnamesh.

It was, the Aspect-Emperor explained, but the first of many tests.

The days began to thaw what the nights yet froze. Preparations intensified. The order to march was a fervent occasion of tears and joyous shouts. There is a taste to these things. The wills of men coalesce, become one, and the *air knows*. The God did not only create the created, He created the *act* of creation as well, the souls that dwell within men. Should it be any surprise that the world of things answered the world of intents? The Great Ordeal marched, and the very earth, rising from dreary winter slumber, bent knee and rejoiced. The Men of the Ordeal could feel it: an approving world, a judging world.

The host advanced in two stages. King Saubon of Caraskand, one of the Holy War's two Exalt-Generals, marched first, taking the quicker elements of the host—the Kianene, the Girgashi, the Khirgwi, and the Shrial Knights—and none of the slower, which included the sorcerous Schools. The Aspect-Emperor's second eldest son, Anasûrimbor Kayûtas, rode with him, leading the famed Kidruhil, the most celebrated heavy calvary cohort in the Three Seas. The Sakarpic host melted away before them, leaving only several companies of Long-Riders, their fleet and devious skirmishers, to harass their advance. The decisive engagement the Exalt-General hoped for never happened.

King Proyas of Conriya, the Ordeal's other Exalt-General, followed with the bulk of the host. Jubilant, the Men of the New Empire marched into the Kathol Passes, which formed the armature of two great mountains ranges, the Hethantas to the west and the Osthwai to the east. The column was too long for any real communication between its forward and rear elements—no rider could press through the masses quickly enough. The scarps climbed to either side, stacked to the timberline.

It snowed the fourth night, when the priests and judges led ceremonies commemorating the Battle of the Pass, where an ancient alliance of refugee Men and the Nonmen of Cil-Aujas had defeated the No-God in the First Apocalypse, so purchasing the World a year of precious respite. Nothing was said of the subsequent betrayal and the extermination of the Nonmen at the hands of those they had saved.

They sang of their devotion, the Men of the Ordeal, heart-breaking hymns composed by the Aspect-Emperor himself. They sang of their own might, of the doom they would deliver to the faraway gates of their enemy. They sang of their wives, their children, about the smaller pockets of the wider world they marched to save. In the evenings, the great bell they called the Interval tolled, and the Singers cried out the calls to prayer, their sweet voices rising across the far-flung fields of tents and pavillions. Hard men shed their gear and gathered beneath Circumfix banners. Noble knelt with slave or menial. The Shrial Priests gave their sermons and benedictions, and the Judges watched.

They spent several days filing through the final stages of the Pass, then descended the sill of the mountains. They crossed the thawing fields of Sagland, where the retreating Sakarpi had burned anything that could be of use to them. Overmatched, the King of Sakarpus had no recourse save the ancient and venerable weapon of hunger.

Few Three Seas Men had ever seen grassland steppes, let alone the vast and broad-backed Istyuli. Beneath grey skies, with tracts still scabbed with snow, it seemed a trackless and desolate place, a precursor to Agongorea, about which they had heard so much in endless recitations of *The Sagas*. Those raised on the coasts were reminded of the sea, of horizons as flat as a rule, with nothing but limits for the eye to fasten upon. Those bred along desert margins were reminded of home.

It was raining when the multitudes climbed into the broad scuffs of land that lifted the Lonely City above the plain. At last, the two Exalt-Generals clasped arms and set about planning the assault. They scowled and joked and shared reminiscences, from the legendary First Holy War to the final days of the Unification. So many cities. So many campaigns.

So many proud peoples broken.

The Emissary arrived in the pre-dawn cold, demanding to see Varalt Harweel II, the King of Sakarpus.

Unable to sleep for fear of the morrow, Sorweel was already awake when his menial came to rouse him. He regularly attended all important audiences—his father insisted on it as part of his princely education. But until recently, "important" had meant something quite different. Skirmishes with the Sranc. Insults and apologies from Atrithau. Threats from disgruntled nobles. Sorweel could not count the times he had sat at the stone bench in the shadow of his father's throne swinging his bare feet in what seemed mortal boredom.

Now, only a year shy of his first Elking, he planted his boots and stared at the man who would destroy them all: King Nersei Proyas of Conriya, Exalt-General of the Great Ordeal. Gone were the courtiers, the functionaries, the partisans of this or that petty interest. Vogga Hall stood vacant and dim, though for some reason, the cavernous aisles and galleries failed to make the outlander look small. From across the terra cotta reliefs that sheathed the walls and columns, Sorweel's ancestors seemed to watch with graven apprehension. The air smelled of cold tallow.

"*Thremu dus kapkurum*," the outlander began, "*hedi mere' otas cha*—" The translator, some mangy herdsman from the Saglands by the look of him, quickly rendered his words into Sakarpic.

"Our captives have told us what you say of him."

Him. The Aspect-Emperor. Sorweel silently cursed his skin for pimpling.

"Ah, yes," King Harweel replied, "our blasphemy . . ." Even though the ornate arms of the Horn-and-Amber Throne concealed his father's face, Sorweel knew well the wry expression that accompanied this tone.

"Blasphemy . . ." the Exalt-General said. "*He* would not say that."

"And what would *he* say?"

"That you fear, as all men fear, to lose your power and privilege."

Sorweel's father laughed in an offhand manner that made the boy proud. If only he could muster such careless courage.

"So," Harweel said merrily, "I have placed my people between your Aspect-Emperor and my throne, is that it? Not that I have placed my throne between your Aspect-Emperor and my people . . ."

The Exalt-General nodded with the same deliberate grace that accompanied his untranslated speech, but whether in affirmation or appreciation, Sorweel could not tell. His hair was silver, as was his plaited beard. His eyes were dark and quick. His finery and regalia made even his father's royal vestments seem like crude homespun. But it was his bearing and imperturbable gaze that made him so impressive. There was a melancholy to him, a sadness that lent him an unsettling gravity.

"No man," Proyas said, "can stand between a God and the people."

Sorweel suppressed a shudder. It was unnerving the way they *all* referred to him as such, Three Seas Men. And with such thoughtless conviction.

"My priests call him a demon."

"Hada mem porota—"

"They say what they need to keep their power safe," the translator said with obvious discomfort. "They are, truly, the only ones who stand to lose from the quarrel between us."

For Sorweel's entire life, it seemed, the Aspect-Emperor had been an uneasy rumour from the South. Some of his earliest memories were of his father dandling him on his knee while he questioned Nansur and Galeoth traders from the World-beyond-the-Plains. With looks at once ingratiating and guarded, they would always demur, protest they had ears only for trade and eyes only for profit, when what they really meant was that they had tongues only for gold. In many ways, Sorweel owed his understanding of the world to Twelve-Pelt caravaners and their struggle to render the South into Sakarpic. The Unification Wars. The Thousand Temples. All the innumerable nations of the Three Seas.

And the coming of the False Prophet who preached the end of all things.

"He will come for us," his father would tell him.

"But how can you know, Da?"

"He is a Ciphrang, a Hunger from the Outside, come to this world in the guise of man."

"Then how can we hope to resist him?"

"With our swords and our shields," his father had boasted, using the mock voice he always used to make light of terrifying things. "And when those fail us, with spit and curses."

But the spit and the curses, Sorweel would learn, always came first, accompanied by bold gestures and grand demonstrations. War was an extension of argument, and swords were simply words honed to a blood-letting edge. Only the Sranc began with blood. For Men, it was always the conclusion.

Perhaps this explained the Emissary's melancholy and his father's frustration. Perhaps they already *knew* the outcome of this embassy. All doom required certain poses, the mouthing of certain words—so said the priests.

Sorweel gripped the edge of his bench, sat as still as his quailing body would allow. The Aspect-Emperor *had come*—even still he could scarce believe it. An itch, a name, a principle, a foreboding, something so far across the horizon that it had to seem both childish and menacing, like the wights Sorweel's nurse would invoke whenever he had vexed her. Something that could be dismissed until encircled by shadows.

Now, somewhere out in the darkness that surrounded their hearts and their walls, somewhere out there, *he* waited, a Hunger clothed in glorious manhood, propped by the arms of grovelling nations. A Demon, come to cut their throats, defile their women, enslave their children. A Ciphrang, come to lay waste to all they knew and loved.

"Have you not read *The Sagas?*" his father was asking the

Emissary, his voice incredulous. "The bones of our fathers survived the might of the Great Ruiner—Mog-Pharau! I assure you, they haven't grown too brittle to survive you!"

The Exalt-General smiled, or at least tried to. "Ah, yes . . . Virtue does not burn."

"What do you mean?"

"A saying in my country. When a man dies, the pyre takes everything save what his children can use to adorn their ancestor scrolls. All men flatter themselves through their forebears."

Harweel snorted not so much at the wisdom, it seemed, as the relevance. "And yet the North is waste and Sakarpus still stands!"

Proyas's smile was pained, his look one of dull pity. "You forget," he said with the air of disclosing a prickly truth, "*my Lord has been here before*. He broke bread with the men who raised these very halls, back when this was but a province of a greater empire, a backwater frontier. Fortune saved these walls, not fortitude. And Fortune, as you so well know, is a *whore*."

Even though his father often paused to order his thoughts, something about the ensuing silence chilled Sorweel to the bowel. He knew his father, knew that the past weeks had taken their toll. His rallying words were the same, and his booming laugh was nothing if not more frequent. But something had changed nonetheless. A slouch in his shoulders. A shadow in his gaze.

"The Great Ordeal stands at your gate," the Exalt-General pressed. "The Schools are assembled. The hosts of a hundred tribes and nations beat sword against shield. Doom encircles you, brother. You *know* you cannot prevail, even with the Chorae Hoard. I know this because your knuckles are as scarred as my own, because your eyes are as bruised by war's horror."

Another ashen silence. Sorweel found himself leaning

forward, trying to peer around the Horn-and-Amber Throne. What was his father doing?

"Come . . ." the Exalt-General said, his voice one of genuine entreaty. "Harweel, I beg of you, take my hand. Men can no longer afford to shed the blood of Men."

Sorweel stood, stared aghast at his father's blank visage. King Harweel was not an old man, but his face seemed slack and rutted about his hanging blond moustaches, his neck bent by the weight of his gold-and-iron crown. Sorweel could feel the impulse, errant and unbidden, the overwhelming urge to cover for his father's shameful indecision, to lash out, to . . . to . . .

But Harweel had recovered both his wits and his voice.

"Then decamp," he said in dead tones. "March to your death in Golgotterath or return to your hot-blooded wives. Sakarpus will not yield."

As though deferring to some unknown rule of discourse, Proyas lowered his face. He glanced at the bewildered Prince before returning his gaze to the King of Sakarpus. "There is the surrender that leads to slavery," he said. "And there is the surrender that sets one free. Soon, very soon, your people shall know that difference."

"So says the slave!" Harweel cried.

The Emissary did not require the translator's sputtering interpretation—the tone transcended languages. Something in his look dismayed Sorweel even more than the forced bluster of his father's response. *I am weary of blood,* his eyes seemed to say. *Too long have I haggled with the doomed.*

He stood, nodding to his entourage to indicate that more than enough breath had been spent.

Sorweel had expected his father to draw him aside afterwards, to explain not only the situation, but the peculiarities of his demeanour. Though he knew well enough what had happened—the King and the Exalt-General had exchanged one final round of fatuous words to sanctify the inevitable conclusion—his sense of shame forced a kind of confusion upon him. Not only had his father been frightened, he had been *openly* so—and before the most dire enemy his people had ever faced. There had to be some kind of explanation. Harweel II wasn't simply King, he was also his *father*, the wisest, bravest man Sorweel had ever known. There was a reason his Boonsmen looked upon him with such reverence, why the Horselords were so loath to invite his displeasure. How could *he* of all Men be afraid? His father . . . His father! Was there something he wasn't telling him?

But no answer was forthcoming. Soldered to the bench, Sorweel could only stare at him, his dismay scarcely concealed, as Harweel barked orders to be relayed to his various officers—his tone brusque in the way of men trying to speak their way past tears. Not long afterwards, just as dawn broke behind impenetrable woollen clouds, Sorweel found himself tramping through mud and across cobble, hustled forward by his father's hard-eyed companions, his High Boonsmen. The narrow streets were swollen with supplies gathered from the surrounding country as well as refugees from the Saglands and elsewhere. He saw men butchering cattle, scraping viscera with honed shoulder blades. He saw mothers walking dumbfounded, their arms too short to herd their rag-bundled children. Feeling useless and depressed, Sorweel wondered about his own Boonsmen, though they would not be called such until his first Elking next spring. He had pleaded with his father the previous week that they be allowed to fight together, but to no avail.

The watches lurched one into the next. The rain, which had fallen lightly and sporadically enough to be taken for water blown from the trees, began in earnest, swallowing the distances in sheets of relentless grey. It slipped through his mail, soaking him first to the leathers, then to the felt. He began shivering uncontrollably—until his rage at the thought of others seeing him shake burned him to the quick. Though his iron helm kept his scalp dry, his face became more and more numb. His fingers seemed to ache and sting in equal measure. Just when he thought he couldn't be more miserable, his father finally called for him, leading him into an emptied barracks so they might warm their hands side by side before the last remnants of a hearth fire.

The barracks was one of the ancient ones, with the heavy lintels and low chapped ceilings, and the stables built in, so that the men could sleep with their horses—a relic of the days when Sakarpi warriors worshipped their steeds. The candles had guttered so that only the dying hearth provided illumination, the kind of orange light that seemed to pick out details at whim. The battered curve of an iron pot. The cracked back of a chair. The face of a troubled king. Sorweel did not know what to say, so he simply stood, gazing at the luminous detail of coals burning into snowy ash.

"Moments of weakness come upon all Men," Harweel said without looking at his son.

The young Prince stared harder into the glowing cracks.

"You must see this," his father continued, "so that when your time comes you will not despair."

Sorweel was speaking before he even realized he had opened his mouth. "But I *do*, Father! I do desp—!"

The tenderness in his father's eyes was enough to make him choke. It knocked his gaze down as surely as a slap.

"There are many fools, Sorwa, men who conceive hearts in simple terms, absolute terms. They are insensible to the war within, so they scoff at it, they puff out their chests and they pretend. When fear and despair overcome them, as they must overcome us all, they have not the wind to *think* . . . and so they break."

The heat enclosed the young Prince, thinning the moisture

that slicked his skin. Already his palms and knuckles were dry. He dared look up at his father, whose bravery, he realized, burned not like a bonfire, but like a hearth, warming all who stood near its wisdom.

"Are you such a fool, Sorwa?"

The fact that the question was searching, genuine, and not meant as a reprimand cut Sorweel to the quick.

"No, Father."

There was so much he wanted to say, to confess. So much fear, so much doubt, and remorse above all. How could he have doubted his father? Instead of lending his shoulder, he had become one more burden—and on this day of days! He had recoiled, stricken by thoughts of bitter condemnation, when he should have reached out—when he should have said, "*The Aspect-Emperor. He comes. Hold tight my hand, Father.*"

"Please . . ." he said, staring into that beloved face, but before he could utter another word the door flew open, and three of the greater Horselords called out.

Forgive me . . .

Even upon the walls, the famed and hallowed walls of Sakarpus, the heat of the barracks stayed with him, as though he had somehow carried away a coal in his heart.

Standing with his father's High Boonsmen upon the northern tower of the Herder's Gate, Sorweel stared out across the miserable distances. The rain continued to spiral down, falling from fog skies. Though the plains ringed the horizon with lines as flat as any sea, the land about the city was pitched and folded, like a cloak cast upon a vast floor, forming a great stone pedestal for Sakarpus and her wandering walls. Several times, Sorweel leaned forward to peer between the embrasures, only to push himself back, dizzied by the sheer drop: a plane of pocked brick that dropped to sloping foundations that hung over grass-and-thistle-choked cliffs. It seemed impossible that any might assail them. Who could overcome such towers? Such walls?

When he stared down their length, with the iron-horned crenelations and lines of bovine skulls set into the masonry, a mixture of pride and awe swelled through him. The Lords of the Plains, draped in the ancient armour of their fathers, crowded by the longshields of their clans. The batteries of archers hunched over their bows, struggling to keep the strings dry. Everywhere he looked, he saw his father's people—his people—manning the heights, their faces grim with determination and expectant fury.

And out there, across the grass slopes, only void, the grey of distances lost through sheet after sheet of gossamer rain. The Aspect-Emperor and his Great Ordeal.

Sorweel rehearsed the prayers his father had taught to him, the Demanding, meant to loosen the sword of Gilgaöl's favour, the Plea to Fate, meant to soften the hard look of the Whore. It seemed he could hear others among the High Boonsmen whispering prayers of their own, summoning the favour they would need to wrest their doom from the Aspect-Emperor's grasping hand.

He's a demon, Sorweel thought, drawing strength from the remembered tenor of his father's voice. *A Hunger from the Outside. He will not prevail . . .*

He cannot.

Just then, a single horn pealed from the rain-shrouded horizon, long drawn and low, of a tone with the call of bull mastodons. For several heartbeats, it seemed to hang suspended over the city, solitary, foreboding. It trailed into silence, one heartbeat, two, until it seemed its signification had ended. Then it was joined by a chorus of others, some shrill and piercing, some as deep as the previous night's thunder. Suddenly the whole world seemed to shiver, its innards awakened by the cold cacophony. Sorweel could see men trade apprehensive looks. Mumbled curses and prayers formed a kind of counterpoint, like bracken about a monument. Blare and rumble, a sound that made a ceiling of the sky—that made water sharp. Then the horns were gone, leaving only the hoarse cries of the lords and officers along the wall, shouting out encouragement to their men.

"Take heart," Sorweel heard an old voice mutter to someone unseen.

"Are you sure?" a panicked boy-voice whispered in reply. "How can you be sure?"

A laugh, so obviously forced that Sorweel could not but wince. "A fortnight ago, the Hunter's priests found a nest of warblers in the temple eaves. *Crimson* warblers—do you understand? The Gods are with us, my son. They watch over us!"

Peering after the voices, Sorweel recognized the Ostaroots, a family whom he had always thought hangers-on in his father's Royal Company. Sorweel had always shunned the son, Tasweer, not out of arrogance or spite, but in accordance with what seemed the general court attitude. He had never thought of it, not really, save to make gentle sport of the boy now and again with his friends. For some reason, it shamed Sorweel to hear him confessing his fears to his father. It seemed criminal that he, a prince born to the greatest of privileges, had so effortlessly judged Tasweer's family, that with the ease of an exhalation, he had assessed lives as deep and confusing as his own. And found them wanting.

But his remorse was short-lived. Shouts of warning drew his eyes back in the direction of the pelting rain, toward the first shadows of movement across the plain. The siege towers appeared first, each within toppling distance of the others, little more than blue columns at the misty limits of his vision, like the ghosts of ancient monoliths. There was no surprise at the number of them—fourteen—since Sorweel and countless others had watched their faraway assembly over the preceding days. The surprise, rather, was reserved for their scale, and for the fact that the Southerners had borne them disassembled across so many trackless leagues.

They moved in echelon, crawling as though perched on tortoises. Slowly, the finer details of their appearance resolved from the mist, as did the rhythmic shouts of the thousands that pressed them forward. They were sheathed in what appeared to be scales of tin, and almost absurdly tall, to the point of tottering, rising to a slender peak from bases as broad as any Sakarpic bastion—unlike any of the engines Sorweel had seen sketched in the *Tomes of War*. Each bore the Circumfix, the mark of the Aspect-Emperor and his sham divinity, painted in white and red across their middens: a circle containing the outstretched figure of an upside-down man—Anasûrimbor Kellhus himself, the rumours said. The sign tattooed into the flesh of the missionaries Sorweel's father had ordered burned.

There was a breathlessness to their approach, which Sorweel attributed to the fact that it was at last *beginning*, that all the worrying and bickering and preparing and skirmishing of the previous months was finally coming to a head. In the towers' wake, the immaculate ranks of the Great Ordeal resolved into gleaming solidity, row after marching row of them, reaching out across field and pasture, their far flanks lost in the rainy haze.

Once again the horns unnerved the sky.

Sorweel stood numb, one of ten thousand faces, concentrated with rancour, dread, disbelief, even ardour, watching as ten times that number—more!—marched through the dreary downpour, bearing the exotic arms of distant peoples, following the devices of a dozen different nations. Strangers come from sweaty shores, from lands unheard of, who knew not their language, cared nothing for their ways or their riches . . .

The Southron Kings, come to save the world.

How many times had Sorweel dreamed of them? How many times had he imagined them reclining half-nude in their grand marble galleries, listening bored to polyglot petitioners? Or riding divans through spicedusted streets, heavy-lidded eyes scanning the mercantile bustle, searching for girls to add to their dark-skinned harems? How many times, his heart balled in child anger, had he told his father he was running away to the Three Seas?

To the land where Men yet warred against Men.

He had learned quickly to conceal his fascination, however. Among the officials of his father's court, the South was the object of contempt and derision—typically. It was a fallen place, where vigour had succumbed to complexity, to the turmoil of a thousand thousand vyings. It was a place where subtlety had become a disease and where luxury had washed away the bourne between what was womanish and what was manly.

But they were wrong—so heartbreakingly wrong. If the defeats of the previous weeks had not taught them such, then surely they understood now.

The South had come to teach them.

Sorweel cast about looking for his father. But like a miracle, King Harweel was already beside him, standing tall in his long skirts of mail. He gripped his son's shoulder, leaned reassuringly. When he grinned, jewels of water fell from his moustaches.

The tapping drone of rain. The peal of outland horns.

"Fear not," he said. "Neither he nor his Schoolmen will dare our Chorae. We will fight as Men fight." He looked to his High Boonsmen, who had all turned to watch their King give heart to his son.

"Do you hear me?" he cried out to them. "For two thousand years, our walls have stood unbroken. For two thousand years, the line of our fathers has reached unbroken! We are their culmination. We are the Men of Sakarpus, the

Lonely City. We are survivors of the Worldfall, Keepers of the Chorae Hoard, a solitary light against the pitch of Sranc and endl—!"

The sound of swooping wings interrupted him. Eyes darted heavenward. Several men even cried out. Sorweel instinctively raised a hand to his mail-armoured stomach, pressed the sorcery-killing Chorae about his waist so that it pinched cold into his navel.

It was a stork, as white and as long as a tusk, flying when it should have sheltered from the rain. Men shrank in horror from the battlement it landed upon, crowded back into one another. It turned the knife of its head toward them, its long bill pressed low to its neck.

The King's hand fell from his son's shoulder.

The stork regarded them with porcelain patience. Its black eyes were sentient and unfathomable.

Raindrops tinkled across iron, pattered against leather.

"What does it want?" some voice cried.

King Harweel pushed himself to the fore of his men. Sorweel stood transfixed, blinked at the rain blowing into his eyes, tasted the cold spill across his lips. His father stood alone, his woollen mantle soaked, his hands slack below the shining lines of his vambraces. The stork stood nearly on top of him, legs like sticks, wings folded into the polished vase of its body, its sage face bent down to regard the King at its feet . . .

Then, hanging in the cloud-swollen distance to the right of the bird, a star appeared, a scintillating point of light. Sorweel could not but glance in its direction, as did all those crowded about him. When he looked back to his father, the stork was gone—gone!

Suddenly he found himself jostled forward by the High Boonsmen, pressed hard against the embrasures. Everybody seemed to be shouting, to his father, to one another, to the horn-filled sky. The siege towers had continued their inexorable approach, as had the Southron men, whose formations now made a dread tapestry of the surrounding plains. The point of light, which flared from deeper distances, suddenly flickered out . . .

Only to reappear above the Ordeal's forward ranks, hanging half again the height of the ponderous towers. Sorweel gasped, tried to step back. It seemed a fearful thing to look up when he already stood so high. The point was no longer a point, but a figure of the purest white striding through a nimbus of blue incandescence. A man or a god.

Sorweel found himself clutching the pitted stone of the battlements.

The Aspect-Emperor.

The rumour. The lifelong itch . . .

"Father!" Sorweel cried, unable to see past the shoulders and shields about him. Gusts tumbled down from the west, blowing the rain into veils of mist, which floated like mountainous apparitions over the walls and their sodden defenders. The cold was like knives. "Father!"

He heard the crack of firing ballistae, but with the wet, the Choraetipped bolts sank far short of the hanging spectre. Shouts and curses erupted all along the wall. Then he heard the *words*, words remembered but not understood, making haze of pools and puddles, stinging skin and making teeth ache.

Sorcery.

Silver lines appeared about the figure's outstretched hands, began scrolling into emptiness . . .

Incandescent geometries, a sun-bright filigree, scaling the rain to the dark-bellied clouds. And a hiss like no other, like the millennial pounding of the surf condensed into the span of heartbeats. Out and out the lines reached, making glory of the sky, a glittering canopy that reached over the walls and across the city. Ghoulish reflections rolled and glimmered across every sword and shield.

"He makes mist," Sorweel murmured to no one. "He blinds us!"

Southron voices, roaring thousands of them, unitary and ecstatic. Hymns—they were singing hymns! The towers continued their relentless approach, driven by trains of bent-back thousands. Someone had to do something! Why was no one doing anything?

Then his father was before him, grasping him by the arms. "Go to the Citadel," he said, his expression strange. The light of the Aspect-Emperor glittered in his eyes, rimmed the lines of his nose and cheek in blue. "It was a mistake bringing you to the walls."

"What do you mean? Father, how cou—"

"Go!"

Sorweel could feel the corners of his face waver and crumple.

"Father—*Father!* My bones are your bones!"

Harweel raised his hand to Sorweel's cheek. "Which is why you must go. *Please*, Sorwa. Sakarpus stands at the ends of the world. We are the last outpost of Men! He needs this city! He needs *our people*! That means he needs you, Sorwa! You!"

The Prince looked down, cowed by his father's fury and desperation. "No, Father," he mumbled, suddenly feeling twig-thin—far younger than his sixteen years. "I won't leave you . . ." When he looked up, cool rain flooded the hot of his tears. "I won't leave you!"

His voice hung raw and shrill, defiance yanked to the sinew. Then the song of the invaders swelled, the throats of the joyous thousands come to burn, to kill.

His father's blow took him in the jaw, sent him skidding into the men behind him, then to his hands and knees onto the wet stone. "Don't shame me with your impertinence, boy!" He turned to one of his High Boonsmen. "Narsheidel! Take him to the Citadel! See that no harm comes to him! He will be our final swordstroke! Our vengeance!"

Without a word Narsheidel hoisted him to his feet by the scruff of his mail harness, began dragging him through the assembled warriors. Pulled backward, Sorweel watched them close ranks in his wake, saw their looks of pity. "Nooo!" he howled, tasting clean cold water on his tongue. Across sodden shoulders and glistening shield-rims, he glimpsed his father staring back at him, his eyes as blue and crisp as the summer sky. For one inscrutable heartbeat, his father's look pierced him. Sorweel saw him turn just as the wall of fog encompassed the parapets.

"Nooooooo!"

The clamour of arms descended upon the world.

He tried to struggle, but Narsheidel was indomitable, an iron shadow that scarcely bent to his thrashing. Through the dark spiral of the tower stair, it seemed all he could see were his father's eyes, loving eyes, judging eyes, regretting a heavy hand, celebrating a tickling laugh, and watching, always watching, to be sure his second heart beat warm and safe. And if he looked close, if he dared peer at those eyes the way he might gems, he knew he would see *himself*, not as he was, but mirrored across the shining curve of a father's pride, a father's hope that he might live with greater grace through the fact of a son.

Thunder shivered about them, cracking ancient mortar, loosing showers of grit from the low-vaulted ceilings. Narsheidel was shouting, something, something taut with more than fear. A warrior already mourning.

Then they were past the iron door, skidding on stones in the Gate's monumental shadow. Rearing horses. Warriors running through fog, their white shields across their backs. The foundations of buildings that vanished into grey. The void of ancient streets opening between them.

And a solitary figure in the midst of the confusion, crouched like a beggar, only clothed in too much shadow . . .

And with eyes that blinked light.

Crying out, Narsheidel hauled him down to the hard wet stone.

Diagrams of burning white, making smoke of the rain. The great bronze plates of the Herder's Gate flashed with sun-brilliance, then fell away, bent like woodchips, twirling like flotsam in a stream.

Shouting, always shouting, Narsheidel pulled him to his feet, yanked him to a run.

He saw the beggar become someone priestly and luminescent, then vanish in a twinkle. He saw his countrymen rally to stem the breach. He saw tall Droettal and his company of Gilgallic Priests roaring as the tide of dark-faced outlanders engulfed them. He saw the Eithmen, whipping their caparisoned chargers through panick-packed streets. He saw gutters rushing with pink and crimson waters. He saw one of the siege towers lurching above the crest of the walls, the ghosts of dragonheads rising from slots in its metallic hide. He saw ropes of men, Longshields and Horselords alike, vanish screaming in roiling light.

Again and again, he threw himself against Narsheidel's strength, sobbing, raving, but the High Boonsman was unconquerable, driving him ever forward, bellowing at the madness to make way. And through it all, he saw his father's summer-blue eyes, beseeching . . .

Please, Sorwa . . .

They ran down labyrinthine alleyways, through endless curtains of rain. Behind them, the shouts and screams multiplied into a senseless white roar, punctuated only by braying horns and the inside-out mutter of sorcery.

The winding streets were so deep they couldn't see the black-walled Citadel until they were almost upon it, hunched against the sky above them, its rounded towers no taller than the soaring walls. Weeds hung from the joints of its sloped and fluted base. Its northern quarters, where the ancient

Sakarpi Kings had once resided, hung in ruin, windows like eye sockets revealing the gutted hollows within. They reeled toward it. The ramparts climbed to encompass a greater part of the sky. Sorweel glimpsed a star flaring high above the black-stone rim, as bright as the Nail of Heaven—only *beneath* the clouds. The light made diamonds of the falling rain.

Even Narsheidel stumbled in terror, face held up, pressing Sorweel before him. "Quick, boy, *quick!*" Then they were through the vault doors, sheltered in deep sockets of black stone. Guards and ashen-faced attendants flocked to them. Sorweel found himself staggering in circles, fending away their fussing hands. "The King?" an old retainer cried. "What has become of the King?"

"There must be a way!" Narsheidel was shouting at some mail-armoured steward. "This place must have secrets! Everything *old* has secrets!"

Then Sorweel was being hustled up tight-winding stairs, through hot, wood-panelled corridors, across low-ceilinged rooms, some too bright, others too dim. Turning-crossing-climbing. Everything, tapestries, batteries of candles, chapped walls, seemed to swim in his periphery.

What was *happening*?

"No!" Sorweel cried, shaking away ushering hands like a lunatic dog. "Stop this! *Stop!*"

They stood in some kind of antechamber, with a hemispherical wall that found its apex in a bricked-in passageway. Narsheidel and two others—an aging Longshield and Baron Denthuel, the one-legged Horselord assigned to command the Citadel—stood back, their hands out, their faces wary or placating or worried or pleading or . . .

"Where's my father?" he cried.

Only Narsheidel, his soaked armour shining silver and black in the uncertain light, dared speak.

"King Harweel is dead, boy."

The words winded him. Even still, Sorweel heard his own voice say, "That means *I am King*. That I'm your master!"

The High Boonsman looked down to his palms, then out and upward, as though trying to divine the direction of the outer roar—for it had not stopped.

"Not so long as your father's words still ring in my ears."

Sorweel looked into the older man's face, with its strong-jawed proportions and water-tangled frame of hair. Only then, it seemed, did he realize that Narshiedel too had loved ones, wives and children, sequestered somewhere in the city. That he was a true Boonsman, loyal unto death.

"King Harweel is—"

Explosion. Only afterwards, sputtering, scrambling across the floor, would the young Prince understand what happened. Bricks exploding outward, as though a tree-sized hammer had struck the round wall's far side, taking Lord Denthuel in the head and neck, swatting him broken to the ground.

Dust carried on the back of shiver-cold air. Pale out-of-doors light. Ears ringing, Sorweel turned to the gaping hole . . .

He might have called out, but he wouldn't remember.

He looked through the breach into the husk of the Citadel's ruined galleries. Something golden hung in the floorless hollows, something that boiled with impossible light. Against a backdrop of empty windows and long-gutted walls, it walked across open air. Walked. Rain plummeted in lines about it, as though down a well.

But no dampness touched him.

The Aspect-Emperor.

The shining demon crossed the threshold, framed by gloom and deluge.

The nameless Longshield simply turned and ran, disappearing into the halls. Raising his greatsword high, Narsheidel cried out, charged the luminescent figure . . .

Who simply stepped to the side, impossibly, like a dancer

avoiding a drunk. Whipping his arms like rope, the figure brought his curved blade up over his scalp, then snapped it back in a perfect arc. Narsheidel's body and head continued careering forward, joined only by a flying thread of blood.

The demon's eyes had remained fixed on Sorweel the entire time. Only . . . they did not seem a demon's eyes.

Too human.

On his knees, Sorweel could do naught but stare.

The man seemed cut from a different place, one with a brighter sun, as though he stood both here amid the ruin that was Sakarpus and upon a mountain summit at the edge of dawn. He was tall, a full hand over Sorweel's father, draped in a priest's gold-panelled vestments, armoured in mail so fine it seemed silk—nimil, some absent part of Sorweel realized, Nonman steel. His hair fell in sodden ringlets about his long, full-lipped face. His flaxen beard was plaited and squared in the manner of the Southron Kings pictured on the most ancient of the Long Hall's reliefs. The severed heads of two demons, their skin blotched and aglow, hung from his girdle, making fishmouths about black-nail teeth.

Scabs of salt crusted his bare sword-hand.

"I am," the vision said, "Anasûrimbor Kellhus."

It started with the shaking, the hot flush of urine. Then his bones became serpents, and Sorweel collapsed to the floor. On his belly . . . On his belly! He spat at the blood greasing his chin.

Fuh-Fuh-Father!

"Come," the man said, crouching to place a hand on his shoulder. "Come. Get up. Remember yourself . . ."

Remember?

"You are a *King*, are you not?"

Sorweel could only stare in horror wonder.

"I-I d-d-don't understand . . ."

A friendly scowl, followed by a gentle laugh. "I'm rarely

what my enemies expect, I know." Somehow, he was already helping him to his feet.

"Buh-buh-but . . ."

"All this, Sorweel, is a tragic mistake. You must believe that."

"Mistake?"

"I'm no conqueror." He paused as though to frown at the very notion. "As mad as it sounds, I *really have* come to save Mankind."

"Lies," the Prince murmured through his confusion. "*Liar!*"

The Aspect-Emperor nodded, closed his eyes in the manner of a long-suffering parent. His sigh was both honest and plain. "Mourn," he said. "Grieve as all Men must. But take heart in the fact of your forgiveness."

Sorweel gazed into the summer-blue eyes. *What was happening?*

"Forgiven? Who are *you* to forgive?"

The scowl of an innocent twice wronged.

"You misunderstand."

"Misunderstand what?" Sorweel spat. "That you think yourse—!"

"Your father loved you!" the man interrupted, his voice thick with a nigh irresistible paternal reprimand. "And that *love*, Sorwa, is forgiveness . . . *His* forgiveness, not mine."

The young King of Sakarpus stood dumbstruck, staring with a face as slack as rainwater. Then perfumed sleeves enclosed him, and he wept in the burning arms of his enemy, for his city, for his father, for a world that could wring redemption out of betrayal.

Years. Months. Days. For so long the Aspect-Emperor had been an uneasy rumour to the South, a name as heaped in atrocity as it was miracle . . .

No more.

CHAPTER TWO

Hûnoreal

We burn like over-fat candles, our centres gouged, our edges curling in, our wick forever outrunning our wax. We resemble what we are: Men who never sleep.

—ANONYMOUS MANDATE SCHOOLMAN,
THE HEIROMANTIC PRIMER

Early Spring, 19 New Imperial Year (4132 Year-of-the-Tusk), southwestern Galeoth

There would have been nightmares aplenty had Drusas Achamian been able to dream a life that was his own. Nightmares of a long, hard war across deserts and great river deltas. Nightmares of sublimity and savagery held in perfect equipoise, though the cacophony of the latter would make all seem like misery. Nightmares of dead men, feeding like cannibals on their once strong souls, raising the impossible on the back of atrocity.

Nightmares of a city so holy it had become wicked.

And of a man who could peer into souls.

But he could not dream of these things. No. Though he had renounced his School, cursed his own brothers, he still wore the great yoke that broke the backs of them all. He still bore within him a second, more ancient soul, Seswatha, the hero and survivor of the First Apocalypse. He still dreamed, as they dreamed, of the World's crashing end. And he still awoke gasping another man's breath . . .

The feast was a greasy, raucous affair—another celebration of the Hunt-Glorious. The High-King, Anasûrimbor Celmomas, reclined the way he always did when too far into his cups: legs askew, shoulders slumped into the left corner of the Urthrone, forehead planted against a slack fist. His Knight-Chieftains bickered and cavorted across the long trestle-table set before him, raising gobs of seared meat in shining fingers, drinking deep from golden cups stamped in the likeness of animal totems. Light danced from the bronze tripods set across the floor about them, making the table a place of shadows and silhouettes, and illuminating the curtain of freshly killed deer that rose behind the revellers to either side. Beyond, the mighty pillars of the Yodain, the King-Temple raised by Trysë's ancient rulers, rose higher still, into the obdurate blackness.

More toasts rang out. To Clan Anasûrimbor, to the Great Kin Lines represented at the table, to the Bardic Priest and his uproarious account of the day's escapade. Honey mead was poured and spilled into cups and smacking lips alike. But Achamian, alone at the very end of the booming table, lifted his vessel only to the water-bearer. He nodded at the warlike exclamations, laughed at the ribald jokes, grinned the sly grin of the learned in the company of fools, but he did not participate. Instead, with eyes that seemed more bored than cunning, he watched the High-King—the man he still called his best friend—drink himself into unconsciousness.

Then he slipped away, without care or notice. Who could fathom the ways of a sorcerer?

Seswatha passed through the shadowy, industrious network of servants that kept the feast in belching good humour, then left the King-Temple for the closeted maze of palace apartments.

The door was ajar—as promised.

Squat candles had been set on the floor along the passageway, spreading fans of illumination across the decorative mosaics above. Figures roped in and out of the gloom, the shadows of men warring against animals. Breathing deep, Achamian chipped shut the door, listened for the rasp of iron. The heavy stone of the Annexes had swallowed all sound save the spit of candle flames twirling in the wake of his passage. Resinous perfumes steeped the air.

When he found her—Suriala, glorious and wanton Suriala—he knelt in accordance with the very Laws he was about to break. He knelt before her beauty, before her hunger and her passion. She raised him to her embrace, and he glimpsed their entwined reflection in the contours of a decorative shield. They looked as bent and desperate as they should, he thought. Then he pressed her to the bed . . .

Made love to his High-King's wife—

A convulsive gasp.

Achamian bolted forward from his blankets. The darkness buzzed with exertion, moaned and panted with feminine lust—but only for a moment. Within heartbeats the chorus call of morning birdsong ruled his ears. Throwing aside his blankets, he leaned into his knees, rubbed at the ache across his jaw and cheek. He had taken to sleeping on wood as part of the discipline he had adopted since leaving the School of Mandate, and to quicken the transition between his nightmares and wakefulness. Mattresses, he had found, made waking a form of suffocation.

He sat for a while, trying to will his arousal away, to banish the memory of her nakedness sheering against his own. Had he still been a Mandate Schoolman, he would have run shouting to his brothers. But he was not, and he had dwelt with too many revelations for too long. Insights that would have once wired his body with horror or exultation now merely throbbed. Discovery, it seemed, had become but another ache.

Snuffling and coughing, he walked across the plank floor to the square corona of white outlining the shutters. "Shed some sun on this," he muttered to himself. "Yes-yes . . . Light is never a bad thing."

He closed his eyes against the explosive brilliance, breathed deep the many layers of morning: the bitter of budding leaves, the damp of forest loam. The cries of children rang up from below, claiming, daring—the singsong of careless souls. "*I don't-don't believe you!*" Banished from the lower floors by their parents—Achamian's slaves—they always ran rampant about the tower's shadow in the morning, racing and twittering like combative starlings. For some reason, hearing them today seemed a profound miracle, so much so he almost wished he could stand such—here, now, eyes closed and all else open—for the remainder of his life.

It would be a good end, he thought.

Squinting against the brightness, he turned to his room, to its racks and rough-hewn tables, to the endless sheaves of scribbling stacked in precarious piles across random surfaces high and low. The broad curve of the stone walls embraced the morning gloom, its mortices lending the appearance of a Galeoth millery. A broad fireplace stood fallow opposite his plank bed. Immense ceiling timbers ran overhead, black with pitch, the spaces between insulated with layers of animal pelts—wolf, deer, even hare and marten.

He smiled a sad upside-down smile. Some small memory winced at the barbarity of the place, for he had spent a good portion of his life travelling the fleshpots of the South. But it had been home for far too long to seem anything other than safe. For nearly twenty years he had slept, studied, and supped in this room.

He walked different roads now. Deeper roads.

How long had he travelled?

All his life, it seemed, though he had been a Wizard for only twenty.

Breathing deep, drawing fingers from his balding scalp to his shaggy white beard, he walked to his main worktable, braced himself for the concentrated recital to come . . .

The meticulous labour of mapping Seswatha's labyrinthine life.

He had hoped to write a detailed account of everything he could remember. He had developed a talent, over the years, for recollecting what he dreamed. He had literally accumulated thousands of recitals, each the focus of innumerable critiques and speculations. Writing from memory was treacherous enough: Sometimes it seemed as though only the bones of things were actually remembered and that the flesh had to be invented anew with each resurrection. But when it came to the Dreams, everything carried the taint of contrivance, even when they tossed him whole into the heart and bowel of Seswatha's life. The key, he had learned, was to start writing immediately, before the afterimage found itself shouldered into obscurity by the brute insistence of the waking world.

But instead, all he could write was,

NAU-CAYÛTI?

He found himself staring at this ink scribble throughout the morning, the name of Celmomas's famed son, whose theft of the Heron Spear would lead to the No-God's ultimate destruction. In the libraries of the Mandate, dozens if not hundreds of tomes were dedicated to his exploits, the predictable stuff mostly: the Slaying of Tanhafut the Red, his string of victories after the disaster at Shiarau, his death at the hands of his wife, Iëva, and of course the endless interpretations of the Theft. But a few scholars—at least two that Achamian could remember—had focused their attention on the sheer frequency of the Dreams involving Nau-Cayûti, which seemed far out of proportion to his short-lived role in the Apocalypse.

But if Seswatha had bedded his mother . . .

The revelation of adultery was significant in its own right—and it stung the old Wizard for reasons he dare not ponder. But the possibility that Seswatha might be Nau-Cayûti's father? Not all facts are equal. Some hang like leaves from the branching of more substantial truths. Others stand like trunks, shouldering the beliefs of entire nations. And a few—a desperate few—are seeds.

He was running through all the details that might allow him to date the dream—which Knight-Chieftains still had favour at the High-King's table, which rings Seswatha wore, the fertility tattoos on the Queen's inner thighs—when one of the children's voices piped through the drone of his failing concentration. "*Yeah, but from how faaaaaar?*" A girl's warbling, squeezed into a reed by the distance. Little Silhanna, he realized.

A woman replied, something tender and inaudible.

It was the accent more than the voice that sent him stumbling to the open window. He found himself blinking, gripping the cracked and pitted sill against the sudden vertigo. It was Sheyic, the common tongue of the New Empire, but lilting with southern nuances. Nansur? Ainoni?

He glanced out to the horizon, across what had once been the Galeoth province of Hûnoreal. The skies were iron grey with the chill-spring promise of summer blue. Climbing and falling canopies jostled across the near distance, a patchwork of tender greens so new that swales of ground could be seen through them. The morning sunlight was still barred from the ravines, so the landscape possessed an oceanic quality; the sunbathed summits and ridge lines resembled yellow islands in a shadowy sea. Even though he couldn't make out the white-backed tributaries of the Rohil, he could see their winding stamp on the disposition of the distant hills, like cables laid across love-tossed sheets.

Strange, the way distances grew in the chill.

The ground immediately below fell away in a series of stubbed terraces, so that looking directly down made it feel as though he were being tugged out the window. There were the outbuildings, little more than lean-tos actually, staking out their humble circle of habitation, and the nearer trees, elms and oaks, winding to heights that would have been eye level had the ground been even. And there were the bare stretches, whose bald stone carried premonitions of smashing melons and broken skulls. He could see nothing of the children, though he did spy a mule staring with daft concentration at nothing in particular.

The voices continued to chirp and giggle somewhere to the left, on a blade of level earth that formed the foundation for several hoary old maples.

"*Momma! Momma!*" he heard young Yorsi cry. Then he spied him through the weave of branches, barrelling up the slope. His mother, Tisthanna, strolled down toward him, wiping her hands on her apron and quite—Achamian was relieved to note—unconcerned. "*Look!*" Yorsi cried, waving something small and golden.

Then he saw a petite woman climbing in Yorsi's wake, laughing at the four blond children who danced around her, their questions rising in chiming counterpoint. "*What's your mule called?*" "*Can I chop your sword?*" "*Can I? Can I? Can I?*" Her hair was Ketyai black and half-cropped, and she wore a leather cloak whose many-panelled manufacture shouted caste-noble even from such a distance. But given his high vantage and the way she looked down at her little interlocutors, Achamian could see nothing of her face.

He felt a tickle in his throat. How long had it been since their last visitor?

In the beginning, when it had just been him and Geraus, only the Sranc had come. He had lost count of how many times he had lit up the hillside with the Gnosis, sending the vile creatures howling back into the forest deeps. Every tree within bowshot carried some scar of those mad battles: A sorcerer poised on the edge of a half-ruined tower, raining brilliant destruction down on fields of what looked like raving, white-skinned apes. Geraus still suffered nightmares. Afterwards, with the end of the Unification Wars, it had been the Scalpoi, the innumerable Men—Galeoth, Conriyans, Tydonni, Ainoni, even Kianene—who had come to collect the Aspect-Emperor's bounty on Sranc scalps. For years it seemed some blood-mad camp of theirs lay within a day's distance of them. And on more than a few occasions, Achamian had to resort to the Gnosis to cut short their drunken depredations. But even they moved on after time, hunting their vicious prizes into the wilderness's truly primeval deeps. Periodically a troop of them would happen upon the tower, and if they were hungry or otherwise broken by the horrors of their trade, some kind of woe was certain to follow. But then even they ceased coming.

So what had it been? Five, maybe six years since the last visitor had climbed to the foot of their tower?

It had to be. That long at least. There had been those two starving Scalpoi who had come shortly after Geraus had taken Tisthanna for his wife, but after? Certainly not since the last of the children had been born.

No matter, the rule had been simple over the years: Visitors meant grief, the Gods and their laws of hospitality be damned.

Holding hands with one of the girls, the nameless woman came to a friendly stop before Tisthanna, bowed her head in greeting—precisely how far Achamian couldn't tell because of an obscuring tree limb, though it seemed the inclination proper to caste-menials. He could see her boots through a brace of budding twigs, the toe of her left absently scuffing the winter-flat leaves; they were every bit as fine as her ermine-trimmed cloak.

Perhaps she was only equipped like a caste-noble.

Craning his head, he leaned out perilously far, to the point of breaking out in a cold sweat, but to no effect. He heard Tisthanna's whinnying laugh, and it relieved him—somewhat. Tisthanna was nothing if not sensible.

Then the two women were walking side by side into the clearing that encircled the tower's foundation, talking loudly enough to be overheard, but in that close, feminine tone that seemed to baffle masculine ears. Nodding at something, Tisthanna, her blonde hair stacked upon her apple-round face, looked up and gestured to him in the window. Achamian, who leaned stooped out like yard and tackle, tried to pull himself into a more dignified posture. His left foot slipped. The sill-stone beneath his left palm cracked free the rotten mortar—

He nearly followed it clacking down.

Tisthanna let loose an involuntary "*Ooop!*" then chortled as Achamian, his long white beard dragging along the stones, carefully palmed his way back to safety.

"*Mast-Master Akka!*" the children called out in a broken chorus.

The stranger looked up, her delicate face bemused and open and curious . . .

And something in Achamian suffered a greater fall.

There is a progression to all things. Madness, miracles, even dreams broken into their most feverish extremes follow some thread of association. The unexpected, the astonishing, are always the effect of ignorance, no matter how absolute they may seem. In this world, everything has its reasons.

"So," she said, her tone balanced between many things, hope and sarcasm among them, "the Great Wizard."

There was a strangeness to her, something like the stare of children with ill-mannered smiles.

"What are you doing here?" Achamian snapped.

He had sent Tisthanna and the children away and now stood with the woman in the sunlight to the lee of the tower, on the broad white stone the children called the Turtle Shell. For years they had been drawing on it with the tips of burnt sticks: grotesque faces, oddly affecting pictures of trees and animals, and, lately, the letters Achamian had taught them to write. There was an order to the drawings, with the steadier lines of symbol and verisimilitude struck across the pale remnants of fancy, like the record of the soul's long, self-erasing climb.

She had instinctively sought out the highest point—something that inexplicably irritated him. She was short, obviously lithe beneath her leather and woollens. Her face was dark, beautiful, with the colour and contours of an acorn. Save for the green irises and a slight elongation of the jaw, she was exactly as he remembered her . . .

Except that he had never seen her in his life.

Was *she* the reason why Esmenet had betrayed him? Was she why his wife—his wife!—had chosen Kellhus over a sorcerer, a broken-hearted fool, all those years ago?

Not because of the child she carried, but because of the child she had lost?

The questions were as inevitable as the pain, the questions that had pursued him beyond civilization's perfumed rim. He could have continued asking them, he could have yielded to madness and made them his life's refrain. Instead he had packed a new life about them, like clay around a wax figurine, then he had burned them out, growing ever more decrepit, ever more *old*, about their absence—more mould than man. He had lived like some mad trapper, accumulating skins that were furred in ink instead of hair, the lines of his every snare anchored to this silent hollow within him, to these questions he dared not ask.

And now here she stood . . . Mimara.

The answer?

"I wondered if you would recognize me," she said. "I *prayed* you would, in fact."

The morning breeze sifted through the dark edges of her hair. After so much time spent in the company of Norsirai women, Achamian found himself struck by memories of his mother and sisters: the warmth of their olive cheeks, the tangle of their luxurious black hair.

He rubbed his eyes, dragged fingers through his unkempt beard. Shaking his head, he said, "You look like your mother . . . Very much."

"So I'm told," she said coolly.

He held out a hand as though to interrupt her, then lowered it just as quickly, suddenly conscious of its knob-knuckled age. "But you never answered me. What are you doing here?"

"Searching for you."

"That much is obvious. The question is *why*."

This time the anger shone through, enough to make her blink. Achamian had never stopped expecting the assassins, whether sent by the Consult or the Aspect-Emperor. But even still, the world beyond the horizon's rim had grown less and less substantial over the years. More abstract. Trying to forget, trying not to hear when your deepest ears were continually pricked was almost as difficult as trying to hate away love. At first nothing, not even holding his head and screaming could shut out the murderous bacchanal. But somehow, eventually, the roar had faded into a rumble, and the rumble had trailed into a murmur, and the Three Seas had taken on the character of a father's legendary exploits: near enough to be believed, distant enough to be dismissed.

He had found peace—real peace—waging his strange nocturnal war. Now this woman threatened to overthrow it all.

He fairly shouted when she failed to answer. "*Why?*"

She flinched, looked down to the childish scribble at her feet: a gaping mouth scrawled in black across mineral white, with eyes, nose, and ears spaced across its lipless perimeter.

"B-because I wanted . . ." Something caught her throat. Her eyes shot up, as though requiring an antagonist to remain focused. "Because I wanted to know if . . ." Her tongue traced the seam of her lips.

"If you were my father."

His laughter felt cruel, but if was such, she showed no sign of injury—no outward sign.

"Are you sure?" she asked, blank in voice and expression.

"I met your mother sometime after . . ."

In a blink Achamian had seen it all, written in a language not so different from the charcoal scrawlings beneath their feet. It was inevitable that Esmenet would do this, that she would use all her power as Empress to recover the child she had forbidden him to mention all those years ago . . . To find the girl whose name she would never speak.

"You mean after she sold me," the girl said.

"There was a famine," he heard himself reply. "She did what she did to save your life, and forever wrecked herself as a result."

He knew these were the wrong words before he finished speaking. Her eyes suddenly became old with exhaustion, with the paralysis that comes from hearing the same hollow justifications over and over again.

The fact that she refused to reply to them said it all.

Esmenet had recovered her some time ago—that much was obvious. Her manner and inflection were too studied, too graceful, not to have been honed over years in the court. But it was just as obvious that Esmenet had found her too late. The damaged look. The rim of desperation.

Hope was ever the great foe of slavers. They beat it from your lips, then they pursued it past your skin. Mimara, Achamian knew, had been hunted to the ground—many, many times.

"But why do I remember you?"

"Look—"

"I remember you buying me apples—"

"Child. It wasn't—"

"The street was busy, loud. You were laughing because I kept smelling mine instead of biting. You said that little girls shouldn't eat through their nose, that it wasn't—"

"It wasn't me!" he exclaimed. "Look. The daughters of whores . . ."

She flinched once again, like a child startled by a snapping dog. How old would she be? Thirty summers? More? Nonetheless, she looked like the little girl she said she remembered, joking about apples on a crowded street.

"The daughters of whores . . ." she repeated.

Achamian gazed at her, filled to his fingertips, suffused by an anxious prickle.

"Have no fathers."

He had tried to say this as gently as he could, but in his ears his voice had grown too harsh with age. The sun limned her in gold, and for a moment she seemed a native of the morning. She lowered her face, studied the lines scraped about them, etched in burnt black. "You said that I was clever."

He ran a slow hand across his face, exhaled, suddenly feeling ancient with guilt and frustration. Why must everything be too big to wrestle, too muddy to grasp?

"I feel sorry for you, child—I truly do. I have some notion of what you must have endured . . ." A deep breath, warm against the bright cool. "Go home, Mimara. Go back to your mother. We have no connection."

He turned back toward the tower. The sun instantly warmed his shoulders.

"But we do," her voice chimed from behind him—so like her mother's that chills skittered across his skin.

He paused, lowered his head to curse his slippered feet. Without turning, he said, "It's not *me* you remember. What you believe is your affair."

"But that's not what I mean."

Something in her tone, the windy suggestion of a snicker or a laugh, forced him to look back. Now the sun drew a line down her centre, violated only by the creases of her clothing, whose contours smuggled light and dark this way and that. The wilderness rose behind her, far more pale but likewise divided.

"I can distinguish between the created and uncreated," she said with something between embarrassment and pride. "I am one of the Few."

Achamian whirled, scowling both at her and the brightness.

"What? You're a *witch*?"

A deliberate nod, made narrow by a smile.

"I didn't come here to find my father," she said, as though everything until now had been nothing but cruel theatre. "Well . . . I thought you might be my father, but I really didn't . . . care . . . that much, I think." Her eyes widened, as though turning from the inner to the outer on some invisible swivel.

"I came to find my *teacher*. I came to learn the Gnosis."

There it was, her reason.

There is a progression to all things. Lives, encounters, histories, each trailing their own nameless residue, each burrowing into a black, black future, groping for the facts that conjure purpose out of the cruelties of mere coincidence.

And Achamian had had his fill of it.

She sees his face slacken, despite the matted wire of his beard. She sees his complexion blanch, despite the sun's morning glare. And she knows that what her mother once told her is in fact true: Drusas Achamian possesses the soul of a teacher.

So the old whore didn't lie.

Almost three months have passed since her flight from the Andiamine Heights. Three months of searching. Three months of hard winter travel. Three months of fending against Men. She travelled inland as much as possible, knowing that the Judges would be watching the ports, that their agents would be ranging the coastal roads, hungry to please her mother, their Holy Empress. It seems a miracle whenever she recalls it. That time in the high Cepalor when the wolves paced her step for weary step, little more than feral ghosts through the soundless snowfall. The mad ferryman at the Wutmouth crossing. And the brigands, who tracked her only to turn away when they saw the caste-noble cut of her clothes. There was fear in the land, fear everywhere she turned, and it suited her and her needs well.

She spent innumerable watches lost in revery during this time, her soul's eye conjuring visions of the man she secretly named her father. When she arrived, it seemed that everything was the way she imagined it. Exactly. A lonely hillside spilling skyward, trees scarred with sorcery's dread murmur. An even lonelier stone tower, a makeshift roof raised across its collapsed floors, grasses growing from rotten-mortar seams. Stacked-stone outbuildings, with their heaped wood, drying fish, and stretched pelts. Slaves who smiled and talked like caste-menials. Even children skipping beneath great-boughed maples.

Only the sorcerer surprises her, probably because she has expectations aplenty of him. Drusas Achamian, the Apostate, the man who turned his back on history, who dared curse the Aspect-Emperor for love of her mother. True, he seemed entirely different in each of the lays sung about him, even in the various tales told by her mother, by turns stalwart and doubt-ridden, learned and hapless, passionate and cold-handed. But it was this contradictory nature that had so forcefully stamped his image in her soul. In the cycle of historical and scriptural characters that populated her education, he alone seemed *real*.

Only he isn't. The man before her seems to mock her soft-bellied imaginings: a wild-haired hermit with limbs like barked branches and eyes that perpetually sort grievances. Bitter. Severe. He bears the Mark, as deep as any of the sorcerers she has seen glide through the halls of the Andiamine Heights, but where they drape silks and perfume about their stain, he wears wool patched with rancid fur.

How could anyone sing songs about such a man?

His eyes dull at the mention of the Gnosis—the inward look of concealed pity, or so it seems. But when he speaks, his tone is almost collegial, except that it's hollow.

"Is it true, what they say, that witches are no longer burned?"

"Yes. There's even a new School."

He does not like the way she says that word, "School." She can see it in his eyes.

"A School? A School of *witches*?"

"They're calling themselves the Swayal Compact."

"Then what need do you have of me?"

"My mother will not allow it. And the Swayali will not risk her Imperial displeasure. Sorcery, she says, leaves only scars."

"She's right."

"But what if scars are all you have?"

This, at least, gives him pause. She expects him to ask the obvious question, but his curiosity seems bent in a different direction.

"Power," he says, glaring at her with an intensity she does not like. "Is that it? You want to feel the world crumble beneath the weight of your voice."

She knows this game. "Was that how it was for you in the beginning?"

His glare seems to falter over some inner fact. But it means less than nothing, winning arguments. The same as with her mother.

"Go home," he says. "I would sooner be your father than your teacher."

There is set manner to the way he turns his back this time, one that tells her that no words can retrieve him. The sun pulls his shadow long and profound. He walks with a stoop that says he has long outlived the age of bargaining. But she hears it all the same, the peculiar pause of legend becoming actuality, the sound of the crazed and disjoint seams of the world falling flush.

He *is* the Great Teacher, the one who raised the Aspect-Emperor to the heights of godhead. Despite his words to the contrary.

He is Drusas Achamian.

That night she builds a bonfire not because she means to, but because she cannot overcome the urge to burn down the Wizard's tower. Since this is impossible, she begins—quite without thinking—to burn it in effigy. After throwing each hewn branch, she stands so that the walls appear to rise miniature from the crackling incandescence, crouching just enough for the flames to garland the little window where she thinks he sleeps.

When she's finished, she stands in its blazing presence, takes comfort in the stink of her exertions, and tells herself the fire is in fact a living thing. She does this quite often: pretends that worldly things are magic, even though she knows otherwise. It reminds her that sorcery is something she can see.

That she is a witch.

She scarcely notices the first drops of rain. The fire seems to beat them into steam, to lap them from her clothing and skin with invisible tongues. Lightning flashes, so bright the flames become momentarily invisible. Then the black heavens open up. The surrounding forest lets loose a vast white roar.

For a time she crouches against the downpour, her leather hood hitched over her head, the fire spitting and steaming immediately before her. The water sends long tendrils through the crease and seam of her cloak, cold roots that gradually sink to the depth of fabric and skin. The dimmer the bonfire becomes, the more the misery of her circumstance oppresses her. To suffer so much, travel so far . . .

She never recalls standing, and certainly not drawing back her cloak. It seems that one moment she's sitting before her fire, her teeth clenched to prevent their chatter, then she's standing several paces away, soaked to drowning, fairly floating in her clothes, staring up at the crippled contours of the Wizard's tower.

"Teach me!" she hollers. "*Teach meee!*"

Like all involuntary cries, it seems to encompass her, to gather her like leaves and cast her into the sheering wind.

"Teach me!"

He simply *has* to hear, doesn't he? Her voice cracking the way all voices crack about the soul's turbulent essentials. He needs only to look down to see her leaning against the slope, wet and pathetic and defiant, the image of the woman he once loved, framed by steam and fire. Pleading. Pleading.

"*Teeeeeach!*"

"*Meeee!*"

But only the unseen wolves answer from somewhere on the higher hills, scoring the wash with cries of their own. Mocking her. *Owoooooo!* Poor little slit! *Owooooooooo!* Their laughter stings, but she is used to it, the hilarity of those who celebrate her pain. She has long ago learned how to break it into kindling, to cast it upon the bonfires behind her eyes.

"Teach me!"

Thunder cracks—the God's hammer striking the shield of the world. It echoes through the hiss of rain across the granite slopes. Hiss-hiss-hiss, like a thousand serpents warning. Mists rise like smoke.

"Curse you!" she shrieks. "You *will teach me!*"

She pauses in the marauding manner of those well practised at provocation, searching for any sign of reaction. Then, through the veils, she sees it. The great door opens, rimmed by an upside-down L of interior light. A shadow watches her for several heartbeats, as though weighing her lunacy against the chill. Then it slips out into the rain.

She knows that it is him immediately, from his hobbling gait, from his bent shape, from the burning in the pit of her throat. From the deep, sorcerous bruise, like a darkness untied to any worldly light. He leans on a staff, setting it in the crooks between boulders to keep from slipping. The rain parts about him like string, and she can see it, the sense of eyes angling, of something not quite complete, that mars all sorcery from the epic to the petty.

He descends the slope like a stair, halting only when he stands immediately before and above her. They stare at each other for a moment, the young woman, standing as though risen from the sea, and the old Wizard, waiting between the lines of falling water. She swallows at the impossibility of him, his beard frayed and feathery, his cloak dust dry in light of her fire. The forests roar about them, a never-ending rain-world.

His eyes are hard and incurious. For a moment, she struggles with a strange embarrassment, like someone caught cursing an animal in tones reserved for people. She spits water from her lips.

"Teach me," she says.

Without a word, he hefts his staff, which she could now see is made not of wood, but of bone. Quite unprepared, she watches him swing it like a mace—

An explosion against the side of her skull. Then sliding palms, knuckles scraped and skinned, arms and legs tangled rolling. She slams to a stop against a molar-shaped rock. Gasps for air.

Stunned, she watches him pick his way back up the shining slope. She tastes blood, bends her face back to let the endless rain rinse her clean. The drops seem to fall out of nowhere.

She begins laughing.

"Teeach meeeee!"

CHAPTER THREE

Momemn

On my knees, I offer you that which flies in me. My face to earth, I shout your glory to the heavens. In so surrendering do I conquer. In so yielding do I seize.

—NEL-SARIPAL, DEDICATION TO *MONIUS*

Early Spring, 19 New Imperial Year (4132 Year-of-the-Tusk), Momemn

When Nel-Saripal, the famed Ainoni poet, finished copying the final revised verses of his epic retelling of the Unification Wars, *Monius*, he had his body-slave run the manuscript to a specially commissioned galley waiting in the harbour. Seventy-three days later it was delivered to his divine patroness, Anasûrimbor Esmenet, the Blessed Empress of the Three Seas, who grasped it the way a barren woman might grasp a foundling babe.

Nel-Saripal's epic cycle would be read aloud the following morning with the entire Imperial Court in attendance. "'Momemn,'" the orator began, "'is the fist in our breast, the beating heart.'"

These words struck Esmenet as surely as a husband's slap. Even the reader, the celebrated mummer Sarpella, faltered at their utterance, they seemed so obviously seditious. Whispers and serpentine glances were traded among those in attendance, and the Blessed Empress fumed behind her painted smile. To say that Momemn was the heart was to say that Momemn was the centre, the capital, something at once factual and laudable. But the word "fist," did that not intimate violence? And to subsequently say that Momemn was the "beating" heart, did that not divide the meaning in troubling ways? Esmenet was no scholar, but after twenty years of rabid reading, she thought she knew something of words and their supernatural logic. Nel-Saripal was saying that Momemn maintained its power through brutality.

That it was a thug.

The poet was playing some kind of game—that much was obvious. Nevertheless, the elegance and imagistic splendour of the ensuing story quickly swept her away, and she decided to overlook what was at most a gesture to impertinence. What great artist failed to punish their patron? Afterwards she would decide that the insult was rather clumsy, no more subtle than the slit gowns worn by the Priestess-Whores of Gierra. Had Nel-Saripal been a greater poet, a rival to Protathis, say, the attack would have been more devious, more cutting—and well nigh impossible to punish. *Monius* would have been one of those deliciously barbed works, cutting those with the fingers to touch, and baffling the palms of all the others.

But her misgivings continued to plague her. Again and again, during whatever thoughtful lull her schedule permitted, she found herself reciting the line: *Momemn is the fist in our breast, the beating heart . . . Momemn . . . Momemn . . .* At first she took his reference to Momemn at face value—perhaps because of the way the city and its convolutions encircled her apartments on the Andiamine Heights. Nel-Saripal, she assumed, had restricted his symbolic mischief to the latter half of the formula: The literal Momemn was the metaphoric heart. But the substitutions, she realized, went deeper, the way they always did when it came to poets and their obscure machinations. Momemn wasn't the heart, it was the *heart's location*. It too was a cipher . . .

Momemn was *her*, she finally decided. Now that her divine husband had taken the field against the Consult, *she* was the fist in her people's breast. She was the heart that beat them. Nel-Saripal, the thankless ingrate, was calling her a thug. A tyrant.

"You . . ." That was how *Monius* truly began.

"You are the fist that beats us."

That night, tossing alone on the muslin planes of her bed, she found herself running in the manner of dreams, where distance, the jolt of earth, and rushing movement were little more than an inconsistent jumble. She could hear Mimara calling to her on the wind. Closer and closer, until the cries seemed to fall from the stars. But instead of her daughter, she found an apple tree, its branches bowed into skirts by the weight of crimson-shining fruit.

She fell very still. An aura of whispering sentience enclosed her. The imperceptible sway of branches. The listless flutter of black-green leaves. Sunlight showered down, pressing bright fingertips into the tree's shaded bowers. She could not move. The fallen apples seemed to glare at her, shrunken heads, withered heads, cheeks to the dirt, watching from the shadows with wormhole eyes.

She screamed when the first of the fingers and knuckles broke earth. They were as cautious as caterpillars at first, scabrous, rotted into spear points, tattered flesh wound like sackcloth about bones. Then blackened arms thrust upward, bearing hands like crabs. The meat of the fruit cracked. Branches were yanked down like fishing rods, then snapped up swishing.

The dead and their harvest.

She stood breathless, motionless, her limbs glassed with

horror. And she could only think, *Mimara . . . Mimara . . .* A mumbling thought, nebulous with the confusion that hums through all dreams. *Mimara . . .*

Then she was blinking at the grey of night's slow retreat. The tree was gone, as were the arms reaching from earthen pits. But the terrible thought remained, no more clear for the fact of waking.

Mimara.

Esmenet wept as though she were her only child. Found, then lost.

The following afternoon sunlight streamed through the fretted walls behind her, embossing the table and its sheets of parchment with brilliant white squares. The secretaries, deputations from a number of different offices, uniformly squinted as they approached with the documents that required her seal. Brocaded tusks and circumfixes shimmered from their sleeves. Grids of light rolled across their backs as they bent to kiss the polished wood of the kneeling floor.

As bored as she was, Esmenet listened attentively to their petitions, typically this or that minor legislative declaration: a clarification of the Slaver Protocols, a revised order of precedence for the Chamber of Excises, and on and on. The New Empire, she had long since learned, was a kind of enormous mechanism, one that used men as gears, thousands upon thousands of them, their functions determined by the language of law. The inevitable maintenance required ever more language, all of it underwritten by the authority of her voice.

As always, she relied heavily on Ngarau, who had been Grand Seneschal since the days of the extinct Ikurei Dynasty, to interpret the import of the requests. They had developed a comfortable rapport over the years, eunuch and Empress. She would ask brief questions, and he would respond either by answering to the best of his ability or by interrogating the petitioning functionary in his turn. If the request was granted—and the vetting process required to reach her penultimate level assured that most of them were—he would dip his ladle in the bowl of molten lead that continually warmed her left side and pour the flashing metal for her to stamp with her Seal. If, as was sometimes the case, some kind of influence peddling or bureaucratic infighting was suspected, the petitioners would be directed to the Judges down the hall. The New Empire tolerated no corruption, no matter how petty.

Mankind was at war.

Several emergency funding requests from Shigek, "tokens of the Empress's generosity," proved tricky to parse. For whatever reason, the rumours that Fanayal ab Kascamandri and his renegade Coyauri prowled the deserts about the River Sempis refused to die. Aside from this, the session had proved uneventful—thankfully. The chill air carried the promise of renewal, and the repetitive nature of the suits made her decisions seem trivial. Though she knew full well that lives turned on her every breath, she welcomed the opportunity to pretend otherwise.

For twenty years she had been Empress. For almost as long as she could read.

Sometimes the unmapped immensity of it all would come crashing through the tedium. The mundane circuit would peel open, the matter of course would evaporate into the hollow of a million mortal obligations. Women. Children. Wilful men. A crazed anxiousness would seize her. If she were walking, she would reel like a drunk, clutch at her vertigo with outstretched hands. If she were talking, she would trail into silence, avert her face and simply breathe, as though that were the endangered thread. *I am Empress*, she would think, *Empress*, and the title would speak not to the glory, but to the horror and the horror alone.

But typically the combination of routine and abstractions kept her afloat. To condense all the administrative details into the "Ministrate" or all the ecclesiastical confusion into the "Thousand Temples" was a powerful and a comforting thing. She would consult the appropriate officials and that was that. *Yes, I understand. Do your best.* Sometimes it even felt *simple*, like a library with all the books inventoried and titled—all she need do was make the proper entries. Of course, some crisis would quickly remind her otherwise, that she was simply confusing the handle for the pot, as the caste-menials would say. The details would always come leaking through—in their multitudes.

Part of her would even laugh, convinced that it was simply too absurd to be real. She, Esmenet, a battered peach from the slums of Sumna, wielding an authority that only Triamis, the greatest of the Ceneian Emperors, had known. Souls in the *millions* traded coins with her profile. *Oh what was that, you say? Thousands are starving in Eumarna. Yes-yes, but I have an insurrection to deal with. Armies, you see, simply must be fed. People? Well, they tend to suffer in silence, sell their children and whatnot. So long as the lies are told well.*

At such a remove, so far from the gutters of living truth, how could she not be a tyrant? Not matter how balanced, thoughtful, or sincerely considered her judgments, how could they not crack like clubs or pierce like spears?

Exactly as Nel-Saripal had implied, the wretch.

Without warning, a small voice piped through the officious murmur. "Thelli! Thelli! Theliopa found another one!" Esmenet saw her youngest, Kelmomas, barrelling through the secretaries, then around the grand table. He ran across his reflection to throw his arms around her waist. She hugged him, laughing.

"Sweetling . . . What do you mean?"

At times his beauty struck her breathless, his features avid beneath a mop of lavish blond curls. But when he surprised her like this, the bouncing perfection of him fairly hummed through her, made her throat thicken for pride.

With Kelmomas she could almost believe the Gods had relented.

"A *skin-spy*, Momma. Among the new slaves for the stables—Theliopa found another one!"

Esmenet involuntarily stiffened. Captain Imhailas appeared on the heel of these words, fairly swinging through the entrance to fall onto his knees. "Your Glory!"

"Leave us," Esmenet commanded Ngarau. The old Imperial Seneschal clapped his hands in dismissal, and a retreating commotion descended on the chambers.

"How is it my *son* bears this news to me?" she asked, gesturing for the Exalt-Captain to take his feet.

"I beg mercy, your Glory." Imhailas was extraordinarily attractive in a way that only Norsirai men could be. It seemed to render his embarrassment all the more ludicrous. "I set out to inform you immediately! I have no idea how—!"

"Can I *seeee*, Momma? Please!"

"No, Kel. You certainly may not!"

"But I *need* to see these things, Momma. I need to know. Someday I'll need to know!"

Scowling, she looked from the boy to the Captain, who stood armour agleam in the broken light. Through the propped doors, she could see the last of the functionaries fleeing into the palace's polished depths. One of the laggards stumbled on the hem of his robes, and for an instant, she glimpsed the tar-black bottoms of his silk slippers.

She blinked, focused on the Exalt-Captain. "What do you think?"

Imhailas hesitated for a moment, then with an air of quotation said, "Calloused hands suffer no tender eyes, your Glory."

Esmenet frowned at the hackneyed quote. *Only an idiot*, she found herself thinking, *asks an idiot for advice*. But her dismissal caught in her throat when she looked at Kelmomas. Squares of light graphed his clothes and skin, bright and oblong where not undone entirely by the compact curves of his body.

For an instant, he seemed so very *soft*, the world's most vulnerable thing, and her heart heaved with the dwarfing confusion that mothers call love. Mere months had passed since his Whelming—since the assassination attempt on the Scuari Campus. All she wanted was to protect him. She would will herself into a cocoon if she could, an impervious and eternal shield . . .

But she knew that she could not. And she was wise enough not to confuse her want for her world.

"Please, Momma," he said, his blue eyes glittering with teary eagerness. The sun seemed to shine through his flaxen curls. "*Please*."

She composed her face and looked back to Imhailas. "I think . . ." she said with a heavy sigh. "I think you're quite right, Captain. The time has come. Both my sweet cherries should see Thelli's latest discovery."

Another skin-spy in the court. Why now, after so many years?

"*Both* boys, your Glory?"

She ignored this, the way she ignored all the tonal differences that seemed to colour references to Kelmomas's twin, Samarmas. In this one thing, she would refuse the world its inroads.

With Kelmomas in tow—he had become much more reluctant at the mention of his brother—Esmenet set off in search of her other darling, Samarmas. The galleries at the summit of the Andiamine Heights were not so very large, but they had the habit of becoming labyrinthine whenever she needed to find someone or something. Of course she could have dispatched slaves to search for him—even now her train of attendants followed at a discrete distance—but she was wary of delegating too much in the way of trivial tasks: It seemed madness enough to be dressed by strange hands in the morning, let alone never having to hunt for her own children. Power, she had come to realize, had the insidious habit of inserting others between you and your tasks, rendering your limbs little more than decorative mementoes of a more human past. Her only organs remaining, it sometimes seemed, were those belonging to statecraft: a tongue attached to a devious soul.

She paused at the juncture of every corridor, the instinctive way parents do not so much look for their children as make themselves visible. Each time figures fell to their faces down the length of the marble shafts, the slaves like hairless dogs, the functionaries like piles of lavish fabric. Gilded corbels gleamed. Decorative columns shone with lines curved to the positioning of lanterns or ceiling apertures.

Not much had changed since the days when the Ikurei Dynasty had presided over the Andiamine Heights. Certainly, the palace had grown in measure with the Empire—or her hips, as it sometimes seemed. Momemn had been one of the few Three Seas cities with wisdom enough to throw itself upon the mercy of her husband. There had been no smoke on the wind, no blood on the flagstones, when she had first walked these halls. And what a wonder it had seemed then, that people could encase themselves in such glorious luxury. Marbles looted from Shigeki ruins. Gold beaten into foils, cast into figures both human and divine. The famed frescoes, such as the *Blue Hubris* by the suicide, Anchilas, or the anonymous *Chorus of the Seas* in the Mirullian Foyer. The white-jade censers. The Zeumi tapestries. The carpets so long, so ornate, that lifetimes had been spent weaving them . . .

All it had lacked was power.

A kind of mute inattention dogged her as she walked. She found herself turning down *the* hall almost without realizing, though she had been able to hear the screams for some time. *His* screams, Inrilatas. One of her middle children, youngest save for the twins.

She paused before the great bronze door to his room,

stared with distaste at the Kyranean Lions stamped into its panels. Even though she passed it several times every day, it always seemed larger than she remembered. She ran her fingertips along the greening rims. She could feel nothing of his cries in the cool metal. No warmth. No hum. The frantic sound seemed to rise more from the cold floor at her feet.

Kelmomas leaned against her thigh, mooning for her attention. "Uncle Maithanet thinks you should have him sent away," he said.

"Your uncle said that?" An itch always accompanied references to Maithanet, a premonition too indistinct to be called a worry. Because he was so much like Kellhus, she supposed.

"They're frightened of us, aren't they, Mommy?"

"Them?"

"Everybody. They're all afraid of our family . . ."

"Why would that be?"

"Because they think we're mad. They think father's seed is too strong."

Too strong for the vessel. Too strong for me.

"You've heard . . . them . . . talking?"

"Is that what happened to Inrilatas?"

"It's the God, Kel. The God burns strongly in all of you. With Inrilatas he burns strongest of all."

"Is that why he's mad?"

"Yes."

"Is that why you keep him here?"

"He is my child, Kel, as much as you. I will never abandon my children."

"Like Mimara?"

An unearthly sound burrowed from the polished stone, a shriek meant to pass sharp, cutting things. Esmenet flinched, certain he was *there*, Inrilatas, just on the other side of the door, his lips mashed against the portal's marmoreal frame. She thought she could hear teeth gnawing at the stone. She looked from the door to the slender cherub that was her other son. Kelmomas. Godlike Kelmomas. Healthy, loving, devoted to the point of comedy . . .

So unlike the others.

Please let it be.

Her smile seemed proper to the tears in her eyes. "Like Mimara," she said.

She couldn't even think the name without a series of inner cringings, as though it were a weight that could be drawn only with ill-used muscles. Even now she had her men scouring the Three Seas, searching—searching everywhere except the one place where she knew Mimara would be.

Keep her safe, Akka. Please keep her safe.

Inrilatas's shriek trailed into a series of masturbatory grunts. On and on they continued, each sucking on the one prior, all possessing a hairless animality that made her clutch Kelmomas's shoulder. She knew this was something no child should hear, especially one as impressionable as Kelmomas, but her horror immobilized her. There was something . . . *personal* in the jerking sounds—or so it seemed. Something meant for her and her alone.

The cry of "Momma!" snapped her from her trance.

It was Samarmas. He burst from his nursemaid's grasp, identical to Kelmomas in every respect, save for the slack pose of his face and the outward bulge of his eyes, so like those on ancient Kyranean statuary.

"My boy!" Esmenet cried, scooping the boy into her arms. With an "*Ooof!*" she swung him onto her hip—he was getting too big!—beamed mother-love into his idiot gaze.

My broken boy.

The nursemaid, Porsi, had followed in his stomping wake, eyes to the ground. The young Nansur slave knelt, face to the floor. Esmenet should have thanked the girl, she knew, but she had wanted to find Sammi herself, perhaps even to spy for a bit, in the way of simpler parents watching through simpler windows.

Inrilatas continued screaming through polished stone—forgotten.

Stairs. Endless stairs and corridors, from the reserved splendour of the summit, to the monumental spectacle of the palace's lower, more public reaches, thence to the raw stone of the dungeons, with troughs worn into the floor stones for the passage of innumerable prisoners. In one courtyard they crossed, Samarmas hugged the backs of everyone who fell to their faces. He was always indiscriminate with his loving gestures, particularly when it came to slaves. He even kissed one old woman on her nut-brown cheek—Esmenet's skin pimpled at the sound of her joyous sobbing. Kelmomas babbled the entire way, reminding Samarmas in his stern big brother way that they must be *warriors*, that they must be strong, that only honour and courage would earn the love and praise of their father. Listening, Esmenet found herself wondering at the Princes-Imperial they would become. She found herself fearing for them—the way she always feared when her thoughts were bent to the future.

As they descended the final stair, Kelmomas began describing skin-spies. "Their bones are soft like a *shark*'s," he said, his voice lilting in wonder. "And they have claws for faces, claws they can squeeze into any face. They could be you. They could be me. At any second they could strike you down!"

"*Monsters*, Mommy?" Samarmas asked, his eyes aglow with tears. "Sharks?" Of course he already knew what skin-spies were: She herself had regaled him with innumerable stories about their sinister role in the First Holy War. But it was part of his innocence to respond to everything as though encountering it for the very first time. Repetition, as she had discovered on many cross-eyed occasions, was a kind of drug for Samarmas.

"Kel, that's quite enough."

"But he needs to know too!"

She had to remind herself that his cleverness was that of a *normal* child, and not like that of his siblings. Inrilatas, in particular, had possessed his father's . . . gifts.

She wished she could put these worries to rest. For all her love, she could never lose herself in Kelmomas the way she could Samarmas, whose idiocy had become a kind of perverse sanctuary for her. For all her love, she could not bring herself to trust the way a mother should.

Not after so many . . . experiences.

As she feared, a carnival of personages great and small clotted the corridors leading to the Truth Room. The whole palace, it seemed, had found some excuse to see their latest captive. She even saw her *cook*, a diminutive old Nilnameshi named Bompothur, pressing toward the door with the others. The voice of Biaxi Sankas, one of the more powerful members of the Congregate, reverberated across the hooded stone spaces. "*Let me pass, you caste-menial fool!*"

The scene troubled her perhaps more than it should. To be Empress of the Three Seas was one thing, to be the wife of the *Aspect-Emperor* was quite another. In his absence, absolute authority fell to her—but how could it not bruise and break when the fall was so far? Even where one would expect her rule to be absolute—such as her own palace—it was anything but. In Kellhus's absence, the Andiamine Heights seemed nothing so much as a squabbling mountain of bowing, scraping, insinuating thieves. The Exalt-Ministers. The caste-nobles of the High Congregate. The Imperial Apparati. The visiting dignitaries. Even the slaves. It sickened her the way they all lined up moist-eyed with awe and devotion whenever Kellhus walked the halls, only to resume their cannibalistic rivalries the instant he departed—when *she* walked the gilded halls. *Word has it, Blessed Empress, that so-and-so is questioning the slave reforms, and in the most troubling manner . . .* On and on, back and forth, the long dance of tongues as knives. She had learned to ignore most of it, the palace would be on the brink of revolt if even a fraction of what was said was true. But it meant that she would never know if the palace were about to revolt, and she had read enough history to know that this was every sovereign's most mortal concern.

She cried out, "Imhailas!"

Whether it was her or some perverse trick of the stone, the ringing of her voice had the character of a screech. A herd of apprehensive faces turned to her and the twins. There was a comical scuffle as they all struggled to kneel in the absence of floor space. She could not but wonder at what Kellhus would say about this lack of discipline. Who would be punished and how? There was always punishment where the Aspect-Emperor was involved . . .

Or as he pretended to call it, education.

"Imhailas!" she cried again. She squeezed Samarmas's hand in reassurance, smiled at him. He had a tendency to cry whenever she raised her voice.

"Yes, your Glory," the Exalt-Captain called from the blockaded threshold.

"What are all these people doing here?"

"It's been some time, your Glory. Almost two years since the last—"

"This is foolish! Clear everyone out save your guards and the pertinent ministers."

"At once, your Glory."

Of course Imhailas scarce needed to utter a word: Everyone had heard her anger and her rebuke.

"They're more afraid of Father," young Kelmomas whispered at her side.

"Yes," Esmenet replied, at a loss as to how to respond otherwise. The insights of children were too immediate, too unfiltered not to be unwelcome. "Yes, they are."

Even a child can see it.

She drew the boys to the wall to make way for the file of

men—a parade of seditious souls draped in ingratiating skins, or so it seemed. She acknowledged their anxious and perfunctory bows as they scurried past, wondering how she could possibly rule when her instruments so sickened her. But she had been too political for far too long not to recognize an opportunity when she saw one. She stopped Lord Sankas as he made to pass, asked him if he would assist her with the twins. "They've never seen a skin-spy before," she explained. She wondered how she could have forgotten how tall he was—even for a caste-noble. Her own height had always been a source of shame for her, given the way it shouted her caste-menial origins.

"Indeed," he said with a gloating smile. Most men were only too eager to embrace evidence of their importance, but when they were as old as Sankas, it seemed more unseemly for some reason. He looked down, winked at her sons. "The horrors of the world are what make us men."

Esmenet smiled up at the Lord, knowing this little piece of advice to her sons would endear them to him. Kellhus was forever reminding her to seek the counsel of those whose friendship could be advantageous. Men, he was always saying, liked to see their words proved right.

"Are we going to see the monster now, Momma?" Samarmas asked in a voice as small as his eyes were wide. She looked to the child, grateful for the excuse to ignore the mob. Over the past year, ever since deciding the twins were not like the others, she had found herself retreating from the mad polity around her into the realm of maternal cares. It was more instinctive, and certainly more gratifying.

"There's no need for you to fear," she said, smiling. "Come. Lord Sankas will protect you."

Though the name was the same, the Truth Room was one of the palace chambers, subterranean or otherwise, that had been drastically expanded in the years since Kellhus's uncontested march into Momemn. The original Truth Room had been little more than the personal torture chamber of the old Ikurei Emperors, and every bit as dark and closeted as their peevish souls. The enormous chamber she now entered with her children was nothing less than an organ of state, a pit with walls tiered by walkways, some possessing cages for prisoners, others lined with various instruments of interrogation, and one, the uppermost, adorned with columns and marble veneers—a gallery for observers from the land of light. It was, the architect had told her, an inverted replica of the Great Ziggurat of Xijoser, carved so that the mighty monument on the Sempis Delta would fit if tipped into its hollow. Esmenet could remember Proyas quipping something to the effect that "sometimes Men must reach down" when seeking the Truth.

She led the children to the ornate balustrade of the highest tier, where the others awaited her. Her Master-of-Spies, Phinersa, and her Vizier, Vem-Mithriti, knelt with their faces to the floor, while Maithanet and Theliopa stood with their faces lowered in greeting. Imhailas was ushering out the last of the stragglers, his humour at once officious and curiously apologetic, the air of someone executing the irrational demands of another.

Theliopa, her eldest daughter by Kellhus, bowed in a stiff curtsy as they approached. Perhaps she was the strangest of her children, even moreso than Inrilatas, but curiously all the more safe for it. Theliopa was a woman with an unearthly hollow where human sentiment should be. Even as an infant she had never cried, never gurgled with laughter, never reached out to finger the image of her mother's face. Esmenet had once overheard her nursemaids whispering that she would happily starve rather than call out for food, and even now she was thin in the extreme, tall and angular like the God-her-father, but emaciated, to the point where her skin seemed tented over the woodwork of her bones. The clothes she wore were ridiculously elaborate—despite her godlike intellect, the subtleties of style and fashion utterly eluded her—a gold-brocaded gown fairly armoured in black pearls.

"Mother," the sallow blonde girl said in a tone that Esmenet could now recognize for attachment, or the guttering approximation of it. As always the girl flinched at her touch, like a skittish cat or steed, but as always Esmenet refused to draw back, and held Theliopa's cheek until she felt the tremors calm.

"You've done well," she said, gazing into her pale eyes. "Very well." It was strange, loving children who could see the movements of her soul through her face. It forced a kind of bitter honesty on her, the resignation of those who know they cannot hide—not ever—from the people they needed to hide from the most.

"I live to please you, Mother."

They were what they were, her children. Bits and pieces of their father. The *truth* of him—perhaps. Only Samarmas was the exception. She could see it in his every stitch, in the ardent affection with which he clung to Lord Sankas's hand, in the round way his eyes probed the shadows beyond the rail, in the anxiousness that warbled through his limbs. Only Samarmas could be . . .

Trusted.

Recoiling from these thoughts, she turned to the others and pronounced the customary greeting, "Reap the morrow." She felt Kelmomas's small fingers squeeze her palm.

"Reap the morrow," they intoned in response. Phinersa jumped to his feet with bandy-legged alacrity. He was a brilliant but nervous man, one who could bloom and wilt in the course of speaking a single sentence. He was one of those men who were far too conscious of their own eyes. They had the habit of darting around the point of your own, but more ritually than randomly, as though they followed some formal rule of avoidance, rather than any instinctive antipathy to the prick of contact. Those rare times he did manage a level gaze, it was with a penetration and intensity that boiled away to nothing in a matter of heartbeats and left you feeling at once superior and strangely exposed.

She found herself bending to assist old Vem-Mithriti, the Grandmaster of the Imperial Saik, to his feet. He smiled and murmured shamefaced thanks, more like a shrinking-voiced adolescent than one of the most powerful Exalt-Ministers in the New Empire. Sometimes Kellhus chose people for their wit and strength, as was the case with Phinersa, and sometimes for their weakness. She often wondered whether old Vem was his Gift to her, since Kellhus himself had no difficulty handling the wilful and ambitious.

Maithanet, her brother-in-law and the Shriah of the Thousand Temples, towered next to the two Exalt-Ministers, dressed in a plain white tunic. The oiled plaits of his beard gleamed like jet in the lantern light. His height and force of presence never failed to remind Esmenet of her husband—the same light, only burning through the sackcloth of a human mother.

"Thelli found it during a surprise inspection of the new slaves," he said, his voice so deep and resonant that it somehow blotted out the memory of the others. With a broad gesture, he drew her eyes out over the balustrade to the iron apparatus several lengths below . . .

Where it hung naked in a pose reminiscent of the Circumfix: the skin-spy.

Slicked in perspiration, its black limbs flexed against the iron brackets that clamped each of its joints—wrists, elbows, shoulders, waist. Even so immobilized, it seemed to *seethe* somehow, as though reflexively testing various points of leverage. The rusty grind and creak of the apparatus spoke to its ominous strength. Muscle twined like braided snakes.

A single gold pin had been driven into its skull, which, according to the arcane principles of Neuropuncture, had forced the thing to unclench its face. Masticating limbs waved where features should have been. They hooked the air like a dying crab, some flanged with disconnected lips, others bearing a flaccid eyelid, a hanging nostril, a furred swatch of brow. Perpetually shocked eyes glared from the pulpy shadows between. Teeth glistened from bared gums.

Esmenet clenched her teeth against the bile rising into her throat. Even after so many years, there was something about the creatures, some violation of fundamentals, that struck her to the visceral quick. As a reminder of the threat that loomed over her and her family, she kept one of their skulls in her personal apartments. It had a great hole where the eyes of a human would hang over the bridge of the nose. The rim of the hole possessed sockets for each unnatural finger. And the fingers, which some artisan had wired into a semblance of their natural pose, folded together in elaborate counterpoise, some curved and interlocking across the forehead, others bent into complex signs about the eyes, mouth, and nose. Every morning she glanced at it—and found herself not so much afraid as *convinced.*

It had long since become an argument for suffering her husband.

And now, here was another one, wrapped in shining meat. One of the Consult's most lethal weapons. A skin-spy. A living justification. The threat that forgave her tyranny.

"Black-skinned?" she said, turning to Maithanet. "Have we ever captured a Satyothi before?"

"This is the first," the Holy Shriah replied, nodding toward Theliopa as he spoke. "We think it might be a test of some kind."

"A plausible assumption," Theliopa said, her voice high and cold. "If the threshold of detection were a near thing, it might have been successful. For all the Consult knows, the subtle differences between complexions and bone structure could have rendered this one undetectable. It would explain the seven hundred and thirty-three days that have elapsed since their last attempt to infiltrate the court."

Esmenet nodded, too unnerved by her daughter's vacant and all-seeing gaze to work through the implications.

She checked on the boys. On his tiptoes, Kelmomas stared with something resembling rapt indecision, as if trying to decide whether the thing below them was a match for his wilder imaginings. Samarmas had abandoned Lord Sankas to join his twin at the balustrade. He stared between his fingers, his face held partially averted. They seemed wise and imbecilic versions of the same child, one modern, the other antique, almost as though history had folded back on itself. Without warning, Kelmomas turned to gaze into her face: In so many little ways, he was still his father's son—and it worried her.

"What do you think?" she asked with a forced smile.

"Scary."

"Yes. Scary."

As though sensing some kind of permission in this, Samarmas threw his arms around her waist and began blubbering. She held his cheek against her midriff and cooed to him in a soft, shushing voice. When she looked up, Phinersa and Imhailas were watching her intently. She supposed with Theliopa present she had no need to fear their intent, but even still, there always seemed to be a glimpse of malice in their look.

Or a lust that amounted to the same.

"What do you wish, your Glory?" Phinersa asked.

Without Kellhus, there was nothing they could learn from this creature. Skin-spies possessed no souls, nothing for Vem-Mithriti's sorcerous Cants to compel. And torments simply . . . aroused them.

"Sound the Plate," she said with weary decisiveness. "Let the People be reminded."

Maithanet nodded in sage assent. "A most wise decision."

Everyone stared at the monstrosity for a wordless moment,

as if committing its form to memory. No matter how many skin-spies she saw, they never ceased to unnerve her with their devious impossibility.

Imhailas cleared his throat. "Shall I make preparations for *your* attendance, your Glory?"

"Yes," she replied absently. "Of course." The People needed to be reminded of more than what threatened them, they needed to be reminded of the discipline that kept them safe as well. They needed to recall the *disciplinarian*.

The tyrant.

She held Samarmasa tight, pressed her fingers through his hair, felt his scalp as soft and as warm as a cat beneath her palm. Such a little soul. So defenceless. Her eyes strayed to Kelmomas, who now crouched, his face pressed against the stone spindles, to better study the gasping monstrosity below.

Though it pained her, she knew her duty. She knew what *Kellhus* would say . . . By the mere fact of his blood, they would live lives of mortal danger. For their own sakes, they would need to become ruthless . . . as ruthless as she had failed to become.

"And for my children as well."

"You're thinking about yesterday's recital," the Holy Shriah of the Thousand Temples said.

After giving the twins back to Porsi, Esmenet had joined her brother-in-law on the long walk to the palace's postern entrance, where his bodyguard and carriage awaited. This had become something of a tradition ever since Kellhus had left to lead the Great Ordeal against Sakarpus. Not only did Maithanet's station make him her social and political equal, his counsel had become a source of comfort—sustenance, even. He was wise in a manner that, although never quite so penetrating as Kellhus, always struck her as more . . . human.

And, of course, his blood made him her closest ally.

"The way Nel-Saripal begins," Esmenet replied, staring absently at the figures engraved in marble panels along the walls. "Those first words . . . 'Momemn is the fist in our breast, the beating heart . . .'" She turned to look up at his stern profile. "What do you think?"

"Significant," Maithanet conceded, "but only as a signal, the way birds tell sailors of unseen land."

"Hmm. Yet another unfriendly shore." She studied his expression, watched the smoke tailings of an oil-lamp break about his hair and scalp. She had said this as a joke, but her scrutiny made it seem more of a test.

Maithanet smiled and nodded. "With my brother and his stalwarts gone, all the embers that we failed to stamp out during the Unification will leap back into flame."

"What Nel-Saripal dares, others will also?"

"There can be no doubt."

She found herself frowning. "So the Consult should no longer be our first priority? Is that what you're saying?"

"No. Only that we need to throw our nets wider. Think of the host my brother has assembled. The first sons of a dozen nations. The greatest magi of all the Schools. Short of the No-God's resurrection, nothing can save Golgotterath. The Consult's only hope is to fan the embers, to throw the New Empire into turmoil, if not topple it altogether. The Ainoni have a saying, 'When the hands are strong, attack the feet.'"

"But who, Maitha? After so much blood and fire, who could be so foolish as to raise arms against Kellhus?"

"The well of fools has no bottom, Esmi. You know that. You can assume that for every Fanayal who opposes us openly, there are ten who skulk in the shadows."

"Just so long as they're not so canny," she replied. "I'm not sure we could survive ten of *him*."

Twenty years ago, Fanayal had ranked among the most cunning and committed foes of the First Holy War. Though the heathen Empire of Kian had been the first to topple at the Aspect-Emperor's feet, Fanayal had somehow managed to avoid his nation's fate. According to Phinersa's briefings, songs of his exploits had reached as far as Galeoth. The Judges had already burned a dozen or so travelling minstrels at the stake, but the lays seemed to spread and reproduce with the stubbornness of a disease. The "Bandit Padirajah," they were calling him. By simply drawing breath, the man had immeasurably slowed the conversion of the old Fanim governorates.

The Shriah and the Empress walked in silence for several moments. Their journey had taken them into the Apparatory, where the residences of the palace's senior functionaries were located. The girth of the halls had narrowed, and the mirror sheen of marble had been replaced with planes of lesser stone. Many of the doors they passed stood ajar, leaking the sounds of simpler, more tranquil existences. A nurse singing to a babe. Mothers gossiping. Those few people they encountered in the hall literally stood slack-jawed before throwing their faces to the ground. One mother viciously yanked her son, an olive-skinned boy perhaps two or three years younger than the twins, to the floor at her side. Esmenet heard his crying more in her belly than in her ears, or so it seemed.

She clutched Maithanet's arm, drew him to a halt.

"Esmi?"

"Tell me, Maitha," she said hesitantly. "When"—she paused to bite her lip—"when you . . . look . . . into my face, what do you see?"

A gentle smile creased his plaited beard. "Not so far or so deep as my brother."

Dûnyain. It all came back to this iron ingot of meaning. Maithanet, her children, everyone near to her possessed some measure of Dûnyain blood. Everyone watched with a portion of her husband's all-seeing eyes. For a heartbeat, she glimpsed Achamian as he had stood twenty years earlier, a thousand smoke plumes scoring the sky beyond him. *"But you're not thinking! You see only your love for him. You're not thinking of what he sees when he gazes upon you . . .*"

And with a blink both he and his heretical words were gone.

"That wasn't my question," she said, recovering herself.

"Sorrow . . ." Maithanet said, probing her face with warm, forgiving eyes. He lifted her small, slack hands in the thick cage of his own. "I see sorrow and confusion. Worry for your first, for Mimara. Shame . . . shame that you have come to fear your children more than you fear *for* them. So very much happens, Esmi, both here and in places remote . . . You fear you are not equal to the task my brother has set for you."

"And the others?" she heard herself ask. "Can the others see this as well?"

Dûnyain, she thought. *Dûnyain blood.*

The Shriah squeezed her hands in reassurance. "Some sense it, perhaps, but only in a dim manner. They have their prejudices, of course, but their sovereign and saviour has made *you* their road to redemption. My brother has built a strong house for you to keep. I hesitate to say as much, but you truly have no cause to fear, Esmi."

"Why?"

"For the same reason I have no fear. The *Aspect-Emperor* has chosen you."

A Dûnyain. A Dûnyain has chosen you.

"No. Why do you hesitate to tell me?"

His eyes unfocused in calculation, then returned to her. "Because if I see your fear, then *he* has seen it also. And if he has seen it, then he counts it as a strength."

She tried in vain to blink away the tears. His image sheered and blurred, Maithanet seemed an elusive, predatory presence. A concatenation of liquid shadows. "You mean he's chosen me *because* I'm weak?"

The Shriah of the Thousand Temples shook his head in

calm contradiction. "Is the man who flees to fight anew weak? Fear is neither strong nor weak until events make it so."

"Then why wouldn't *he* tell me as much."

"Because, Esmi" he said, drawing her back down the hall, "sometimes ignorance is the greatest strength of all."

For a thing to seem a miracle, it cannot quite be believed.

The following morning Esmenet awoke thinking of her children, not as the instruments of power they had become, but as babies. She often found herself shying away from thoughts of the early years of her motherhood, so relentless had Kellhus been in his pursuit of progeny. Seven children she had conceived by her husband, of which six had survived. Add to that Mimara, her daughter from her previous life, and Moënghus, the son she had inherited from Kellhus's first wife, Serwë, and she was the mother of eight . . .

Eight!

The thought never ceased to surprise and to dizzy her, so certain she had been that she would live and die barren.

Kayûtas had been the first, born close enough to Moënghus that the two had been raised as fraternal twins. She had delivered him in Shimeh upon the Holy Juterum, where the Latter Prophet, Inri Sejenus, had ascended to the Heavens two thousand years previous. Kayûtas had been so perfect, both in form and in temperament, that the Lords of the Holy War had wept upon seeing him. So perfect, like a pearl, she sometimes thought, taking in the world's shadowy jumble and reflecting only a generic, silvery light. So smooth that no fingers could grasp him, not truly.

It had been Kayûtas who had taught her that love was a kind of imperfection. How could it be otherwise, when he was perfect and could feel no love? Simply holding him had been a heartbreak.

Theliopa had come second, born in Nenciphon while

Kellhus waged the first of many wars against the drugged princes of Nilnamesh. After Kayûtas, how could Esmenet not hope against hope? How could she not clutch this new babe and pray to the Gods, please, *please*, give me but one human-hearted child? But even then, her daughter's limbs still slick with the waters of passage, she had known she had born another . . . Another child who could not love. With Kellhus at war, she stumbled into a kind of bottomless melancholy, one that made her envy suicides. If it had not been for her adopted son, little Moënghus, it might have ended then, this queer fever dream that had become her life. He at least had needed her, even if he was not her own.

That was when she began demanding resources, real resources, for her search for Mimara—whom she had sold to slavers in the shadow of starvation so very long ago. She could remember staring at Theliopa in her bassinet, a pale and wan approximation of an infant, thinking that if Kellhus denied her, she would have no choice but to . . .

Fate truly was a whore, to deliver her to such thoughts.

Of course, she found herself almost immediately pregnant, as though her womb had been a hidden concession in the deal she had struck with her husband. Her third child by Kellhus, Serwa, was born in Carythusal with the smell of the Zaudunyani conquest still on the wind—soot and death. Like Kayûtas, she had seemed perfect, flawless, and yet unlike him she had seemed capable of love. What a joy she had been! But when she was scarce three years old, her tutors realized that she possessed the Gift of the Few. Despite Esmenet's threats, despite her entreaties, Kellhus sent the girl—still a babe!—to Iothiah to be raised among the Swayal witches.

There had been bitterness in that decision, and no few thoughts of heresy and sedition. In losing Serwa, Esmenet learned that worship could not only survive the loss of love, it possessed room for hatred as well.

Then came the nameless one with eight arms and no eyes,

the first to be delivered on the Andiamine Heights. The labour had been hard, life-threatening even. Afterwards would she learn that the physician-priests had drowned it, according to Nansur custom, in unwatered wine.

Then came another son, Inrilatas—and there was no doubt that he could love. But Esmenet had developed instincts for these things, as mothers who bear many children sometimes do. From the very beginning, she had known something was wrong, though she could never name the substance of her misapprehensions. But it became plain to his nurses by his second year. Inrilatas was three when he first began speaking the little treacheries that dwelt in the hearts of those about him. The entire court walked in terror of him. By the age of five he could summon words so honest and injurious that Esmenet had seen hard-hearted warriors blanch and reach for their blades. She would never forget the time when, after singing to him in his bed, he had looked up with his too-nimble face and said, "Don't hate yourself for hating me, Mommy. Hate yourself for who you are." *Hate yourself for who you are*, spoken in the dulcet tones of child adoration. By the time he was six, only Kellhus could fathom, let alone manage, him, and he had not the time for anything more than a cursory relationship. She still shuddered whenever she recalled the rare conversations they shared, father and son. Afterwards, it was as if Inrilatas, who had always walked the perimeter of sanity, simply tripped and tumbled in the wrong direction. The veil of utter madness was drawn down.

She had prayed for the passing of her fertility during this time, for what the Nansur called *meseremta*, the "dry season." But Yatwer's Water continued to flow, and she so dreaded coupling with Kellhus that she actively sought out surrogates for him, women of native intellect like herself. But if his divine seed was a burden she could scarce bear, then it broke all the others. Of the seventeen concubines he impregnated, ten died in childbirth, and the others gave birth to more . . . nameless ones. Thirteen in sum, all drowned in wine.

Esmenet sometimes wondered how many hapless souls had been assassinated to keep this secret. A hundred? A thousand?

News of Mimara's discovery arrived shortly after Inrilatas's final breakdown. For almost ten years Esmenet's men, soldiers of the Eöthic Guard who had sworn to die before returning to their mistress empty-handed, had scoured the Three Seas. In the end they found Mimara in a brothel, dressed in paste and foil to resemble none other than Esmenet herself, so that low men might couple with their dread Empress. All Esmenet could remember of the news was the cruelty of the floor.

They had found her daughter, her only child sired by a man instead of a god. And if the manner of her discovery had not broken Esmenet's heart, then the hatred she saw in Mimara's eyes upon their reunion most certainly had . . . Mimara, sweet Mimara, who as a child would only hold her mother's thumb when they walked hand in hand, who would cry inexplicably at the sight of solitary birds, or squeal at the glimpse of rats flitting from crack to crevice. She had come back to her mother broken, another bruised and battered peach, and quite as mad as any of Esmenet's other more divine daughters and sons.

As it turned out, Mimara also possessed the Gift of the Few. But where Kellhus had turned a deaf ear to Esmenet with Serwa, this time he left the matter in her selfish hands. She would not lose another daughter to the witches, even if it destroyed any chance of mending the tattered history between them. She would not sell Mimara a second time—no matter how vicious the young woman's rantings. Even the Schoolmen Esmenet consulted had told her that Mimara was too old to master the painstaking meanings sorcery required. But as so often happens in family quarrels, the grounds were entirely incidental to the *conflict*. Mimara simply needed to punish her, and she in turn had needed to be punished—or so Esmenet had assumed.

The twins arrived during this time, and with them one final spear-throw at Fate.

There had been much cause for despair in the beginning. Though as perfect in form as their eldest brother, Kayûtas, they could not be separated without lunatic squalls of anguish. And when they were left together, all they ever did was stare into each other's eyes—watch after watch, day after day, month after month. The physician-priests had warned her of the risks of bearing children at her age, so she had prepared herself for . . . oddities, she supposed, peculiarities over and above what she had already experienced. But this was so strange as to be almost poetic: two children with what seemed a single soul.

It was Kellhus who purchased the slave who would save them—and her. His name was Hagitatas, famed among the Conriyan caste-nobility as a healer of troubled souls. Somehow, through tenderness, wisdom, and incalculable patience, he managed to pry her two little darlings apart, to give them the interval they required to draw their own breath, and so raise the frame of individual identities. Such was her relief that even the subsequent discovery of Samarmas's idiocy seemed cause for celebration.

These sons *loved*—there could be no question that they loved!

At last the Whore of Fate, treacherous Anagkë, who had lifted Esmenet from ignorance and brutality of the Sumni slums to the pitch of more profound torments, had relented. At last Esmenet had found her heart. She was an old mother now, and old mothers knew well the tightfisted ways of the world. They knew how to find largesse in its meagre capitulations.

How to be greedy with small things.

There was hope in her apprehension as her body-slaves dressed and painted her. When Porsi brought Kelmomas and Samarmas to her anteroom festooned like little generals, she laughed with delight. With the two of them in mutinous tow, she descended the stairs and landings to the lower palace, then hurried through the subterranean corridor that ran beneath the Scuari Campus. Periodically she heard the deep clap of the Plate thrumming across the city's quarters, calling all those who would witness this latest abomination. And at turns she caught hints of a deeper sound, more human in its register, legion in its tones.

By the time they surfaced in the limestone gloom of the Allosium Forum, the roar had become a deafening wash that hummed through the pillars and lintels. They stood motionless as the vestiaries fussed with creases and other unsightly defects in their clothing. Then, following an aisle between dark columns, Esmenet led her sons into light and fury.

The crest of the monumental stair seemed the summit of a mountain, a place so high that it made haze of the world below. The sun was dry and cool. The broad expanse of the Scuari Campus seethed beneath it, a dark sea scarped by the hazy contours of the city. As one, untold thousands cried out in jubilation, with abandon, as though she were the throw of the number-sticks that had saved all of their lives.

Esmenet was always conscious of her unreality at moments such as this. Everything, even the cosmetics smeared across her skin, possessed the weight of fraud. She was not Esmenet, and nor were her children Kelmomas and Samarmas. They were images, semblances drawn to answer the mob and their anxious fantasies. They were Power. They were Justice. They were mortal flesh draped about the dread intent of God.

Authority in all its myriad incarnations.

She stood with a twin to either side, pretending to bask in the thunder of their adulation. Everywhere she looked she saw open mouths, black holes no wider than a woman's first, no deeper than a boy's arm. And though the air quivered with sound, each of them seemed as soundless as a gaping fish, sucking at air too thin not to suffocate.

The silence, when it finally came, tickled her with its abruptness. She hesitated, heard the strange hum of unvoiced expectations, of endless eyes watching. Finally a solitary cough broke the hanging spell, and she started down the monumental stair, led the twins past the mirrored shields of the assembled Eöthic Guardsmen, then around the folds of the great crimson curtain that had been raised about the scaffold.

The swish of her gowns seemed to blot out all other noise. She could smell them now, her people, raw and sour. The uniformity of their faces seemed to dissolve into insulting details. The painted hauteur of the caste-nobility assembled immediately below. The woollen leers of the caste-menials crowding the innumerable distances beyond.

How many of them, she wondered, harboured souls that would see her and her children dead?

She glanced at the twins, trying to smile for their sakes. Kelmomas looked . . . blank. Tears silvered Samarmas's cheeks.

Eight of them, she thought.

Theliopa hid in her soulless apartments, far too fragile for ceremonial carnivals such as this. Moënghus, Kayûtas, and Serwas marched with their father in the Great Ordeal, at a distance appropriate to children who were strangers. Inrilatas screamed from the prison of his room. And Mimara . . . wandered.

Eight. And only these two boys loved.

Whispering, "Come," she led them to their gilded and cushioned seats. A call rang out as they sat, and all across the depths of the vista before them, the masses fell to their knees. Unable to reach over the arms of her throne, she relinquished her sons' hands. The golden claws of twin Kyranean Lions arched above her, signifying the continuity of empires from the present back to the murk of Far Antiquity. Upon her left shoulder, she bore a grand ruby brooch, symbolizing the divine blood of her husband, which had passed through his seed into her, and thence into their children. Across her right shoulder, she wore a sash of felt, blue chased with gold, the sign of her command of the Eöthic Guard, the protectors of the Imperial Precincts, and in the absence of the Aspect-Emperor, her own private army, bound to her by oaths of life and death.

She heard rather than saw the release of the curtains that concealed the scaffold behind her. Shouts like a thunderclap. The mobs surged, not so much forward as *outward*. Hands were raised in air-pummelling exultation. Lips curled. Teeth flashed with sunlit spittle.

Somehow, through the roar, she could hear Samarmas bawling to her right. When she looked, she saw him huddling, shoulders in and chin down, as though trying to squeeze through some hidden passage within himself. A kind of maternal hatred clamped her jaw tight, a wild urge to order the Guardsmen into the masses, to cut and beat them from her sight. How dare they frighten her child!

But to be a sovereign is to be forever, irrevocably, cut into many. To be a matron, simple and uncompromising. To be a spy, probing and hiding. And to be a general, always calculating weakness and advantage.

She fought the mother-clamouring within, ignored his distress. Even Samarmas—who she was certain would become nothing more than a dear fool—even he had to learn the madness that was his Imperial inheritance.

For him, she told herself. *I do this for his sake!*

The mobs continued howling, not at her or her sons, but at the sight of the Consult skin-spy, which she knew would be strung like a spitted pig through the centre of the scaffold above and behind her. According to tradition, her eyes were too holy for such a horrific sight, so a lottery was held among the caste-nobility to see who would be granted the honour of bringing her the hand mirror she would use to actually witness the creature's purification. With some surprise she saw Lord Sankas approach, his elbows pressed together before his cuirass, so that the mirror could lay flat across his inner forearms.

Samarmas flew from his seat and hugged him about the waist. For a moment the old caste-noble teetered. Gales of laughter passed through the crowds. Esmenet hastened to detach him, wiped his cheeks and kissed his forehead, then directed him back to his little throne.

Grinning in embarrassment, Biaxi Sankas knelt so that he might offer up the mirror. Nodding to show Imperial favour, she took it from his arms, raised it so that she saw flashing sky, then her own face. Her beauty surprised her—large dark eyes on an oval face. She could not remember when it happened, when she starting feeling older and uglier than she in fact was. She had always been popular as a whore, even in a city renowned for its white-skinned tastes. She had always been beautiful—and in that down-to-the-bones way that somehow followed certain women even into their decrepitude.

She had never been a match for her face.

A pang made her avert the mirror, and she glimpsed the uppermost timbers of the scaffold hanging in a pool of bald sky. Tilting the handle, she followed beams to where the chains were anchored, then followed the chains until the skin-spy occupied the mirror's centre. With pinched breaths, she gazed at what she had already seen in the multitude of faces before her: coin for the toll their Aspect-Emperor had exacted from them.

The thing bucked and thrashed, bouncing like a stone tied to a bowstring. Perched on separate boarded platforms, two of Phinersa's understudies ministered to the thing, the one already making the incisions required to peel back the skin, the other flicking the Neuropuncture needles that controlled the abomination's reaction—the thing would simply cackle and climax otherwise. Like a chorus of burning bulls it screamed, its spine arched, the radial limbs of its face yanked back like the petals of a dying flower.

Both the twins had climbed into their seats to gaze over the back, Kelmomas pale and expressionless, Samarmas with his shining cheeks pressed to the cushion. She wanted to shout at them to turn away, to look back to the shrieking mob, but her voice failed her. Even though the mirror was meant to protect her, holding it the way she did seemed to make it all the more real, into something that *rubbed* against the soft-skin of her terror.

The brand was drawn from an iron-bowl of coals that had been raised into the scaffold. The thing's eyes were put out.

With a kind of rapt horror she found herself wondering at her circumstances. What kind of whore was Fate, to throw her into this place, this time, to make her the vessel of cruel godlings and the bar of world-breaking events? She believed in her husband. She believed in the Great Ordeal. She believed in the Second Apocalypse. She believed in all of it.

She just couldn't believe that any of it happened.

She whispered to herself in that paradoxical voice we all bear within us, the one that speaks the most wretched truths and the most beguiling lies, the one that is most us, and so not quite us at all. She whispered, "*This is a dream.*"

Sarmarmas wept and Kelmomas, who otherwise seemed so strong for a child his age, trembled like an old man's dying words. At last she relented. Setting down the mirror, she reached over the arms of her throne to squeeze both their hands. The feel of small fingers closing tight about her own brought tears to her eyes. It was a sensation so primeval, so *right*, that it almost always daubed the turmoil from her soul.

But this time it felt more like an . . . admission.

The masses roared in exultation, becoming in some curious way, the iron that burned, the blade that peeled. And Esmenet sat painted and rigid, gazing out across their furious regions.

Thug. Tyrant. Empress of the Three Seas.

A miracle not quite believed.

Chapter Four

Hûnoreal

For He sees gold in the wretched and excrement in the exalted. Nay, the world is not equal in the eyes of the God.

—SCHOLARS, 7:16, *THE TRACTATE*

Early Spring, 19 New Imperial Year (4132 Year-of-the-Tusk), southwestern Galeoth

There is no other place. It is as simple as that.

She cannot go back, not to the brothel that is her mother's palace, nor to the brothel that is a brothel. She was sold so very long ago, and nothing—no one—can buy her back.

She pilfers wood from the shed—little more than a wall cobbled from the debris fallen from the upper tower—and watches his slave curse and scratch his woolly head, then strike out to replace it. She makes fires, even though she has nothing to cook or to burn, and she sits before them, poking them like an anthill or staring at them, as though it were a little baby kicking and clawing at an impossible sky. She lets her mule, whom she calls Foolhardy, wander free, thinking or maybe even hoping that it would run away. Each night, she hugs herself in shame and guilt, certain that Foolhardy will be taken down by the wolves or at least spooked into running by their endless howls. But each morning, the brute is still there, standing close enough to be hit by a stone, flicking its ears at flies, staring off in any direction but hers.

She cries.

She continues to watch her fire, gazes at it with a new mother's fascination, gazes at it until her eyes are pinched dry. There is something *proper* about flames, she thinks. They possess a singularity of purpose that can only be called divine . . .

Flare. Wax. Consume.

Like a human. Only with grace.

One of the children, the youngest of the girls, creeps down to her to explain they have been forbidden to speak or play with her because she is a witch. Was it true she's a witch?

As a joke Mimara grimaces and croaks, "*Yeeaasss!*"

After the little girl flees, she sees them from time to time, hiding behind a fence of weeds or the ridged edge of some immense tree trunk, crawling and peering and running with faux-screams whenever they realize that she sees them watching.

She can see the Wards set about the tower, though she can only guess at their purposes. And she notes the scattered signs of more violent, more ephemeral sorceries—a gash in a monstrous elm, scorching across plates of stone, earth cooked to glass—proof that the Wizard has resorted to his prodigious skills. Always and everywhere she sees the ontic *plenitude* of things—the treeness of trees, the essence of water and stone and mountains—mostly pristine, but sometimes wrecked thanks to Schoolmen and their savage croon. The eyes of the Few were with her always, prodding her onto this path she has chosen, fortifying her resolve.

But more and more the *different eye* seems to open, one that has perplexed her for many years—that frightens her like an unwanted yen for perversion. Its lid is drowsy, and indeed it slumbers so deep she often forgets its presence. But when it stirs, the very world is transformed.

For moments at a time, she *can see them* . . . Good and evil.

Not buried, not hidden, but writ like another colour or texture across the hide of everything. The way good men shine brighter than good women. Or how serpents glow holy, while pigs seem to wallow in polluting shadow. The world is unequal in the eyes of the God—she understands this with intimate profundity. Masters over slaves, men over women, lions over crows: At every turn, the scriptures enumerate the rank of things. But for terrifying moments, the merest of heartbeats, it is unequal *in her eyes* as well.

It's a kind of madness, she knows. She has seen too many succumb in the brothels to think she is immune. Their handlers were loath to mark the skin, so they punished the soul. She was no exception.

It *has* to be madness. Even still, she cannot but wonder how Achamian will appear in the light of this more discerning eye.

The morning sun rears from the bulk of the hill and lances across the trees with their limbs like frozen ropes, spilling pools of bright through the thatched gloom. And she watches and watches, until the colours pale into coral evening.

And she thinks the tower was not so tall. It only seems such because it occupies higher ground.

The world hates you . . .

The thought comes upon her, not with stealth or clamour, but with the presumption of a slave owner, of one who sees no boundaries save their own.

The suffering follows quick upon the heels of her vigil—she had exhausted the last of her provisions before reaching the tower—and something within her rejoices. The world *does* hate her—she does not need a small brother's tearful confession to know that. "*It hurts Momma to even look at you!*

She wishes she would have drowned you instead of sold you . . ." Here she sits, starving and shivering, staring and croaking at the inscrutable window beneath the tower's demolished crown. This one thing she wants—to become a witch, to exact what she has paid . . .

So of course she must be denied.

There is no other place. So why not cast her life across the Whore's table? Why not press Fate to the very brink? At least she will die knowing.

She weeps twice, though she feels nothing of the sorrow that moves her: once glimpsing one of the little girls crouched peeing beneath sunshot bowers, and again seeing the Wizard's silhouette pacing back and forth across his open window—back and forth. She literally cannot remember the last time she has been at one with her weeping. In her childhood, she supposes. Before the slavers.

At the very end of the heart's exhaustion lies a kind of resignation, a point where resolve and surrender become indistinguishable. Wavering requires alternatives, and she has none. The world is in rout. To leave would be to embark on a flight without refuge, to lead an itinerant existence, aimless, with nothing to credit one far-flung road over another, since despair has become all directions. She has no choice because all her choices have become the same.

A broken tree, as her brothel-master once told her, can never yield.

Two days become three. Three become four. Hunger makes her dizzy, while the rain makes her clay-cold. *The world hates you*, she thinks, staring at the broken tower. *Even here.*

The last place.

And then one night he simply comes out. He looks haggard, not just like an old man who never sleeps, but one who never forgives—himself or others, it does not matter. He bears rank wine and steaming food, which she falls upon like a thankless animal. Then he sits opposite her fire and begins talking. "The *Dreams*," he says with the intensity of someone who has waged long war against certain words.

She stares at him, unable to stop fingering food into her mouth, which she swallows against the sob in the back of her throat. The firelight seems to have grown shining porcupine quills. For a moment, she fears she might swoon for relief.

He speaks of the Dreams of the First Apocalypse, the nightmares that all Mandate Schoolmen share thanks to the derelict memories of their ancient founder, Seswatha, and the long dark horror of his war against the Consult. "Over and over," he mutters, "as if a life can be writ like a poem, torments fashioned into verses . . ."

"Are they that bad?" she asks in the lame silence. She can scarce see him past the combination of her tears and the fire's glare: an old and rutted face, one that has seen much—too much—and yet has not forgotten how to be tender or honest.

He winks at her before gazing down to fiddle with his pouch and pipe. He stuffs the bowl, his look both pensive and sealed. He picks up a twig from the fire's edge; a small flame twirls from the end of it.

"They used to be," he says, lighting the pipe. He goes cross-eyed, staring at the touch of fire and bowl.

"I don't understand."

He draws deeply on the stem; the bowl glows like a molten coin.

"Do you know," he asks, exhaling a cloud of sweet-smelling smoke, "why Seswatha left us his dreams?"

She knows the answer. Her mother always resorted to talk of Achamian to salve the abrasions between her and her embittered daughter. Because he was her real father, Mimara had always thought. "To assure the School of Mandate never forgets, never loses sight of its mission."

"That's what they say," Achamian replies, savouring his smoke. "That the Dreams are a goad to action, a call to arms. That by suffering the First Apocalypse over and over, we had no choice but to war against the possibility of the Second."

"You think otherwise?"

A shadow falls across his face. "I think that your adoptive father, our glorious, all-conquering Aspect-Emperor, is right." The hatred is plain in his voice.

"Kellhus?" she asks.

An old man shrug—an ancient gesture hung on failing bones. "He says it himself, Every life *is a cipher* . . ." Another deep inhalation. "A riddle."

"And you think Seswatha's life is such."

"I know it is."

And then the Wizard tells her. About the First Holy War. About his forbidden love for her mother. About how he was prepared to gamble the very World for the sanctuary of her arms. There is a candour to his telling, a vulnerability that makes it all the more compelling. He speaks plaintively, lapsing time and again into the injured tone of someone convinced others do not believe them wronged. And he speaks slyly, like a drunk who thinks he confides terrible secrets . . .

Even though Mimara has heard this story many times, she finds herself listening with an almost childish attentiveness, a willingness to be moved, even hurt, by the words of another. He has no idea, she realizes, that this story has become song and scripture in the world beyond his lonely tower. *Everyone* knows he loved her mother. *Everyone* knows that she chose the Aspect-Emperor and that Achamian subsequently fled into the wilderness . . .

The only secret is that he still lives.

With these thoughts her wonder quickly evaporates

into embarrassment. He seems overmatched, tragically so, wrestling with words so much larger than himself. It becomes cruel to listen as she does, pretending not to know what she knows so well.

"She was your morning," she ventures.

He stops. For a heartbeat his eyes seem to lose something of their focus, then he glares at her with a kind of compressed fury. He turns to tap his pipe against a stone jutting from the matted leaves.

"My what?"

"Your morning," Mimara repeats hesitantly. "My mother. She used to tell me that . . . that she was your morning."

He holds the bowl to the firelight for inspection. "I no longer fear the night," he says with an absent intensity. "I no longer dream as Mandate Schoolmen dream." When he looks up, there is something at once flat and decisive in his eyes. The memory of an old and assured resolution.

"I no longer pray for the morning."

She leans back to pluck another log for the fire. It lands with a rasping thump, sends a train of sparks twirling up through the smoke. Watching their winking ascent to avoid his gaze, she hugs her shoulders against the chill. Somewhere neither near nor far, wolves howl into the bowl of the night. As though alarmed, he glances away into the wood, into the wells of blackness between the variant trunks and limbs. He stares with an intensity that makes her think that he *listens* as much as he hears, to the wolves and to whatever else—that he knows the myriad languages of the deep night.

It is then that he tells his tale in earnest . . .

As though he has secured permission.

Her mother had waited for him like this, so very long ago.

Over the days and nights since Mimara's arrival, Achamian had told himself many things. That he was angry—how could he reward such impudence? That he was prudent—what could be more dangerous than harbouring a fugitive Princess-Imperial? That he was compassionate—she was too old to master the semantics of sorcery, and the sooner she understood this, the better. He told himself many things, acknowledged many passions, save the confusion that was the truth of his soul.

Her mother, Esmenet, had waited for him on the banks of the River Sempis over twenty years previous. Not even word of his death could turn her from her vigil, so obstinate, so mulish was her love. Not even sense could sway her.

Only Kellhus and the appearance of honesty.

Even before Mimara began her watch—or siege, as it sometimes seemed—Achamian knew that she shared her mother's stubbornness. It was no small feat travelling alone from Momemn the way she had; his skin prickled at the thought of it, this small woman daring the Wilds to find him, spending night after night alone in the scheming dark. So even before he had shut his doors against her, commanded his slaves to avoid her, he knew she would not be so easily driven away. Even that night when he had struck her in the rain.

Something more was needed. Something deeper than sense.

He told himself that she was mad enough to do it, that she would literally waste to nothing waiting for him to climb down from his tower. He told himself he needed only to be *honest*, to confess the truth in all its mangled detail, and that she would see, realize that her vigil could win only the destruction of two souls. He told himself these things because he still loved her mother, and because he knew that one never stood still, even while waiting. That sometimes the sheathed knife could cut the most throats of all.

So he came in kindness, with the food she so obviously needed, and with an openness that itched because of its premeditation. He certainly hadn't anticipated *losing* himself in story and conversation. It had been so long since he had truly spoken. For nigh twenty years, his words had always skipped without sinking.

"I'm not even sure when it began happening, let alone why," he said, pausing to draw a palsied breath. "The Dreams began to change . . . in strange, little ways at first. Mandate Schoolmen claim to relive Seswatha's life, but this is only partially true. In fact, we dream only portions, the long trauma of the First Apocalypse. All we dream is the spectacle. 'Seswatha,' the old Mandate joke goes, 'does not shit.' The banalities—the substance of his life—is missing . . . The *truth* of his life is missing."

All the things that were forgotten, he realized.

"In the beginning, I noticed a change in the *character*, perhaps, but nothing more. A slight difference in emphasis. When the dreamer is remade, won't the dreams change also? Besides, the dread spectacle was simply too overwhelming to care all that much. When thousands are screaming, who pauses to count bruises on an apple?

"Then it happened: I dreamed of him—Seswatha—stubbing his toe . . . I fell asleep, this world folded in on itself the way it always does, and *his* world rose into its place. I was he, crossing a gloomy room racked with what seemed to be thousands of scrolls, mumbling, lost in thought, and I stubbed my toe on the bronze foot of a brazier . . . It was like a fever dream, the ones that travel like a cart in a circle, happening over and over. Seswatha stubbing his toe!"

Without thinking, he had leaned forward and clutched the tip of his felt-slippered foot. The leather was fire hot. Mimara simply stared at him, her eyes placid above fine-boned cheeks, looking for all the world like the past, like *her* staring out over the smoke of a harsher fire. Another abject listener. Either she remained silent out of irritation—perhaps he had spoken too long or too hard—or she kept her counsel, understanding that his story was a living thing, and as such could only be judged as a whole.

"When I awoke in the morning," he continued, "I had no idea what to make of it. It didn't strike me as a revelation of any kind, only a curiosity. There are always anomalies, you see. If this were Atyersus, I could show you whole tomes cataloguing the various ways in which the Dreams misfire: the inversions, substitutions, alterations, corruptions, and on and on. More than a few Mandate scholars have spent their lives trying to interpret their significance. Numerological codes. Prophetic communications. Ethereal interferences. It's an easy obsession, considering the suffering involved. They convince nobody save themselves in the end. As bad as philosophers.

"So I decided the toe-stubbing dream was my *own*. Seswatha never stubbed his toe, I told myself. I stubbed my dream toe while dreaming that I was Seswatha. After all, it was *my* toe that ached all morning! It never happened, I told myself. Not really . . .

"And of course the next night it was back to the Dreams as I knew them. Back to the blood and the fire and the horror. A year passed, maybe more, before I dreamed another banality: Seswatha scolding a student on a veranda overlooking the Library of Sauglish. I dismissed this one the same as the first.

"Then two months after that, I dreamed yet another trivial thing: Seswatha huddled in a scriptorium, reading a scroll by the light of coals . . ."

He trailed, though whether to let the significance settle in or to savour the memory, he did not know. Sometimes words interrupted themselves. He pinched the hem of his cloak, rolled the rough-sewn seam between thumb and forefinger.

Mimara ran the blade of her hand across the bowl's interior curve to scoop out the last of her gruel—like any slave or caste-menial. It was strange, Achamian noted, the way she alternately remembered and forgot her *jnanic* manners. "What was the scroll?" she asked, swallowing.

"A lost work," he replied, absent with memories. He blinked. "Gotagga's *Parapolis* . . . The title means nothing to you, I know, but for a scholar it's nothing short of . . . well, a miracle. *The Parapolis* is a lost work, famous, the first great treatise on politics, referenced by almost all the writers of Far Antiquity. It was one of the greater treasures lost in the First Apocalypse and *I dreamed of reading it*, as Seswatha, sitting in the cellars of the Library . . ."

Mimara paused for one last pass of her tongue along the bowl's rim. "And you don't think you invented this?"

Irritation marbled his laugh. "I suppose my tongue is sharp enough to count me clever, but I'm no Gotagga, I assure you. No. No. There was no question. I awoke in a mad haste, searching for quill, hide, and horn so I could scratch down as much as I could remember . . ."

Her meal forgotten, Mimara watched him with same shrewd canniness that had so honed her mother's beauty. "So the dreams were *real* . . ."

He nodded, squinting at the memory of the miracle that had been that morning. What a wondrous, breathless scramble! It was as though the answer was already there, wholly formed, as clear as the steam rolling off his morning tea: He had started dreaming *outside* the narrow circle of his former Mandate brothers. He had begun dreaming Seswatha's *mundane life*.

"And no one," she asked, "no Mandate Schoolman, has ever dreamed these things before?"

"Bits maybe, fragments, but nothing like this."

How strange it had been, to find his life's revelation in the *small* things; he who had wrestled with dying worlds. But then the great ever turned upon the small. He often thought of the men he'd known—the warlike ones, or just the plain obstinate—of their enviable ability to overlook and to ignore. It was like a kind of wilful illiteracy, as if all the moments of unmanly passion and doubt, all the frail details that gave substance to their lives, were simply written in a tongue they couldn't understand and so *needed* to condemn and belittle. It never occurred to them that to despise the small things was to despise *themselves*—not to mention the truth.

But then that was the tragedy of all posturing.

"But why the change?" she asked, her face a delicate oval hanging warm and motionless against the black forest deeps. "Why you? Why *now*?"

He had inked these questions across parchment many times.

"I have no idea. Perhaps it's the Whore—fucking Fate. Perhaps it's a happy consequence of my madness—for one cannot endure what I've endured day and night without going a little mad, I assure you." He made her laugh by blinking his eyes and jerking his head in caricature. "Perhaps, by ceasing to live my own life, I'd began living his. Perhaps some dim memory, some spark of Seswatha's soul, is reaching out to me . . . Perhaps . . ."

Achamian blinked at the crack in his voice, cleared his throat. Words could soar, dip, and dazzle, and sometimes even cross paths with the sun. Blind and illuminate. But the voice was different. It remained bound to the earth of expression. Not matter how it danced, the graves always lay beneath its feet.

On the back of a heavy breath, he said, "But there is a far greater question."

She hugged her knees before the pop and swirl of the fire, blinking slowly, her expression more careful than impassive. He knew how he must look, the challenge in his glare, the defensiveness, the threat of punishing surrogates. He looked like a venomous old man, balling up his reasons in uncertain fists—he knew as much.

But if there were judgment in her eyes, he could detect nothing of it.

"My stepfather," she said. "Kellhus is the question."

He imagined he must be gaping at her, gawking like a stump-headed fool.

He had spoken to her as if she were a stranger, an innocent, when in point of fact she was joined to him at the very root. Esmenet was her mother, which meant that Kellhus was her stepfather. Even though he had known this, the significance of that knowing had completely escaped him. Of course she knew of his hatred. Of course she knew the particulars of his shame!

How could he be so oblivious? The Dûnyain was her father! The *Dûnyain*.

Did this not instantly make her an instrument of some kind? A witting or unwitting spy? Achamian had watched an entire army—a *holy* war—succumb to his dread influence. Slaves, princes, sorcerers, fanatics—it did not matter. Achamian himself had surrendered his love—his wife! What chance could this mere girl have?

How much of her soul was hers, and how much had been replaced?

He gazed at her, tried to scowl away the slack from his expression.

"He sent you, didn't he?"

She looked genuinely confused, dismayed even. "What? Kellhus?" She stared at him, her mouth open and wordless. "If his people find me, they would drag me home in chains! Throw me at the feet of my fucking mother—you *have* to believe that!"

"He sent you."

Something, some mad note in his voice perhaps, rocked her backward. "I'm not ly-lying . . ." Tears clotted her eyes.

A strange half-crook bent her face to the side, as though angling it away from unseen blows. "I'm not *lying*," she repeated with a snarling intensity. A twitch marred her features. "No. Look. Everything was going so well . . . Everything was going so well!"

"This is the way it works," Achamian heard himself rasp in an utterly ruthless voice. "This is the way he sends you. This is the way he *rules*—from the darkness in our own souls! If you were to *feel* it, know it, that would simply mean there was some deeper deception."

"I don't know what you're talking about! He-he's always been kind—"

"Did he ever tell you to forgive your mother?"

"What? What do you mean?"

"Did he ever tell you the shape of your own heart? Did he ever speak salving words, healing words, words that helped you see yourself more clearly than you had ever seen yourself before?"

"Yes—I mean, no! And yes . . . Please . . . Things were going so—!"

There was a grinding to his aspect, an anger that had become reptilian with age. "Did you ever find yourself in awe of him? Did something whisper to you, This man is more than a man? And did you feel gratified, gratified beyond measure, at his merest tenderness, at the bare fact of his attention?"

He was shaking as he spoke now, shaking at the memories, shaking at the nakedness of twenty years stripped away. It seemed to hang about the edges of his vision, the lies and the hopes and the betrayals, the succession of glaring suns and uproarious battles.

"Akka . . ." she was saying. So like her whore-mother. "What are you talki—?"

"When you stood before him!" he roared. "When you *knelt in his presence*, did you feel it? Hollow and immovable, as if you were at once smoke and yet possessed the bones of the world? Truth? Did *you feel Truth?*"

"Yes!" she cried. "Everyone does! *Everyone!* He's the Aspect-Emperor! He's the Saviour. He's come to save us! Come to save the Sons of Men!"

Achamian stared at her aghast, his own vehemence ringing in his ears. Of *course* she was a believer.

"He sent you."

It was too late, he realized, staring at the image of Mimara across the fire. It had already happened. Despite all the intervening years, despite the waning violence of the Dreams, she had returned him to the teeth of yesterday. To simply gaze upon her was to taste the dust and blood and smoke of the First Holy War.

He understood her look—how could he not when he so readily recognized it as his own? Too many losses. Too many small hopes denied. Too many betrayals of self. The look of someone who understands that the World is a peevish judge, forgiving only to render its punishments all the more severe. She had suffered a moment of weakness when she had seen him clambering down the slopes with food; he could see that now. She had let herself hope. Her soul had taken her body's gratitude and made it its own.

He believed her. She was not a willing slave. If anything she reminded him of the Scylvendi, of a soul at once strong and yet battered beyond recognition. And she looked so much like her mother . . .

She was precisely the kind of slave Kellhus would send to him. Part cipher. Part opiate.

Someone Drusas Achamian could come to love.

"Did you know I was there when he first arrived in the Three Seas," he said, broaching the silence of dark forests and rustling flames. "He was no more than a beggar claiming princely blood—and with a Scylvendi as his companion no less! I was there from the very first. It was *my back* he broke climbing to absolute power."

He rubbed his nose, breathed deep as though preparing for the plunge. It never ceased to strike him as strange, the fits and starts of the body and its anxieties.

"Kellhus," he said, speaking the name in the old way, with the intonations of familiarity and wry trust. "My student . . . My friend . . . My prophet . . . It was my wife he stole . . .

"My morning."

He glared, challenging her to speak again. She simply blinked, wriggled as though to adjust her position. He could see her swallow behind the line of her lips.

"The only thing," he continued, his voice wrung ragged with conflicting passions. "The only thing I took with me from my previous life was a simple question: Who is Anasûrimbor Kellhus? *Who?*"

Achamian stared at the bed of coals pulsing beneath the blackened wood, paused to allow Mimara fair opportunity to respond, or so he told himself. The truth was that the thought of her voice made him wince. The truth was that his story had turned into a confession.

"Everyone knows the answer to that question," she ventured, speaking with a delicacy that confirmed his fears. "He's the Aspect-Emperor."

Of course she would say this. Even if she hadn't been Kellhus's adoptive daughter, she would have said precisely the same thing. They so wanted it to be simple, believers. "*It is what is!*" they cried, sneering at the possibility of other eyes, other truths, overlooking their own outrageous presumption. "*It says what it says*," spoken with a conviction that was itself insincerity. They ridiculed questions, for fear it would make their ignorance plain. Then they dared call themselves "open."

This was the iron habit of Men. This was what shackled them to the Aspect-Emperor.

He shook his head in slow deliberation. "The most important question you can ask any man, child, is the question of *his origin*. Only by knowing what a man has been can you hope to say what he *will* be." He paused, brought up short by an old habit of hesitation. How easy it was to hide in his old pedantic ruts, to recite rather than talk. But no matter how woolly, his abstractions always became snarled in the very needling particularities he so unwittingly tried to avoid. He had always been a man who wanted to digress, only to find himself bleeding on the nub.

"But everyone knows the answer to that question," she said with same care as before, "Kellhus is the Son of Heaven." *What else could he be?* her over-bright eyes asked.

"Yet he is flesh and blood, born of a father's seed and a mother's womb. He was reared. He was taught. He was sent out into the world . . ." He raised his eyebrows as though speaking something crucial but universally overlooked. "So tell me, where did all this happen? *Where?*"

For the first time, it seemed, he glimpsed real doubt gnawing her gaze. "They say he was a prince," she began, "that he comes from Atrith—"

"He does not come from Atrithau," Achamian snapped. "I know this on a dead man's authority."

The Scylvendi. Cnaïür urs Skiötha. As always, the man's words came back to him: "*With every heartbeat they war against circumstance, with every breath they conquer! They walk among us as we walk among dogs, and we yowl when they throw out scraps, we whine and whimper when they raise their hand . . . They make us love!*"

They. The Dûnyain. The Tribe of the Aspect-Emperor.

"But what about his bloodline?" Mimara asked. "Are you saying his name is false as well?"

"No . . . He *is* an Anasûrimbor, I grant you that—the coincidences would be stacked too high were it otherwise. That is our only clue."

"How so?"

"Because it means the question of his birthplace is the question of where the Line of Anasûrimbor could have survived."

She seemed to consider this. "But if not Atrithau, then where? The North is more than ruined, more than wilderness—or so my tutors always say. How could anyone survive with . . . *them?*"

Them. The Sranc. Achamian thought of the multitudes, clawing the earth in frustration, throwing up gouts of dirt in the absence of warding limbs, stamping and howling, stamping and howling across the endless tracts.

"Exactly," he said. "If the Line were to survive, it had to be within a refuge of some kind. Something secret, hidden. Something raised by the Kûniüric High Kings, ere the First Apocalypse . . ."

"*Then listen!*" the Scylvendi cried. "*For thousands of years they have hidden in the mountains, isolated from the world. For thousands of years they have bred, allowing only the quickest of their children to live. They say you know the passing of ages better than any, sorcerer, so think on it!* Thousands *of years . . . Until we, the natural sons of true fathers, have become little more than children to them.*"

"A sanctuary."

Achamian knew he was speaking too desperately now, even though he measured his words the way hungry mothers dolloped out butter. Such words could not come slow enough. *The Aspect-Emperor a liar?* Her face was blank in the way of those grievously offended, whose retort remained bottled by the fear of unstopping too many passions. His soul's eye and ear cried out for her: *Jealous old fool! He stole her*, Esmenet! *That is the sum of your pathetic case against him. He stole the only woman you've loved! And now you lust only for his destruction, to see him burn, though all the world is tinder . . .*

He breathed deeply, leaned back from the fire, which

suddenly seemed to nip him with its heat. He resolved to refill his pipe, but could only clench his fists against the tremors.

My hands shake.

His voice grows more shrill. His gesticulations become wilder. His discourse develops a pinned-in-place savagery that makes him difficult to watch and impossible to contradict.

Her heart rejoices at first, certain that he has relented. But the *tone* of his voice quickly tells her otherwise. The excitement. The wry delivery of his observations, as though to say, *How many times?* The way people speak is a bound thing, as far from free as a slave or a horse. Place binds it. Occasion binds it. But other people rule it most of all; the shadow of names lies hidden in every word spoken. And the longer he talks, the more Mimara realizes that he is speaking to someone other than her . . .

To Esmenet.

The irony stings for some reason. She had taken him to be her father, and now he takes her to be her mother. *He's mad . . . Mad the same as me.*

The Wizard is not so much her father, she realizes, as her *brother*. Another child of Esmenet, almost as broken, and every bit as betrayed.

She has been wrong about him in every way, not simply with regard to demeanour and appearance. Her mother styled him a scholar and a mystic, someone who spent his exile lost in arcane researches. Mimara has read enough about sorcery to know the importance of meanings, that semantic purity is a Schoolman's perennial obsession. And yet nothing could be further from the case. As he explains to her, he cares *nothing* for the Gnosis, not even as a tool. He has retired from the Three Seas for heartbreak—this much is true.

But the *reason*, the rule that makes his life rational in his own eyes, is simple vengeance.

The truth of Anasûrimbor Kellhus, he insists, was to be found in the secret of his origins—in the secret of something called the Dûnyain. "The Scylvendi was his mistake!" Achamian cries, his eyes wild with unkempt passions. "The Scylvendi knew what he was. *Dûnyain!*" And the secret of the Dûnyain, he claims, though Mimara understands instantly that this is little more than a hope, was to be found in the detail of Seswatha's life.

His Dreams. His Dreams had become the vehicle for his vengeance. Here, on the very edge of the wilderness, he has bent all his efforts to decoding their smoky afterimages. Twenty years he has laboured, mapping, drawing up meticulous inventories, sifting through the debris, the detritus of a dead sorcerer's ancient life, searching for the silver needle that would see his wrongs avenged.

It's more than a fool's errand; it is a madman's obsession, on a par with those ascetics who beat themselves with strings and flint, or who eat nothing but ox-hides covered in religious writings. Twenty years! Anything that could consume so much life simply has to be deranged. The hubris alone . . .

His hatred of Kellhus she finds understandable, though she herself bears no grudge against her stepfather. She barely knows the Aspect-Emperor, and those rare times she found herself alone with him on the Andiamine Heights—twice—he seemed at once radiant and tragic, perhaps the most immediate and obvious soul she had ever encountered.

"*You think you hate her,*" he once said—referring to her mother, of course.

"*I know I do.*"

"*There's no knowledge,*" he had replied, "*in the shadow of hate.*"

Now, watching and listening to this old man, she thinks she understands those words. Cooped in his desolate tower, trapped between the banks of his soul, how could Achamian not bring the two great currents of his life together? His Dreams and his Hatred. Contained too long in too little space, how could they not become entangled in a single turbulent stream? To resent is to brood in inaction, to pass through life acting in a manner indistinguishable from those who bear no grudges. But hatred hails from a wilder, far more violent tribe. Even when you cannot strike out, you strike nonetheless. Inward, if not outward, as if such things have direction. To hate, especially without recourse to vengeance, is to besiege yourself, to starve yourself to the point of eating your own, then to lay wreaths of blame at the feet of the accused.

Yes, she decides. Drusas Achamian is her brother.

"So all this time," she says, daring to speak into one of the few silences he affords her, "you've been dreaming his life, cataloguing it, searching for clues as to my stepfather's origin . . ."

"Yes."

"What have you found?"

The question shocks him; that much is plain. He draws clawed fingers through his great and grizzled beard. "A name," he finally says with the sullen resentment of those forced to admit the disproportion between their boasts and their purse.

"A name?" She nearly laughs.

A long sour glare.

She reminds herself to take care. Her instinct, given all that she has endured, is to be impatient with the conceits of others. But she needs this man.

An inward look of concentration, then he says, "Ishuäl."

He almost whispers it, as though it were a jar containing furies, something that could be cracked open by a careless tongue.

"Ishuäl," she repeats, simply because his tone seems to demand it.

"It's derived from a Nonman dialect," he continues. "It means 'Exalted Grotto,' or 'High Hidden Place,' depending on how literal the translation."

"Ishuäl? Kellhus is from Ishuäl?"

It troubles him, she can tell, to hear her refer to her stepfather as such—as someone familiar.

"I'm certain of it."

"But if it's a hidden place . . ."

Another sour glare. "It won't be long," he mutters with old man dismissiveness. "Not now. Not any more. Seswatha . . . His life is opening . . . Not just the small things, but *the secrets as well.*"

A life spent mining the life of another, pondering glimpses of tedium through the lense of holy and apocalyptic portent. Twenty years! How can he hope to balance the proportions? Grub through dirt long enough and you *will* prize stones.

"Like he's yielding," she forces herself to say.

"Exactly! I know I sound mad for saying it, but it's almost as *if he knows.*"

She finds nodding difficult, as though pity has seized the hinge of her neck and skull. What reservoirs of determination would it take? To spend so long immersed in a task not only bereft of any tangible profit, but without any appreciable measure of progress—how much would it require? Year after year, wrestling with the imperceptible, wringing hope out of smoke and half-memory. What depths of conviction? What kind of perseverance?

Certainly not any the sane possess.

Faces. All conduct is a matter of wearing the appropriate faces. The brothel taught her that, and the Andiamine Heights simply confirmed the lesson. It's as though expressions occupy various positions, a warning here, a greeting there, with the distance between measured by the difficulty of forcing one face from the other. At this moment nothing seems so difficult as squeezing pity into the semblance of avid interest.

"No other Mandate Schoolman has ever experienced anything like this?" She has asked this already, but it bears repeating.

"Nothing," he replies, his face and posture true to his frailty. He has shrunk into the husk of hides that clothe him. He seems as lonely as he is, and even more isolate. "What can it mean?"

She blinks, strangely offended by this open display of weakness. Then it happens.

The Mark already blasts him, renders him ugly in the manner of things rent and abraded, as though his inner edges have been pinched and twisted, pinched and twisted, his very substance worried from the fabric of mundane things. But suddenly she sees more, the hue of judgment, as though blessing and condemnation have become a wash visible only in certain kinds of light. It hangs about him, *bleeds* from him, something palpable . . . evil.

No. Not evil. Damnation.

He is damned. Somehow she knows this with the certainty with which children know their hands. Thoughtless. Complete.

He is damned.

Another blink, the different eye closes, and he is an old Wizard once again. The illuminated surfaces are as impervious as before.

Sorrow wells through her, at once abstract and tidal, the resignation one feels when losses outrun numbers. Clutching her blanket, she presses herself to her feet, scuttles to sit on the cold ground beside him. She looks at him with the eyes she knows so well, the gaze that promises to roam wherever. She knows that he is hopeless, the wreck of what was once a mighty man.

But she also knows what she needs to do—to give.

Another lesson from the brothel. It's so simple, for it's what all madmen yearn for, what they crave above all things . . .

To be believed.

"You have become a prophet," she says, leaning in for the kiss. Her whole life she has punished herself with men. "A prophet of the past."

The memory of his power is like perfume.

The recriminations come later, in the darkness. Why is there no place so lonely as the sweaty slot beside a sleeping man?

And at the same time, no place so safe?

Bundling a blanket about her nakedness, she crawls to the dim bed of coals, where she sits, rocking herself between clutched arms and rough folds, trying to squeeze away the memory of skidding skin, the wheezing of old man exertions. The dark is complete, so much so the forest and the stoved-in tower seem painted in pitch. The warmth of the gutted fire only sharpens the chill.

The tears do not come until he touches her—a gentle hand across her back, falling like a leaf. Kindness. This is the one thing she cannot bear. Kindness.

"We have made our first mistake together," he says, as though it were something significant. "We will not make it again."

No forest slumbers in silence, even in the dead of a windless night. The touch of twigs and leaves, the press of forking branches, the sweep of limbs endlessly interlocking, incorporating more and more skirted trunks, creating a labyrinth of hollows, with only sudden scarps to interrupt them. Somehow it all conspired to create a whispering dark.

The coals tinkle like faraway glass.

"Am I broken?" she sobs. "Is that why I run?"

"We all bear unseen burdens," he replies, sitting more behind her than beside. "We are all bent somehow."

"You mean you," she says, hating herself for the accusation. "The way you are bent!"

But the hand does not retreat from her back.

"The way I must be . . . I must discover the truth, Mimara. More than my spite turns upon what I do."

Her snort is convulsive, phlegmatic. "What difference will it make? Golgotterath will be destroyed within the year. Your Second Apocalypse will be over before it even begins!"

His fingertips draw away.

"What do you mean?" he says, his tone both light and brittle.

"I mean that Sakarpus will have already fallen." Why does she suddenly hate him? Was it because she seduced him, or because he failed to resist? Or was it because laying with him made no difference? She gazes at him, unable or unwilling to hide the triumph her eyes. "The plans were afoot ere I fled the cursed Heights. The Great Ordeal marches, old man."

Silence. Remorse comes crashing in.

Can't you see? something shrieks within her. *Can't you see the poison I bring? Strike me! Strangle me! Pare me to the core with your questions!*

But she laughs instead. "You have shut yourself away for too long. You have found your revelation too late."

CHAPTER FIVE

Momemn

Where luck is the twist of events relative to mortal hope, White-Luck is the twist of events relative to divine desire. To worship it is to simply will what happens as it happens

—ARS SIBBUL, *SIX ONTONOMIES*

Early Spring, 19 New Imperial Year (4132 Year-of-the-Tusk), Iothiah

Psatma Nannaferi sat in the dust, rocking to whispered prayers, her crooked hand held out to the train of passers-by. Though she counted their shadows, she took care not to probe their eyes, knowing that whatever moved them to give, be it pity, the bite of guilt, or simply the fear of an unlucky coin, it must be their own. The blessed words of the Sinyatwa were clear on that account: "From seed to womb, from seed to furrow. The right hand cannot give to the left . . ."

To give was to lose. It was an arithmetic with only one direction.

This was the miracle of the Ur-Mother, Yatwer, the Goddess of Fertility and Servitude, who moved through the world in the form of more and more and more. Unasked for bounty. Undeserved plenitude. She was the pure Gift, the breaking of tit for tat, the very principle of the birthing world. It was She who made time flesh.

Which was why Nannaferi realized she had to move. More and more the copper talents came to her palm, rather than to those other beggars raised beside her. More and more they landed with a knowing clink, a momentary hesitation. One young girl, a Galeoth slave, even gave her an onion, whispering, "Priestess-Mother."

It always happened this way, even in cities as great as Iothiah. The human heart was ever bent on exchange. Even though people knew the purpose of the Beggar's Sermon, they were still drawn to her once the rumours of her presence spread. They felt the pinch of their offering, and assumed that this made it Gift enough. If you asked them whether they were trying to purchase the Goddess's favour, they would insist they only wanted to give. But their eyes and expressions always shouted otherwise.

Such a strange thing, giving, as if the arms of beggars could be the balance of the world.

So Nannaferi would be forced to move, to find someplace where anonymity could assure the purity of the offerings she received. To take from those angling for dispensations was a kind of pollution. And more importantly, it saved no souls. For adherents to the Cult of Yatwer, ignorance was the royal road to redemption.

She undid the veil from her old and cratered face, pocketed the coins in her sack-cloth robe. As though to verify her conclusion, three more coins plopped into the dust before her, one of them silver. Excess generosity was ever the sign of greed. She left them in their small oblong craters. Other Yatwerian priestesses, she knew, would have taken them, saying waste not want not or some other trite blasphemy. But she was not one of the others—she was Psatma Nannaferi.

She grabbed her cane and with shaking elbows out began to hoist herself to her feet . . .

Only to be struck to her knees.

It began as it always did, with a curious buzzing in the ears, as though dragonflies swarmed about her head. Then the ground bucked and flopped like cloth thrown over fish, and watercolour haloes swung about every living form. And she saw *her*, though she could not turn to look, a shadow woman, spoked in sun-silver, walking where everything and everyone exploded like clay urns, a silhouette so sharp it cut eyes sideways. A hand reached out and pressed the side of her hooded head, irresistibly gentle, forcing her cheek down to the pungent earth.

"*Mother*," she gasped.

The shadow held her, as though pinning her below unseen waters. "**Be still, child**," it said in a voice that crawled like beetles up out of the heart of things. It seemed that she would crack open, that her marrow would climb out and wrap her in a newer skin.

"Your brother has finally arrived. The White-Luck Warrior has come."

The hand leaned down upon her, a sun-swallowing mountain.

"So soon?"

"No, my love. On the anointed day."

Her body was but a string tied about an infinite iron nail, woollen tailings that trembled in an otherworldly wind.

"And the D-D-Demon?"

"Will be driven to his doom."

Then the roar vanished, sucked up like smoke from the opium bowl. The blasted streets became a wall of onlookers, peopled by vendors, teamsters, harlots, and soldiers. And the shadow became a man, a Nansur caste-noble by the look of him, with concerned yet gentle eyes. And the hand was his hand, rubbing her poxed cheek the way you might massage a sleeping limb.

He does not fear to touch—

"It's okay," he was saying. "You were seized, but it's passing. How long have you suffered the Falling Disease?"

But she ignored him—and all the others. She clawed aside his hovering hands. She fairly beat herself a path with her cane when she clambered to her feet.

What did they know of *giving?*

The city of Iothiah was ancient. Not so old as Sumna perhaps, but certainly older than the Thousand Temples—far older. As was the Cult of Yatwer.

The recently built Chatafet Temple in the northeast of the city was where most of Iothiah's faithful congregated to worship, mourn, and celebrate. By all accounts, it was one of the most successful Yatwerian temples in the Three Seas, bolstered by the ever-growing number of converts among what had been, until the First Holy War, a largely heathen population. But for those initiated in the greater mysteries of the Cult, it was little more than a point of administrative pride. The true importance of lothiah lay in the funerary maze of the Ilchara Catacombs, the great Womb-of-the-Dead.

The once famed Temple of Ilchara had been destroyed by the heathen Fanim, its marble and sandstone looted over the centuries of their tenure. Now it was little more than a gap in the rambling network of tenements surrounding it. All that remained were gravel heaps hazed by desert scree. Here and there ragged blocks rose pale as ice from the shag of grasses. Sandy tracks marked the paths taken by generations of playing children. Were it not for the black banners stitched with Yatwer's sacred sign—a harvest sickle that was at once a pregnant belly—nothing immediate would have identified it as hallowed ground.

Psatma Nannaferi led her sisters across a flower-covered mound toward the Catacomb entrance. Their sandalled feet swished through the grasses, adding a strange melancholy to their sporadic conversation. Nannaferi said nothing, concentrated on holding her head high despite her bent back. It seemed she wore her revelation rather than the black-silk gowns of her holy station, so palpable it had become. She could feel it billow about her in winds that only souls could sail. Immortal attire. She was certain the others glimpsed it, even if their eyes remained ignorant. They glanced more than they should, more quickly than they should, the side-long appraisals of the envious and overawed.

Even scarred and diminutive, Nannaferi was and always had been imposing, a will of oak among hearts of balsa. In her youth, the senior priestesses never failed to overlook her when doling out the reprimands they used to confirm their superior station. Others they scolded and whipped, but they always passed by the "Shigeki pox-girl," as they called her, in silence. Small as she was, she seemed a weight too great for their flimsy nets. Something about her eyes, perhaps, which always seemed fixed on their tipping point. Or her voice, whose flawless edge called attention to the cracks and twists in their own.

Gravitas, the ancient Cenieans would have called it.

No one dared hate her, for that would have carried too much admission. And all respected her, for that was the only ingress she allowed, the only way to avoid suffocating in her implacable gaze. So she rose through the layered hierarchies of the Cult of Yatwer the way a stone dropped through flotsam. In twenty short years, she became the Matriarch, the Cult's titular leader, answering only to the Shriah in Sumna. Fourteen years after that, she was declared Mother-Supreme, a station outlawed when the Thousand Temples brought the Cults to heel long ago but maintained in secret for almost sixteen centuries.

A broad trench yawned before the priestesses. Forced to descend the earthen ramp in single file, they momentarily crowded the edge, flummoxed by the delicate question of precedence. Nannaferi ignored them, reached the bottom before the first of them had dared follow. A band of armed men, local caste-menials chosen for their fanatical zeal, fell to their knees as she strolled into their midst. She glanced across their sun-shining backs, nodded in approval as each murmured the ritual invocation, "*Hek'neropontah . . .*"

Gift-giver.

Gift-giver, indeed, she silently mused. A Gift they could scarce comprehend, let alone believe.

She paused before the entrance, knelt to one knee so that she might taste Goddess-earth.

Aside from excavating the ancient gate, the Cult had done nothing to undo the sacrilege wrought by the heathen. Looters had stripped the black-marble panels with the friezes depicting the Goddess in her various guises, Sowing, Tilling, and Harvesting, and they had pried off the bronze snakes that had wound about the flanking columns. They had taken little else otherwise. According to local lore, the Fanim had been loath to enter the Catacombs, especially after the Grandee charged with mapping its depths had failed to return. Apparently the Padirajah himself had ordered the place sealed, calling it in his accursed tongue *Gecca'lam*, or Pit of the She-Demon.

They were as wretched as madmen, the heathen, and as deserving of pity, their delusions ran so deep. But one thing, at least, they saw with admirable clarity.

The Goddess was to be feared.

Even the Elder Scriptures, the *Higarata* and *The Chronicle of the Tusk*, gave the Goddess short shrift, so drunk were the poets on masculine virtues. The reason was obvious enough: Yatwer, more than any of the Hundred, celebrated the poor and the weak, for *they* were the growers and the makers, the toiling multitudes who carried the caste-nobility like a foul slime upon their backs. She alone celebrated them. She alone held up her hands to grant them a second, more shadowy life. Celebrated and avenged.

Even her brother War, it was said, feared her. Even Gilgaöl shrank from Yatwer's bloody gaze.

And well he should.

Planting her cane before her, Psatma Nannaferi strode into the shadow of the ancient sandstone lintels. She entered the worldly womb of the Ur-Mother, descended into the company of her long-dead sisters.

The subterranean cemetery wound deep beneath the ruined foundations of its namesake temple, level wheeling beneath level, making a vast drum of the earth. The lantern-light revealed an endless series of brick-vaulted recesses, each packed with urns, some so ancient the script they bore could not be read. For thousands of years, since the days of the Old Dynasty, the ashes of Yatwer's priestesses had been brought here to slumber in holy community.

The Womb-of-the-Dead.

Psatma Nannaferi could sense the awe in her sister high-priestesses. They shuffled after her in small, solemn clots, the young assisting the old, the awestruck walking in a kind of stupor, as though only now delivered to the truth of their calling—and so seeing their sham piety for the vanity that it was. Only the bitch that posed as the Chalfantic Oracle, Vethenestra, dared affect boredom. Heavens forfend an oracle who has not seen it all.

Take-take-take. It was a wickedness, a *pollution*, that knew no bounds.

It was the very essence of the Demon.

Nannaferi held on to this passion as she guided them into the void that was the Charnal Hall. Her middle anger, she sometimes called it, where her judgment smouldered just enough to singe the hearts of the weak. Everything was sinful, everything was accountable; this was simply the truth of an unruly and disordered world. The Goddess was surfeit, the Goddess was wilderness, only beaten with hoe and plow into the feeding of the world. Nannaferi was the hoe. Nannaferi was the plow. And before these entombed proceedings were completed, her sisters would find themselves weeded and tilled . . . fertile soil for the White-Luck Warrior.

There was no vanity in her task. The Goddess had made her into the rule with which the world would be measured—no more, no less. Who was Nannaferi to take heart or pride in this, let alone question the why and wherefore? The knife, as the Galeoth saying went, was no greater for the skinning.

Only more doused in blood.

She told them to space their lanterns throughout the vaulted hollow, then directed them to take seats about the immense stone table in the chamber's heart: the legendary Struck Table, where the Ur-Mother herself had once chastised her wayward daughters. Nannaferi took the place of the Goddess, so that the cracks that sundered its ancient planes radiated from her withered breast. A fissure seemed to fork and vein its way to each of her sisters, which was good, she thought, for she would be the light that revealed the fractures in them all.

She sat perfectly immobile, waited patiently for the last of their conversations to fade. Several present had only recently arrived from across the Three Seas; there were more than a few old enmities and friendships here, interrupted by appointments abroad. Since friendship was one of the Goddess's most blessed gifts, she tolerated their banter. It was a rare thing, she knew, to find oneself in the company of peers when you reached the highest echelons of the Cult. Loneliness was ever the cold price of authority, and it showed in these women. Eleva, in particular, seemed desperate to speak.

But the pall of enormity was quick to silence even her. Soon all twelve sat with the same rigid austerity as their Mother-Supreme: the Oracle and the eleven High Priestesses of the Cult. Everyone save the Matriach, Sharacinth—a fact that none could have missed.

"Only once since the time of the heathen," Nannaferi said, her voice throat-smoky with age, "has the Struck Table been convened. Many of you were here that day. It was a joyous time, a time of celebration, for at last the Cult had regained this place, our Great Goddess's earthly womb, where the long line of our sisters dwell, awaiting their Second Birth in the Outside. At that time we celebrated the Shriah and his Holy War, thinking only of what we might regain. We did not see the Demon that slumbered in its belly, that would possess it, transform it into an instrument of oppression and blasphemous *tyranny*."

She allowed her outrage to twist this final word.

"We did not see the Aspect-Emperor."

She slapped her cane of sacred acacia flat on the table. Her sisters jumped at the crack. Then she reached into her gown, whose silken folds seemed almost moist where they bunched against the bent joints of her body, and withdrew a small sphere of iron, no larger than a dove's egg, ringed with indecipherable script. She raised it high between thumb and forefinger, gingerly set it on the table before her . . .

A Chorae. A Holy Tear of God.

As though following some irresistible logic, the women's gazes moved in perfect tandem from the Chorae to her face. To be addressed in such a bald manner was shock enough: The Inaugurals, the ceremonial rites and prayers of initiation, were mandatory on such occasions. Now they stared at her in outright astonishment. They were beginning to understand, Nannaferi noted with grim satisfaction.

Their Goddess girded for war.

"But first," she said, resting her right hand on the shaft of her cane, "we must deal with the matter of the witch."

With the Chorae before her, the implication was plain: She meant *one of them*.

Several gasped. Maharta, the youngest of their number (and a political concession to Nilnamesh), actually cried out. Sharhild, with her piggish eyes and radish cheeks, watched with the expression of bland stupidity she always used to conceal her cleverness. Vethenestra, of course, nodded as though she'd known all along. What kind of Oracle would she be otherwise?

A hush fell upon them, so complete it seemed they could hear the dead ashes breathe.

"B-but Holy Mother," Maharta fairly whispered. "How could you know?"

Psatma Nannaferi closed her eyes, knowing they would be globes of crimson when they snapped opened.

"Because the Goddess," she murmured, "lets me see."

Shouting clamour. The clinking thump of a stone stool falling. Eleva leapt to her feet, her arms outstretched, her eyes and mouth shining sun-white, her hair and robes boiling in some intangible tempest. An uncanny mutter fell from the arches, the walls, from the circumference of all things seen—a voice that crumpled thought like paper. Sharhild flew at her, knife out and stabbing, only to be tossed back, thrown like soiled clothes into the corner. Spectral walls parsed the Charnal Hall, the ghosts of cyclopean bricks. Screams rang through the closeted deep. The priestesses scrambled, scattered. Shadows twisted about the hinges of things.

The thwack of iron on wood. A blinding incandescence. A sucking roar.

Moans and small cries of disbelief rose through the sulphurous reek. Maharta sobbed, crouched beneath the eaves of the Struck Table. "Eleva!" someone cried. "*Eleva!*"

"Has been dead for days," Nannaferi spat. She alone had not moved. "Maybe longer."

The cane tingled in her hands, as if still shivering from the impact. Using it, she walked up to the fallen witch, stared down at the cracked statue of salt across the floor. An anonymous girl, forever frozen in anxious, arrogant white. Buxom. Improbably young.

With an involuntary groan Nannaferi knelt to retrieve her Chorae from the powdered floor. Her blessed Tear of God.

"They hunt us with witches," she said, her hatred warbling through her voice. "What greater proof could we have of their depravity?"

Witches . . . The School of Swayal. Yet another of the Aspect-Emperor's many blasphemies.

Several stunned heartbeats passed before her sisters collected themselves. Two helped Sharhild back to her seat, full of praise for the old Thunyeri shield-maiden's ferocity and courage. Others crept forward to look at the dead witch who but moments earlier had been Eleva—one of their favourites, no less! Maharta continued crying, though she had been shamed into snuffles. Vethenestra resumed her seat, cast blank looks of apprehension about the Table.

Then, as though once again answering to some collective logic, they erupted in questions and observations. The low-lintelled ceiling of the Charnal Hall rang with matronly exclamations. Apparently Vethenestra had dreamt this would happen a fortnight ago. Did this mean the Shriah and the Thousand Temples scrutinized them? Or was this the work of the Empress? Phoracia claimed to see Eleva touch a Chorae not more than three months previous in Carythusal, during the solstice observances. That meant the witch had replaced her recently, did it not? Sometime close to the secret summons they all received . . .

But how could that be? Unless . . .

"Yes," Nannaferi said, her tone filled with a recognition of menace that cleared the room of competing voices. "The Shriah knows of me. He has known of me for quite some time."

The Shriah. The Holy Father of the Thousand Temples.

The Demon's brother, Maithanet.

"They have tolerated me because they believe secret knowledge a valuable thing. They accumulate conspiracies the way caste-merchants do ledgers, thinking they can control what they can number."

A hard-faced moment.

"Then we're doomed!" Aethiola abruptly cried. "Think of what happened to the Anagkians . . ."

Five assassins, convinced they were enacting Fate, had attempted to murder the Empress on the day of her youngest son's Whelming. It had been a failure and, more importantly, a blunder, one that had threatened all the Orthodox, no matter what their Cult. The rumours of the Empress's revenge were predictably inconsistent: The Anagkian Matriarch had either been flayed alive, or sewn into a sack with starving dogs, or stretched into human rope on the rack. The only certain thing was that she and all her immediate subordinates had been arrested by the Shrial Knights, never to be seen again.

Nannaferi shook her head. "We are a different Cult."

This was no vain conceit. With the possible exception of Gilgaöl, none of the Hundred Gods commanded the mass sympathy enjoyed by Yatwer. Where other Cults were not so different than their temples, surface structures that could be pulled down, the Yatwerians were like these very halls, the Womb-of-the-Dead, something that could not be pulled down because it was the earth. And just as the Catacombs had tunnels, abandoned Old Dynasty sewers, reaching as far out as the ruins of the Sareotic Library, so did they possess far-reaching means, innumerable points of entry, hidden and strategic.

Wherever there were caste-menials or slaves.

"But Mother-Supreme," Phoracia said. "We speak of the *Aspect-Emperor*."

The name alone was the argument.

Nannaferi nodded. "The Demon is not so strong as you might think, Phori. He and his most ardent, most fanatical followers march in the Great Ordeal, half a world away.

Meanwhile, all the old grievances smoulder across the Three Seas, waiting for the wind that will fan them to flame." She paused to touch each of her sisters with the iron of her gaze. "The Orthodox are everywhere, Sisters, not just this room."

"Even the heathens grow more bold," Maharta said in support. "Fanayal continues to elude them in the south. Scarcely a week passes without riots in Nenciph—"

"But still," Phoracia persisted, "you haven't *seen him* as I have. You have no inkling of his power. *None* of you do! *No one* kno—" The old priestess caught herself with a kind of seated lurch. Phoracia was the only one of their number older than Nannaferi, at that point where the infirmities of the body could not but leach into the soul. More and more she was forgetting her place, overspeaking. The intermittent impertinence of the addled and exhausted.

"Forgive me," she murmured. "Holy Mother. I-I did not mean to imply . . ."

"But you are correct," Nannaferi said mildly. "We indeed have no inkling of his power. This is why I summoned you *here*, where the souls of our sisters might shroud us from his far-scyring eyes. *We* have no inkling, but then we are not alone. Not as he is alone."

She let these words hang in the sulphur-stained air.

"The Goddess!" sturdy old Sharhild hissed. A bead of blood dropped from her scalp to her brow, tapped onto the pitted stone of the table. "We all know that She has touched you, Mother. But She *has come to you* as well, hasn't she?" The dread in her accented voice outlasted the wonder, seemed to hone the sense of mountainous weight emanating from the ceiling.

"Yes."

Once again the Charnal Hall erupted in competing voices. Was it possible? Blessed event! How? When? Blessed, blessed event! What did she say?

"But what of the Demon?" Phoracia called above the others.

The sisters fell silent, deferring as much to their embarrassment as to her rank. "The *Aspect-Emperor*," the prunish woman pressed. "What does *she* say of him?"

And there it was, the fact of their blasphemy, exposed in the honesty of an old woman's muddled soul. Their fear of the Aspect-Emperor had come to eclipse all other terrors, even those reserved for the Goddess.

One could only worship at angles without fear.

"The Gods . . ." Nannaferi began, struggling to render what was impossible in words. "They are not as we are. They do not happen . . . all at once . . ."

Her eyes narrowed in fatuous concentration, Aethiola said, "Vethenestra claims—"

"Vethenestra knows nothing," Nannaferi snapped. "The Goddess has no truck with fools or fakers."

The Struck Table fell very still. All eyes followed the wandering crack that led to the Chalfantic Oracle, Vethenestra, who sat in the tight pose of someone at war with their own trembling. For the Mother-Supreme to refer to any of them by *name* was disaster enough . . .

The woman paled. "H-Holy Mother . . . If I-I had cause to dis-displease you . . ."

Nannaferi regarded her as if she were a broken urn. "It is the Goddess who is displeased," she said. "I simply find you ridiculous."

"But what have I—?"

"You are no longer the Oracle of Chalfantas," she said, her voice parched with regret and resignation. "Which means you have no place at this table. Leave, Vethenestra. Your dead sisters await."

An image of her own sister came to Nannaferi, her childhood twin, the one who did not survive the pox. In a heartbeat it all seemed to pass through her, the whooping laughter, the giggling into shoulders, the teary-eyed shushing. And it ached, somehow, to know that her soul had once sounded such notes of joy. It reminded her of what had been given . . .

And those few things that remained.

"Awa-await?" Vethenestra stammered.

"*Leave*," Nannaferi repeated. There was something about the way she held her hand, an unnerving gestural inflection that implied destination rather than direction.

Vethenestra stood, her hands clutching knots of fabric against her thighs. Her first steps were backward, as if expecting to be called back, or to wake, for she looked at them with a stung and stupefied glee, a face that had forgotten what was real. She turned to the black maw of the entrance. Each of them felt it, an ethereal squeezing, a wringing of empty air. They blinked in disbelief, gazed in horror at the issue. Ribs of menstrual crimson wound like smoke through the dark. Glistening curlicues, twining into nothingness.

Oblivious, Vethenestra crossed the threshold. But she didn't so much step into the shadows as step *out*, as though she were no more than her image, twisting away in directions indescribable to the eye, like a pool soaked out of existence. One heartbeat she was, and the next she was not.

Something like speech seemed to rattle in the corners beyond their hearing—or perhaps it was a shriek.

Silence. The very air seemed animate. The excavated hollows that surrounded them, hall after honeycombed hall, hummed with emptiness, the deadness of space. Watching her sisters, Nannaferi could see it slacken the last of their eyes, the comprehending, the standing *underneath* what they had lived the entirety of their shallow lives. The *Goddess*, not the name they used to sugar their lips, not the vague presence that tickled their vanity or itched the underbelly of their sins, but the *Goddess*, the Blood of Fertility, the monstrous, ageless Mother of Birth.

Here, lending her fury to the blood dark.

Without warning, Maharta fell to her knees, pressed

tear-streaked cheeks to the soiled floor. Then they were all kneeling, all hissing or murmuring prayers.

And Nannaferi spoke to the ceiling, crooked hands held out. "Your daughters are clean, Mother . . .

"Your daughters *are clean*."

They were abject now, staring at her with mewling eyes, adoring and horrified eyes, for they saw now that their Goddess was *real*, and that Psatma Nannaferi was her chosen daughter. Maharta hugged her about the thighs, bent to kiss her knees. The others crowded near, trembling with wonder and zeal, and the Mother-Supreme pressed closed her unpainted lids, savoured the rain of their gentle touches, felt corporeal and incorporeal, like someone invisible finally seen.

"Tell them," she said to her sisters, her voice hoarse with the passion to dominate. "In whispers, let your congregations know. Tell them the White-Luck turns against their glorious Aspect-Emperor."

They had to take such gifts that were given. Even those beyond their comprehension . . .

"Tell them the Mother sends her Son."

Or that would see them dead.

Momemn . . .

Kelmomas liked to pretend that the Sacral Enclosure, the octagonal garden situated in the heart of the Imperial Apartments, was nothing less than the roof of the world. It was easy enough, given the way the surrounding structures obscured the expanse of Momemn to the west or the great plate of the Meneanor to the east. From almost any position along the colonnades or verandas overlooking the Enclosure, all you could see was the long blue tumble of the sky. It lent a sense of altitude and isolation.

He stared at the greening sycamores, their crowns nodding

in a chill wind that could scarce reach him where he sat on the balcony. The grand old trees fascinated him. The wending lines of trunks parsed into great hanging limbs. The leaves twittering like minnows in the sun. The arrhythmic back and forth against iron-bellied clouds. There was a power to them, a power and a stillness, that seemed to dwarf the staid background of marble columns and walls and shadowy interior spaces stacked three storeys high.

He would very much like to be a tree, Kelmomas decided.

The secret voice murmured, as though proposing lame solutions to an all-conquering boredom. But Kelmomas ignored it, concentrated instead on the sound of his mother's fluting dialogue. By lying on his belly and pressing his face against the cold polish of the balustrades, he could almost see her sitting at the edge of the East Pool, the only place where the Enclosure opened onto the expanse of the Sea.

"*So what should I do?*" she was saying. "*Move against the whole Cult?*"

"*I fear Yatwer is too popular,*" his uncle, the Holy Shriah replied. "*Too beloved.*"

"*The Yatwerians, yes-yes,*" his sister, Theliopa, said in her spittle-laden, words-askew way. "*Father's census figures indicate that some six out of ten caste-menials regularly attend some kind of Yatwerian rite. Six-out-of-ten. Far and away the most popular of the Hundred. Far-far. Far-far.*"

The pause in Mother's reply said it all. It wasn't so much that she reviled her own daughter—Mother could never hate her own—only that she could find no reflection of herself, nothing obviously human. There was no warmth whatsoever in Theliopa, only facts piled upon facts and an intense aversion to all the intricacies that seal the intervals between people. The sixteen-year-old could scarce look at another's face, so deep was her horror of chancing upon a gaze.

"*Thank you, Thel.*"

His older sister was like a dead limb, Kelmomas decided,

an extension into insensate space. Mother leaned on her intellect only because Father had commanded it.

"*I remember what it was like*," Mother continued. "*I shudder to think how many coppers I tossed to beggars, thinking they might have been disguised priestesses. The Goddess of the Gift . . .*" A laugh, at once pained and rueful. "*You have no idea, Maitha, what a salve to the heart Yatwer can be . . .*"

Piqued by the undertones of anxiousness and melancholy in her voice, Kelmomas craned his head, pressed against the marble posts until his cheeks ached. He saw her, reclining in her favourite divan, little more than a teary-eyed silhouette against the glassy expanse of the pool. She seemed so small, so blow-away frail, that he found it difficult to breathe . . .

She needs us, the voice said.

Just then his nursemaid, Porsi, arrived with his twin brother, Samarmas. Popping to his feet with little-boy effortlessness, Kelmomas skipped from the veranda into the redolent gloom of the playroom. Samarmas's grin ate up his angelic face the way it always did, turning him into a leering childhood version of an Ajoklian idol. Porsi, her acne scars like dappled wine stains, her fingers resting possessively on his brother's golden maul, immediately began speaking in her now-the-twins-are-together voice. "Would you like to play *parasta?* Would you like to do that? Or, something different? Oh, yes, how could I forget? Such *strong* boys—growing too old for parasta, aren't we? Something warlike, then. Would that be better? I know! Kel, you could be sword while Sammi plays shield . . ."

On and on she would go, while Kelmomas would smile or sulk or shrug and stare into her face and ponder all the small terrors that he saw there. Usually, he would play along, making games of the games she organized for the two of them. While playing parasta, he would modulate his tantrums over the course of successive days, gauging the variables that informed her response. He found that the very same words could make her laugh or grit her teeth in frustration, depending on his tone and expression. He discovered that if he abruptly walked up to her and placed his head on her lap, he could summon mist, even tears to her eyes. Sometimes, while Samarmas drooled and mumbled over some ivory toy, he would turn his cheek from her thigh and stare in a lazy, all-is-safe way into her face, smelling the folds of her crotch through her gown. She would always smile in nervous adoration, thinking—and he knew this because he somehow could see it—that a little god stared up from her lap. And he would say curious, child-like things that filled her heart with awe and wonder.

"You are just like him," she would reply every so often. And Kelmomas would exult, knowing that she meant Father.

Even slaves can see it, the voice would say. It was true. He was able to hold so much more in the light of his soul's eye than the people around him. Names. Nuances. The rate at which various birds beat their wings.

So he knew, for instance, everything about the sickness the physician-priests called Moklot, or the Shudders. He knew how to simulate the symptoms, to the point where he could fool even old Hagitatas, his mother's court physician. All he need do was think about becoming feverish, and he became feverish. The trembly-shake-shake, well, even his halfwit brother could do that. He knew that when he told their Porsi that his calves were cramping she would rush off to fetch his medicine, an obscure and noxious leaf from faraway Cingulat. And he knew that she would not find it in the infirmary, because how could she, when it was hidden beneath her own bed? So he knew she would begin searching . . .

Leaving him alone with his twin brother, Samarmas.

"*But why, Maitha?*" Mother was saying. "*Are they mad? Can't they see that we're their salvation?*"

"*But you know the answer to this, Esmi. The Cultists themselves are no more or no less foolish than other* Men. *They see only what they know, and they argue only to defend what they cherish. Think of the changes my brother has wrought . . .*"

Porsi would be gone for a long time. She would never think to look under her pallet because she had never placed it there. She would search and search, growing ever more bah-bah-teary-eyed, knowing that she would be called to account.

Smiling, Kelmomas sat cross-legged and contemplated his brother, who had his head to the maroon carpets, staring up at a dragon from some miniature perspective. Though his hands dwarfed the dragon's palm-worn head, he seemed diminutive, like a soapstone figurine playing with elaborately carved grains of sand. A toy Prince-Imperial poking toys that were smaller still.

Only the lazy battle of boredom and awe in his expression made him seemed real.

"*So this business of the White-Luck?*" his mother's distant voice asked.

"*White-Luck-White-Luck,*" Theliopa said. Kelmomas could almost see her rocking on her stool, her joints twitching, her hands climbing from her elbows to her shoulders then back again. "*A folk belief with ancient Cultic origins—ancient-old-ancient. According to Pirmees, the White-Luck is an extreme form of providence, a Gift of the Gods against worldly tuh-tuh-tyranny.*"

"White-Luck-White-Luck," Samarmas chimed in unison, then gurgled in his chin-to-windpipe way. Kelmomas glared him into silence, knowing that their uncle, at least, was entirely capable of hearing him.

As was anyone who shared their father's incendiary blood.

"*You think it's nothing more than a self-serving fraud?*" his mother asked his uncle.

"*The White-Luck? Perhaps.*"

"*What do you mean, 'perhaps'?*"

Samarmas had ambled to and from the toy trunk, bearing several more figures, some silver, others mahogany. "Mommy," he murmured in a world-does-not-exist voice, extracting the figurine of a woman cast in aquiline silver. He held her to the hoary dragon so they could kiss. "Kisses!" he exclaimed, eyes lit with gurgling wonder.

Kelmomas had been born staring into the deluge that was his twin's face. For a time, he knew, his mother's physicians had feared for him because it seemed he could do little more than gaze at his brother. All he remembered were the squalls of blowing hurt and wheezing gratification, and a hunger so elemental that it swallowed the space between them, soldered their faces into a single soul. The world was shouldered to the periphery. The tutors and the physicians had droned from the edges, not so much ignored as overlooked by a two-bodied creature who stared endlessly into its own inscrutable eyes.

Only in his third summer, when Hagitatas, with doddering yet implacable patience, made a litany of the difference between beast, man, and god, was Kelmomas able to overcome the tumult that was his brother. "Beasts move," the old physician would rasp. "Men reflect. Gods make real." Over and over. "Beasts move. Men reflect. Gods make real. Beasts move . . ." Perhaps it was simply the repetition. Perhaps it was the palsied tone, the way his breath undid the substance of his words, allowing them to soak into the between places, the gem-cutting lines. "Beasts move . . ." Over and over, until finally Kelmomas simply turned to him and said, "Men reflect."

A blink, and what was one had become two.

He just . . . understood. One moment he was nothing, and another he was staring, not at himself, but *at a beast*. Samarmas, Kelmomas would later realize, was wholly what he would later see lurking in all faces: an animal, howling, panting, lapping . . .

An animal that, because of his unschooled sensitivities and its sheer immediacy, had devoured him, made a lair of his skull.

A blink, and what had absorbed suddenly repelled. Afterwards, Kelmomas could scarcely bear looking into the carnival of Samarmas's face. Something about it wrenched him with disgust, not the grimace-and-look-away variety, but the kind that pinched stomach walls together and launched limbs in wild warding. It was as though his brother wore his bowels on the outside. For a time, Kelmomas wanted to cry out in warning whenever Mother showered Samarmas with coos and kisses. How could she not see it, the unsheathing of wet and shiny things? Only some instinct to secrecy had kept him silent, a will, brute and spontaneous, to show only what needed to be shown.

Now he was accustomed to it, of course. The beast that was his brother.

The dog.

"Hey, Sammi," he said, wearing his mother's mouth-watering smile. "Watch . . ."

Bending over, he placed a single palm on the floor and raised his feet in the air. Grinning upside down, he bounced one-handed toward him, from indifferent carpet to cold marble.

Samarmas gurgled with delight, covered his mouth and pointed. "Bum-bum!" he cried. "I see your bum-bum!"

"Can't you do this, Sammi?"

Samarmas pressed his cheek to his shoulder, smiled bashfully down. "Nothing," he conceded.

"*The Gods did not see the First Apocalypse*," Uncle Maithanet was saying, "*so why would they see the Second? They are blind to the No-God. They are blind to any intelligence without soul.*"

Again the imperceptible pause before Mother's reply. "*But Kellhus is a* Prophet . . . *How—?*"

"*How could he be hunted by the Gods?*"

Kelmomas lingered upside-down next to his brother, his heels swaying above.

"Isn't there *anything* you can do, Sammi?"

Samarmas shook his head, still doing his gurgle-laugh-gurgle at his brother's ridiculous pose.

"*Lord Sejenus*," Maithanet was saying, "*taught us to see the Gods not as entities unto themselves, but as fragments of* the God.

This is what my brother hears, the Voice-Absolute. This is what has renewed the Covenant of Gods and Men. You know this, Esmi."

"*So you're saying the Hundred could very well be at war with the God's designs—with their very own sum?*"

"Yes-yes," Theliopa interjected. "*There are one hundred and eighty-nine references referring to the disparate ends of the Gods and the God of Gods, two from the Holy Tractate itself. 'For they are like Men, hemmed in by darkness, making war on the shadows of they know not what.' Schol-Scholars, thirty-four, twenty. 'For I am the God, the rule of all things . . .'*"

Kelmomas swung his feet down to sit cross-legged before Samarmas, shimmied close enough to touch knees. "I *know*," he whispered. "I know something you can do . . ."

Samarmas flinched and jerked his head, as though hearing something too remarkable to be believed.

"What? What? What?"

"*Think of your own soul*," Uncle Maithanet was saying. "*Think of the war within, the way the parts continually betray the whole. We are not so different from the world we live in, Esmi . . .*"

"*I know—I know all this!*"

"How about balance?" Kelmomas said. "You know how to *balance*, don't you?"

Moments later, Samarmas was perched tottering on the balcony's broad stone rail, deep spaces yawing out beyond and beneath him. Kelmomas watched from the playroom, standing just behind the line of sunlight across the floor, grinning as though astonished by his skill and daring. The distance-filtered voices of his uncle and mother seemed to fall from the sky.

"*The White-Luck Warrior*," his uncle was saying, "*need not be real. The rumours alone constitute a dire threat.*"

"*Yes, I agree. But how do you battle rumours?*"

Kelmomas could almost see his uncle's simulated frown.

"*How else? With more rumours.*"

Samarmas whooped in whispering triumph. Cotton-white

arms out and waving. Toes flexed across a marmoreal line. The sycamores rearing behind, dark beneath sunlit caps, reaching up as though to catch some higher fall.

"*And the Yatwerians?*" Mother asked.

"*Call a council. Invite the Matriarch herself here to the Andiamine Heights.*"

The sudden dip and lean. The stabilizing twitches. The small looks of bodily panic.

"*Yes, but you and I both know she isn't the real leader of the Cult.*"

"*Which might work to our advantage. Sharacinth is a proud and ambitious woman, one who chafes at being a figurehead.*"

Quick recovery steps. Feet swishing over polished stone. A gurgling laugh caught in an anxious, reflexive swallow.

"*What? Are you suggesting we bribe her? Offer to make her Mother-Supreme?*"

"*That's one possibility.*"

The slender body bent about an invisible point, one which seemed to roll from side to side.

The surrounding air deep with the promise of gravity.

"*As Shriah you hold the power of life and death over her.*"

"*Which is why I suspect she knows little or nothing of these rumours, or what her sisters plan.*"

Eyes avid and exultant. Hands cycling air. A breathless grinning.

"*That's something we can use.*"

"*Indeed, Esmi. As I said, she is a proud woman. If we could induce a schism in the Cult . . .*"

Samarmas tottering. A bare foot, ivory bright in the glare, swinging out from behind the heel of the other, around and forward, sole descending, pressing like a damp cloth across the stone. A sound like a sip.

"*A schism . . .*"

The shadow of a boy foreshortened by the high angle of the sun. Outstretched hands yanked into empty-air clutches.

Feet and legs flickering out. A silhouette, loose and tight-bundled, falling through the barred shadow of the balustrade. A gasp flecked with spittle.

Then nothing.

Kelmomas stood blinking at the empty balcony, oblivious to the uproar rising from below.

Just like his father, he was able to hold so much more in the light of his soul's eye than the people around him. It had been this way ever since Hagitatas had taught him the difference between beast, man, and god—ever since he first had looked *away* from his brother's face. Beasts move, the old man had said.

Men reflect.

So he knew the love and worship Samarmas bore him, knew that he would do anything to close the abyss of insight and ability between them. And he knew precisely where the Pillarian Guards fixed their sandalled feet, where they planted the butt of their long spears . . .

Alarums rang through the Enclosure, clawed up to the sky. Soldiers, their martial voices hoarse with grief and terror. The guarded babble of slaves.

As though stunned, Kelmomas walked to the marble railing, leaned over the point where his brother had fallen. He looked down, saw his brother in an armoured circle of guardsmen, his eyes rolled back, his right arm coiled like rope, his torso twitching about the spear-shaft that pierced his flank.

The young Prince-Imperial was careful to wipe the olive oil from the rail. Then he howled the way a little boy should.

Why? the voice asked. The secret voice.

Why didn't you kill me sooner?

He saw his mother beat her way through the Pillarian Guards, heard her inconsolable scream. He watched his uncle, the Holy Shriah, grasp her shoulders as she fell upon her beloved son. He saw his sister Theliopa, absurd in her black gowns, approach in fey curiosity. He glimpsed one of his own tears falling, a liquid bead, falling, breaking upon his twin's slack cheek.

A thing so tragic. So much love would be required to heal.

"Mommy!" he cried. "*Mommeeeeeeee!*"

Gods make real.

There was such love in the touch of a son.

The funerary room was narrow and tall, plated with lines of blue-patterned Ainoni tile, but otherwise unadorned. Light showered through air like steam. Idols glared from small niches, almost, but never quite forgotten. Gold-gleaming censers wheezed in the corners, puffing faint ribbons of smoke. The Empress leaned against the marble pedestal in the room's centre, looking down, staring at the inert lines of her littlest.

She began with his fingers, humming an old song that made her slaves weep for recognition. Sometimes they forgot she shared their humble origins. Smiling, she looked at them as though to say, *Yes, I've been you all along . . .*

Just another slave.

She raised a forearm, cleansed it with long gentle strokes, elbow to wrist, elbow to wrist.

He was cold like clay. He was grey like clay. Yet, no matter how hard she pressed, she could not rob him of his form. He insisted on remaining her son.

She paused to cry. After a time she swallowed away the ache, cleared her throat with a gentle cough. She resumed her work and her humming. It almost seemed that she carved him more than she cleansed, that with every stroke he somehow became more real. The flawless lines and moist divets. The porcelain gleam of skin. The little mole beneath his left nipple. The constellation of freckles that reached like a shawl from shoulder to slender shoulder.

She absorbed all of it, traced and daubed and rinsed it, with movements that seemed indistinguishable from devotion.

There was such love in the touch of a son.

His chest. The low curve of his abdomen. And of course his face. Sometimes something urged her to prod and to shake, to punish him for this cruel little game. But her strokes remained unperturbed, slow and sure, as if the fact of ritual were some kind of proof against disordered souls.

She wrung the sponge, listened to the rattle of water. She smiled at her little boy, wondered at his beauty.

His hair was golden.

He smelled, she thought, as though he had been drowned in wine.

Kelmomas pretended to weep.

She bundled him tight against her breast, and he squirmed clear of the blankets crowded between them. He pressed himself against her shuddering length. Her every sob welled through him like waves of lazy heat, washed him with bliss and vindication.

"*Don't let go!*" she gasped, pressing her cheek back from his damp hair. "Never-never-please!"

Her face was his scripture, written with looms of skin, muscle, and tendon. And the truths he read there were holy.

He knew it so intimately he could tell whenever a mole had darkened or a lash had fallen from her eyelids. He had heard the priests prattle about their Heavens, but the truth was that paradise lay so much nearer—and tasted of salt.

Her face eclipsed him, the ligaments of anguish, the trembling lips, the diamonds streaming from her eyes.

"Kel," she sobbed. "Poor baby . . ."

He keened, squashed the urge to kick his feet in laughter. *Yes!* he cried in silent glee, the limb-wagging exultation of a child redeemed. *Yes!*

And it had been so easy.

You are, the secret voice said, *her only love remaining.*

Chapter Six

Marrow

Ask the dead and they will tell you. All roads are not equal. Verily, even maps can sin.

—EKYANNUS 1, 44 *EPISTLES*

What the world merely kills, Men murder.

—SCYLVENDI PROVERB

Early Spring, 19 New Imperial Year (4132 Year-of-the-Tusk), the River Rohil

The Wizard picked his way through the cool forest deeps, his bones as old as his thoughts were young. He huffed and grimaced, but there was a knowing cadence to his hobble, proof of prior years spent travelling. Four days he had trudged, wending between the pillar trees, squinting at the sun's glare through the spring-thin canopy, using the slow crawl of distant landmarks to guide him to his destination . . .

Marrow.

All Achamian knew of this place was what his Galeöth slave, Geraus, had told him. It was a Scalpoi entrepôt located at the westward end of the long navigable stretch of the River Rohil, a place where the companies of scalpers who worked the hinterland could collect their bounties and purchase supplies. As the nearest centre of any description to the tower, this was where Geraus would come, three or four times a year, to sell his pelts and, with the gold Achamian gave him, secure those goods they could not improvise for themselves. An even-tempered, slow-speaking man, Geraus had always taken wary delight in telling them the stories of his visits. Perhaps because the journey was both arduous and perilous—Tisthanna rarely forgave Achamian the weeks of Geraus's absence—or perhaps because they simply marked a deviation from the routine of his life, Geraus was given to foot-stomping airs for the days immediately following his return. Only when his tales were completed would he retreat to the borders of his gentle and dependable self. They had always been his time to shine, for the slave of the great Wizard to be "world-shouldered," as the Galeoth say.

For the most part, the visits seemed to be skulking, secretive affairs, transactions made between trusted men and trusted men only. A bag of beans, to hear Geraus speak of it, was as valuable and fraught with complication as a purse of gold or a bale of scalps. He made no secret of his discretion—in fact, he seemed to take great pride in it. Even when his children were infants, Geraus seemed bent on impressing them with the inestimable survival value of humility. The greatest virtue of any slave, he always seemed to be saying, was the ability to pass unnoticed.

No different than a spy, Achamian could not help reflecting.

To think he had believed those days dead and gone, wandering the Three Seas, passing from court to court, holding his head high before sneering kings and potentates—a Schoolman still. Even though he had shed the fat, even though he wore wool and animal skins instead of muslin and myrrh, the simple fact of striking for unseen horizons had brought his past back to prickling life. Sometimes, when he glanced up through greening limbs, he would see the turquoise skies of Kian, or when he knelt to refill his waterskin, the heaving black of the northern Meneanor. Blinks had become glimpses, each with its own history, its own peculiar sense and beauty. Caste-noble courtiers laughing, their faces painted white. Steaming delicacies served by oiled slaves. Fortifications sheathed in enamelled tiles, gleaming beneath arid suns. A black-skinned prostitute drawing high her knees.

Twenty years had slipped away, and not a day had passed.

He already found himself mourning Geraus and his family, far more than he would have imagined. Slaves were funny that way. It was as though the fact of ownership shrouded certain obvious and essential human connections. You assumed it would be the *conveniences* you would miss, not the slaves who provided them. Now, Achamian could care less about the comforts—they seemed contemptible. And something inner shook whenever he thought of their faces—laughing or crying, it did not matter—something jarred loose by the knowledge he would never sit with them again.

It made him feel like a weepy grandfather.

Perhaps it was good, this suicidal turn his life had taken.

He paused, savoured the gilded granduer of the evening wilderness seen from afar. The escarpment scrawled along the horizon, a long-wandering band of vertical stone mellowing in the dusk, buttressed by scree-and-boulder-choked ramps that descended into the forests below. He could see the Long-Braid Falls, so named because of the way the River Rohil divided about a great head of stone on the scarp's edge, twisting down in two thundering cataracts.

Marrow lay immediately below, soaked in the waterfall's rose-powder haze. The original town, according to Geraus, had been built downriver but had crept like a caterpillar to the escarpment's base as scalp broker after scalp broker vied to be the first to greet the westward-bound Scalpoi. Now, hacked out of the surrounding forest, it looked like a sore scabbed in pitch and wood, huts piled upon shanties, all clapped together using logs and orphaned materials, packed along the riverbank, encrusting the lower terraces of the cliff.

It was fully dark before Achamian reached the town's derelict outskirts. Timber posts were all that remained of the original Marrow. He could see them standing in the surrounding bracken, as silent as the moonlight that illuminated them, some rotted, some leaning, all of them possessing a funereal solitude that he found unnerving. Various characters and random marks scored those nearest the track, the residue of uncounted travellers with their innumerable vanities and frustrations. Shining between gaps in the darkling clouds, the Nail of Heaven allowed him to decipher several. "I FUCK SRANC," one said in fresh-cut Gallish. "HORJON FORGOT TO SLEEP WITH HIS ASS TO THE WALL," another claimed in Ainoni pictograms—beside a blot that could have been sun-cooked blood.

The roar of the falls climbed high into the night, and the first of the mists beaded his skin. A sense of menace ringed the lights of habitation before him. How long had it been since he had last braved a place like this? The carnival of strangers.

His mule in tow, Achamian trudged into what appeared to be the main thoroughfare. He was half-breathless by this time, his body suffused with the falling-forward hum of slogging through distances of mud. His cloak seemed lined with ingots of lead, so pendulous it had become. The town's name was appropriate, he decided. Marrow. He could almost imagine that he tramped through the muck of halved bones.

Shadowy men reeled through the ruts around and beside him, some alone, their eyes hollow and alert, others in cackling groups, their lips and looks relaxed by a consciousness of numbers. Everyone was sodden. Everyone shouted over the thunder of the falls. Most were armed and armoured.

Many were caked in blood, either because they were wounded or because they were unwashed.

These were the Scalpoi, sanctioned by the writ of the Aspect-Emperor, drawn from the four corners of the New Empire: wild-haired Galeoth, smooth-cheeked Nansur, great-bearded Tydonni, even lazy-lidded Nilnameshi—they were all here, trading scalps for Imperial kellics and shrial remissions.

Feeling harried by a succession of long looks, Achamian hunched deeper into the hood of his cloak. He knew he was anything but conspicuous, that part of him had simply forgotten how to trust in anonymity. Even still he found himself shrinking from the touch of other eyes, belligerent or curious, it did not matter. There was an unruliness in the air, a whiff of some profound lawlessness, which he initially ascribed to the release of pent urgencies. The Scalpoi spent months far from any hearth, warring and hunting Sranc through the trackless Wilds. He could scarce imagine a more savage calling, or a greater warrant for excess.

But as the mad parade thickened, he realized that the abandon was more than simply a matter of glutting frustrated lusts. There were too many men from too many different castes, creeds, and nations. Castenobles from Cingulat. Runaway slaves from Ce Tydonn. Fanim heretics from Girgash. It was as though common origins were all that guaranteed civilization, a shared language of life, and that everything was fury and miscommunication otherwise. Hungers—that was all these men had in common. Instincts. What had made these men wild wasn't the wilderness, or even the mad savagery of the Sranc, it was the inability to trust anything more than the bestial in one another.

Fear, he told himself. *Fear and lust and fury . . . Trust in these, old man.* It seemed the only commandment a place such as Marrow could countenance.

He trudged onward, more wary than ever. He smelled

whisky, vomit, and shallow latrines. He heard songs and laughter and weeping, the ghostly notes of a lute plucked from the bowl of the night. He glimpsed smiles—the glint of gold from yellow-rotted teeth. He saw lantern-limned interiors, raucous, illuminated worlds, filled with hard words and mad, murderous looks. He saw the glimmer of naked steel. He watched a roaring Galeoth man hammer another, over and over, until the man was little more than a blood-soaked worm flexing and squirming in the muck. A drunk harlot, her flabby arms bruised and bare, accosted him. "Fancy a peach?" she drawled, groping between his thighs.

He felt the flare of dwindled memory, the twitch of old, life-preserving habits, no less prudent for becoming vestigial. He gripped the pommel of his knife beneath his cloak.

He passed the lightless Custom House with its threadbare Circumfix hanging slack in the windless gloom. Marrow was an outpost of the New Empire—it wouldn't do to forget that. He passed a lazaret with its aura of astringent, feces, and infection. He passed a low-raftered opium den, as well as several booming taverns and two half-tented brothels, oozing moans and mercantile giggles into the general night. He even happened upon a wooden post-and-lintel temple to Yatwer, filled with chimes and chants—some evening ceremony, Achamian supposed. All the while the cataract whooshed and rumbled, the motionless blast of water against stone. Clear beads dripped from the rim of his cowl.

He tried not to think of the girl. Mimara.

By the time he found the inn Geraus had mentioned, the Cocked Leg, he was almost accustomed to the uproar. Marrow, he decided while leading his mule into the rear courtyard, was not so different from the great polyglot cities of his youth. More vicious, roughed in timber instead of monumental stone, and lacking the size that allowed indifference and mass anonymity to congeal into urban tolerance—there was no unspoken agreement to overlook one another's perversions here. Anyone could be judged at any moment. But even still, it possessed the same sense of *possibility*, accidental and collective, humming across every public threshold, as though the congregation of strangers was all it took to generate alternatives . . .

Freedom.

A night in such a place could have a million endings, Achamian realized. That was its wonder and horror both.

A night in Marrow.

The room was small. The woollen bedding reeked of mould and must. The innkeeper had not liked the looks of him, that much was certain. Show the pauper to the pauper's room—that was the ancient rule. Nevertheless, Achamian found himself smiling as he doffed his dripping cloak and squared his supplies and belongings. It seemed he had set out for Marrow a sleeping hermit and had arrived an awakening spy.

This was good, he told himself as he followed the stairs and halls toward the thunder of the Cocked Leg's common room. Most auspicious. Now all he required was some luck.

He grinned in anticipation, did his best to ignore the bloody handprints decorating the wall.

Achamian's adventurous mood evaporated as soon as he pressed his way into the smoky, low-timbered room. The shock nearly struck him breathless, so long had it been since he had last observed other men with his arcane eyes. There was another *sorcerer* here—an old and accomplished one given the black and blasted depth of his Mark—sitting in the far corner. And there was someone carrying a Chorae as well. A cursed Tear of God, so-called because its merest touch destroyed sorcerers and their desecrations.

Of course, he could see the Mark whenever he looked to his own hands or glimpsed his reflection in sitting water, but it was like his skin, something too near to be truly visible. Seeing its eye-twisting stain on another—especially after so many years immersed in the clarity of the Uncreated, the World as untouched by sorcerers and their blasphemous voices—made him feel . . . young.

Young with fear.

Turning his back on the presence, Achamian made his way to the barkeep, whom he easily recognized from his slave's description. According to Geraus, his name was Haubrezer, one of the three Tydonni brothers who owned the Cocked Leg. Achamian bowed his head, even though he had yet to see anyone observing *jnan* since arriving here. "My name is Akka," he said.

"Ya," the tall, stork-skinny man replied. His voice wasn't so much deep as it was dark. "You the old pick. This no land for the slow and crooked, ya know."

Achamian feigned an old man's baffled good humour. It seemed absurd that the venerable Norsirai slur for Ketyai, "pick," could still sting after so many years.

"My slave, Geraus, said you could assist me."

Coming to Marrow had always been the plan—as had hiring a company of Scalpoi. Mimara had simply forced him to abbreviate his timetable, to begin his journey before knowing his destination. Her coming had rattled him in more ways than he cared to admit—the suspicions, the resemblance to her mother, the pointed questions, their sad coupling—but the consequences of her *never* coming would have been disastrous.

At least now he knew why Fate had sent her to him—as a boot in the rump.

"Yaa," Haubrezer brayed. "Good man, Geraus." A searching look, rendered severe by the angularity of his face. He struck Achamian as one of those men whose souls had adapted to the peculiarities of their body. Stooped and long-fingered, mantislike both in patience and predatoriness. He did not hunt, Achamian decided, so much as he waited.

"Indeed."

Haubrezer stared with an almost bovine relentlessness—bored to tears, yet prepared to die chewing his cud. The man seemed to have compensated for his awkwardness by slowing everything down, including his intellect. Slowness had a way of laying out the grace that dwelt in all things, even the most ungainly. It was the reason why proud drunks took care to walk as though under water.

At last, the large eyes blinked in conclusion. "Ya. The ones you look for . . ." He lowered his veined forehead toward the back corner, on the far side of the smoking central hearth.

Toward the sorcerer and the Chorae that Achamian had sensed upon entering the common room.

But of course . . .

"Are you sure?"

Haubrezer kept his head inclined, though it seemed that he stared at his eyebrows rather than the grim-talking shadows beyond the smoke.

"Ho. No mean Scalpoi, those. They the Veteran's Men. The Skin Eaters."

"The Skin Eaters?"

A sour grin, as though the man had been starved of the facial musculature needed to pull his lips from his teeth. "Geraus was right. You hermit, to be sure. Ask anyone here around"—he gestured wide with a scapular hand—"they will tell you, ya, step aside for the Skin Eaters. Famed. The whole River know. They bring down more bales than *rutta*—anyone. Ho. Step aside for the Skin Eaters, or they strike you down. *Hauza kup*. Down but good."

Achamian leaned back to appraise what suddenly seemed more a hostile tribe than another alehouse trestle. Though all the other long-tables were packed, the three men Haubrezer referred to sat alone, neither rigid nor at their ease, yet with a posture that suggested an intense inward focus, a violent disregard for matters not their own.

The image of them wavered in the sparked air above the hearth: the first—the bearer of the Chorae—with the squared-and-plaited beard of an Ainoni or a Conriyan; the second with long white hair, a goatee, and a weather-pruned face; and the broad-shouldered third—the sorcerer—cowled in black-beaten leather.

Achamian glanced back up at Haubrezer. "Do I require an introduction?"

"Not from the likes of me."

An acute sensitivity to his surroundings beset Achamian while crossing the common room, which for him amounted to a kind of bodily awareness of some imminent undertaking—some reckless leap. He winced at the odour of sweat festering in leather. The outer thunder of the Long-Braid Falls shivered through air and timber alike, so that the room seemed a motionless bubble in a torrent. And the guttural patois everyone spoke—a kind of mongrel marriage of Gallish and Sheyic—struck him with an ancient and impossible taste: the First Holy War, twenty long years gone by.

He thought of Kellhus and found his resolution rekindled.

The pulse of a fool . . .

Achamian had no illusions about the men he was about to meet. The New Empire had signalled the end of the once lucrative mercenary trade, but it did not signal the end of those willing to kill for compensation. He had spent the greater part of his life in the proximity of such men—in the company of those who would think him weak. He had long ago learned how to mime the proper postures, how to redress the defects of the heart with the advantages of intellect. He knew how to treat with such men—or so he thought.

His first heartbeat in their presence told him otherwise.

The cowled man, the sorcerer, turned to him, but only

far enough to reveal a temple and jawline as white and as smooth as boiled bone. Obdurate black shrouded his eyes. The small, silver-haired man graced him with a nimble, shining look and a smile that seemed to welcome the derision to come. But the square-bearded one, the man Haubrezer had identified as the Captain, continued staring into his wine-bowl as before. Achamian understood instantly he was the kind of man who begrudged others everything.

"Are you the Ainoni they call Kosoter?" he asked. "Ironsoul. The Captain of the Skin Eaters?"

A moment of silence, far too thick to connote shock or surprise.

The Captain took a deliberate drink, then fixed him with his narrow brown eyes. It was a look Achamian recognized from the massacres and privations of the First Holy War. A look that saw only dead things.

"I know you," was all he said in a voice with a hint of a papyrus rasp.

"You will address the Captain as 'Veteran,'" the silver-haired man exclaimed. He was diminutive but with wrists thick enough to promise an iron grip. And he was old, at least as old as Achamian, but it seemed the years had stripped only the fat of weakness from him, leaving spry fire in the leather that remained. He was a man who had been shrivelled strong. "After all," he continued with a slit-eyed laugh, "it's the *Law*."

Achamian ignored him.

"You know me?" he said to the Captain, who had resumed his study of his inscrutable drink. "From the First Hol—"

"Sir," the small man interrupted. "Please. Allow me to introduce myself. I am Sarl—"

"I need to contract your company," Achamian continued, staring intently at the Captain. Definitely Ainoni. He looked archaic, like something risen from a burial mound.

"Sir," Sarl pressed, this time with a cut-throat gleam in his eye. "*Please* . . ."

Achamian turned to him, frowning but attentive.

His grin hooked the ruts of his face into innumerable lines. "I have, shall we say, a certain facility for sums and figures, as well as the finer details of argument. My illustrious Captain, well, let us just say, he has little patience for the perversities of speech."

"So *you* make the decisions?"

The man burst into a beet-faced cackle, revealing the arc of his gums. "No," he gasped, as though astounded that anyone could ask a question so uproariously thick. "No-no-no! I do the singing. But I assure you, it is the *Captain* who inks the verse." Sarl bowed to the Ainoni in embellished deference—who now watched Achamian with something poised between curiosity and malice. When Sarl turned back to Achamian, his lips were pursed into a *see-I-told-you-so* line.

Achamian snorted dismissively. This was one thing he didn't miss about the civilized world: the addiction to all things indirect.

"I need to contract your Captain's company."

"Such a strange request!" Sarl exclaimed, as though waiting to say as much all along. "And daring, very daring. There are no more wars, my friend, save the two that are holy. The one that our Aspect-Emperor wages against wicked Golgotterath, and the more tawdry one we wage against the Sranc. There are *no more mercenaries*, friend."

Achamian found himself glancing back and forth between the two men. The effect was unnerving, as though the division of attention amounted to a kind of partial blindness.

For all he knew, this was the whole point of this ludicrous exercise.

"It isn't mercenaries I need, it's scalpers. And it isn't war that I intend, it's a journey."

"Ahhh, *very* interesting," Sarl drawled. His eyes collapsed into fluttering slits every time he smiled, as if blinking at some kind of comical grit. "A journey requiring scalpers is a journey *into the wastes*, no?"

Achamian paused, disconcerted by the ease of the man's penetration. This Sarl was every bit as nimble as he looked.

"Yes."

"As I thought! Very, *very* interesting! So tell me, just *where* in the North do you need to go?"

Achamian had feared this question, as inevitable as it was. Who was he fooling?

"Far . . ." He swallowed. "To the ruins of Sauglish."

Another spittle-flecked spasm of laughter, this one carving every vein, every web of wrinkles in succinct shades of purple and red. He even yanked his wrists together as though bound, shook up and down, fingers flicking. He looked to the cowled man as though seeking confirmation. "Sauglish!" he howled, rolling his face back. "Oh ho, my friend, my poor, poor lunatic friend!" He reclined back in his chair, sucking air. "May the Gods"—he shook his head in a kind of astonished dismissal—"keep your bowls warm and full and whatever."

Something in his look and tone said, *Leave while you still can . . .*

Achamian's fists balled of their own volition. It was all he could do to keep from burning the pissant to cinders. Arrogant monkey-of-a-man! Only the Captain's Chorae and the indigo Mark of his cowled companion stayed his tongue.

A hard moment of fading smiles.

Sarl scratched the pad of his thumb with the nail of his index finger.

Then the Captain said, "What lies in Sauglish?"

The words fairly knocked the blood out of Sarl's ruddy face. Perhaps there were consequences for misreading the Captain's interest. Perhaps the man had simply wandered too far out on a drunken limb. For some reason, Achamian had the impression that Lord Kosoter's voice always had this effect.

"What do you know of it?" Achamian asked. He immediately realized this was a grievous mistake, answering a question with a question when discoursing with the Captain. Nevertheless, he felt the need to match, flint for flint, the man's unearthly look, to communicate his own ability to see the atrocity at the heart of all things.

He stared into Lord Kosoter's shining eyes. He could hear Sarl breath, a shallow-chested sound, like a dog dreaming. He found himself wondering if the cowled man had moved. A ringing sidled into the room, high-pitched and hazy, and with it came a premonition of lethality, a wheedling apprehension. The stakes of this contest, part of him realized, involved far more than dominance or respect or even identity, but the very possibility of being . . .

I am the end of you, the eyes in his eyes whispered. And they seemed a thousand years old.

Achamian could feel himself wilt. Wild-limbed imaginings flickered through his soul, hot with screams and blood. He could feel tremors knock through his knees.

"Go easy now, friend," Sarl murmured in what seemed genuine conciliation. "The Captain here can piss halfway cross the world, if need be. Just *answer* his question."

Achamian swallowed, blinked. "The Coffers," some traitor with his voice said. Glancing at Sarl seemed like breaking the surface of a drowning.

"Coffers," Sarl repeated strangely. "Perhaps"—a quick glance at Lord Kosoter—"you should tell the Captain what you meant by the Coffers."

Achamian could see the man's implacable eyes, like Scrutiny incarnate, leaning against his periphery. He found himself glancing at the cowled figure, then looking away, down to the accursed floor.

It wasn't supposed to be like this!

"No," he said, breathing deep, then glaring at all three in turn. The way to deal with the Captain, he realized, was to make him one of a number. "I shall try my luck elsewhere." He made to leave, feeling faint and sweaty and more than a little nauseous.

"You're the *Wizard*," Lord Kosoter called out in a growl.

The word hooked Achamian like a wire garrote.

"I remember you," the grave face continued as he turned. "I remember you from the Holy War." He slid his wine-bowl to one side, leaned forward over the table. "You *taught him*. The Aspect-Emperor."

"What does it matter?" Achamian said, not caring whether he sounded bitter.

The almost black-on-black eyes blinked for what seemed the first time.

"It matters because it means you were a Mandate Schoolman . . . once." His Sheyic was impeccable, bent more to some inner dialect of anger than to the lilting cadences of his native Ainoni tongue. "Which means you *really do know* where to find the Coffers."

"So much the worse for you," Achamian said. But all he could think was *how* . . . How could a scalper, any scalper, know about the Sohonc Coffers? He found himself glancing at the leather-cowled man to the Captain's left . . . The sorcerer. What was his School?

"I think not," Lord Kosoter said, leaning back. "There's scalpers aplenty in Marrow, sure. Any number of companies." He hooked his wine-bowl with two calloused fingers. "But none who know *who you are* . . ." His grin was curious, frightening. "Which means none who will even entertain your request."

The logic of his claim hung like an iron in the air, indifferent to the swell of background voices. Truth was ever the afterlife of words.

Achamian stood dumbstruck.

"I have this leaf," Sarl said, his eyes bright with just-between-friends mischief. "You place it against your anus—"

The cowled man erupted in faceless laughter. Achamian saw his left eye as he tilted his head back, a glimpse of a pupil set in watery grey. But it was the guttural arrhythmia of his laugh that told him what he was . . .

"Just *twooo*," Sarl howled, his purple brows nearly pinched to his apple-red cheeks. "*Tw-twooo ensolariis!*"

Achamian sneered as much as smiled. The Anus Leaf was an old joke, an expression referring to charlatans who peddled hope in the form of false remedies.

The Captain watched him with imperturbable care.

They were right, he realized. Derision was all he could expect here in Marrow—or even worse. The Skin Eaters were his only hope.

And they had already struck him down.

Achamian took the proffered bowl in both hands just to be sure it didn't shake. He drained it and gasped. Unwatered wine from some bitter Galeoth soil.

"The Coffers!" Sarl crowed. "Captain! He wants to loot the *Coffers*!"

Achamian smacked his lips about the burning in his gullet, wiped a rasp-woollen sleeve across his beard and mouth. It was strange, the way a single drink could make you part of someone's company. "It was *him*," Achamian said to the Captain while nodding in the direction of the cowled figure. "Wasn't it? He told you about the Coffers . . ."

Another mistake. Evidently, the Captain refused to recognize even the most innocent conversational impositions. Hint, innuendo, implication; all of it accused with a glare, then condemned with onerous silence.

"We call him Cleric," Sarl said, tilting his head toward the man—a mock covert gesture.

The black, leather-rimmed oval seemed to stare back at Achamian.

"Cleric," Achamian repeated.

The cowl remained motionless. The Captain resumed staring into his wine.

"You should hear him in the Wilds," Sarl exclaimed. "Such sweet sermons! And to think I once thought myself eloquent."

"And yet," Achamian said carefully, "Nonmen have no priests."

"Not as Men understand them," the black pit replied.

Shock. Its voice had been pleasant, melodious, but marbled with into-nations alien to the human vocal range. It was as though the tones of a deformed child had been woven into it.

Achamian sat rigid. "Where are you from?" he asked, his lungs pressed against his backbone. "Ishterebinth?"

The hood bowed to the tabletop. "I can no longer remember. I have known Ishterebinth, I think . . . But it was not called such then."

"I see your Mark. You wear it fierce and deep."

The hood lifted, as though raising hidden ears to some faraway sound. "As do you."

"Who was your Quya Master? From which Line do you hail?"

"I . . . I cannot remember."

Achamian licked his lips in hesitation, then asked the question that had to be asked of all Nonmen. "What can you remember?"

An odd hesitation, as though to the syncopation of an inhuman heart.

"Things. Friends. Strangers and lovers. All of them heart-breaking. All of them horrific."

"And the Coffers? You remember them?"

An almost imperceptible nod. "I was at the Library of Sauglish when it fell—I think. I remember that terror all too well . . . But why it should cause me such sorrow, I do not know."

The words pimpled Achamian's skin. He had dreamed the horrors of Sauglish far too many times—he need only close his eyes to see the burning towers, the fleeing masses, the Sohonc battling iron-scaled Wracu in skies wreathed in smoke and flame. He had tasted the ash on the wind, heard the wailing of multitudes. He had wept at his own cowardice . . .

This made him unique among Men, to have lived the span of two lives—two eye blinks, Seswatha and Achamian, flung across the millennia. But this Nonman before him, his life straddled a hundred human generations. He had lived the entire breadth of those nation-eating ages. From then to now—and even more. From the twilight of the First Apocalypse to the dawn of the Second.

He was in the presence of a *living line*, Achamian realized, of eyes that had witnessed all the intervening years between his two selves, between Achamian, the Wizard-Exile, and Seswatha, the Grandmaster of the Sohonc. This Nonman had lived the two-thousand-year sleep between . . .

It almost made Achamian feel whole.

"And your name?"

Sarl whispered some kind of curse.

"Incariol," the cowled figure said with an air of inward grappling. And then again, "*Incariol* . . ." as though testing its sound on his tongue. "Does that sound familiar?"

Achamian had never heard of it, not that he could remember. Even still, it was plain these Scalpoi had no inkling of who or what rode with them. How could any mortal fathom such a cavernous soul?

As old as the Tusk . . .

"So you're an Erratic."

"Am I? Is that what I am?"

How did you answer such a question? The creature

before him had lived so long his very identity had collapsed beneath him, dropped him into the pit of his own lifetime. His was a running-over soul, where every instance of love or hope or joy drained into the void of forgetfulness, displaced by the more viscous passions of terror, anguish, and hate.

He was an Erratic, addicted to atrocity for memory's sake.

"He's calling you mad," Sarl said, a little too quickly given the gravity of their silence.

The hood turned to him.

"Yes . . . I *am* mad."

Sarl waved his hands in affectionate contradiction. "Come now, Cleric. No need to—"

"*Memories* . . ." the black pit interrupted. A word struck in wincing tones of woe. "Memories make us sane."

"See!" Sarl exclaimed, whirling to Achamian. "Sermons!" His face was pinched red about a manic smile, as though he were the kind of man who made claims compulsively and so gloated over every instance of their confirmation.

"This one night in the Wilds, one of our number asks Cleric here what's the greatest treasure he's heard tell. Gold, as you might imagine, is quite a popular topic among us Scalpoi, especially when we're hunting on the dark—without campfires, that is. Warms the bones as sure as any flame, talk of peaches and gold."

There was something—the turn of his face, maybe, the aura of antagonism in the way he leaned forward, or the twist of insincerity in his tone—tone—that told Achamian that "sermons" were the least of the man's concerns.

"So Cleric here," Sarl rasps, "obliges us with another sermon. He mentions *several* glories, for he's seen things we mortals can scarce conceive. But for some reason it was the *Coffers* that stuck. The hoard hidden beneath the Library of Sauglish, ere it was destroyed in the First Apocalypse. The Coffers, we say. The Coffers—any time we're loath to mention that unluckiest of words, 'hope.' Coffers. Coffers.

Coffers. We trek out to run down the skinnies, give them a trim, but we always say we're searching for the *Coffers*."

The face-wrinkling amiability suddenly dropped from his face, revealing something cold and hateful and implausibly profound.

"And now, here *you* are, as sure as Fate."

There was something, Achamian decided, altogether too mobile about the man's expressions.

"You're a learned man," Sarl added, speaking through strings of phlegm. An uncommon intensity had fixed his rodent features—as if some life-or-death opportunity were on the verge of slipping from his grasp. "Tell me, what do you think of the concept of *coincidence*? Do you think things happen for reasons?"

A perplexed look. A depleted smile. Achamian could summon no more.

Sarl leaned back, nodding and laughing and petting his white goatee. *Of course you do!* his squinty look shouted, as though Achamian had given him the oh-so-predictable book-learned response.

Achamian did his best not to gape. He had forgotten what it was like, the succession of trivial surprises that was part and parcel of joining the company of strangers. In the company of strangers it was so easy to forget the small crab-like histories that held others together and set you apart.

But this was no trivial surprise.

From Marrow to the wastes of Kûniüri was a journey of months across Sranc-infested Wilds. Were it not for the Great Ordeal, the trek would be simply impossible: Over the centuries, the School of Mandate had lost more than a few expeditions trying to reach either Sauglish or Golgotterath. But even with the Great Ordeal drawing the Sranc like a lodestone, Achamian knew he could not make his way alone—not so far, not at his age. This was the whole reason why he had come to Marrow: to recruit the assistance he would need. He had simply struck upon the Sohonc Coffers as an inducement, if not an outright ruse . . . And now this.

Could it simply be coincidence?

Lord Kosoter watched Sarl with eyes of glassy iron.

The small man blanched. His face squinted along plaintive lines. "If this is no coincidence, Captain, then it's *the Whore*. Anagkë. Fate." He looked around as if encouraged by imaginary fellows. "And the Whore, begging your pardon, Captain, fucks everyone in the end—*everyone*. Foe, friend, fuzzy little fucking woodland creatures . . ."

But his words were for naught. The Captain's silence boomed as much.

And Achamian found himself wondering just when the agreement had been struck—and just how the men he had hoped to *hire* had become his partners. Was he simply one more Skin Eater?

Should he be grateful? Relieved? Horrified?

"I remember . . ." the blackness wrapped by the cowl said. "I remember the slaughter of . . ."

A peculiar sound, like a sob thumbed into the shape of a cackle.

"Of *children*."

"A man," the Captain grimly noted, "has got to remember."

That night Achamian dreamed in the old way. He dreamed of Sauglish.

The Wracu came first, as they always did, dropping from the clouds with claws and wings askew. Their roars seemed to fall from all directions, curiously hollow, like children screeching into caverns, only infinitely more savage.

Vertigo. Seswatha hung with his Sohonc brothers above their sacred Library, whose towers and walls yawed out below them, perched on the Troinim, the three hills that commanded the great city's westward reaches. They awaited the frenzied descent, their figures hazed blue by their Gnostic Wards. Light sparked from their eyes and mouths, so that their heads seemed cauldrons. Their feet braced against the ground's echo, they sang their blasphemous song.

Psalms of destruction.

Lines of brilliant white mapped the gaping spaces, striking geometries, confining geometries, lights that made smoke of hide and fury. Rearing back to bare claws and spew fire, the dragons plummeted into the arcane glitter, shrieking, screaming. Then they were through, bleeding smoke, some writhing and convulsing, one or two toppling to their deaths. The singing became more frantic. Threads of incandescence boiled against iron scales. Unseen hammers beat against wings and limbs.

Then the Wracu were upon them.

And for an instant, Seswatha *became Achamian*, an old man born of another age, his eyes rolling like a panicked horse. Somehow forgotten, he jerked his gaze side to side, from the white robed men hanging frail in their glowing spheres to the black-maned beasts that assailed them, burning and rending. Wings bellied like sails in the tempest. Eyes narrowed into sickle-shaped slits. Wounds smoked. The Wracu hammered and clawed the curved planes, and things not of this world sheared. The antique Schoolmen shouted, cried out in horror and frustration. A dragon fell, gutted by blue flame. A sorcerer, young Hûnovis, was stripped to bone by burning exhalations, and twirled like a burning scroll into the vista below. The glare of sorcery and fiery vomit intensified, until all that Achamian could see were ragged silhouettes twisting serpentine over the void.

The city pitched across the distances, a patchwork of labyrinthine streets and packed structures. To the east, he saw the shining ribbon of the River Aumris, the cradle of

Norsirai glory. And to the west, beyond the fortifications, he saw the alluvial plains blackened by hordes of whooping Sranc. And beyond them, the *whirlwind*, howling across the horizon, monstrous and inexhaustible, framed by the rose-gold of more distant skies. Even when obscured by smoke Achamian could feel it . . . Mog-Pharau, the end of all things.

Roars scored the heights to arch of heaven, reptilian fury wrapped about the inside-out mutter of sorcery—the glory of the Gnosis. The dragons raged. The sorcerers of the Sohonc, the first and greatest School, fought and died.

He did not so much see those below as he remembered them. Refugees packing the rooftops, watching the slow advance of doom. Fathers casting their own babes to the hard cobble of the streets. Mothers cutting their children's throats—anything to save them from the fury of the Sranc. Slaves and chieftains howling, crying out to heavens shut against them. The broken staring into the dread west, numb to everything save the whirlwind's roping approach . . .

Their High-King was dead. The wombs of their wives and their daughters had become graves. The greatest of their thanes and chieftain-knights, the flower of their armed might, had been struck down. Pillars of smoke scored the distance across the earth's very curve.

The world was ending.

Like choking. Like drowning. Like a weight without substance, sinking cold through him, a knife drawn from the snow, even as he fell slack into its bottomless regions. Friends, brothers, shaken apart in grinning jaws. Strangers flailing in fiery blooms. Towers leaning like drunks before crashing. Sranc encrusting distant walls, like ants on slices of apple, loping into the maze of streets. The cries, shrieks, screams—thousands of them—rising like steam from burning stones. Sauglish dying.

Hopelessness . . . Futility.

Never, it seemed, had he dreamed a *passion* with such vehemence.

Undone, the surviving Sohonc fled the skies, took shelter in the Library with its net of great square towers. Batteries of ballistae covered their retreat, and several of the younger Wracu foundered, harpooned. Achamian stood abandoned in the sky, gazing at mighty Skafra, scars like capstan rope, limbs like sinuous timbers, and leprous wings beating, obscuring the distant No-God with every laborious *whump-whump*. The ancient Wracu grinned its lipless dragon grin, scanned the near distances with eyes of bloody pearl . . .

And somehow, miraculously, looked *through him*.

Skafra, near enough for his bulk to trigger bodily terror. Achamian stared helplessly at the creature, watched the bright crimson of its rage drain from its scales and the rising blooms of black that signified dark contemplation. The conflagration below glittered across its chitinous lines, and Achamian's eyes were drawn downward, to the plummet beneath his feet.

The sight of the Holy Library burning stuck pins into his eyes. Beloved stone! The great walls sheathed in obsidian along their sloped foundations, rising high and white above. The copper roofs, stacked like massive skirts. And the deep courtyards, so that from the sky the structure resembled the halved heart of some vast and intricate beast. Sunbright sputum washed across ensorcelled stone, knifed through seams and cracks. Dragonfire rained across the circuit, a spray of thunderous eruptions.

But where? Where was Seswatha? How could he dream without—

The old Wizard awoke crying out thoughts from the end of a different world. *Sauglish! We have lost Sauglish!*

But as his eyes sorted the darkness of his room from the afterimages, and his ears dredged the roar of the falls from the death-throe thunder, it seemed he could hear the madwoman . . . Mimara.

"*You have become a prophet* . . ." Was that not what she had said?

"*A prophet of the past.*"

The next day Sarl collected Achamian and brought him to what must have been one of the Cocked Leg's largest rooms. Though he moved with the same spry impatience, the old cutthroat seemed surprisingly quiet. Whether this was due to the previous night's drink or discussion, Achamian could not readily tell.

Another man awaited them in addition to Kosoter and Cleric: a middle-aged Nansur named Kiampas. If Sarl was the Captain's mouth, then Kiampas, Achamian realized, was his hand. Clean-shaven and elegantly featured, he looked somewhat younger than the fifty or so years Achamian eventually credited to him. He was definitely more soldier than warrior. He had a wry, methodical air that suggested melancholy as much as competence. Because of this, Achamian found himself almost instantly trusting both his instincts and his acumen. As a former Imperial Officer, Kiampas was a devotee of plans and the resources required to bring them to fruition. Such men usually left the issue of overarching goals to their superiors, but after listening to Achamian explain the mission to come, his manner betrayed obvious doubt if not out-and-out dismay.

"So just when did you hope to reach these ruins?" His speech had a well-practised insistence—a first-things-first air—that spoke of many long campaigns.

"The Wards protecting the Coffers are peculiar," Achamian lied, "geared to the heavenly spheres. We must reach Sauglish *before* the autumn solstice."

All eyes raked him, searching, it seemed, for the telltale glow of deceit in the blank coals of his face.

"Sweet Sejenus!" Kiampas cried in disbelief. "The end of summer?"

"It's imperative."

"Impossible. It can't be done!"

"Yes," the Captain grated, "it *can*."

Kiampas paled, seemed to glance down in unconscious apology. Though he was cut of different cloth entirely, Achamian wasn't surprised to see him sharing Sarl's reaction to the chest-tightening rarity of their Captain's voice.

"Well then," the Nansur continued, apparently searching for his equilibrium in the matter at hand. "The choice of routes is straightforward then. We should travel through Galeoth, up through—"

"That cannot be done," Achamian interrupted.

The studied lack of expression on Kiampas's face would be Achamian's first glimpse of the man's escalating disdain.

"And what route do you suggest?"

"Along the back of the Osthwai."

"The back of the . . ." The man possessed a sneering side, but then, so did most ironic souls. "Are you fucking mad? Do you realize—"

"I cannot travel anywhere in the New Empire," Achamian said, genuinely penitent. Of all the Skin Eaters he had met thus far, Kiampas was the only one he was prepared to trust, if only at a procedural level. "Ask Lord Kosoter. He knows who I am."

Apparently the lack of contradiction in the Captain's glare was confirmation enough.

"So you wish to avoid the Aspect-Emperor," Kiampas continued. Achamian did not like the way his eyes drifted to the Captain as he said this.

"What of it?"

His impertinent smile was rendered all the more injurious by the dignity of his features. "Rumour has it Sakarpus has fallen, that the Great Ordeal even now marches northward."

He was saying they would have to cross the New Empire no matter what. Achamian bowed his face to the jnanic degree that acknowledged a point taken. He knew how absurd he must look, an old, wild-haired hermit dressed in a beggar's tunic, aping the etiquette of a faraway castenobility. Even still, this was a courtesy he had yet to extend to any of the others; he wanted Kiampas to know that he respected both him and his misgivings.

Something told him he would need allies in the weeks and months to come.

"Look," Achamian replied. "Were it not for the Great Ordeal, an expedition such as this would be madness. This is perhaps the one time, the *only* time, that something like this can be attempted! But just because the Aspect-Emperor clears our way, doesn't mean we must cross his path. He shall be far ahead of us, mark me."

Kiampas was having none of it. "The Captain tells me you're a fellow Veteran, that you belonged to the First Holy War. That means you know full well the sluggish and capricious ways of great hosts on the march."

"Sauglish lies out of their way," Achamian said evenly. "The chances of encountering any Men of the Circumfix are exceedingly slim."

Kiampas nodded with slow skepticism, then leaned back, as if retreating from some disagreeable scent.

The smell of futility, perhaps.

After that second meeting, the watches of the day and the days of the week passed quickly. Lord Kosoter commanded a muster of the full company the following morning. The Skin Eaters assembled among the posts of old Marrow, far enough from the mists for their jerkins to harden in the sun. They were a motley group, some sixty or so strong, sporting all manner of armour and weaponry. Some were fastidious, obviously intent on reclaiming as much civilization as they could during their brief tenure in Marrow. One was even decked in the crisp white gowns of a Nilnameshi caste-noble and seemed almost comically concerned with the mud staining his crimson-threaded hems. Others were savage-slovenly, bearing the stamp of their inhuman quarry, to the point of almost resembling Sranc in the case of some. A great many seemed to have adopted the Thunyeri custom of wearing shrunken heads as adornment, either about their girdles or sewn into the lacquered faces of their shields. Otherwise, the only thing they seemed to share in common was a kind of deep spiritual fatigue and, of course, an abiding, almost reverential fear of their Captain.

When they had settled into ranks, Sarl described, in terms grandiloquent enough to flirt with mockery, the nature of the expedition their Captain was in the course of planning. Lord Kosoter stood off to the side, his eyes scavenging the horizon. Cleric accompanied him, somewhat taller and just as broad, his face hidden in his cowl. The cataracts boomed in the distance, a great murky hiss that reminded Achamian of the way the Inrithi hosts had roared in response to Kellhus some twenty years previous. Birdsong braided the nearby forest verge.

Sarl explained the extraordinary perils that would face them, how they would be travelling ten times the distance of a standard "slog," as he called it, and how they could expect to live in the "pit" for more than a year. He paused after mentioning this last as though to let its significance resonate. Achamian reminded himself that the wilderness was not so much a *place* to these men, as an art with its own well of customs and lore. He imagined that scalpers traded stories of companies gone missing returning after so many months in the "pit." Those words, "more than a year," he realized, likely carried dismaying implications.

But again and again, the old, wire-limbed man came back to the Coffers. "Coffers," spoken like the title of some great king. "Coffers," murmured like the name of some collective aspiration. "Coffers," spat as though to say, "How long shall we be denied our due?" "Coffers," hollered over and over like the name of some lost child. "Coffers," invoked as though it were something lost and holy, another Shimeh crying out for reconquest . . .

But more real than any of these things in that it could be divided into equal shares.

A lie carved at the joints.

Sarl explained all, his face reddening, then reddening again, his head bobbing to the more strident turns of speech, his body given to illustrative antics, standing at attention, trotting in place, pacing while the voice pondered. And all was disciplined silence throughout, something which, given the crazed composition of the Skin Eaters, Achamian would have thought a miracle had he not shared bowls with their Captain.

"You have until tomorrow morning to decide," Sarl announced in wide-armed conclusion. "Tomorrow to decide whether to risk all *to become a prince!* or cradle your pulse and die a slave. Afterwards, departures will be considered desertion—*desertion!*—and Cleric, here, will be set to the hunt. You know the rule of the slog, boys. The knee that buckles pulls ten men down. The knee that buckles pulls ten men down!"

Watching them break ranks and fall to talking among themselves, Achamian found himself comparing them to the hard-bitten men of the First Holy War, the warriors whose zeal and cruelty had allowed Kellhus to conquer all the Three Seas. The Skin Eaters, he decided, were a far different breed than the Men of the Tusk. They were not ruthless so much as they were vicious. They were not hard so much as they were numb. And they were not driven so much as they were hungry.

They were, in the end, *mercenaries* . . . albeit ones touched by the gibbering ferocity of the Sranc.

Lord Kosoter seemed to acknowledge as much over the course of the rare glances Achamian exchanged with him. It was a bond between them, Achamian realized, their shared experiences of the First Holy War. They alone possessed the measuring stick, they alone knew the rule. And it had made them kinsmen of a sort—a thought that at once awed and troubled Achamian.

During that night's obligatory revels, Sarl approached him. "The Captain has asked me," he said, "to remind you these men are Scalpoi. Nothing more. Nothing less. The legend of the Skin Eaters resides *in him*."

Achamian thought it strange, a man who despised speaking confiding in a man who could do nothing else. "And you? You believe this?"

The same eye-pinching grin. "I've been with the Captain since the beginning," he cackled. "From before the Imperial Bounty, in the wars against the Orthodox. I've seen him stand untouched in a hail of arrows, while I cringed behind my shield. I was at his side on the walls of Meigeiri, when the fucking Longbeards fell over themselves trying to flee from his blood-maddened gaze. I was *there*, after the battle of Em'famir. With these two ears I heard the *Aspect-Emperor*—the Aspect-Emperor!—name him Ironsoul!" Sarl laughed with purpling mania. "Oh, yes, he's mortal, to be sure. He's a man like other men, as many an unfortunate peach has discovered, believe you me. But something watches him, and more important, *something watches through him . . .*"

Sarl seized Achamian's elbow, smashed his wine-bowl into Achamian's hard enough to shatter both. "You would do well . . ." he said, a mad blankness on his face. He eased backward step by unreal step, nodding as though to a tune or a truth that only rats could hear, "to respect the Captain."

Achamian looked down to his soaked hand. The wine had run from his fingers as thick as blood.

To think he had worried about the Nonman's madness.

The presence of the Erratic concerned Achamian, to be sure, but on so many levels that the resulting anxieties seemed to cancel one another out. And he had to admit, aside from the bardic romance of a Nonman companion, there was a tremendous practical advantage to his presence. Achamian had few illusions about the odyssey that confronted them. It was a long and bitter *war* they were about to undertake as much as it was an expedition, a protracted battle across the breadth of Earwa. He had much to learn regarding this Incariol, true, but there were few powers in the world that could rank a Nonman Magi.

Lord Kosoter kept him close for good reason.

At the ensuing muster the following morning, only some thirty or so Skin Eaters reported—half the number of those assembled the previous day. Lord Kosoter remained as inscrutable as ever, but Sarl seemed overjoyed, though it was unclear whether it was because so many or so few had "cleaved to the slog," as he put it. The defections may have halved his chances of survival, but they also had doubled the value of his shares.

With the composition of the company decided, the following days were dedicated to outfitting and supplying the expedition. Achamian quite willingly surrendered what remained of his gold, a gesture that seemed to impress the Skin Eaters mightily. The fortune spent seemed to speak of the far greater fortune to be made—even Sarl joined in the general enthusiasm. It was ever the same: Convince a man to take a single step—after all, what earthly difference could *one* step make?—and he would walk the next mile to prove himself right.

How could they know Achamian had no expectation of return? In a sense, leaving the Three Seas was the real return. He might no longer be a Mandate Schoolman, but his heart belonged to the Ancient North all the same. To the coiling insinuations of the Dreams . . .

To Seswatha.

"It is always like this," Kiampas told him one evening at the Cocked Leg. The two of them had been sitting side by side wordlessly eating while the trestle before them boomed and cackled with revelling Skin Eaters—Sarl in the celebratory thick of them.

"Before going on a slog?" Achamian asked.

Kiampas paused to suck at the tip of a rabbit bone. He shrugged.

"Before anything," he said, glancing up from the carcass scattered across his plate. There seemed to be genuine sorrow in his look, the regret of kings forced to condemn innocents in the name of appeasing the masses. "Anything involving blood."

Weariness broke across the Wizard, as if a consciousness of years were an integral part of understanding the man's meaning. He turned to the illuminated tableau of scalpers before them: nodding, leaning, shaking with laughter, and, with the exception of Sarl and a few others, brash with rude youth. For the first time, Achamian felt the cumulative weight of all the lies he had told, as though the prick of each had been tallied in lead. How many would die? How many would he use up in his quest to learn the truth of the man-god whose profile graced all the coins they so coveted?

How many pulses had he sacrificed?

Are you doing this for the sake of vengeance? Is that it?

Guilt palmed his gaze toward the incidental background, toward those untouched by his machinations. Across the haze of the room's central hearth, he saw Haubrezer watching the Skin Eaters as well. When he realized that Achamian had seen him, the thin man jerked to his feet, then lurched through the door, his wrists paddling the air with every loping step.

Achamian thought of the innkeep's warning. "*Stand aside for the Skin Eaters*," he had said.

They strike you down but good.

"I have built a place," the High-King said.

It was strange, the way Achamian knew he dreamed, and the way he knew it not at all, so that he lived this moment as a true now, as something unthought, unguessed, unbreathed, as *Seswatha*, speaking with another man's selfsame spontaneity, every heartbeat counting out a unique existence, veined and clothed and clotted with urgent and indolent passion. It was strange, the way he paused at the forks of the moment and made *ancient* decisions . . .

How could it be? How could he feel all the ferment of a free soul? How could he live a life *for the first time* over and over?

Seswatha leaned over a small table set between glowering tripods. Snake-entwined wolves danced in a bronze rim around the lip of each, so that the light cast by their flames was fretted by struggling shadows. It made staring at the *benjuka* plate and its occult patterns of stone pieces difficult. Achamian suspected his old friend had done this deliberately. Benjuka, after all, with its infinite relationships and rule-changing rules, was a game of prolonged concentration.

And no man loathed losing more than Anasûrimbor Celmomas.

"A place," Achamian repeated.

"A refuge."

Seswatha frowned, bent his gaze up from the plate.

"What do you mean?"

"In case the war . . . goes wrong."

This was uncharacteristic. Not the worry, for indecision riddled Celmomas to the core, but the worry's expression. Back then, no one save the Nonmen of Ishterebinth understood the stakes of the war that embroiled them. Back then, "apocalypse" was a word with a different meaning.

Achamian nodded in Seswatha's slow and deliberate way. "You mean the No-God," he said with a small laugh—a laugh! Even for Seswatha, that name had been naught but a misgiving, more abstraction than catastrophe.

How did one *relive* such ancient ignorance?

Celmomas's long and leonine face lay blank, indifferent to the geography of pieces arranged between them. The totem braided into his beard—a palm-sized countenance of a wolf cast in gold—seemed to pant and loll in the uncertain light.

"What if this . . . this *thing* . . . is as mighty as the Quya say? What if we are too late?"

"We are not too late."

Silence fell upon them as in a tomb. There was something subterranean about all the ancillary chambers of the Annexes, but none more so, it seemed, than the Royal Suites. No matter how thick the decorative plaster, no matter how bright the paint or gorgeous the tapestries, the lintelled ceilings hung just as low, humming with the weight of oppressive stone.

"You, Seswatha," the High-King said, returning his gaze to the plate. "You are the only one. The only one I *trust*."

Achamian thought of his Queen, her buttocks against his hips, her calves hooked hot and hungry about his waist.

The High-King moved a stone, a move that Seswatha had not foreseen, and the rules changed in the most disastrous way possible. What had been opportunity found itself twisted inside out, stamped into something as closed and as occluded as the future.

Achamian was almost relieved . . .

"I have built a place . . . a refuge . . ." Anasûrimbor Celmomas said. "A place where my line can outlive me."

Ishuäl . . .

Sucking musty air, Achamian shot upright in bed. He grabbed his white maul, pressed his head to his knees. The Long-Braid Falls thundered beyond the timbered walls, a white background roar that seemed to give the blackness mass and momentum. "Ishuäl," he murmured. "A place . . ." He looked up to the heavens, as though peering through the obscurity of his room's low ceiling. "But where is it?"

Whining ears, sorting through the fibres of sound: laughter from the floor, breaking like a bubble in boiling pitch; shouts calling out the streets, daring and proclaiming.

"*Where?*"

The truth of men lay in their origins. He knew this as only a Mandate Schoolman could. Anasûrimbor Kellhus had not come to the Three Seas by accident. He had not found his half-brother waiting for him as Shriah of the Thousand Temples by accident. He had not conquered the known world by accident!

Achamian swung his feet from his blankets, sat on the edge of his straw-mattressed bed. The words from some ribald song floated up through the joists in the floor.

Her skin was rough as brick,
Her legs were made of rope.
Her gut was plenty thick,
And her teeth were soft as soap.

But her peach was cast in gold.
Aye! No! Aye!
T'were her peach that had me sold!

Waves of gagging laughter. A muffled voice raised to the Coffers. A ragged, ululating cheer, soaking through wood.

The Skin Eaters, singing before they shed blood.

For the longest time, Achamian sat motionless save for the slow saw of his breathing. It seemed he could see the spaces beneath, that he hung upon glass over close limb-jostled air. The Captain was absent, of course, as remote as his godlike authority required. But he could see Sarl, his ink-line eyes, age-scorched skin, and gum-glistening smile, see him using his rank to enforce the pretence that he was one of them. That was his problem, Sarl, his refusal to acknowledge his old man crooks, the flabby reservoirs of regret and bitterness that chambered every elderly heart.

And then there were the men, the Skin Eaters proper as opposed to their mad handlers, spared the convolutions of long life, lost in the thoughtless fellowship of lust and brute desire that made the young young, flaunting the willingness to fuck or to kill under the guise of whim, when in truth it all came down to the paring eyes of the others. Recognition.

He could see all of it through night and floors.

And the Wizard realized, with the curious fate-affirming euphoria of those who discover themselves guiltless. He would burn a hundred. He would burn a thousand.

However many fools it took to find Ishuäl.

The company stomped to the foot of the escarpments, in the chill of the following morning, a long bleary-eyed train bent beneath packs and leading mules, and began climbing out of the squalid precincts of Marrow. The switchback trail was nothing short of treacherous, smeared as it was in donkey shit. But it seemed appropriate, somehow, that spit and toil were required to leave the wretched town. It made palpable the limits they were scaling, the fact that they had turned their backs on the New Empire's outermost station, the very fringe of civilization, both wicked and illumined.

To leave Marrow was to pass out of history, out of memory . . . to enter a world as disordered as Incariol's soul. Yes, Achamian thought, willing his old and bandy limbs step by puffing step. It was proper that he should climb.

All passages into dread should exact some chastising toll.

Mimara has learned much about the nature of patience and watching.

And even more about the nature of Men.

She realizes quite quickly that Marrow is no place for the likes of her. She understands her fine-boned beauty, knows in intimate detail the way it hooks, burrlike, the woollen gaze of men. She would, she knows, be endlessly accosted, until some clever pimp realized she had no protection. She would be drugged, or set upon by numbers greater than she could handle. She would be raped and beaten. Someone would comment on her uncanny resemblance to the Holy Empress on an uncut silver kellic, and she would be trussed in cheap-dyed linens, foil, and candy jewels. For miles around, every scalper with a copper would walk away with some piece of her.

She knows this would happen . . . In her marrow, you might say.

Her slavery moves through her, not so much a crowd of flinching years as an overlapping of inner shadows. It is always there—always *here*. The whips and fists and violation, a clamour shot through with memories of love for her sisters, some weaker, some stronger, pity for the torment in the eyes of some, those who would weep, "*Just a child . . .*" They used her, all of them used her, but somehow the bottom of the jar never dried. Somehow a last sip remained, enough to moisten her lips, to dry her eyes.

This was how her mother's agents found her years ago, dressed like their Holy Empress, emptied save for a single sip. Apparently thousands had died, such was Anasûrimbor Esmenet's outrage. A whole swath of the Worm in Carythusal had been razed, the male population indiscriminately slaughtered.

But it was never clear just whom Mother was avenging.

Mimara knows what will happen. So rather than follow Achamian into the town, she circles around and climbs the escarpments instead. This time, she really does leave her mule, Foolhardy, to the wolves. She takes up a position well away from the eastward tracks—not a day passes, it seems, without some company trudging in from the horizon—and she watches the town the way an idle boy might study a termite-infested stump. It looks like a toy woven of rotted grass. The trees and bracken opening about a great lesion of open mud. The rows of swollen-wood structures ribbing the interior. The great white veils floating like some ghostly afterimage from the falls, encompassing the strings of fuzzing smoke . . .

From high above she watches the town and waits. Sometimes, when the wind blows just so, she can even smell the place's fetid halo. She watches the coming and going, the ebb and flow of miniature men and their miniature affairs, and she understands that the infinite variety of Men and their transactions is simply a trick of an earthbound vantage, that from afar, they simply *are* the mites they appear to be, doing the same things over and over. Same pains, same grievances, same joys, made novel by crippled memory and stunted perspective.

Finitude and forgetfulness, these are what grace Men with the illusion of the new. It seems something she has always known, but could never see; a truth obscured by the succession of close leaning faces.

She dares no fire. She hugs herself warm. From lips of high-hanging stone, she watches and waits for *him*. She has no other place to go. She is, she decides, every bit as rootless as he. Every bit as mad.

Every bit as driven.

Chapter Seven

Sakarpus

. . . conquered peoples live and die with the knowledge that survival does not suffer honour. They have chosen shame over the pyre, the slow flame for the quick.

—TRIAMIS I, *JOURNALS AND DIALOGUES*

Early Spring, 19 New Imperial Year (4132 Year-of-the-Tusk), Sakarpus

It was a thing of wonder.

While the citadels and strong places of Sakarpus still smoked, innumerable storks began clotting the southern horizon, not the field-sized flocks that the Men of the Ordeal were accustomed to, but high-flying mountains of them, darkening the sky, settling like salt in water across the surrounding hills. Even for men familiar with momentous sights, it was remarkable to behold: the whooshing descent, the starved elegance, the twitch and turn of avian scrutiny, multiplied over and over across every sky. Since storks meant many different things to the many different nations of the Great Ordeal, few could agree what the bird's arrival augured. The Aspect-Emperor said nothing, save issuing an edict to protect the birds from becoming either food or ornament. Apparently the Sakarpi held them holy: The men guarded them against foxes and wolves, while the womenfolk gathered their guano for a concoction called char soot, a long-burning fuel they used in lieu of wood.

The Judges were kept busy. Several hangings were required, and one Ainoni sergeant, who had been killing birds to make and sell pillows, was even publicly flayed. But eventually the Men of the Ordeal became accustomed to the squawking, white-backed hills, and ceased heckling the conquered men and women who tended to them. In the parlance of the camp, "eating stork" became synonymous with any reckless and self-indulgent act. Soon it seemed obvious—even to those, like the Kianene, who thought storks were vermin—that these birds with their thin-necked conceit were in fact holy, and that the hills were a kind of natural temple.

Meanwhile, preparations for the ensuing march continued. In the Council of Names, the kings and generals of the Great Ordeal debated points of supply and strategy beneath the all-seeing eyes of their Aspect-Emperor. Even though flushed with pious excitement—a great number of them had spent years waiting for this very day—they harboured few illusions about the trials and perils that awaited them. Sakarpus stood at the very edge of the mannish world, the point where, as King Saubon of Enathpaneah would say, "Men are more lamb than lion." Sranc ruled the land beyond the northern horizon, scratching a vicious existence from the ruined cities of the long-dead High Norsirai. And that land, the Lords of the Ordeal knew, stretched for more than two thousand miles. Not since the wars of Far Antiquity had so many attempted such an arduous journey. "Between this march and the Consult," their Aspect-Emperor told them, "the march will prove far deadlier."

For more than a decade, a greater part of the New Empire's resources had been bent toward the arduous trek to Golgotterath. Even before Sakarpus had fallen, the Imperial Engineers had begun building a second city below the ancient first: barracks, smithies, lazarets, and dozens of sod-walled storehouses. Still others staked the course of the broad stone road that would, in a matter of weeks, connect the ancient city to faraway Oswenta. Even now, an endless train of supplies wound in from the southern horizon, bearing arms, wares, rations, and more rations. Infantrymen, no matter their rank, were limited to strict portions of *amicut*, the campaign fare of the wild Scylvendi peoples to the southwest. The castenobility could count on somewhat heartier provisions but were reduced to riding shaggy-maned ponies that required no grain to preserve their strength. Vast herds of sheep and cattle, bred solely to accompany the march, were also beaten across the horizon, so many that some Men of the Ordeal began calling themselves ka Koumiroi, or the Herdsmen—a name that would later become holy.

But even with all these preparations, there was simply no way the Great Ordeal could bear the food required to reach Golgotterath. The ponderous herds, the great packs borne by the infantrymen, and the mile-long mule trains would only take them so far. At some point, the columns would have to fan out and fend for themselves. The Lords of the Ordeal knew they could depend on game for their men and wild fodder for their horses: thousands of the now legendary Imperial Trackers had given their lives mapping the lands ahead. But foraging armies moved far more slowly than supplied ones, and if winter struck before the Ordeal could overcome Golgotterath, the result would be catastrophic. A second problem, and the point that was endlessly argued in the Councils, was that no one knew how many of the countless Sranc clans the Enemy would be able to rally. Despite the Imperial Bounty, despite collecting enough scalps to clothe entire nations, the number of Sranc remained beyond reckoning. But without the dread will of the No-God, the creatures were governed only by their terror, hatred, and hunger. Not even the Aspect-Emperor could say how many the Consult might recruit or enslave to oppose them. If the answer was many, then the day the Ordeal divided to begin foraging could very well be the day of its doom.

It was *this* that made Sakarpus so crucial, and not, as so many assumed, her famed Chorae Hoard. This was why Men of the Ordeal were killed so that birds might live. Where the hard rod of Imperial authority had been used to batter other nations into submission, only the soft hand of Imperial favour could be used here, where the people called themselves the Hoosverûl, or the Unconquered. The Lords of the Ordeal could ill-afford even a single week of riot and rebellion, let alone grinding months. Sakarpus was the nail from which their future would hang. After the public Councils, when the Aspect-Emperor retired to confer privately with his two Exalt-Generals, King Saubon of Enathpaneah and King Proyas of Conriya, Sakarpus and the temper of her people were often discussed.

This was how the fateful decision was made to place the young King of Sakarpus, Sorweel, in the care of the Aspect-Emperor's two eldest sons, Moënghus and Kayûtas.

"When he becomes a brother to them," his Arcane Holiness explained to his old friends, "he will be as a son to me."

The knock came mere moments after Sorweel's attendants had finished dressing him, a single rap, hard enough to rattle the hinges. The young King turned to see the door swing wide. Two men walked in without so much as an imploring look, the one fair and "royal boned," as the Sakarpi said of tall gracile men, the other dark and powerfully built. Both were dressed in the martial finery of the New Imperium, with long white vests hanging over *hauberks* of nimil-chain. Cloth-of-gold tusks glimmered in the dull morning light.

"Tomorrow," the fair one said in flawless Sakarpic, "you

will report to me . . ." He strolled to the one open panel along the suite's shuttered balcony, glanced out over the conquered city before turning on his heel. The dawning light caught his hair, transformed it into a luminous halo. "You ride with us . . . apparently."

The other plucked a string of fat from the tray that bore the remains of Sorweel's breakfast, dropped it into his mouth. He scrutinized Sorweel with murderous blue eyes as he chewed, absently wiped the pads of his fingers along his kilt.

Sorweel knew who they were—there was no mistaking the lethal strength of the one or the unblinking calm of the other. He probably could have guessed their names even before their father had sacked his city. But he resented their manner and tone and so replied with the cold outrage of a lord insulted by his lessers. "You don't look like horses."

Moënghus growled with what may have been laughter, then muttered something in Sheyic to his taller brother. Kayûtas snorted and grinned. They both watched Sorweel as though he were an exotic pet, a novelty from some absurd corner of the world.

Perhaps he was.

An uncomfortable silence followed, one that seemed to swell with every passing heartbeat.

"My elder brother," Kayûtas said eventually, as though recovering from a momentary lapse in etiquette, "says that's because we're wearing our breeches."

"What?" Sorweel asked, flushing in confusion and embarrassment.

"Why we don't look like horses."

Despite himself, Sorweel smiled—and so lost this first battle. He could feel it, humming through the two brothers' laughter, a satisfaction scarcely concerned with humour.

They're hunters, he told himself, *sent to run down my heart*.

He felt it most at night, when the ranging concerns of the day shrunk to the clutch of limbs beneath cold blankets and the mourning could seize his face without fear of discovery. Small. Alone. A stranger in his father's home. *I am a king of widows and orphans*, he would think, as the faces of his father's dead Boonsmen floated before his soul's eye. It all came crowding back, the sights and sounds, the horror, the jerk and tumble of violent futility. Children weeping in the doorways, beloved buildings cupped in shining flame, the bodies of Horselords twisted in the streets.

I am a captive in my own land.

But as desolate as these sleepless watches were, Sorweel found a kind of reprieve in them. Here, huddled beneath the heavy weave, there was certainty, an assurance that his sorrow and hatred were not a kind of misplaced inevitability. Here, he could see his father clearly, he could hear his long low voice, as surely as he could those nights when he pretended to sleep, and his father had come to sit at the foot of his bed, to speak of his dead wife.

"*I miss her, Sorwa. More than I dare let you know.*"

But his days were . . . more confusing.

Sorweel did as he was told. He presided over the farce that was his court. He attended the ceremonies, spoke the holy words that would see his people "safe," bore the witless accusation in the eyes of priest and petitioner alike. He walked and gestured with the listless grace of those who moved through a fog of betrayal.

He learned that he lacked the ability to do and to believe contradictory things. Where a nobler soul would have found consistency in his acts, he seemed to find it in his *beliefs*. He simply believed what he needed to believe in order to act as his conquerors wished him to act. While he muddled through the schedule his foreign secretaries arranged for him, while he sat in their perfumed presence, it really seemed that things *were* as the Aspect-Emperor claimed, that the world turned beneath the shadow of the Second Apocalypse, and that all Men must act of one accord to preserve the future, no matter how much it might offend their pride.

"*All Kings answer to holy writ,*" the godlike man had told him. "*And so long as that writ is otherworldly, they willingly acknowledge as much. But when it comes to them as I come to them, wearing the flesh of their fellow man, they confuse the sanctity of obeying the Law with the shame of submitting to a rival.*" A warm laugh, like a dear uncle admitting a harmless folly. "*All men think themselves closer to the God than others. And so they rebel, raise arms against the very thing they claim to serve . . .*

"*Against* me."

The young King still lacked the words to describe what it was like, kneeling in the Aspect-Emperor's presence. He could only think that knees were somehow not enough, that he should fall to his belly like the ancient supplicants engraved on the walls of Vogga Hall. And his voice! Melodious. By turns gentle, bemused, penetrating, and profound. The Anasûrimbor need only speak, and it would seem obvious that Sorweel's father simply had succumbed to his conceit, that Harweel, like so many men before him, had confused his pride for his duty.

"*This is all a tragic mistake . . .*"

Only afterwards, as his handlers led him through the general clamour of the encampment, would his father's words return to him. "*He is a Ciphrang, a Hunger from the Outside, come in the guise of man . . .*" And suddenly he believed the precise opposite of what he had believed a mere watch before. He would curse himself for being a kitten-headed fool, for breaking the only faith that remained to him. Despite the pain, despite the way it limned his face with the threat of sobs, he would recite his father's final outburst: "*He needs this city! He needs our people! That means he needs you, Sorwa!*"

You.

And all would be confusion. For Sorweel understood that if his father had spoken true, then *everyone* about him—the Ainoni with their white cosmetics and plaited beards, the Schoolmen with their silk-print coats and airs of omniscience, the Galeoth with their long flaxen hair knotted above their right ear, all the thousands who sought redemption through the Great Ordeal—had gathered for naught, had conquered for naught, and now prepared to war against the Great Ruiner's successors, all for naught. It seemed that delusion, like the span of arches, could only reach so far before collapsing into truth. It seemed impossible that *so many* could be so thoroughly deceived.

King Proyas had told him the stories about the Aspect-Emperor, about the miracles he had witnessed with his own eyes, about the valour and sacrifice that had "cleansed" the Three Seas. How could Harweel's claim gainsay such rampant devotion? How could his son not fear, in the bullying presence of such conquerors, that the matter only seemed undecided because he secretly held his finger on the scale?

During the day, every word, every look seemed to argue his father's foolhardy conceit. Only at night, lying in the solitary dark, could Sorweel take refuge in the simpler movements of the heart. He could let his lips tremble, his eyes fill with tears like hot salted tea. He could even sit at the end of his bed as his father had sat, and pretend he spoke to someone sleeping.

"*I dreamed of her again, Sorwa . . .*"

At night, the young King could simply close his eyes and refuse. This was the secret comfort of orphans: the ability to believe according to want and not world—whatever it took to numb the ache of things lost.

I miss her too, Da . . .

Almost as much as I miss you.

They sent a slave for him the following morning, an old, dark-skinned man almost comically bundled against the spring chill. Sorweel saw the dismayed looks traded between his Householders—slaves were anathema in Sakarpus—but he affected no anger or outrage. Even though no porters could be found, the outlander insisted, in the exasperated hand-waving way of demands made across linguistic divides, that he come immediately. Sorweel consented without argument, secretly relieved he wouldn't have to lead a procession out of the city—that he could pretend this was a mere outing rather than the abdication it seemed.

More than walls had been overthrown with the coming of the Aspect-Emperor.

The slave said nothing as they rode through the city. Sorweel followed with his eyes fixed directly forward, more to avoid the questioning gazes of his countrymen than to study anything in particular—save maybe the blasted heights of the Herder's Gate as they rose and fell out of view. He thought of the naive faith his people had put in their ancient fortifications—after all, who was the Aspect-Emperor compared to Mog-Pharau?

He thought of his father's blood cooked into the stone.

The Inrithi encampment lay a short distance beyond the pocked and blackened walls, its tented precincts sprawling across miles of field and pasture. It seemed at once mundane and legendary: a migratory city of wood, twine, and cloth, where the stink of latrines hedged every breath, as well as a vast assemblage, a vehicle great enough to carry the dread weight of history. The Men of the Ordeal trudged to and fro, supped at firepits, rolled armour in barrels of gravel, tended to gear and horses, or simply sat about the entrances to their tents, deep in eyes-to-the-horizon conversation. They paid scant attention to Sorweel and his guide as they wended through the avenues and byways of the camp.

The old slave led without hesitation. He pressed through

this or that commotion—a brawl, a wain buried to the axles in muck, two stalled mule-trains—with the calm assertiveness of a caste-noble, turning down lesser mud tracks only when marching companies blocked their passage entirely. Without a word, he led Sorweel deeper and deeper into the encampment. The grim stares of Thunyerus became the exotic canopies of Nilnamesh became the haggling bustle of Cironj. Every turn, it seemed, delivered them to another of the world's far-flung corners.

Before meeting the Aspect-Emperor, Sorweel would have thought it impossible that one man could make an instrument of so many disparate souls. The Sakarpi were a sparse people. But even with their meagre numbers, not to mention common language and traditions, King Harweel had found it difficult to overcome their feuds and grudges. The more Sorweel pondered it, the more miraculous it seemed that all the Men of the Three Seas, with their contradictory tongues and ancient animosities, could find common purpose.

Everywhere he looked, he could see it, hanging slack in the windless morning: the Circumfix.

Wasn't there proof in miracles? Isn't that what the priests said?

Swaying to the canter of his horse, Sorweel found himself glancing at face after face, a stranger for every heartbeat, and finding bleak comfort in the careless way their looks skipped past him. There was a kind of safety, he realized, in the Great Ordeal's clamour. In the press of so many, how could he not be forgotten? And it seemed that this was the only true desire that remained to him: to be forgotten.

Then, in the uncanny way that familiar faces rise out of the anonymity of strangers, he saw Tasweer, the son of Lord Ostaroot, one of his father's High Boonsmen. Two Conriyan knights led him staggering, each holding chains welded to a collar about his skinned neck. His wrists were cruelly bound. His elbows had been wrenched back about a wooden rod.

His hair was as wild as his eyes, and his *parm*, the traditional padded tunic of Sakarpi noblemen, hung stained, ragged, and beltless above bare knees.

The mere sight of him clutched the breath from Sorweel's throat, returned him to the rain-swept battlements, where he had last seen Tasweer—and his father. He could almost hear the crowing horns . . .

The young man did not recognize him, but rather stared with the unfixed intensity of those beaten back into the depths of themselves. To his shame, Sorweel looked away—to judge the weather across the horizon, he told himself. Yes, the weather. His horse felt reed-legged beneath him, like something wavering in the summer heat. The world smelled of mud cooking in the morning sun.

"Y-you?" a voice croaked from below.

The young King could not bear to look.

"Sorweel?"

Compelled to look down, he saw Tasweer gazing up at him, his once open face almost bewildered, almost horrified, even almost glad of heart, but in truth none of these things. The captive reeled to a halt, blinking.

"Sorweel," he repeated.

His Conriyan escorts cursed, flicked his chains in warning.

"No!" the prisoner cried, leaning against the links. A stubborn and helpless noise. "Nooo!" as they yanked him to his knees in the muck. "Sorweel! S-s-sorweel! Fight them! Y-you have to! Cut their throats while they sleep! Sorweel! Sor—!"

One of the square-bearded knights struck him full in the mouth, knocked him into rolling half-consciousness.

As had happened so many times since the city's fall, Sorweel found himself divided, struck into two separate souls, one real, the other ethereal. In his soul's eye he slipped from his saddle, his boots slapping into wheezing mud, and shouldered his way past the Conriyans. He pulled Tasweer to his knees, held his head behind the ear. Blood pulsed from the captive's nostrils, clotted the coarse growth rising from his jaw. "Did you see?" Sorweel cried to the broken face. "Tasweer! Did you see what happened to my father?"

But the bodily Sorweel simply continued after his guide, his skin porcelain with chill.

"Noooo!" pealed hoarse into air behind him, followed by raucous laughter.

The young King of Sakarpus resumed his study of the nonexistent weather. The true horror of defeat, a kernel of him realized, lay not in the fact of capitulation, but in the way it kennelled in the heart, the way it loitered and bred and bred and bred.

The way it made fate out of falling.

Eventually they came to the northern perimeter of the encampment, to a broad field whose greening expanse was marred by broad swaths of hoof-mudded turf and ornamented by stretches of blooming yellow-cress. Small groups of horsemen rode patterns at various intervals, answering to the booming cries of their commanders. They were doing squad drills, Sorweel realized, riding a hearty breed not so different from those used by Sakarpi Horselords.

The slave led him along a row of white-canvas tents, most of them stocked with various kinds of stores. Where the two of them had passed largely unnoticed before, now they drew stares, largely from clots of loitering cavalrymen. Several even called out to them, but Sorweel affected not to notice. Even well-wishes became insults when shouted in an unfamiliar tongue.

Finally the slave reined to a halt and dismounted before an expansive white pavilion. A crimson standard had been hammered into the ground beside the entrance. It bore a black Circumfix over a golden horse: the sign of the Kidruhil, the heavy cavalry that had caused Harweel and his High Boonsmen so much grief in the skirmishes preceding the Great Ordeal's arrival. A guard armoured in a gold-stamped cuirass stood motionless beside it; he merely nodded at the slave as he led Sorweel across the threshold.

A strange aroma permeated the interior air, pleasant despite the bitter overtones. Like orange peels burning. He stood rigid, his eyes adjusting to the enclosed light. The recesses of the pavilion were largely unfurnished and unadorned: simple reed mats for flooring, various accouterments hanging from posts, a wicker-and-wood cot covered with empty scroll cases. The Circumfixes embroidered into the ceiling canvas cast vague shadows across the ground.

Anasûrimbor Kayûtas sat at the corner of a camp-table set against the centre post, alone save for a bald secretary who mechanically inked lines of script, apparently adding to the stacks of papyrus spread about him. The Prince-Imperial leaned back in his chair, his sandalled feet kicked out and crossed on the mats before him. Rather than acknowledge Sorweel, he gazed from one papyrus sheet to another, as though following the thread of some logistical concern.

Sorweel's wizened guide knelt, pressing his forehead to the stained mats, then withdrew the way he had come. Sorweel stood alone and breathless.

"You're wondering," Kayûtas said, his eyes fixed on the vertical bars of script, "whether it was a deliberate insult . . ." He set a final sheet down, following it with still-reading eyes as he did so. He looked to Sorweel, paused in appraisal. "Having a slave bring you here like this."

"An insult," Sorweel heard himself reply, "is an insult."

A handsome smirk. "I fear no court is so simple."

The Prince-Imperial leaned back, raised a wooden bowl to his lips—water, Sorweel noted after he set it down.

It was no small thing, to stand before the son of a living god. Even with his hair trimmed so close and so curiously to the contours of his skull, Kayûtas closely resembled his father. He had the same long strong face, the same pearl-shining eyes. He even possessed the same unnerving manner. His every movement, it seemed, followed pre-ordained lines, as though his soul had mapped all the shortest distances beforehand. And when he was still, he was utterly still. But for all that, Anasûrimbor Kayûtas still possessed a *mortal* aura. There could be no doubt that he faltered as other men faltered, that his skin, if pressed, would be thin and warm . . .

That he could bleed.

"Tell me," the Prince-Imperial continued, "what do your countrymen call it when men trade useless words?"

Sorweel tried to breath away his hackles. "Measuring tongues."

The Prince-Imperial laughed at the cleverness of this. "Excellent. A name for jnan if there ever was one! Let us dispense with 'tongue measuring' then. Agreed?"

The secretary continued scratching characters across papyrus.

"Agreed," Sorweel replied warily.

Kayûtas smiled with what seemed genuine relief. "Let me speak to the matter then: My father needs more than your city, he needs the obedience of her people as well. I suppose you know full well what this means . . ."

Sorweel knew, though it had become more and more difficult to contemplate. "He needs me."

"Precisely. This is why you're here, to give your people a stake in our glorious undertaking. To make Sakarpus part of the Great Ordeal."

Sorweel said nothing.

"But of course," the Prince-Imperial continued, "we remain the enemy, don't we? Which I suppose makes all this little more than a cunning ploy to win your loyalty . . . a way to dupe you into betraying your people."

It was too late for that, Sorweel could not help but think. "Perhaps."

"Perhaps," Kayûtas repeated with a snort. "So much for not measuring tongues!"

A dull and resentful glare.

"Well, no matter," the Prince-Imperial continued. "I'll keep *my* end of our bargain at least." He winked as though at a joke. "I may not have the Gift of the Few, but I am my father's son, and I possess many of his strengths. I find languages effortless, as I suppose this conversation demonstrates. And I need only look at your face to see your soul, not so clearly as Father, certainly, but enough to sound the measure of you or anyone else before me. I can see the depth of your pain, Sorweel, and though I think your people have simply reaped the consequences of their own foolishness, I *do understand*. If I fail to commiserate, it's because I hold you to the same standards of manly conduct as would *your* father. Men weep to wives and pillows . . .

"Do you understand me?"

Sorweel blinked in sudden shame. Did they have spies watching him sleep as well?

"Excellent," Kayûtas said, like a field captain pleased by the vigour of his company's response. "I should also tell you that I *resent* this charge of my father's. I even resent this interview, not simply because I lack the time, but because I think it beneath me. I detest politics, and this relationship my father has forced upon us is nothing if not political. Even still, I recognize that these passions are a product of my own weakness. I will not, as other men might, hold you accountable for them. My father wants me to be as a brother to you . . . And since my father is more God than Man, I will do exactly as he wishes."

He paused as though to leave room for Sorweel to reply, but the young King could scarce order his thoughts, let alone speak. Kayûtas had been every bit as direct as he had promised, and yet at the same time his discourse seemed bent to the point of deformity, charged with a too-penetrating intelligence, pleated with an almost obscene self-awareness . . .

Who were these people?

"I can see the embers of sedition in your eyes," Kayûtas resumed, "a wild hunger to destroy yourself in the act of avenging your father." His voice had somehow scaled the surrounding canvas panels, so that it seemed to fall from all directions. "At every turn you struggle, because you know not whether my father is a demon, as your priests claim, or the Saviour the Men of Three Seas *know* him to be. I do not begrudge you this, Sorweel. All I ask is that you inquire with an open heart. I fear proof of my father's Holy Mission will come soon enough . . ."

He paused as though distracted by some unexpected thought. "Perhaps," he continued, "if we're fortunate enough to survive that proof, you and I can have a different conversation."

Sorweel stood rigid, braced against the sense of futility that whelmed through him. *How?* was all he could think. *How does one war against foes such as this?*

"In the interim," the Prince-Imperial said with an air of turning to more practical matters, "you need to learn Sheyic, of course. I will have an instructor arranged for you. And you need to show my Horse-masters that you're a true son of Sakarpus. You are now a captain of the Imperial Kidruhil, Sorweel, a member of the illustrious Company of Scions . . ." He lowered his chin in a curious smile. "And I am your general."

Another long, appraising pause. The old secretary had paused to cut a new tip on his quill, which he held in fingers soaked black with ink. Sorweel caught him stealing a quick glance in his direction.

"Is this agreeable to you?" Kayûtas asked.

"What choice do I have?"

For the first time something resembling compassion crossed the Prince-Imperial's face. He breathed as though gathering wind for crucial words. "You are the warlike son of a warlike people, Sorweel. Remain in Sakarpus, and you will be little more than a carefully managed captive. Even worse, you will never resolve the turmoil that even now chokes your heart. Ride with me and my brother, and you will see, one way or another, what kind of king you must be."

He scarce understood what was happening, so how could he know what he should or shouldn't do? But there was heart to be found in the sound of resolution. And besides, he was developing a talent for petulant remarks. "As I said," Sorweel replied, "what choice."

Anasûrimbor Kayûtas nodded, rather like a field surgeon regarding his handiwork, Sorweel thought.

It is enough that I obey . . .

"The slave who brought you here," the Prince-Imperial continued in a by-the-way tone, "is named Porsparian. He's from Shigek, an ancient land to the south of—"

"I know where it is."

Had it come to this? Had it come to the point where interrupting his oppressors could count as vengeance?

"Of course you do," Kayûtas replied with a partially suppressed grin. "Porsparian has a facility with tongues. Until I find you an instructor, you will practise your Sheyic with him . . ." Trailing, the man leaned across the table to lift a sheaf of papyrus between his fore and index fingers.

He held it out to Sorweel, saying, "Here."

"What is it?"

"A writ of bondage. Porsparian is now yours."

The young King blinked. He had stared at the slave's back so long he could scarcely remember what he looked like. He took the sheet in his hands, stared at the incomprehensible characters.

"I know," Kayûtas continued, "that you will treat him well."

At that, the Prince-Imperial returned to his reading, acting for all the world as if their conversation had never happened. Numb save where the sheet burned his fingertips, Sorweel retreated. Just as he turned to cross the threshold, Kayûtas's voice brought him up short.

"Oh, yes, and one final thing," he said to the papyrus. "My elder brother, Moënghus . . . Beware him."

The young King tried to reply but came to a stammering halt. He grimaced, breathed past the hammering of his heart, then tried again. "Wh-why is that?"

"Because," Kayûtas said, his eyes still ranging the inked characters, "he's quite mad."

Stepping from the Prince-Imperial's pavilion, Sorweel told himself he blinked for the sharpness of the sun. But his burning cheeks and aching throat knew better, as did his sparrow-light hands.

What am I to do?

The shouts of the cavalrymen carried on the wind, followed by a caw-cawing of a horn, high and shrill above the bone-deep din that was the Great Ordreal. The sound seemed to cut, to peel, expose him past the skin.

How many kings? How many grim-souled men?

What was Sakarpus compared to any nation of the Three Seas, let alone the might and majesty that was the New Empire? A god for an emperor. The sons of a god for generals. An entire world for a bastion. Sorweel had heard the reports of his father's spies in the weeks preceding the Ordeal's assault on the city. Shit-herders. This was what the Men of the Three Seas called him and his kinsmen . . .

Shit-herders.

A blank feeling reached through him, like forgetting to

breathe, only more profound. What would his father say, seeing him unmanned time and again, not because of the wiles or the ruthlessness of their enemy, but because of . . . because of . . .

Loneliness?

The slave, Porsparian, watched him from the shadow of their horses. Not knowing what to do, Sorweel simply walked up and passed the writ of bondage to him.

"I . . ." he started, only to gag on welling tears. "I-I . . ."

The old man gawked in voiceless alarm. He grasped Sorweel's forearms and gently pressed the writ against the padded fabric of his parm tunic. And Sorweel could only think, Wool, here stands the King dressed in woollen rags.

"*I failed him!*" he sobbed to the uncomprehending slave. "*Don't you see? I failed!*"

The old Shigeki gripped him by the shoulders, stared long and hard into his anguished eyes. The man's face, it seemed, was not so different from the writ Sorweel held against his breast: smooth save where scored with lines of unknown script, across the forehead, about the eyes and snout, as dark as any ink, as if the god who had carved him had struck too deep with the knife.

"What do I do?" Sorweel murmured and gasped. "What do I do now?"

The man seemed to nod, though the yellow eyes remained fixed, immobile. Gradually, for reasons Sorweel could not fathom, his breathing slowed and the roaring in his ears fell away.

Porsparian led him to his quarters, taking too many turns for Sorweel to ever hope to remember. The tent was large enough for him to stand in, and furnished with nothing more than a cot for himself and a mat for his slave. For most of the afternoon, he laid in a bleary reverie, staring at the white fabric, watching it rise and fall like the shirt of a slumbering little brother. He paid no attention to the porters when they arrived with his meagre collection of things. He held his father's torc for a time, an age-old relic of the Varalt Dynasty, stamped with the seal of his family: the tower and two-headed wolf. He pulled it to his breast, clutched it so tight he was sure the sapphires had cut him. But when he looked there was no blood, only a quick-fading impression.

King Proyas arrived as the tent panels became waxen in the failing light. He said a few jocular words in Sheyic, perhaps hoping to hearten with his tone. When Sorweel failed to respond, the Exalt-General stared at the young King with a kind of magisterial remorse, as though seeing in him some image from his own not-so-kindly past.

Porsparian knelt with his forehead to the ground for the entirety of visit.

After Proyas left, the two sat in utter silence, king and slave, pondering the way the rising dark made everything transparent to the encampment's evening chorus. Singing warriors. Churlish horses. Then, when the darkness was almost complete, they heard someone, a Kidruhil trooper, relieving himself behind the tent's far corner. Sorweel found himself smiling at the old Shigeki, who was little more than a silhouette sitting on the ground a length away. When the trooper farted, Porsparian abruptly cackled, rocked to and fro with his spindly legs caught in his arms. He laughed the way a child might, gurgling against the back of his throat. The effect was so absurd that Sorweel found himself howling with the mad old man.

Afterwards, Sorweel sat on the end of his cot while Porsparian busied himself lighting a lantern. Everything seemed bare in the light, exposed. Without explanation, the old Shigeki disappeared through the flap, into the dread world that murmured and rumbled beyond the greased canvas. Sorweel stared at the lantern, which was little more than a wick in a bronze bowl, until it seemed his sight must be marred forever. The point of light seemed so clear, so whispering pure, that he could almost convince himself that burning was the most blissful death of all.

He looked away only when Porsparian returned bearing unleavened bread and a steaming bowl—some kind of stew. The scent of pepper and other exotic spices bloomed through the tent, but Sorweel, as gaunt as he was, had no appetite. After some urging, he finally convinced the slave to eat the entire meal instead of, as Sorweel surmised, waiting on whatever scraps he might leave.

He thought it strange the way Men did not need to share a language to speak about food.

He sat on the end of his cot as before, watching the diminutive Shigeki. Without a whisper of self-consciousness, the man pulled aside one of the rough-woven reed mats, revealing a patch of bruised turf. He parted the grasses, cooing in a strange voice as he combed his fingers through them, then he began praying over the line of bare earth he had uncovered. In a moment of almost embarrassing intensity, Porsparian pressed his cheek against the ground, hard, the way an adolescent might grind against a willing lover. He muttered something—a prayer, Sorweel supposed—in a language far more guttural than Sheyic. Holding his hand like a spatula, he pressed a slot into the black soil—a ritual mouth, Sorweel realized moments afterwards, when Porsparian placed a small portion of bread into it.

By some trick of the light, it actually seemed as if the earthen mouth *closed*.

Smacking his lips with satisfaction, the cryptic little man rolled onto his rump and began fingering the food into his own grey-and-yellow-toothed mouth.

Though Porsparian ate with crude honesty of a Saglander, Sorweel could not help but see a kind of sad poetry to his feasting. The inward pleasure of his eyes, the crook in his wrists as he raised each stew-soaked gob of bread, the slight, backward tilt of his head as he opened his dark-brown lips.

The young King wondered how it could be that two men so dissimilar, a world apart in age, station, and origin, could *share* such a moment. Neither of them talked—what could they say, with their tongues wrapped around different sounds for similar meanings? But even if they could have spoken to each other, Sorweel was certain they would have said nothing. Everything, it seemed, was manifest.

Nothing needed to be spoken because all could be seen.

Sitting as he sat, watching as he watched, a kind of wild generosity seized him, that glad-hearted madness that emptied coffers and pockets. Without thinking, he reached under the cot and retrieved the writ of bondage that Kayûtas had given him that very morning. What did it matter, he thought, when he was already dead? For the first time he thought he understood the freedom that lay concealed in the cold bosom of loss.

Porsparian, suddenly wary, had set down his bowl to watch him. Sorweel stepped past him to squat over the lantern, strangely conscious of the way his shadow swallowed the rear quarters of the tent. He held the papyrus out, so the light glowed through the pulped lines of the reeds used to make the sheets. Then he touched it to the tear-drop flame . . .

Only to have the writ snatched away by a stamping and cursing Porsparian. Sorweel jumped upright, even raised his hands—for a bewildered moment he thought the old slave was about to strike him. But the man merely flapped the sheet until the flame went out. Its uppermost edges were curled and blackened, but it was otherwise intact. Breathing heavily, the two regarded each other for a crazed moment, the king slack and bewildered, the slave braced with old man defiance.

"We are a free people," Sorweel said, warring against a renewed sense of dread and futility. "We don't trade Men like cattle."

The yellow-eyed Shigeki shook his head in a slow and

deliberate manner. As though relinquishing a knife, he set the writ onto the mussed blankets of Sorweel's cot.

Then he did something inexplicable.

Bending at the waist over the lantern, he drew his finger along the edges of the flame, oblivious to the heat. Straightening, he pulled aside his tunic, revealing an old man's sunken chest—wild grey hairs across nut-brown skin. With the lamp-black on his fingertip, he traced what Sorweel immediately recognized as a sickle over his heart.

"Yatwer," the man breathed, his eyes alight with a kind of embittered intensity. He reached out, gripped the young King by the arm. "*Yatwer!*"

"I-I don't understand," Sorweel stammered. "The Goddess?"

Porsparian let his hand slide down Sorweel's arm—a strangely possessive gesture. He grasped the young King's wrist, ran a thumb along his horsing bracelet before turning his hand palm outward. "Yatwer," he whispered, his eyes brimming with tears. Drawing Sorweel's palm between them, he leaned forward and kissed the soft-skinned basin.

Fire climbed the young King's skin. He tried to yank his hand back, but the old man held him with the strength of newly cast stocks. He rolled his age-creased face above Sorweel's palm, as if drowsing to some unheard melody. A single tear tapped the spot where his lips had touched . . .

It seemed to burn and cut all at once, like something molten falling through snow.

Then the slave uttered a single word in Sakarpic, so sudden and so clear that Sorweel nearly jumped.

"*War . . .*"

He was in awe of these people. Their devious refinement. Their labyrinthine ways. Their faith and their sorcery. Even their slaves, it seemed, possessed enigmatic power.

For watch after watch, Sorweel lay rigid in his cot, holding his own hand, pressing the impossible blister on his palm. Porsparian slept across the ground in the near darkness, his breathing broken by a periodic cough and wheeze. When he at last learned their language, Sorweel decided, he would tease the man for snoring like an old woman.

The sounds of the Great Ordeal subsided, drew out and away until the young King could almost believe that only his tent remained, solitary on a trampled plain. There was, it seemed, a moment of *absolute* silence, a moment where every heartbeat hesitated, every breath paused, and the numb immobility of death fell upon all things.

He asked it to take him. It was as close as he had come to prayer since the day his father had died.

Then he heard something. It was almost too broad to be distinguished from the quiet at first, as if wings, spread too wide, simply became the sky. But slowly, contours resolved from the background, a kind of porous roar, something without a singular origin, but rather born of many. For the longest time, he could not place it, and for a panicked moment he even imagined that it came from the city, the combined screams and cries of his people, dying beneath the swords of their dark-skinned conquerors.

Then in a rush he realized . . .

The storks.

The storks called from across the nocturnal hills. They always did this, every spring. Legend said that each of them sang to a different star, naming their sons and daughters, beseeching, cajoling, guiding the gosling descent of innumerable stick-limbed souls . . .

Sorweel finally dozed, warm with thoughts of his mother and his first childhood visit to the Viturnal Nesting. He could remember her beauty, wane and pale. He could remember how cold her hand had seemed about his own—as though fate had begun prying loose her grasp on life even then. He could remember gazing in wonder at the storks, untold thousands of them, making white terraces of the hillsides.

"Do you know why they come here, Sorwa?"

"*No, Mama . . .*"

"Because our city is the Refuge, the hinge of the Worldly Wheel. They come here as our forefathers once came, Darling . . ."

Her smile. It had always seemed the world's most obvious thing.

"They come so that their children might be safe."

Later that night, he awoke in jerking horror, like a guard caught napping on the night of a great battle. Everything reeled in alarm and disorder. He sat up with a breath that was a cry, and at the foot of his cot he saw his *father* sitting, his back turned to him, weeping for his dead wife.

Sorweel's mother.

"It's okay, Da," he rasped, swallowing against his own tears. "She watches . . . She watches over us still."

At that, the apparition went rigid, in the way of proud men grievously insulted, or of broken men mocked for the loss that had overwhelmed them. Sorweel's throat clenched, became hot and thin as a burning reed, to the point where he could not breathe . . .

The ghost of Harweel turned its burnt head, revealing a face devoid of hope and eyes. Beetles dropped from the joints of his blasted armour, clicked and scuttled in the dark.

The dead, it grated without sound, *cannot see.*

Dawn was no more than a band of grey in the east. Still the innumerable camps had been broken, the tents and pavilions felled, the guy-ropes coiled and stacked, the great baggage-trains loaded. Men caught steaming breath in their hands, stared across the frost-barren distances. Beasts of burden stamped and complained in the gloom.

Drawing a team of twenty oxen, the priests delivered the great wain to the highest point in the vicinity, a knoll stumped with ancient foundation stones. The bed of the vehicle had been constructed from timbers typically used in ship building, such was its size. Each of the eight iron-bound wheels stood as tall as olive trees. Slaves clambered across the frame, undoing the knots that fixed the circumfix-brocaded tarp. They rolled the crimson-and-gold covering back, revealing a horizontally suspended cylinder of iron as long as a skiff. Inscriptions adorned its every surface—verses from the Tusk rendered in the many tongues of the Three Seas—lending it an ancient and wrinkled look.

At the command of the High-Priest, a towering eunuch raised the Prayer Hammer . . . struck. The Interval sounded, a far-reaching, sonorous knell that somehow rose from the silence without breaking it, hung upon the ears before fading in imperceptible degrees.

The assembled Men of the Circumfix looked out to the horizon, waiting. For those across the higher slopes, their numbers scarce seemed possible, so far did the formations reach into the distance. The Nilnameshi phalanxes, with a file of iron-clad mastodons running like a spine through their midst. The Thunyeri with their long-edged axes. The Tydonni with their flaxen beards bound to their girdles. And on and on. High Ainon, Conriya, Nansur, Shigek, Eumarna, Galeoth, Girgash; the hosts of a dozen nations, arrayed about the gleaming standards of their kings, waiting . . .

Some were already on their knees.

Without warning, the Thunyeri began cursing and waving arms, spitting hatred at the North. Their broken shouts spread, resolved into a thundering chorus, one that soon boomed across the entirety of the Ordeal, even though many knew not the words they recited.

Hur rutwas matal skee!
Hur rutwas matal skee!

Men held out their arms as if they could, with their souls, reach out the thousands of miles to Golgotterath and wrestle it to ground with wrath and ardour alone. Each saw the coming tribulation in their soul's eye, and in their heart, their triumph was more than assured, it was decreed . . .

Hur rutwas matal skee!
Hur rutwas matal skee!

The Interval tolled again, resonating through the thousand-throated clamour, and the roar faded into expectant silence. The *ghus*, the oceanic prayer horns, sounded just as the eastern light etched the horizon in brilliant gold, like a cup tipped to overflowing.

Gold paint gleamed. Circumfix banners hung listless in the chill air. A presentiment passed through the assembly, and the cries of defiance and adulation rose once again, the way wind might coax a second rain from sodden trees. Their Aspect-Emperor—they could feel him.

He walked across the vault of heaven, standing bright in a sun that had yet to reach the masses below. Orange and rose painted the eastern flanges of his white-silk robes. His golden hair and braided beard shone. Starlight flashed from his high-hanging eyes. The Men of the Three Seas howled and roared in adoration—a cacophony of tongues. They reached out, lifted fingertips to touch his remote image.

"HOLD MY LIGHT," the hanging figure called in thunder.

The rim of the sun boiled over the horizon, and morning

dawned over the Great Ordeal. Warmth kissed the cheeks of those watching.

"FOR TODAY WE WALK THE WAYS OF SHADOW . . ."

And they fell to their knees—warriors and scribes, kings and slaves, priests and sorcerers, more than two hundred and eighty thousand souls, the greatest gathering of human arms and glory the world had ever seen. So many that it seemed that the floor of the world had dropped with their kneeling. They raised their faces and cried out, for light had come to them . . .

And the sun had followed.

"AMONG ALL PEOPLES, ONLY YOU HAVE TAKEN UP THE YOKE OF APOCALYPSE. AMONG ALL PEOPLES, ONLY YOU . . ."

For the Sakarpi who watched from their broken battlements, it was a thing of wonder and horror. Many felt a kind of hanging consternation, similar to that which afflicts men who make overbearing declarations. Everyone had assumed the Second Apocalypse and the march to Golgotterath was simply a pretext, that the Great Ordeal was an army of conquest, and the assault on Sakarpus another chapter of the Unification Wars, about which they had heard so many atrocious rumours and tales. But now . . .

Did they not witness proof of the Aspect-Emperor's word?

No one dared mock. Not a single jeer was raised against the ecstatic roar. They listened to their conqueror's sky-spanning voice, and though the language defeated them, they thought they understood what was said. They knew the scene before them would be celebrated for a thousand years, that accounts of it would be recited in the manner of *The Sagas* or even *The Chronicle of the Tusk*.

The day the Great Ordeal marched beyond the frontiers of Men.

The proud and the embittered celebrated, thinking that the Southron Kings marched to their doom. But that evening, long after the last of the long-snaking columns had vanished over the northern crests, thousands of Sakarpi went down into the streets to listen to sermons of the white-and-green-clad Judges. They took the lengths of copper wire that were offered to them, to twist into the shape of Circumfixes.

Afterwards, they clutched their crude tokens the way children sometimes moon over baubles that have captured their imagination. The Circumfix. A *living* symbol of a *living* god. It seemed a wonder, all the stories, all the shining possibilities, the golden clamour of a deeper, more forgiving reality. They walked together in whispering clots, glared at those who upbraided them with as much pity as defensive hostility. Pride, the Judges had told them, was ever the sin of fools.

That night they knelt for what seemed the first time, gave voice to the great unanswered ache in their hearts. They held their Circumfixes hot between moist palms, *and they prayed.* And the chill that pimpled their skin seemed holy.

They *knew* what they had seen, what they had felt.

For who could be such a fool as to mistake Truth?

Chapter Eight

The River Rohil

The will to conceal and the will to deceive are one and the same. Verily, a secret is naught but a deception that goes unspoken. A lie that only the Gods can hear.

—MEREMPOMPAS, *EPISTEMATA*

Early Spring, 19 New Imperial Year (4132 Year-of-the-Tusk), the headwaters of the River Rohil

The plan was to follow the tributaries of the River Rohil all the way into the Osthwai Mountains, then cross the Ochain Passes into the trackless Meörn Wilderness, where pretty much all the Scalpoi companies that frequented Marrow hunted their inhuman quarry. It was, Kiampas assured Achamian, an old and oft-travelled route. "As reliable as anything in this wicked trade," he had said. Things wouldn't get interesting, he guessed, until they had "slogged past the Fringe," the Fringe being the fluid and ever-receding border of what Sarl called "skinny country"—land ranged by the Sranc.

The first two nights Achamian made and broke his own camp and prepared his own meals. The third night, Sarl invited him to dine at the Captain's fire, which aside from Lord Kosoter and Sarl, included Kiampas and Incariol. Initially, Achamian had not known what to expect, but then, after dining on a repast of venison and boiled sumac shoots, he realized that he had known how it would be all along: Sarl discoursing on and on about everything and anything, with Kiampas contributing cautious asides, the Nonman adding cryptic and sometimes nonsensical observations, and the Captain staring down the night with nary a word.

The invitation was not extended the following night, and Achamian fumed, not because he had been excluded, but because of the hollow-boned loneliness that accompanied the exclusion. Of all the prospective perils that had plagued his soul's eye, heartsickness had been the least of his worries. And yet here he was, four nights out, moping like the outcast runt at temple. He did his resolute best to keep his eyes fixed on his humble fire. But no matter how vehement his curses, his found his gaze ranging to the talk and laughter emanating from the other camps. Obviously frequented by other companies, the entire area had been cleared of deadfall and bracken, so he could clearly see the rest of the Skin Eaters between the ancient elms, their campfires pitched in the depressions between humps of packed earth, interlocked rings of illumination, anemic and orange, tracing trunks and limbs against the black of the greater forest.

Achamian had almost forgotten what it was like, watching men about their fires. The arms folded against the chill. The mouths smiling, laughing, tongue and teeth peeking in and out of the firelight. The gazes hopping from face to face within the cage of camaraderie, only to return to the furnace coals during the inevitable lulls. At first it struck him as something fearful, an exposing of what humans do when they turn their backs to the world, their interiority laid bare to the vaults of dark infinity, cracked open like oysters, with no walls save a warlike nature. But as the moments passed, he found the sight more and more affecting, to the point of feeling old and maudlin. That in a place so vast and so dark creatures this frail would dare gather about sparks called light. They seemed at once precious and imperilled, like jewels mislaid across open ground, something sure to be scooped up by jealous enormities.

His scrutiny did not go unnoticed. The first time he noticed the man watching him, Achamian simply looked away. But when he glanced back moments afterwards, the man was still staring—intently. Achamian recognized him as the Ketyai who had arrived at the company's initial muster in Marrow fussing over the hems of his white Nilnameshi gowns. What might have been a hard moment passed between them, then the man was standing, talking, and nodding in his direction. As one, most of the others in his eclectic group followed his eyes, some craning their necks, some leaning to see past their fellows—a series of hooded, cursory looks. Achamian had seen them all innumerable times on the trail, wondered about their stories, but he had shared no words with any of them. He imagined it wouldn't much matter even if he had. Like mead-hall tables, campfires seemed to make foreigners of everyone.

The Nilnameshi strode from the others to come crouch by Achamian's humble little flame. He smiled and shrugged, introduced himself as Somandutta. He was relatively young, clean-shaven, as was the custom for Nilnameshi caste-nobles, with amiable eyes and a full-lipped mouth—the kind of man who inspired husbands to be more gracious to their wives. He seemed to blink continually, but it was a habit that only seemed ludicrous the first time you noticed it, then became quite natural after.

"You're not one of them," he said, nodding with raised brows toward the Captain's fire. "And you certainly aren't one of the Herd." He tipped his head to his right, in the direction of three neighbouring firepits, each of them crammed with younger flame-yellowed faces, most sporting long Galeoth moustaches. "That means you must be one of the Bitten."

"The Bitten?"

"Yes," he said, smiling broadly. "One of us."

"One of you."

The generous face regarded him for a moment, as though trying to decide how to interpret his tone. Then he shrugged, smiled like somebody remembering a sensible deathbed promise. "Come," he simply said. "Your beard has the punch of smoke."

Even though he had no clue what the Nilnameshi meant, Achamian found himself following the man. The "punch of smoke," as it turned out, referred to hashish. A pipe was handed to him the instant he stepped up to the fire, and the next thing Achamian knew he was sitting cross-legged at the puffing centre of their attention. Out of nervousness perhaps, he drew deep.

The smoke burned like molten lead. They roared with laughter as he hacked himself purple.

"See!" He heard Somandutta cry. "It wasn't just me!"

"Wizard!" someone growled and cheered. Others took it up—"Wiz-Wiza-Wizard!"—and Achamian found himself smiling and choking and nodding in bleary-eyed acknowledgment. He even waved.

"You get used to it. You get used to it," someone assured him while rubbing the small of his back. "Only the good mud for the slog, my old friend. It has to take us far!"

"See!" Somandutta repeated as though the world's last sane man. "It's *not* me!"

The hashish was already soaking through Achamian's senses by the time Somandutta, or Soma as the others called him, went around the circle with introductions. Achamian had met such groups before, strangers hammered into families by the privations of the road. Once they lowered their hackles, he knew, they would find in him cause to celebrate their fraternity. Every family was eager to prove itself exceptional in some way.

There was Galian, perhaps the eldest member of Bitten. In his youth he had been a soldier in the old Nansur Army; he had even fought in the famed Battle of Kiyuth, where Ikurei Conphas, the last of the Nansur Emperors, had overcome the nomadic Scylvendi. The giant that Soma had earlier called

Ox was Oxwora, a renegade son of the famed Yalgrota, one of the heroes of the First Holy War. There was Xonghis, a Jekki hillman who had been a former Imperial Tracker. He, Soma explained, was the Captain's "peach," by which he meant his most prized possession. "If he gets a chill," the Nilnameshi caste-noble said, "you must surrender your cloak and rub his feet!" The other giant of the group was Pokwas, or Pox as he was called. According to Somandutta, he was a disgraced Zeümi Sword-Dancer, come to eke out a living among the unwashed barbarians of the Three Seas. "It's always Zeüm this or Zeüm that with him," the Nilnameshi explained with mock disgust. "Zeüm invented children. Zeüm invented wind . . ." There was Sutadra, or Soot, whom Achamian had already identified as Kianene because of his goatee and long moustaches. Apparently Soot refused to speak of his past, which meant, Soma said with exaggerated menace, he was a fugitive of some description. "Likely a Fanim heretic." And lastly, there was Moraubon, a rangy Galeoth who had once been a Shrial Priest, "until he discovered that peaches don't grow on prayers." Apparently the question of whether he was "half-skinny" was a matter of ongoing debate.

"He hunts," Pox explained, his grin as broad as his black face, "with both bows strung."

Collectively, the seven of them were the only remaining members of the original company first assembled by Lord Kosoter some ten years previous. They called themselves the Bitten because they had been "gnawed" for so many long slogs. As it so happened, each and every one of them had been literally bitten by Sranc as well—and sported the scars to prove it. Pox even stood and dropped his leggings to reveal a puckered crescent across his left cheek, among other things.

"Sweet Sejenus," Galian exclaimed. "That solves the mystery of Soma's missing beard!"

Raucous laughter.

"Was that where it was hiding?" Achamian asked as innocently as a crafty old man could manage.

The Bitten fell dead silent. For a moment all he could hear was the talk and laughter from the other campfires echoing through the sieve of the surrounding forest. He had taken that step, so fateful in the company of close-knit strangers, between watching and participating.

"Where *what* was hiding?" Xonghis asked.

"The skinny that bit him."

Somandutta was the first to howl. Then all the Bitten joined in, rocking on their mats, trading looks like sips of priceless wine, or simply rolling their eyes heavenward, shining beneath the eternal arches of the night.

And Drusas Achamian found himself friends with the men he had in all likelihood killed.

Ever since striking out from his tower, Achamian had been afraid that his old body would fail him, that he would develop any one of the innumerable ailments that deny the long road to the aged. For some reason, he had assumed that his far thinner frame would also be far weaker. But he was pleasantly surprised to find his legs growing more and more roped with muscle, and his wind becoming deep—to the point where he had no difficulty managing even the most punishing pace.

Walking in file, leading their small mule trains, they followed a broad trail that generally ran parallel to the river. For long tracts it was treacherous going, as the trail had been scuffed deep enough to expose knobbed roots and buried rocks. The Osthwai Mountains loomed vast and magnificent above them, their peaks lost in a dark shoal of clouds as wide as the horizon. They seemed to eat the eastern sky in imperceptible increments.

They passed several inbound companies, lines of lean, lean men, hunched beneath their remaining provisions and cord-threaded scalps, not a beast of burden to be seen. They would have looked macabre, like skeletons marching in stolen skins, were they not so jubilant at the prospect of gaining Marrow.

"They were forced to winter in the Wilds," Soma explained to Achamian. "We were almost caught ourselves. The Ochain Passes have been especially treacherous these past couple of years." He bent his head to his feet, as though inspecting his boots for scuffs. "It's like the world is getting colder," he added after several steps.

Tidings and jibes were shared back and forth as the companies passed. The newest whores. The worsening conditions in the Osthwai. The brokers who kept "forgetting their thumbs" when counting. Rumours of the Stone-Hags, a pirate company cum bandit army that apparently hunted scalpers the way scalpers hunted Sranc. Which tavern-keeps were watering their wine. And as always, the unaccountable cunning of the skinnies.

"The trees!" one particularly hoary Norsirai said. "They came at us out of the trees! Like monkeys with fucking knives . . ."

Achamian listened without comment, both fascinated and dismayed. Like all Mandate Schoolman, he looked at the world with the arrogance of someone who had survived—even if only in proxy—the greatest depravities circumstance could offer. But what happened in the Wilds, whatever it was that edged their voices when the Skin Eaters spoke of it, was different somehow. They too carried the look and posture of survivors, but of something more mean, more poisonous, than the death of nations. There was the wickedness that cut throats, and there was the wickedness that put whole peoples to the sword. Scalpers, Achamian realized, dwelt somewhere in the lunatic in-between.

And for the first time he understood: He had no real comprehension of what was to come.

The point was brought home by the half-starved man he saw slumped, his face between his knees, beneath the hanging veils of a willow. Before he knew what he was doing, Achamian was kneeling at the man's side, pressing him upright. The fellow was as light as kindling pine. His face was sunken in the way

Achamian had seen in Caraskand during the First Holy War, so that the edges and the irregularities of the skull beneath pressed clear through the skin, chipping short the cheeks and pitting the sockets. His eyes were as flat and waxen as any guttered candle.

The man said nothing, seemed to stare into the same.

Pokwas dropped a large hand on Achamian's shoulder, startling him. "Where you fall is where you lie," the Sword-Dancer said. "It's a Rule. No pity on the slog, friend."

"What kind of soldiers leave their comrades to die?"

"Soldiers who aren't soldiers," Pokwas replied with a noncommital shrug. "Scalpers."

Even though the Sword-Dancer's tone said it all—the Wilds were simply a place too hard for ritual observance or futile compassion—Achamian wanted to ask him what he meant. The old indignant need to challenge, to contest, welled sharp within his breast. Instead, he simply shrugged and obediently followed the towering man back into the long-walking file.

Achamian the talker, the asker of questions, had died a long time ago.

But the episode continued to occupy the old Wizard's thoughts, not the cruelty so much as the pathos. He had been away for so long a part of him had forgotten that men could die so ignominiously, like dogs skulking into the weeds to pant their last. The image of the unfortunate refused to fade: the eyes clouding, the lips mouthing the air, the body like sticks in the sack of his skin. How could he not feel like a fool? Between his Dreams of the First Apocalypse and his memories of the First Holy War, he could scarce imagine anyone who had seen more death and degradation than he. And yet there it was, the fact of a dying stranger, like an added weight, a tightness that robbed him of his wind.

Was it some kind of premonition? Or was he simply growing soft? He had seen it many times, the way compassion made rotted fruit of old men's hearts. The vitality of his old bones had surprised him. Perhaps his spirit was what would fail . . .

Something always failed him.

The trail wound on and on through the forest deeps, a track that had seen countless scalpers strut or shamble. Though Somandutta paced him on several occasions, trying to draw him into some inane topic of conversation, Achamian remained silent, walking and brooding.

That night he made a point of sitting next to Pokwas at the fire. The mood was celebratory. Xonghis had felled a doe, which the company then portioned according to rank—the unborn fetus included. Achamian said nothing, knowing that the sacrilege of consuming pregnant game would mean nothing to these men.

"I'm curious," Achamian asked after eating his fill, "about these Rules of the Slog . . ."

The black man said nothing at first. He looked particularly fierce, limned in firelight, his lips drawn back as he tore meat from bone. He chewed in contemplation a moment, then said, "Yah."

"If it were, say, *Galian* lying at the side of th—"

"It would be the same," the Zeümi interrupted through a mouthful of venison. He looked to Galian as he said this, shrugged in mock apology.

"But he's your . . . your *brother*, is he not?"

"Course he is."

Galian made kissing noises from across the fire.

"So," Achamian pressed, "what about the rules of brotherhood?"

This time it was Galian who answered. "The only rules on the slog, Wizard, are the rules *of the slog*."

Achamian scowled, pausing to sort between a number of different questions, but Galian interrupted him before he could speak. "Brotherhood is well and fine," the former Columnary said, "so long as it doesn't cost. As soon as it becomes a luxury . . ." He shrugged, resumed gnawing on the bone he still held in his right hand. "The skinnies," he said with an air of distracted finality.

The Sranc, he was saying. The Sranc were the only rule.

Achamian studied their faces across the firelight. "No liabilities, is that it? Nothing that could afford your opponent any advantage." He raised a finger to scratch the side of his nose. "That sounds like something our glorious Aspect-Emperor would say."

Aside from the vague intuition that discussing the Aspect-Emperor was generally unwise, the old Wizard really didn't know what to expect.

"I would help," Soma blurted. "If *Galian* was dying, that is. I really would . . ."

The eating paused. The ring of faces turned to the young Nilnameshi, some screwed in mock outrage, others sporting skeptical grins.

With a guileless smile, Soma said, "His boots fit as fine as my own!"

There was a moment of silence. Soma's jokes, Achamian had learned, generally occasioned a kind of communal trial and conviction, especially when he was *trying* to be funny. Heads were shaken. Eyes were rolled to heaven. Oxwora, the enormous Thunyeri with shrunken Sranc heads tangled in his shaggy mane, looked up from the glistening rib he had been gnawing, scowling as though his appetite had been ruined. Without a word he tossed the bone at the Nilnameshi. Either by fluke or by dint of grease, the thing slid rather than bounced from his head.

"Ox!" Somandutta cried with real anger, but in the harmless way of the long heckled. The giant grinned, his beard and moustache spackled with flecks of meat.

Suddenly the others were reaching to their feet, and a

haphazard wave of bones peppered the hapless Nilnameshi, who held his arms out, cursing. He made as though to throw several back at this or that figure, but ended up joining the general laughter instead.

"Loot thy brother," the Zeümi said to Achamian in a *there-you-have-it* tone. The Sword-Dancer slapped his back. "Welcome to the slog, Wizard!"

Achamian laughed and nodded, glanced out beyond the circle of illumined faces to the night-hooded world. It was no simple or mean thing, the companionship of killers.

Two days following his introduction to the Bitten, Achamian glimpsed Xonghis jogging along the outside of the trudging line from the rear. The others paid him no attention: He continually roamed while the others marched. Out of boredom more than anything, Achamian asked the man what was wrong, expecting something wry and cutting in reply. Instead, the Jekki slowed his pace to stride beside him. His short-sleeved tunic revealed a grappler's veined arms, brown beneath the reddish hint of sunburn. He was a lean, broad-shouldered man, with the aura of coiled reserve that seemed proper to a former Imperial Tracker.

"We're being followed," he said in his odd accent.

"Followed?"

"Yes . . ." He seemed to weigh his own cryptic options. "By a woman."

Achamian nearly coughed, such was his alarm. "Who else knows?"

The Tracker's almond-shaped eyes narrowed. His Xiuhianni blood was always more pronounced in open daylight. "Moraubon and several of the Herd."

"Moraubon?"

Suddenly Achamian was huffing and gasping, running back along the tangled verge of the trail. The parade of walking scalpers watched him pass with frowning curiosity. Then he was all alone on the trail, running down a boulder-stumped incline, away from the river and into the mute confines of the forest. Several moments passed before he heard the first hoot, a raw laughing call, filled with malice and the open-mouthed eagerness of men bent on rutting. He heard Moraubon shouting a few moments afterwards: instructions to the others racing across the forest floor. He heard a feminine shriek—no, not a shriek, a shrill cry of defiance and frustration.

The sorcerous words were already rumbling from his lips, through the essence of the encircling world, and he was climbing, not air, but the echoes of ground across the sky, up into the interweaving limbs. Branches lashed him as he broke through the canopy, then walked over the forest crown, each step swallowing a dozen cubits, tipping for the vertigo of looking down through the towering trees. He could see the pitch of the surrounding wilderness to the horizon, ridges like wandering fins, tributaries threading dark clefts with silver, mountains looming in white judgment. He saw men running, Skin Eaters, like the shadows of mice beneath meadow thatch. Then he saw her—Mimara—kicking and thrashing in the clutches of three men.

He stepped into their midst.

They had her pulled like living rope across the forest floor. Moraubon was kneeling between her legs, undoing his girdle and breeches. He seemed to be cooing and growling. He whirled to the sound of Achamian's sorcerous muttering . . .

Only to be blown tumbling, kicking up tailings of leaves. An Odaini Concussion Cant.

The other Skin Eaters cried out, scrambled back while tugging at their weapons. Through his rage, Achamian could feel something exult at this first violent exercise. *Let them see!* an inner voice cried. *Let them know!* His voice cracked out, soaked into the surrounding matter and steamed skyward, sourceless, all-encompassing. The Skin Eaters, including Moraubon, retreated in the safety of the great trunks.

The Compass of Noshainrau, an existential glitter, a line of sun-concentrated white, sweeping out like a flail from the axis of his upraised arm, sketching a perfect circle of destruction. Wood charred and exploded. Flame spilled like water across the ancient oaks, elms, and maples. Mountainous groans and creaks—a chorus—then the roar of mighty trees falling, a ring of them crashing into their stone-heavy cousins, chasing the Skin Eaters into the deeper shadows of the forest.

Achamian stood over her, bright in the sudden sunlight, showered by the twirling green of innumerable spring-early leaves. A Wizard draped in wolf skins. The bulk of once great trees lay heaped about them. Forked trunks and limbs gouged the ground beneath shags of greenery.

Mimara spat blood from her lips, tried to pull her torn leggings to her hips. She made a noise that might have been a sob or a laugh or both. She fell to her knees before him, her left thigh as bare and pale as a barked sapling. A laughing grimace. A glimpse of teeth soaked in blood.

"Teach me," she said.

No words were spoken as they hastened back, Achamian fuming in the lead, Mimara shambling in her clutched clothing to keep up. They found the Skin Eaters standing in clots across slopes of earth between wain-sized molars of stone. The river arced and sprayed white beyond them, endlessly pounding the hillside. All eyes turned to them as they approached, lingered for a moment on Mimara's slight figure. Instinctively, Achamian held out his arm and drew her close to his chest. Together they pressed to the fore of the crowd.

They saw Moraubon, obviously winded, climb to Lord Kosoter where he stood, thumbs hooked in his war girdle, on the mottled back of a boulder. A confusion of vertical stone faces rose behind the Captain, crested with bracken and the odd suicidal tree. A great rooster tail of water spouted through the heart of the enclosure, kicked into foam by some powerful twist in the current. The cowled Nonman, Cleric, was nowhere to be seen.

The two men shared inaudible words, with Moraubon glancing at Mimara, as though to say, *Look at her* . . . The Captain remained absolutely motionless. Sarl glared at the Skin Eaters from immediately below.

"The one with the Chorae," Mimara whispered, referring to Lord Kosoter. "Who is he?"

Achamian found himself glancing down the line of warlike faces. "Shush," was all he said.

At first it seemed the Captain had simply reached out and seized Moraubon's chin—so casual was his movement. Achamian squinted, trying to understand the wrongness of the image: Lord Kosoter holding the man mere inches from his face, not so much looking into his eyes as *watching* . . . Achamian only glimpsed the knife jammed beneath the scalper's mandible when Lord Kosoter withdrew his hand.

Moraubon crumpled as if the Captain had ripped out his bones. Blood sheeted the boulder.

"Can *anybody*," Sarl cried out over the river's white thunder, "tell me what the rule is for peaches on the slog?"

"The Captain always gets the first bite," Galian called solemnly.

"And what is it that has made us legends of the Wilds? What allows us *to eat so much skin*?"

"The Rules of the Slog!" a number of them shouted against the roar.

Not in reluctance, Achamian realized, but with dark affirmation. Even the Bitten, even those who had broken bread with the dead man on the boulder.

They're all mad.

Sarl reddened about his mock smile. His eyes became two more wrinkles creasing his face.

Without a glance at his sergeant, the Captain crouched in his ragged Ainoni finery, wiped his blade clean on Moraubon's sleeve. Then he fixed his gaze on Achamian and Mimara. He leapt from the boulder, his balance and bearing shockingly limber. Until that moment, he had seemed carved of living granite.

He strode up to the two of them.

"Who is she?"

"My daughter," Achamian heard himself say.

There was no chance the murderous brown eyes could stare him down—not this time. She felt too much like her mother pressed in the brace of his arm, too much like Esmenet. The Captain glanced to the ground for a meditative moment, seemed to nod, though it could have been a trick of the breeze through his squared beard. After a hooded glance, he turned to make his way back to the head of the trail.

"Either she carries her weight like a man," he shouted as he walked away. "Or she carries *our* weight like a woman!"

Catcalls and whistles from the Skin Eaters. Each of them, it seemed, glanced at Achamian and Mimara as they drifted back to resume the march. Their expressions ran the gamut from accusation to jeering lechery. But it was the blank faces that troubled Achamian the most, the eyes that seemed to commit Mimara's torn leggings to memory.

No one bothered with Moraubon's body, which continued to drain against a backdrop of booming water and towering debris. A white corpse on a red-painted stone.

"Who is he?" Mimara whispered. While Achamian had eyed the others, she had continued gazing at the Captain's receding back.

"A Veteran," he murmured. "The same as me."

They lagged behind the others, passing from broken sunlight to green shadow, arguing over the rush and hiss of the river.

"You cannot stay! This is impossible!"

"Where would you have me go?"

"Go? Go? Where do you think? Back to your mother! Back to the Andiamine Heights where you belong!"

"Never."

"I know your mother. I know she loves you!"

"Not so much as she hates what she did to me."

"To save your life!"

"Life . . . Is that what you call it? Should I tell you the story of my life?

"No."

"All these men. Trust me, I've borne them before. I can bear them again."

"Not *these* men."

"Then I suppose I'm lucky to have *you*."

She was nothing like Esmenet, he had come to realize. She tilted her head the same way, as though literally trying to look around your nonsense, and her voice stiffened into the same reedy bundle of disgust, but aside from these echoes . . .

"Look. You simply *cannot stay*. This is a journey . . ." He paused, his breath yanked short by the sheer factuality of what he was about to say. "This is a journey without any return."

She sneered and laughed. "So is every life."

There was something snide and infuriating about her, he decided, something that begged to be struck—or *dared* . . . He could not tell which.

No. She was nothing like Esmenet. Even the vicious dismissiveness of her snorts—all her own.

"Is that what you've told these scalpers?"

"What do you mean, 'told'?"

"That this journey will see them all killed."

"No."

"What did you tell them?"

"That I can show them the Coffers."

"The Coffers?"

"The legendary treasury of the School of Sohonc, lost when the Library of Sauglish was destroyed in the First Apocalypse."

"So they know nothing of Ishuäl? They have no idea that you hunt the origins of their Holy Aspect-Emperor? The man who pays the bounty on their scalps!"

"No."

"Murderer. That makes you a *murderer.*"

"Yes."

"Teach me, then . . . Teach me, or I'll tell them everything!"

"Extortion, is it?"

"Murder is more wicked by far."

"What makes you certain I wouldn't kill you, if I'm a murderer as you say?"

"Because I look too much like my mother."

"There's a thought. Maybe I should just tell the Captain who you are. A Princess-Imperial. Think of the ransom you would fetch!"

"Yes . . . But then why bleed all the way to Sauglish looking for the Coffers?"

Impudent. An almost lunatic selfishness! Was she born this way? No. She wore her scars the way hermits wore their stench: as a mark of all the innumerable sins she had overcome.

"This is not a contest you can win, Wizard."

"How so?"

"I'm no fool. I know you've sworn by whatever it is you hold sacred to never teach anoth—"

"*I am cursed!* Disaster follows my teaching. Death and betra—"

"But you're mistaken to think that you can use threats or

pleas or even *reason* with me. This Gift I have, this ability to see the world the way *you* see it, it's *the only Gift* I have ever received, the only hope I have ever known. I will be a witch, or I will be dead."

"Didn't you hear me? My teaching is cursed!"

"We're a fine match then."

Impudent! Impudent! Was there ever such a despicable slit?

That night they cast their camp a short distance from the cluster of others. Neither of them spoke a word. In fact, a quiet had fallen across all the Skin Eaters, enough to make the crackle of their fires the dominant discourse. Only Sarl's hashed voice continued to saw on as before.

"Kiampas! Kiampas! That was no pretty night, I tell you!"

Achamian need only look up to see several orange faces lifted in their direction—even among the Bitten. Never in his life, it seemed, had he felt so absurdly conspicuous. He heard nothing, but he listened to them mutter about her all the same: assessing her breasts and thighs, spinning expressions of longing into violent boasts, catalogues of what they would do, the vigour of their penetrations, and how she would scream and whimper; speculating on the whys and wherefores of her presence, how she had to be a whore to dare the likes of them, or how she soon would be . . .

He need only glance at Mimara to know that she listened too. Another woman, a free-wife, or a Princess-Imperial raised in cozened isolation, might be oblivious, simply assume that the white-water souls of men sluiced through the same innocent tributaries as their own, that they shared a common turbulence. But not Mimara. Her ears were pricked—Achamian could tell. But where he felt apprehension, the shrill possessiveness of an overmatched father, she seemed entirely at her ease.

She had been raised in the covetous gaze of men, and

though she had suffered beneath brutal hands, she had grown strong. She carried herself, Achamian realized, with a kind of coy arrogance, as though she were the sole human in the presence of resentful apes. Let them grunt. Let them abuse themselves. She cared nothing for all the versions of her that danced or moaned or choked behind their primitive eyes—save that they made her, and all the possibilities that her breath and body offered, invaluable.

She was the thing wanted. So be it. She would find ways to make them pay.

But for Achamian it was too much. Her resemblance to Esmenet was simply too uncanny. And though he had little or no affection for the daughter—the girl was too damaged—he felt himself falling in love with the mother all over again. Esmenet. Esmenet. Sometimes, when his flame-gazing reveries dipped too deep, he found himself startled by the image of her in his periphery, and the very world would reel as he struggled to sort memories of the First Holy War from the chill dark of the now. *To go back*, he found himself thinking. *I would do anything to go back . . .*

So, with the hollow chest of speaking for the sake of forgetting, Achamian began explaining the metaphysics of sorcery to her—if only to kill the prurient silence with the sound of his own voice. She watched him, wide-eyed, the perfect oval of her face perched on her knees—illuminated and beautiful.

Quite against his intentions, he began teaching her the Gnosis.

The hike into the mountains proved arduous. The trail heaved and plummeted as it strayed farther and farther from the river gorges. The mules clicked across tracts of sheeted gravel and bare stone. The mighty broadleaves of the plateau became ever more spindly. "It's like we're climbing back into winter,"

Mimara breathlessly noted after picking a purple bud from the twigs hanging above her head.

Perhaps because of the accusatorial aura hanging between them, or perhaps just to steer his thoughts away from the burning in his thighs or the stitches in his flank, Achamian began teaching her Gilcûnya, the ancient tongue of all Gnostic Magi. As a student at Atyersus, he had been dismayed to discover that he would have to learn an entire language—not to mention one whose grammar and intonation were scarcely human—before he would be able to sing his first primitive Cant. Mimara, however, took to the task with out-and-out zealotry.

He hadn't the heart to tell her the truth: that the reason the sorcerous Schools were loath to take adults as students had to do with the way age seemed to diminish the ability to learn languages. What had taken him a single year as a child could very well take her several. It could be the case that she would *never* learn to manipulate the meanings with the precision and purity required . . .

Why this should seem a crime was beyond him.

The Skin Eaters watched them whenever opportunity afforded, some more boldly than others. Where the width of the trail allowed, a dozen or so always seemed to gather in loose and fortuitous packs about them. Achamian found himself bristling each time, and not simply because of the endless succession of gazes sliding across her form. They were friendly, courteous to a fault, but there was no mistaking their bullying nearness, or the predatory lag whenever their look crossed his own, that moment too long, pregnant with threat and prowess. He understood the game well enough, the false gallantry of helping her across the more treacherous twists in the trail, the implicit significance of offering him the exact same assistance. *Leave her to us, old man . . .*

Mimara, of course, affected not to notice.

That afternoon a stop was called at the base of an incline.

No one at their end of the line knew the cause of the delay, and everyone was worn out enough to remain incurious. Achamian was doing vocabulary drills with Mimara when Sarl surprised them. "The Captain wants you," the man said, smiling as usual, though more than a little chagrin seemed written into the wrinkles netting his eyes. He grimaced at Mimara as he paused to catch his breath, then looked to the other Skin Eaters milling in the gloom. He lowered his voice to a mutter. "Troubling news."

Achamian did his best to pace the old cutthroat up the incline. By the time he gained the crest of the ridge line, he was breathing hard, pressing his knees with his hands at every step. A cold breeze greeted him, soaking through his beard and clothing. The Osthwai Mountains piled across the horizon in all their glory, titanic flanges of earth and stone rearing into cloud-smothered peaks. The woollen ceiling seemed close enough to touch, and so black that his hackles raised in the expectation of thunder. But the distances remained crisp with silence.

He saw Lord Kosoter standing with Cleric looming at his side. Both were watching Kiampas haggle with a Thunyeri almost as tall as Oxwora, though far older and nowhere as thick-limbed. The two seemed to be speaking some mongrel tongue that combined elements of Sheyic and Thunyeri. At least several dozen of the man's wild countrymen stood watching in the near distance.

The tall one, Sarl explained in a low murmur, was called Feather, though Achamian could see nothing avian about his ornament. Several shrunken Sranc heads adorned his crazed red-and-grey hair. His war girdle used knuckle-bones in the place of beads. Aside from his hauberk, the gold-wire Circumfix hanging about his neck seemed his only concession to civilization. Even paces back, Achamian could smell his furs, the carnivore reek of blood and piss. He was, Sarl continued in a low mutter, the chieftain of one of the so-called tribal companies, most of which were made up of Thunyeri, a people who had warred so long and so hard against the Sranc it had become a missionary calling.

When Kiampas and Feather concluded their business, the tall chieftain reached out to clasp forearms with Lord Kosoter. It struck Achamian as a formidable moment, two storied Scalpoi, each with their own aura of assassination, each garbed in tattered parodies of their nation's battledress. It was the first time he had witnessed the Captain extend anything so precious as respect. With an enigmatic gesture, the chieftain returned to the trail, followed by the long line of his men. His manic blue eyes scraped across Achamian as he passed.

"They plan on camping on the low slopes," Kiampas was saying to Lord Kosoter, "hunting, foraging . . ."

"What's the problem?" Achamian asked.

Kiampas turned to him, his eyes smiling in an otherwise guarded expression, the triumphant look of a man who kept fastidious count of wins and losses. "A spring blizzard in the mountains," he said. "We're stuck here for at least two weeks, probably more."

"What are you saying?" Achamian looked to the glaring Captain.

Kiampas was only too happy to respond. "That your glorious expedition has come to an end, Wizard. We can wait or we can hump round the Osthwai's southern spur. Either way we've no hope of reaching Sauglish by summer's end." There was no mistaking the relief in his eyes.

"The Black Halls," someone said in the tone of contradiction.

It was the Nonman, Cleric. He had his broad back turned to them, his cowl facing east, toward the nearest of the mountains to their right. His voice pimpled the skin, as much for its import as for its inhuman resonances. "There *is* another way through the mountains," he continued, twisting his unseen face toward them. "A way that I remember."

Achamian held his breath, understanding instantly what the Nonman was suggesting but too dismayed to truly consider the implications. Sarl snorted, as if hearing a joke beneath even his vulgar contempt.

Lord Kosoter studied his Nonman lieutenant, stared into the black oval with cryptic intensity.

"Are you sure?"

A drawn silence, filled by the guttural banter of the Thunyeri trudging behind them.

"I lived there," Cleric said, "on the sufferance of my cousins, long ago . . . Before the Age of Men."

"Are you sure *you remember?*"

The cowl bent earthward.

"They were . . . difficult days."

The Ainoni nodded in grim deliberation.

"Captain?" Kiampas exclaimed. "You *know* the stories . . . Every year some fool leads his compa—"

Lord Kosoter had not looked at the sergeant until he mentioned the word *fool*. His eyes were interruption enough.

"The Black Halls it is, then!" Sarl exclaimed in a smoky cackle, the one he always used to blunt his Captain's more murderous inclinations. He seemed to wheeze and laugh at each man in turn. "Kiampas! Can't you see, Kiampas? We're Skin Eaters, man—*Skin Eaters!* How many times have we talked about the Black Halls?"

"And what about the rumours?" the Nansur officer snapped, though with the wariness of a struck dog.

"Rumours?" Achamian asked.

"Bah!" Sarl cackled. "Men just can't countenance mystery. If companies get eaten, they have to invent a Great Eater, no matter what." He turned to Achamian, his face wrinkling in incredulity. "He thinks a *dragon* hides in the Black Halls. A Dragon!" He jerked his gaze back to Kiampas, red face thrust forward, knobby fists balled at his side. "Dragon, my eye! It's the skinnies that get them. It's the skinnies that get us all in the end."

"Sranc?" Achamian asked, even though fire-spitting monstrosities heaved in his soul's eye. How many Wracu had roared through his ancient dreams? "How can you be sure?"

"Because their clans make it through the mountains somehow," Sarl replied, "especially in the winter. Why do you think so many scalpers risk the Black Halls in the first place?"

"I told you," Kiampas persisted. "I met those two from Attrempus, survivors of the High Shields. I'm no fool when it comes—"

"Poofs!" Sarl spat. "Moppers! Trying to soak you for a drink! The High Shields were massacred on the long side of the mountains. Kiampas. *Kiampas!* Everyone knows that! The *Long Side*!"

The two sergeants glared at each other, Sarl in entreaty, like the son who always placates his father for his brother's sake, and Kiampas in incredulous resentment, like the sole sane officer in a host of madmen—which was, Achamian reflected, not all that far from the case.

"We take the Low Road," Lord Kosoter grated. "We enter the Black Halls."

His tone seemed to condemn all humanity, let alone the petty dispute before him. The Nonman continued to stare off into the east, tall and broad beneath his mottled cowl. The mountain climbed the climbing ground beyond him, a white sentinel whispering with altitude and distance.

"Cleric says he remembers."

Achamian returned to find Mimara fairly surrounded by Skin Eaters, most of them Bitten. She stood childlike in the looming presence of Oxwora and Pokwas, her look one of guarded good humour. She was careful to keep her face and posture directed toward the trail, as though she expected to leave their company at any moment, as well as to not look at any one of them for more than a heartbeat. He could tell she was frightened, but not in any debilitating way.

"So you're Ainoni, then?"

"Small wonder the Captain's smitten . . ."

"Maybe he'll stop undressing *us* with his cursed eyes!"

The laughter was genuine enough to make Mimara smile, but utterly unlike the raucous mirth that was their norm. Soldiers, Achamian had observed, often wore thin skins in the presence of women they could neither buy nor brutalize. A light and careless manner, a gentle concern for the small things, stretched across a sorrow and an anger that no woman could fathom. And these men were more than soldiers, more than scalpers, even. They were Skin Eaters. They were men who led lives of uncompromising viciousness and savagery. Men who could effortlessly forget the dead rapist that had been their bosom friend.

And they would try to woo what they could not take.

"It's as I thought," Soma said as Achamian joined them. His look was amiable enough but with an edge that advised no contradictions. "*She's* one of the Bitten as well!"

The smell of contrivance hung about all their looks. They had planned this, Achamian realized, as a way of luring the prize to *their* fire. The question was one of how far the covenant went.

"The Ochain Passes are closed," he said. "Blizzard."

He watched their faces struggle to find the appropriate expressions. There was comedy in all sudden reversals, a kind of immaterial nudity, to find your designs hanging, stripped of the logic that had been their fundament. Their carnal plots depended on the expedition, and the expedition depended on the Passes.

"The decision has been made," he said, trying hard not to sound satisfied.

"We brave the Black Halls of Cil-Aujas."

Chapter Nine

Momemn

A beggar's mistake harms no one but the beggar. A king's mistake, however, harms everyone but the king. Too often, the measure of power lies not in the number who obey your will, but in the number who suffer your stupidity.

—TRIAMIS I, *JOURNALS AND DIALOGUES*

Early Spring, 19 New Imperial Year (4132 Year-of-the-Tusk), Momemn

Her face seemed numb for tingling.

"Does he hear us, Mommy? Does he know?"

Esmenet clutched Kelmomas's little hand so tight she feared she might hurt him. "Yes," she heard herself say. The stone of the Ashery snared her words, held them close and warm, as though she spoke into a lover's neck. "Yes. He's the son of an earthly god."

According to Nansur custom, the mother of a dead male child had to mark her face with her son's ashes each full moon after the cremation: two lines, one down each cheek. *Thraxami*, they were called, tears-of-the-pyre. Only when her tears no longer darkened them could the rite cease. Only when the weeping ended.

Even now, she could feel his residue across her cheeks, burning, accusing, as though transmuted, Samarmas had become antithetical to his mother, a kind of poison that her skin could not abide.

As though he had become wholly his father's.

The tradition was too old, too venerated, to be contradicted. Esmenet had seen engravings of women marked with thraxami dating back to the early days of ancient Cenei, trains of them marching like captives. And in the ritual dramas the temples put on during Cultic festivals, mummers used black lines down a white-painted face to represent desolate women the way they used red horizontal lines, *wurrami*, to depict rage-maddened men. For the Nansur, thraxami were synonymous with mourning.

But where others kept their child's remains in their household shrine, little Samarmas, as a Prince-Imperial, had been interred in the High Royal Ashery of the Temple Xothei. So once again, what was tender and private for others became rank spectacle for her. Thousands had mobbed the gates of the Imperial Precincts, and thousands more the foundations of mighty Xothei, a seething carnival of mourning and anticipation, mothers casting dust skyward and rending their hair, slaves loafing and gawking, boys jumping to snatch glimpses over grown shoulders, and many more. Even here, deep in the temple's mazed bowel, she thought she could hear their anxious hum.

What would they say when they saw that her cheeks were dry? What would they make of an Empress who could not weep for the loss of her dearest child?

Illuminated only by the rare lamp, the walls of the Ashery seemed to hang in a greater black. Each of the niches spoke to the sensibilities of different ages and families. Some were garish with gilding and ornament, while others, like the adjacent niches of Ikurei Xerius and his nephew Ikurei Conphas, were simply chiselled into the raw stone, bereft of the marble facing that graced so many of the others. She tried not to ponder the irony of her son resting so close to Conphas, who had been the Nansurium's last Emperor before the ascension of Kellhus. She likewise ignored the guttered votives and small bowl of grain that had been left on the sill of his niche.

Someday, she thought, *all* her children would rest in this immobile gloom. Static. Speechless. Someday, *she* would reside here, cool dust encased in silver, gold, or perhaps Zeümi jade—something cold, for all the substances that Men coveted were cold. Someday the heat of her would leach into the world, and she would be as dirt to the warm fingers of the living.

Someday she would be dead.

The relief that accompanied the thought was so sudden, so violent, that she almost audibly gasped. A confusion descended upon her, robbing her of memory and volition. She swayed, raised a hand to her blinking eyes. Then she found herself on the floor, sitting in a way that would have horrified her vestiaries it was so common, so undignified—no better than a whore hanging her legs from a window. She saw Kelmomas watching her, tried to smile reassurance. She leaned her head against the unyielding marble, the image of him lingering in her soul's eye. Small. Defenceless. The very image of his dead twin.

She heard his voice.

"Mommy? Does he hear us?"

She simply could not stop seeing him, Samarmas, his blood clotting the grass, his body as small as a dog, slowly relaxing about the spear that pierced it, slowly drifting asleep. Every time she blinked.

Every time she looked upon this other son.

"I told you . . ."

"No . . . I mean when we *think*." He was crying now, a desperate kind of hitching that made him bare his teeth. "D-does Sammy hear us *when we think?*"

She opened her knees and he fell into her arms, burned her

neck with a muffled wail. And she saw—with griveous clarity, it seemed—that Samarmas's death had sundered her soul in two, the one part numb and wondering, the other clinging to this child, this replica, as though trying to absorb his shudders.

How could she protect him? And if she could not, how could she love?

She laid her head across his scalp, blew at the hairs that stuck to the seal of her lips. Her cheeks were wet, but whether the tears were her own she could not tell. No matter. The mob would be appeased. Her Exalt-Ministers would be relieved, for the Yatwerian matter had become far more than a Cultic nuisance. Who would raise voice or hand against a bereaved mother? And Kellhus . . .

She was so tired. So weary.

"The dead hear everything, Kel."

Iothiah . . .

A life lived, now forgotten.

And in its place . . .

A breeze as dry as hot ash. An airy room, clean with tile and paint, the floor canted to drain storm-waters. A woman in a simple linen shift, wedding young, her hair raven-dark, suckling an infant, smiling, asking something sweet and curious. Her head tipped, almond eyes flashing, poised to laugh at something soon to be said, a warm and gentle wit.

Peach-coloured walls trimmed in vining green.

A life forgotten . . .

Concern clouding her dark eyes. A quick glance at the infant against her breast, then again the question.

"Love? Are you okay?"

You look like you're dreaming . . .

A doorway, open onto a vista of tan and blue—pale and soft and oceanic. A blue that does not hang close behind the nodding palms, but opens and opens to the white ribs of heaven. A blue like billowing cotton.

The threshold crossed. Then a courtyard where gnarled old slaves chase chickens. A young scullery girl staring, immovable save for her tracking gaze, her skin as brown as her broom handle.

The gate. The street.

The infant wailing now, swung from a frantic hip, the woman scolding, weeping, crying out: "What are you doing? What has happened?"

Wake up, please! You're scaring me!

A slender clutch knocked aside by a strong, wide-waving arm. Steps taken. Distances rolled up into oblivion. A tugging from spaces unseen. The woman shrieking, "My love! My love, please!"

What have I done?

Two hundred and fifty-seven years before, a Shigeki builder had saved twenty-eight silver talents by purchasing burnt brick from farther up the River Sempis, where the clay was riddled with sand. Aside from the tan hue, the tenement he raised was indistinguishable from the others. Over the course of the following centuries, the flood-waters had twice risen high enough to lave the southernmost pylons. Though the damage appeared minimal, sheets of material had fallen from the base of the outermost support, lending it a gnawed look, which for some reason, seemed to attract urinating dogs.

It toppled exactly when it should, drawing with it an entire quadrant, collapsing four floors of apartments and crushing all the unfortunates within. There was a roar, a collective peal of screams punched into silence. Afterwards, dust sweeping out and up. The earthen clap and tinkle of raining bricks. Then streets packed with shouting passers-by.

The woman and the infant were gone.

A life forgotten . . .

The streets. Miraculous numbers. Miraculous movement,

like threads of sand falling into and through one another without collision or redirection.

The alleyways. The rainbow awnings, cooling the dust, shielding the walking files, dimming the sun to a threaded glare.

The great agora.

A peacock walking holy and unmolested through a parting crowd, iridescent eyes shimmering from its plumage, blessing all those who took care not to match them. A man barking, his face bent low and dangerous, then slapping the boy who walked with him. The click of teeth in paste. Two old men scratching their heads and laughing, lips drawn across gums, over teeth like pieces of broken pottery. A distempered dog limping up the temple steps, crooning low through half-open jaws.

A life . . .

She sat in the dust with the other wretches, a listless row of them in the shade of a temple wall, palms raised to catch rain, infirmities folded beneath tattered cloth or festering in the haze of dust. Indecent with age, threshed of all compassion, she sat begging. She did not look at the passing to and fro of miserly shadows.

One thousand four hundred and twenty-two years before, a Scylvendi marauder had raped a Ceneian woman who had not the courage to take her life as was the tradition. She fled her family, fearing they would kill her to preserve their honour, and bore her child, a son, on the banks of the Great River Sempis. Now a descendant of that son tossed a halved coin exactly when he should, but carelessly, so that the bitten point spun from the outer edge of her thumb, causing her to look out and up . . .

And old woman's paper blink.

Bent knees. The ground rising tidal. Strong hands reaching out for her wrist, drawing it up. Unseen lips against the heat of her palm. The smell of copper and skin.

An ancient look suddenly infantile with wonder.

"My name," she whispered, "is Psatma Nannaferi."

The pulse and fork of blood. A voice so close the speaker could not be seen. The pulse and fork of blood behind this place . . .

"I am the White-Luck . . . I walk. I breathe."

"Yes," she gasped, shaking her wizened head in affirmation. A soul, wrought of iron and cruelty, quivering like a maiden in the flower of her first bleeding. "W-we are siblings, you and I."

Praise be our Mother.

"Siblings . . ."

A trembling hand held out to an unseen cheek. The pads of calloused fingers, touching nothing, spanning out as though across grease or paint. Tears cleansing an old woman's eyes.

Tears for a life forgotten.

"So beautiful."

Tears for what stood in its place.

Momemn . . .

Esmenet was standing before her great silvered mirror when she first glimpsed Kelmomas mooning in the shadowy corners of her dressing room, almost small enough to go unnoticed.

Morning light showered through the unshuttered balcony, so bright it seemed to render her apartments blinking dim beyond the glare it cast across the floor. She appraised her image with the negligent attention of those who spend too much time before mirrors, her thoughts far too occupied with points of strategy to care about her appearance. Maithanet and Phinersa had withdrawn but moments earlier, leaving her with innumerable "suggestions" on how to best disarm, overawe, or even intimidate Hanamem Sharacinth. She was due to meet with the Yatwerian Matriarch within the watch.

She saw his reflection peeking through the silken folds of her hanging gowns, one crimson, the other cerulean blue.

He was a shy, furtive shadow, scarcely more substantial than the fabric hanging about him. She knew instantly that all was not well, but something—habit, or perhaps exhaustion—prevented her from acknowledging him. A pang gripped her throat. Not so long ago it had been a game that both Samarmas and he had played, hiding and seeking through her wardrobe while she was dressed. And now . . .

"Sweetling?" she called. She glimpsed her smile in the mirror: It was so grim that she flushed in shock. Was this how she looked every time she smiled, as though she merely bent her lips?

Kelmomas stared at his toes instead of replying.

She dismissed her body-slaves with a vague flutter of her fingers, turned to look at him directly. Birdsong floated on the cool morning drafts.

"Sweetling . . . Where's Porsi?"

She winced at the question, which she had asked out of habit. Porsi had been scourged and turned out for her negligence. When Kelmomas failed to respond, Esmenet found herself looking back into the mirror, pretending to be preoccupied with the twists of muslin about her waist. Her hands automatically hitched and smoothed, hitched and smoothed.

"I c-can be Sammy . . ."

She heard these words more with her breast it seemed than her ears. A flush of cold about the heart. Even still, she continued to face the mirror.

"What do you mean? Kel, what are saying?"

Our children are so familiar to us that we often forget them, which is why the details of their existence sometimes strike us with discomfiting force. Either because she watched him through the mirror or in spite of it, Esmenet suddenly saw her son as a little stranger, the child of some unknown womb. For a moment, he seemed too beautiful to be . . .

Believed.

"If you don't . . ." Kelmomas began in a pinched voice.

He was twisting the fabric of his tunic against his right hip, causing the hem to ride up his thighs.

At last she turned, sighing as if irritated and feeling instantly ashamed for it. "Sweetling. If I don't *what?*"

His little shoulders jerked in a soundless gasp. He stared down with the fierce concentration that only injured boys seemed able to summon—as though seeing could choke what was seen.

"If you don't w-want me . . . If you don't want . . . Kelmomas, I can be Sam-Sammi."

Heartbreak crashed over her, numbed her to the extremities. In a rush she saw the full compass of her selfishness. Had she even truly mourned for Samarmas, an anguished part of her wondered, or had she simply made him evidence of her own hardship? For whom had she grieved?

She tried to speak, but there was no voice in the sound she made.

Kelmomas warred with his trembling lips. "I l-look . . . look j-just like . . ." He fell to his rump, then slumped into a silken bundle onto the floor. He did not sob, nor did he wail; he keened, a noise every bit as small as his frame and yet animal in its intensity, its honesty.

Abandoning her reflection, Esmenet pressed through cool fabric to kneel over him. Now that she could see her crime, it seemed she had known all along. Trapped in circles of self-pity, pinned by the weight of endless duty and obligation, she had never paused to consider what Kelmomas suffered. As devastated and desolate as she had been the past days, she possessed the same vein of flint that tempered the heart of all mothers, the same hereditary knowledge. Children died. They died all the time, such was the cruelty of the world.

But for Kelmomas. He had lost so much more than a sibling or a playmate. He had lost his days. He had lost *himself*. And he could not comprehend.

I'm all he has left, she thought, stroking his fine, golden hair.

Even still, something dark in her recoiled.

Children. They wept so much.

Save for the long gold-and-white banners depicting the Circumfix, the Imperial Audience Hall on the Andiamine Heights looked much the same as it had during the Ikurei Dynasty. Everything was designed to overawe petitioners and to concentrate the glory and the dignity of those sitting upon the Mantle. The old Nansur Emperors had always aspired to an architectural and decorative opulence at odds with their actual power, perhaps thinking that the illusion, if pursued with enough patience and zeal, could be made manifest.

It was as Kellhus said: Monuments were as much prayers as they were tools, overreaching arrested in dwarfing stone. That the world was littered with their ruins illustrated more than a few uneasy facts regarding the human soul. Men were always inclined to bargain from a position of strength, especially where the Gods were concerned.

Today, Esmenet could not help but reflect, would almost certainly be a case in point.

She had grown quite accustomed to her seat just below the Mantle on the dais, fond of it even. Several paces from her slippered feet, steps descended in broad hemispheric arcs to the Auditory, the main floor where the penitents and courtiers assembled. An arcade of immense pillars soared to either side, diminishing both in perspective and illumination. Ornate tapestries hung motionless between the marble trunks, each a Gift from some province of the New Empire, each featuring the Circumfix as its central motif. Animal totems from Thunyerus. Tigers and twining lotus from Nilnamesh . . .

Everything, it seemed, had been pinned to her position, as though stone and space had faces that could turn, that could lower in obeisance. She was the windless centre, the intangible point of balance.

But it was the missing rear wall that pleased her most, the sense of natural light showering over her shoulders, the knowledge that everyone gathered across the Auditory saw her against the sky-bright firmament. It rendered what could be the most vulnerable position, the place of the effigy, into something too elusive to serve as a convincing target of curses. She loved nothing more than evening audiences, where petitioners often held their hands against the sun to see. It let her act and speak with the impunity of silhouettes.

She even liked the fact that birds continually became fouled in the nearly invisible netting that had been draped over the opening to prevent them from nesting in the vaults. There was something at once sinister and reassuring to the sense of flutter and battle hanging over her periphery. They relieved her, it seemed, of the need to make threats. On any given day, there would only be one or two trapped, their felt-limbed struggles too small and their cries too shrill to bring about any real compassion.

Today there were four.

Sometimes after sunset, she had allowed Samarmas help the slaves set them free. Eyes miracle wide. Hands trembling. His smile was like fear, it was so intense.

The gentle swell of orisons from the upper galleries announced the Matriarch's imminent entrance—one of innumerable hymns to the Aspect-Emperor.

Our souls rise from darkness,
at once near and far.
Our souls fall into darkness,
through gates left ajar.

He comes before,
A candle carried into forever after.
He comes before . . .

Thinking of the twins, Esmenet set her teeth, warred against the pang that threatened to crack her painted face. Kelmomas had been inconsolable, and she had been forced to leave him bawling, begging for her to hold him, promising to become his dead brother for her sake.

"We l-love you, Mom-mommy . . . So-so m-much . . ."

We, he had said, his voice small and forlorn. She could scarce think of the episode without blinking the heat from her eyes. She exhaled slow and deep, doing her best to appear motionless. The great bronze doors swung soundlessly open, and she watched Hanamem Sharacinth, the nominal ruler of the Cult of Yatwer, stride into the abandoned Auditory. The Matriarch was supposed to dress in gunny to signify her poverty, but vertical bands gleamed across her earth-coloured gown with her every step. Maithanet accompanied her, resplendent as always in commodious white and gold.

He comes before,
A candle carried into forever after.
He comes before . . .

The end of the chorus faded into the pitch of ringing stone. The Yatwerian Matriarch stiffly dipped to one knee, then the other. "Your Glory," she said, before pressing her face to her reflection across the marble floor.

Esmenet nodded to demonstrate Imperial Favour. "Rise, Sharacinth. We are all children of the Ur-Mother."

The older woman lifted herself, though not without some effort. "Indeed, your Glory." She looked to Maithanet, as though expecting some kind of assistance, then remembered herself. She was not accustomed, Esmenet realized, to the company of her betters. Esmenet had received many petitioners over the years, long enough to reliably guess the tenor of an audience from the first exchange of words. Sharacinth, she could tell, had made hard habit out of authority, to the point where she could not be trusted to show either grace or deference. Defensiveness hung about the old woman like an odour.

Esmenet cut directly to the point. "What do you know of the White-Luck Warrior?"

"I thought as much," the Matriarch huffed, her eyes narrow with arrogance. Her face was angular and curiously bent, as though it were a thing of clay left too long on one side.

"And why would that be?" Esmenet asked with mock graciousness.

"Who hasn't heard the rumours?"

"The *treason*, you mean."

"The treason, then."

For a moment the outrageousness of her tone quite escaped Esmenet. So often, it seemed, she forgot her exalted station and discoursed with others as though they were her equals. She found herself blinking in indignation. *She hasn't even condoled me for the loss of my son!*

"And what have you heard?"

A calculated pause. Sharacinth's eyes seemed bred to bovine insolence, her lips to a sour line. "That the White-Luck has turned against the Aspect-Emperor . . . Against you."

Esmenet struggled to draw breath around her outrage. Arrogant ingrate! Treacherous old bitch!

Was this what she had imagined all those years ago, sitting on her sill in Sumna, enticing passers-by with a glimpse of the shadows riding up and down her inner thighs? Knowing nothing of power, Esmenet had confused it with its trappings. Ignorance—few things were so invisible. She could remember staring at the coins she had so coveted, those coins that could ward starvation or clothe bruised skin, and wondering at the profile of the man upon them, the Emperor who seemed to stand astride her every bounty and privation. Not hated. Not feared. Not loved. These were passions better spent on his agents. The Emperor himself had always seemed . . . far too far.

In the endless reveries between beddings, she would sort through everything she could remember, all the lore, inchoate and humbling, that a citizen affixes to the subject of their sovereign. And in her soul's eye she would see him, Ikurei Xerius III, sitting *in this very place*.

How could it be possible?

Once, quite on a whim, she had shown Samarmas a silver kellic. "Do you know," she had asked, pointing to the apparition of her own profile across its face, "who that is?" He had a way of opening his mouth when astounded, as though trying to shape his lips about a nail. It was at once comical—and heartbreaking in that it so clearly betrayed his idiocy.

My *son!* she silently cried. Picking wounds had become her path of least resistance, the one effortless thing. But there was no escaping the clamour of her responsibilities, the motions she had to force against the grain of what should be overwhelming grief. She had no choice but to have faith in her painted face.

"But you've heard *more*," she asked in a hard and steady voice—a voice proper to the Empress of the Three Seas. "Haven't you?"

"More. More," Sharacinth muttered. "Of course, I've heard more. When does one not always hear more? Rumours are like locusts or slaves or rats. They breed indiscriminately."

They had known she was a prideful woman. It was the whole reason for summoning the bitch here: Maithanet had hoped the dimensions and reputation of her surroundings would be enough to mellow her hubris into something more malleable, something they could shape to their own purposes.

Apparently not.

"Matriarch, you would do well to recollect the stakes of our conversation."

A sneer—an open sneer! And for the first time, Esmenet glimpsed it, the look that is the terror of all those who command positions of power: the look that says, *You are temporary, no more a passing affliction.* Suddenly she understood the staged calculation behind her throne and its position above the auditory floor. With one look, it seemed, the old woman had thrown it all into stark relief: the truth behind the hierarchy of disparate souls. *Recognition*, Esmenet realized. Power came down to recognition.

It was all naked force otherwise.

"*Matriarch!*" Maithanet boomed, drawing into his voice and aspect all the magisterial authority of the Thousand Temples.

Sharacinth opened her mouth in retort—not even the Shriah could cow her, it seemed. But whatever breath she possessed was sucked from her lungs . . .

Instead she wheezed and stumbled back, raised a hand against the sudden, immolating light that had sparked into existence above the floor before her. It danced and spiked outward, so brilliant it rendered everything dim. Crazed shadows swung from her ankles across the far corners of the Auditory. The point grew and sparkled, chattered with incandescences that possessed intensities beyond the gaze's conception . . .

Esmenet lowered her forearm, blinked at scalded eyes.

There he stood, tall, magnificent and otherworldly, exactly as she remembered him. A white silk tunic fell loose over his armour, embroidered in countless crimson tusks, each the length of a thorn. His beard was braided gold, his mane was long and free-flowing. The two demon heads hung bound to his right hip, mouthing curses without breath . . . There was a mad density to his aspect, a hoarding of reality that denied the world the sharpness of its edges and the substance of its weight.

It seemed the earth should groan beneath his feet. Her husband . . .

The Aspect-Emperor.

Sharacinth stood like a shipwreck survivor leaning to the memory of tossed seas. Two paces behind her and to the right, Maithanet lay supine across the shining floor. The Shriah of the Thousand Temples *kneeling*.

Esmenet knew enough not to watch Kellhus assume the Mantle to her right. Confidence, which in all complicated situations is nothing more than the pretence of premeditation, is ever the outward marker of power. There could be no appearance of improvisation.

"Hanamem Sharacinth," he said, his voice at once mild and permeated with the tones of imminent murder, "do you think you merit standing in my presence?"

The Matriach nearly fell over trying to throw herself to the floor. "N-no!" she sobbed in old woman terror. "M-Most Glorious . . . Pluh-please—"

"Will you," he interrupted, "take steps to assure that this sedition against me, this *blasphemy*, comes to an end?"

"Y-yesssh!" she wailed to the floor. She even hooked her fingers behind her head.

"For, make no mistake, *I shall war* against you and yours." The grinding savagery of his voice swallowed the entirety of the hall, battered the ear like fists. "Your deeds I shall strike from the stones. Your temples I shall turn into funeral pyres. And those that still dare take up breath or arms against me, I shall hunt, unto death and beyond! And my Sister, whom you worship, shall lament in the dark, her memory no more than a dream of destruction. Men shall spit to cleanse their mouths of her name!"

The old woman shook, arched her back as if gagging in terror.

"Do you understand what I say, Sharacinth?"

"Yessssh!"

"Then this is what you shall do. You shall heed your Empress and your Shriah. You shall put an end to the ignoble sham that is your office. You shall make claim to the truth of your station. You shall make war upon the wickedness within your own temple—you shall cleanse the filth from your own altar!"

Somewhere beyond the vaulted ceiling, a cloud engulfed the sun, and everything dimmed save the old woman writhing upon her reflection. Kellhus leaned forward, and it seemed all the world leaned with him, that the pillars themselves tilted, hanging above the Matriach, shivering in catastrophic outrage.

"And you shall hunt this witch you call your mistress, Psatma Nannaferi! You shall put an end to the sacrilege that is your Mother-Supreme!"

Her face averted, her elbows to the floor, she shook two white-palmed hands out in warding.

"No-noooo! Pluh-pluh-pleeeeese—"

"SHARACINTH!" The name crashed through the Hall, boomed through its arched recesses. "WOULD YOU OFFEND ME IN MY OWN HOUSE?"

The Matriarch shrieked something inarticulate. A puddle of urine spread about her knees.

Then, as though exhaling a pent breath, the world resumed its natural lines and proportions. The unseen cloud passed from the unseen sun, and indirect light once again showered blue upon the dais.

"Taste your breath," Kellhus said as he stood. He stepped out to loom patient and fatherly over the woman blinking up at him from the base of the steps. "*Taste it*, Sharacinth, for it is the mark of my mercy. Fight the inclination of your heart, conquer your weakness for pride, for spite. Do not make humiliation of truth. I know you can feel it, the promise of release, the bone-shuddering release. Turn from the shrill poison of your conceit, from the hooked fists and knuckled teeth, from the rod of cold iron that holds you rigid when you should sleep. Turn from these things and embrace the truth of the life—the *life!*—that I offer you."

Esmenet had heard these words so many times they should have seemed more a recitation than something *meant*, an incantation that never failed to undo the knots of pride that so bound men. And yet each time, she found herself sinking through the surface, floating utterly submerged. Each time, she heard them *for the first time*, and she was frightened and renewed.

Over the years, her husband had ceased being many things to Esmenet. But he was a miracle still.

The Matriarch of the Cult of Yatwer wept as a child might, snuffling and mumbling, "F-f-forgive . . . F-f-forgive meeeee . . ." Over and over.

"Comfort her," Kellhus said to his half-brother. Nodding in obeisance, Maithanet stood and crouched at the wailing woman's side.

Smiling, the Aspect-Emperor turned to Esmenet and reached out his hand. He spoke the sun-fiery words. She clutched two of his outstretched fingers, fell into his pulsing embrace. She felt the open spaces about them collapsing, dropping in sheets of ethereal fabric, falling away.

His light consumed her . . .

. . . and they were alone together, in the cool gloom of their private apartments. His legs crumpled, and he leaned and lurched against her. Grunting, Esmenet helped him stagger to their bed.

"Wife . . ." was all he said, rolling onto his back even though he still wore his sword, Certainty, sheathed across his shoulder blades. He raised a heavy hand to his forehead.

More air than light filtered in from the seaward balconies. The rooms were broad and surprisingly low-ceilinged, articulated by a series of steps that divided the bedroom proper from the lower regions. The furnishings were elegant and, with the exception of the crimson-cushioned bed, spare. She often wondered if her antipathy to ornament was more a result of the maddening complexities of her new life or a pining for the simple squalour of her old.

"How many?" she asked, knowing that he could only translocate the space of a horizon, and only then to places he had long studied from a distance or to places he had actually been. He had literally travelled all the way from the Istyuli Plains horizon by horizon.

"Many."

She found herself looking away, blinking. The profile of various cities frescoed the walls, creating the pale illusion that the room occupied some impossible space over Invishi, Nenciphon, Carythusal, Aöknyssus, and Oswenta. Esmenet had commissioned them several years previous—as a physical reminder of her position in political space. It was a decision she had long since regretted.

Simple, her soul whispered. *I must make things simple.*

"You came . . ." she began, shocked to find she was already crying. "You came as s-soon as you heard?" She knew this could not be true. Each and every night Mandate Far-Callers spoke with him in his dreams, apprised him of all that happened on the Andiamine Heights and elsewhere. He had come because of the situation with the Yatwerians, because of Sharacinth. Not because of his idiot son.

There were no accidents with Anasûrimbor Kellhus.

He sat up on the edge of the bed, and somehow she found herself in his arms, immersed in his wide-world husband smell, wracked with sobs.

"We've been cursed!" she gasped. "Cursed!"

Kellhus gently pressed her back into his gaze and somehow above the surface of her immediate grief. She found herself drawing cool and soothing air.

"Misfortune," he said. "Nothing more, Esmi."

When had his voice become a drug?

"But isn't that what the White-Luck means? Mimara has fled, and no one can find her, Kellhus! I have this-this terrible feeling—such a terrible feeling! And now Samarmas! Sweet-sweet Samarmas! Do you know what they're saying in the streets? Do you know that some of them actually celebrate! That—"

"You must take no action against them," he said with stern compassion—the perfect tone. He always spoke in the perfect tone, words like cool plaster trowelled across the cracks of desire and confusion. "Not the Yatwerians. They are not a people that we can massacre or uproot like the Mongilean Kianene. They are too widespread, too diffuse. The Great Ordeal is all that matters, Esmi. It has taken us too long as it stands. Golgotterath must be overcome before the No-God is resurrected. The immediate ever clouds the far, and desire ever twists reason to its own ends. I know these concerns seem to blot out all other considerations—"

"Seem? *Seem*? Kellhus! Kellhus! Our *son is dead!*"

Her voice pealed raw across the polished stone hollows.

Silence. Where for others the lack of response augured wounds scored or truths too burdensome to ignore or dismiss, for her husband it meant something altogether different. His silence was always one with the world about it, monolithic in the way of framing things. Without exception it said, *Hear the words you have spoken*. You. It was never, ever, the mark of error or incapacity.

Which was why, perhaps, she found him so easy to worship and so difficult to love.

Then he uttered her name, "Esmi . . ."

"Esmi," spoken in a voice so warm, so laced with compassion, that she found herself once again crying freely. He kissed her scalp and hair, a divine monster. "Shhhh . . . I'm not asking you to take comfort in abstractions, for there is none. Even still, the Great Ordeal remains the end that maps all others. We cannot allow anything, *anyone*, to take precedence over it. Not riots. Not the collapse of the New Empire . . ." It was as if she stared into her own eyes, his look was so canny—save that he knew her so much better than she knew herself.

"Not even the death of our son."

She had understood this all along. His tone had told her so.

A breeze bellied the dust-violet sheers, drawing them over the hard line of the Meneanor Sea. A finger of light flickered across the mural of Carythusal.

"How much misfortune must there be?" she heard herself crying.

The White-Luck hunt us . . . Hunts us . . .

"All of the woe the world has to offer, if need be. So long as we overcome the only one that is fatal."

The Second Apocalypse.

She was beating his chest softly, pressing her forehead into the jasmine-scented silk. She could feel the reptilian imprint of the nimil-mail beneath. Looking up through tears, he seemed a towering glow and shadow both. "But it's *you* they hunt! What? Do the Gods *want* a Second Apocalypse? Do they want the world shut against them?"

She had chosen Kellhus over Achamian. Kellhus! She had chosen her womb. She had chosen power and sumptuous ease. She had chosen to lay her hand upon the arm of a living god . . . Not this! Not this!

"Come, Esmi. I know Maithanet has explained this to you."

"B-but it seems . . . it s-s-seems . . ."

"Most live on the edge of heartbeats, trusting their betters and the blind eyes of habit to see them further. A rare few can apprehend the span of entire lives. But you and I do not possess either luxury, Esmi. We must act according to the dictates of the ages, or there will be no ages for anyone to live. And this makes us appear cold, merciless, even monstrous, not only to others and ourselves, but to the Hundred as well. *We walk the Shortest Path*, the labyrinth of the Thousandfold Thought. This is the burden the God has laid upon us, and the burden that the Gods begrudge."

She found herself on the surface of his voice, for once hearing it with a musician's cold ear: the tunnelling harmonics, the resonance that forced it into unheard immediacy, the papery rasp that raised it outside the circle of the world.

The voice that had conquered the First Holy War, then all the Three Seas. The voice of the King of Kings, the mortal echo of the God of Gods . . . The voice that had conquered first her thighs and then her heart.

She thought of that final afternoon with Achamian, the day that Holy Shimeh fell.

"I haven't the strength! I ca-can't b-bear losing any-any-m-more . . ."

"You *have* the strength."

"Let Maithanet rule! He's your brother. He shares your gifts. He should rule . . ."

"He is Shriah. He cannot be more."

"But why? Why?"

"Esmi, you have my love, my trust. I know that you have the strength to do this."

A gust from over the dark sea. The violet sheers roiled and billowed, parted like gossamer lips.

"The White-Luck," he whispered in a voice that was the sky, the curve of all horizons, "shall break against you."

She gazed up at his face through sting and tears, and it seemed that in it she could see *every* face, the mien of all those who had bent upon her in Sumna, when she had kept a whore's bed.

"How? How can you know?"

"Because the anguish that makes mud of all your thoughts, because the fear that stains your days, because all your regret and anger and loneliness . . ." A haloed hand cupped her cheek. Blue eyes sounded her to the bottommost fathoms.

"All this makes you pure."

Iothiah . . .

"Cursed!" Nannaferi cried. "Cursed be he who misleads the blind man on the road!"

All old voices failed in some manner; they cracked or they quavered, or they dwindled with the loss of the wind that once empowered them. But for Psatma Nannaferi, the breaking of her voice, which had once made her family weep for its melodic purity, seemed to reveal more than it marred, as though it were but paint, hoary and moulted, covering something furious and elemental. It struck over the surrounding clamour, reached deep into the packed recesses of the Catacombs.

Hundreds had gathered, filling the Charnal Hall with sweat and exertion, crowding the adjacent tunnels, stamping the detritus across the floors. Torches bobbed like buoys at sea, casting ovals of illumination across the bowed ceilings, revealing pockets of expression in the shadowy masses: smiles and howls, mouths fixed about wonder—disbelieving wonder. Smoke pooled in the dark gaps between the lintels. Fingers of light probed the niche-pocked walls and the innumerable urns packed within, cracked and leaning, limned in ages of dust.

"Cursed be the thief!" Nannaferi shrieked. "For he who dines on the fortune of others is a bringer of famine!"

She stood naked before them, wearing her skin like a beggar's rags. White-painted sigils sheathed her arms to the pit and her legs to the crotch, but her torso and genitals gleamed, adorned only in sweat. She stood withered and diminutive before them, and yet she towered, so that it seemed that her blood-soaked hair should brush the low ceilings.

And *he* sat before her, naked and immobile on a beaten chair. A slave's chair.

The White-Luck Warrior.

"Cursed be the homicide, the *murderer*, he who lies in wait to slay his brother!"

She parted her hairless legs, paused so that all could see slick lines of blood running from her shining pudenda. And she grinned a proud and vicious grin, as though to say, *Yes!*

Witness the strength that is my womb! The Great Giver, the Son Bearer, the gluttonous Phallus Eater!

Yes! The Blood of my Fertility flows still!

The ecstatics immediately before her wept at the miracle, stared with the eyes of the strangled, tore their hair and gnashed their teeth. And their rapture became grounds for the rapture of the cohort behind them, and so on, through tunnel after forking tunnel, until a thousand voices roared through the closeted deeps.

"Cursed be *whore*!" she cried, not needing to read the text, the *Sinyatwa*, on the scuffed stone at her feet. "Cursed be she who lies with men for gold over seed, for power over obedience, for lust over love!"

She bent as though to abuse herself. With the blade of her right palm, she scraped a line of blood, drawing it up to the creases of her swollen sex. She huffed in pleasure, then raised her bloody palm for all to see.

"Cursed be the false—the deceivers of men! *Cursed be the Aspect-Emperor!*"

There are pitches of passion that are holy simply for the intensity of their expression. There is worship beyond the eaged world of words. Psatma Nannaferi's hatred had long ago burned away the impurities, the pathetic pageant of rancour and resentment that so often make fools of the great. Hers was the grinding hatred, the homicidal outrage of the betrayed, the unwavering fury of the degraded and the dispossessed. The hatred that draws tendons sharp, that cleanses only the way murder and fire can cleanse.

And at long last she had found her knife.

She stepped over the scriptures, pressed the slack pouches of her breasts against the sweat of his neck and shoulders. She reached around him with her arms. Holding her right palm like a palette, she dipped the third finger of her left hand into her issue, then marked him: a horizontal line along each of his cheeks.

They gleamed menstrual crimson. Wurrami, the ancient counterpart of the thraxami, the lines of ash used by mourning mothers.

"Ever!" she cried. "Ever have we dwelt in the shadow of the Whip and Club. Ever have we been despised—we, *the Givers!* We, *the weak!* But the Goddess knows! Knows why they beat us, why they leash us, why they starve and violate us! Why they do everything save kill!"

She prowled around him, raised her buttocks across his hips. With a shrill cry, she thrust down, encompassed him to his grunting foundation. A broken chorus of cries passed through the congregation, as the penetration was multiplied in heart and eye.

"Because without Givers," she shouted in a voice hoarse for passion—doubly broken, "there is nothing for them to take! Because without slaves, there can be no masters! Because we are the wine that they imbibe, the bread that they eat, the cloth that they soil, the walls that they defend! Because we are the truth of their power! The prize they would conquer!"

And she could feel it: he the centre of her, and she the circumference of him—an ache encircled by fire. Hoe and Earth! Hoe and Earth! She was an old crone splayed across a boy, her eyes the red of blood, his the white of seed. The crowd before them bucked and heaved, a cauldron of avid faces and sweat-slicked limbs.

"We shall stoke!" she moaned and roared. "We shall foment! We shall teach those who give what it means to take!"

And she slid, drawing her loose buttocks across the plate of his abdomen. His was the body of a man newly wed—a father of but one child. Slender, golden for the perfection of its skin. Not yet bent to the harshness of the world, to the toil that all giving exacts.

Not yet strong.

"There is the knife that cuts," she croaked, "and there is the sea that drowns. Always we have been the latter. But now!

Now that the White-Luck has come to us, we are *both*, my Sisters! On our seas they shall founder! And on our knife they shall fall!"

She rode the hook of him harder and harder, until he convulsed and screamed. The earth shook—the unborn kicking at the Mother's womb. Gravel streamed from the ceilings. And she could feel the hot flood him, the outward thrust. And then, with his slumping, a kind of inward breath—and it was her turn to jerk rigid and scream. She could feel her strength fill him, the knitting of muscle across his frame, the scarring, the *aging strong* of a body wracked by years in the world. The soft hands that clawed her chest became horned with calluses, thick with throttling strength, even as her scrotal breasts rounded, lifted in the memory of a more tender youth. The smooth cheek against her neck became leathery with unlived seasons, gravelly with the memory of another's pox.

And as youth washed through her, drawing a thousand thousand wrinkles into smooth swales of skin, the mad faces encircling her surged forward, clutching at the sodden floor beneath their feet . . .

Beaten and battered she had been tipped in libation. And now the dread Goddess raised her, a bowl cast of gold.

A vessel. A grail. A cup filled with the Waters-Most-Holy. The Blood and the Seed.

"Cursed!" she shrieked in a singer's heart-cutting voice, high and pure, yet warmed by the memory of her authoritarian rasp. She watched as the Blood of her Fertility was passed among the throngs, a never-diminishing pool that was passed from palm to palm. She watched the Ur-Mother's children mark their cheeks with the red line of hatred . . .

"Cursed be he who misleads the blind man on the road!"

Chapter Ten

Condia

Look unto others and ponder the sin and folly you find there. For their sin is your sin, and their folly is your folly. Seek ye the true reflecting pool? Look to the stranger you despise, not the friend you love.

—TRIBES 6:42, *THE CHRONICLE OF THE TUSK*

Early Spring, 19 New Imperial Year (4132 Year-of-the-Tusk), Condia

The Istyuli Plains dominated the heart of Eärwa, running from the northern back of the Hethantas to the southern spurs of the Yimaleti. It seemed hard to believe that this region had birthed dynasties and toppled empires before the First Apocalypse and the coming of the Sranc, consisting as it did of nothing more than endless sheaves of arid grassland.

In the days of Far Antiquity, a schism opened between the western Norsirai tribes, the High Norsirai, who under the tutelage of the Nonmen raised the first great literate civilization of Men along the banks of the River Aumris, and their eastern kin, the White Norsirai, who clung to the nomadic ways of their ancient fathers. For an entire age the Istyuli formed the barbaric hinterland of the High

Norsirai nations that rose and fell about the great river cities of the west: Trysë, Sauglish, Umerau, and others. The tribes of White Norsirai who roamed and warred across the plains sometimes raided, sometimes bartered with, and continually despised their earth-tilling cousins to the west. The fewer the roads the harsher the codes, as the ancient Kûniüric proverb had it. And periodically, when united beneath the tyranny of some powerful tribe or personality, they invaded and conquered.

To the north of Sakarpus, the Istyuli Plains still bore the name of one of those conquering peoples, the Cond.

Nothing remained to mark their passing: The Cond, like most pastoral peoples, were primarily remembered for works destroyed rather than works raised. For the Men of the Ordeal, only the name connected the sloped terrain to the legends of their long-dead glory. They were accustomed to the rumour of lost peoples and nations, for their own lands had stacked them deep. But there was a melancholy attached to their thoughts of the Cond. Where the far antique peoples of the Three Seas had been replaced by other peoples, the end of the wild-haired horsemen of the Cond had been the end of Men on these plains. Proof of this lay in those signs of habitation the Inrithi did find: great heaps of bone sucked to the marrow, and swaths of turf overturned not by plows, but by claws hungry for grubs.

Signs of Sranc.

A kind of communal recognition dawned on the host, a realization that abandoned lands could be liberated. To demonstrate this fact, King Hoga Hogrim—the nephew of Hoga Gothyelk, the famed Martyr of Shimeh—commanded his Tydonni to draw stone from a nearby outcropping for a great ring, an immense Circumfix implanted for all time in Condian earth. The Longbeards laboured through the night, their numbers swelling as more and more of their encamped neighbours joined them. The break of dawn revealed not so much a ring as a circular fortress, as wide as five war-galleys set end to end and with walls of unshaped sand-stone standing the height of three men.

Afterwards, the Aspect-Emperor himself walked among the exhausted men, remitting their sins and blessing their distant kith and kin. "Men make such marks," he said, "as their will affords them. Behold! Let the World see why the Tydonni are called the 'Sons of Iron.'"

And so the march wore on. According to conventional military wisdom, a host as vast as the Ordeal should break up and march in separate columns. Not only would this improve the ability of the soldiery to collect forage, be it wild game or the grasses their hardy ponies were bred to survive on, it would drastically increase their rate of advance. But as strange as it sounded, the sloth of the Great Ordeal was a necessity, at least at this stage in the long march to Golgotterath. The plan was to stretch the supply umbilicus between the host and Sakarpus as far as humanly possible, before taking what the Aspect-Emperor's generals grimly referred to as the Leap, marching beyond the point of meaningful contact with the New Empire.

Since the length of this umbilicus depended on the ability of the Imperial supply trains to overtake the Great Ordeal, dividing the host into quicker columns would simply increase the length of the Leap. This would prove disastrous, given the needs of the host and the scarcity of meaningful forage along the length of the Istyuli. Even if the Ordeal were to break into a hundred columns and spread across the width of the plain, it could not be trusted to provide enough game to make an appreciable difference. The host had to carry the supplies required to reach the more abundant lands of what had once been eastern Kûniüri, where, according to the Imperial Trackers, it could easily find enough forage once it scattered.

So it crept forward as all cumbersome armies must, scarcely

travelling more than ten to fifteen miles a march. Aside from numbers, the rivers were the greatest source of delay. Again thanks to the Imperial Trackers, each waterway had been meticulously mapped years in advance. Not only did the Great Ordeal's planners need to know where the best crossing points were, they had to know the state of those fords at various times of the year and during various kinds of weather. A single swollen river could spell doom if it prevented the Great Ordeal from reaching Golgotterath before the onset of winter.

But even mapped, the fords still represented bottlenecks. In some cases, three, even four days were required simply for the host to cross banks no more than a stone's throw apart. These too were scheduled into the sacred host's ever-tightening margins.

In the highest councils of the Aspect-Emperor, the possibility that the Consult might find some way to poison these rivers was a matter of continual concern, if not outright dread. Only the possibility that they might exterminate game along their path troubled them more. As veterans of the First Holy War, both of the Ordeal's Exalt-Generals, King Saubon and King Proyas, were intimately acquainted with the catastrophic consequences of running out of water. Thirst, like hunger or disease, was a vulnerability that increased in proportion to an army's size, which was why it could unravel even the greatest host in a mere matter of days.

But among the rank and file, the absence of Sranc was the only concern voiced about the evening fires, not because they suspected anything devious—what trick could catch their Holy Aspect-Emperor unawares?—but because they longed to put their spears and swords and axes to work. Rumours were traded about the far-ranging exploits of Sibawul te Nurwal, whose Cepaloran lancers had apparently run down several fleeing Sranc clans. Similar tales were told about General Halas Siroyon and his Famiri, or General

Inrilil ab Cinganjehoi and his steel-clad Eumarnan knights. But the tales only seemed to whet their bloodlust and to draw out the trackless tedium of the march. They complained the way warriors complained, about the food, the lack of women, the pitch of the ground they slept across, but they never forgot their sacred mission. They marched to *save the world*, which for most meant saving their wives, their children, their parents, and their lands. They marched to prevent the Second Apocalypse.

And *the God himself* marched with them, speaking through the mouth, glaring through the eyes of Anasûrimbor Kellhus I.

They were plain men—warriors. They understood that doubt was hesitation, and that hesitation was death, not only on the field of war, but on the field of souls as well. Only believers persevered.

Only believers conquered.

What was Sakarpus compared to this? And who was he, but the son of another Beggar King?

These were the questions that Sorweel could not but ask whenever he looked to the shield line of the horizon. Men. Wherever he turned his gaze, he saw more and more armed and armoured Men.

The Great Ordeal.

For Sorweel, it existed in series of circles, each radiating outward, from his squad in the Company of Scions to the very limit of the world. In his immediate vicinity, all was the close tedium of riders on the march, defined more by sound and smell than sight: the must of fresh dung, the equine snorts and complaints, the swishing percussion of endless hooves through grass, the rattle of the small almost chariotlike carts that each of the doughty little horses pulled. A glimpse was all it took to surpass this mundane circle:

Striding legs became scissoring forests, men rocking in their high-backed saddles became slow-filing fields of thousands. And beyond this, individuals vanished into many-coloured masses, their armour winking in the high-sky sun. The shouts and calls and laughter dissolved into a white ambient roar. Mobs congealed into ponderous columns strung with vast trains of mules and teetering ox-carts.

The host did not so much cross the greening pastures as they *encompassed* them, a slow flood of warlike humanity. Everything and everyone became a link in a far greater articulation. Only the high-jutting banners retained their singularity: the signs of tribes and nations, each married in some fashion to the Circumfix. And farther, moving beneath the silence that was the sky, even the banners became abstract, hooked threads on the carpet that had become a darker earth. The *very ground seemed to move*, out to the vanishing line of the plains.

The Great Ordeal. A thing so great that not even the horizon could contain it. And for a boy on the cusp of manhood, a thing that humiliated far more than it humbled.

What honour could dwell in a soul so small?

Officially, the Company of Scions was touted as one of the most elite units in the Kidruhil, but unofficially, it was known to be largely ceremonial. The power of the Aspect-Emperor or more importantly, the *rumour* of his power, was such that many rulers beyond his sway sent their own sons to him as means to guarantee their treaties with the New Empire. They were observers, perhaps even prisoners, but they certainly were not warriors—let alone Men of the Ordeal.

For Sorweel, this was a source of many contradictory passions. His blood ran hot at the prospect of battle—how long had he pestered his father for an opportunity to ride to war? But at the same time, the dishonour—if not the treachery—of riding beneath his enemy's banners alternately gouged his belly with horror and squeezed his heart with abject shame. He even caught himself *taking pride*, in his uniform from time to time: the fine tooling of the leather-stripped skirts, the soft castor of the gloves, the interlocking motifs stamped into the cuirass, even the white cloak of his caste-nobility.

For as long as he could remember, Sorweel had always thought betrayal a kind of *thing*. And as a thing, he assumed, it was what it was, like anything else. Either a man kept faith with his blood and nation, or he didn't. But betrayal, he was learning, was far too complicated to be a mere thing. It was more like a disease . . . or a man.

It was too insidious not to have a soul.

It *crept*, for one thing, not like a snake or a spider, but like spilled wine, seeping into the fractures, soaking everything its own colour. Each betrayal, no matter how trivial, seemed to beget further betrayals. And it *deceived* as well, postured as nothing less than *sense* itself, as reason. "Play along," it told him. "Pretend to be one of their Kidruhil—yes, *pretend*." Wise counsel, or so it seemed. It failed to warn you of the peril, of how each day playing leached your soul of resolution. It said nothing of the slow collapse of pretending into *being*.

He tried to remain vigilant, and in the deep of night, he clung to his recriminations. But it was so hard, so hard to remember the taste of *certainty*.

The Scions were scarcely a hundred strong, far and away the smallest of the Kidruhil's three-hundred-odd companies. They rode with the strange sense of being a sliver in a great fist, an intrusion that inflamed and irritated. Kidruhil troopers were selected according to their skill and their ardour. If anything made the Scions anathema to their fellow Kidruhil, it was their *lack of faith*. Though the officers were always careful to observe the semblance of diplomatic decorum, their men understood, enough to allow a general contempt—and in some cases even outright hatred—to shine through.

But if the Scions were an outcast within the Kidruhil, then Sorweel was even more an outcast within the Scions. Of course everyone knew who he was. How could any Son of Sakarpus not be the talk of the Company, let alone the son of its slain king? Whether it was pity or derision, Sorweel saw in their looks the true measure of his shame. And at night, when he lay desolate in his tent listening to the fireside banter of the others, he was certain he could understand the questions that kept returning to their strange tongues. Who was this boy who rode for those who murdered his father? This Shit-herder, what kind of craven fool was he?

At the end of his sixth day, as he stood so that Porsparian could remove his gear, a black-skinned man with an ashen pallor pressed his face through the flap and begged permission to enter.

"Your Glory . . . I am Obotegwa, Senior Obligate of Zsoronga ut Nganka'kull, Successor-Prince of High Holy Zeüm." He fell to his knees as he said this, making three waving flourishes with each of his hands and lowering his chin to his chest. He was dressed in the finest silks, a padded yellow jacket stencilled with thin black floral motifs. His ebony skin, which was a shock to Sorweel—until the coming of the Great Ordeal, he had never seen any Satyothi—shone in the day's failing light. His receding white hair and high-climbing beard had been trimmed close to the apple-round contours of his skull. There seemed to be a sturdy honesty both to his bearing and his voice, which possessed a raspy earthiness despite its high tone.

As the son of an isolate nation, Sorweel had little grasp of etiquette between nations. Even his own father had seemed at a loss as to how to deal with the Aspect-Emperor's first fateful emissaries. Sorweel found himself flustered by the man's elaborate display, as well as bewildered by his command of the Sakarpic tongue. So he did what all young men did in such circumstances: he blurted.

"What do you want?"

The Obligate raised his face, displayed a grandfather's wise smile. "My Lord Master requests the pleasure of your company at his fire, your Glory."

The young King accepted the invitation, his cheeks burning.

All Sorweel knew of black men was that they hailed from Zeüm, an ancient and great nation in the distant west. And all he knew of Zeüm was that its people were black. He had noted Zsoronga earlier, both during assembly and exercises. The man was difficult to miss, even among the large retinue of black-skinned companions and servants that rode with him. Men born to authority, Sorweel had noticed, often stood apart from others, not merely in appearance, but in demeanour and comportment as well. Some positively swaggered with prominence—or self-importance as the case might be. Though Zsoronga communicated his station with a similar intensity, he did so without any overt gestures whatsoever. You simply looked at his party and *knew* that he was the first among them, as though consciousness of rank possessed a kind of visual odour.

Obotegwa waited outside while Porsparian finished ministering to the young King. The old Shigeki slave muttered under his breath the whole time, periodically fixed him with a yellow-eyed glare. Words or no words, Sorweel would have asked him what was amiss, but too many worries plagued his thoughts. What could this Zsoronga want? Amusement for his cohort? A lesson for his fellows, a living example of how base the blood of nobles could be?

He watched his enigmatic slave scowl over his uniform, swallowed against a sudden, almost maniacal urge to scream. Never. Never in his life had he suffered such consistent uncertainty. It plagued him, like some bone-deep fever of the soul. Everywhere he turned he found himself faced with the unfamiliar, whether it be wondrous, blasphemous, or merely novel. He knew not what was expected of him, by others, by honour, by his Gods . . .

And perhaps even more debilitating, he knew not what to expect of himself.

Certainly something better than this. How could he have been born with such a despicable heart, hesitating like an old man whose life had outrun his trust in his heart and frame? How could Harweel, strong Harweel, *wise* Harweel, have given birth to such a craven fool as he? To a boy who would weep in the arms of his murderer!

"I am no conqueror."

Worry piled upon recrimination. And then, miraculously, he found himself stepping through the canvas flaps into the bustle of the camp. He stood blinking at the streaming files of passers-by.

Obotegwa turned to him with a look of faint surprise. After leaning back to appraise the cut of his padded Sakarpic tunic, he beamed reassurance. "Sometimes it is not so easy," he said in his remarkable accent, "to be a son."

So many sights. So many kinds of Men.

The encampment was in a state of uproar as its countless denizens hastened to take advantage of the remaining daylight. The sun leaned low on Sorweel's left, spoked the sky with arid brilliance. The Great Ordeal thronged beneath it, a veritable ocean of tents, pavilions, and packed thoroughfares, sweeping out across the bowl of the valley. The smoke of countless cooking fires steamed the air. Zaudunyani prayer calls keened over the roar, high feminine voices, filled with sorrow and exaltation. The Standard of the Scions—a horse rearing through a tipped crown on Kidruhil red—lay dead in the motionless air, yet somehow the ubiquitous Circumfix banners seemed to wave as if in some higher breeze.

"Indeed," Obotegwa said from his side, "it is a thing of wonder, your Glory."

"But is it *real*?"

The old man laughed, a brief husky wheeze. "My master will like you, I am sure."

Sorweel continued stealing gazes across the encampment as he followed the Zeümi Obligate's lead. He even stared at the southern horizon for several heartbeats, across miles of trampled earth, even though he knew Sakarpus had receded out of all vision. They had passed beyond the Pale into the Wilds where only Sranc roamed.

"My folk never dared ride this far from our city," he said to Obotegwa's back.

The old man paused to look apologetically into his face. "You must forgive my impertinence, your Glory, but it is forbidden for me to speak to you in any voice save my Master's."

"And yet you spoke earlier."

A gentle smile. "Because I know what it means to be thrown over the edge of the world."

Sorweel brooded over these words as they resumed walking, realizing they inadvertently explained what had pained his eyes when he looked southward. The Lonely City *had become an edge*. It had been more than conquered, its solitude had been consumed. Once an island in wicked seas, it was now a mere outpost, the terminus of something far greater, a civilization—just like the times of the Long Dead.

More than his father had been killed, he realized. His father's *world* had died with him.

He blinked at the heat in his eyes, saw the Aspect-Emperor leaning over him, blond and luminous, a sunlit man in the heart of night. "*I am no conqueror . . .*"

These proved long thoughts for the short walk to Prince

Zsoronga's pavilion. He found himself within the small Zeümi enclave before he was even aware of approaching it. The Prince's pavilion was an elaborate, high-poled affair, roofed and sided in weathered black-and-crimson leather, and chased with frayed tassels that may have once been golden but were now as pale as urine. A dozen or so smaller tents reached out to either side, completing the enclosure. Several Zeümi milled about the three firepits, staring with a directness that was neither rude nor welcoming. Anxious, Sorweel found himself considering the tall wooden post raised in the enclosure's heart. Satyothi faces, stylized with broad noses and sensual lips, had been carved one atop another along its entire length, stacks of them staring off in various directions. This was their Pillar of Sires, he would later learn, the relic to which the Zeümi prayed the same as Sakarpi prayed to idols.

Obotegwa led him directly into an antechamber at the fore of the pavilion, where he bid Sorweel to remove his boots. This proved to be the only ceremony.

They found Prince Zsoronga reclined across a settee in the airy depths of the central chamber. Light filtered down through a number of open slots in the ceiling, blue shafts that sharpened the contrast between the illumined centre of the chamber and the murky spaces beyond. Obotegwa bowed as he had earlier, uttering what Sorweel imagined was some kind of announcement. The handsome young man sat up smiling, set down a codex bound in gold wire. He gestured to a neighbouring settee with a long arm.

"*Yus ghom*," he began, "*hurmbana thut omom* . . ."

Obotegwa's voice rasped into the thread of his with practised ease, so much so it almost seemed Sorweel could understand the Prince directly.

"Appreciate these luxuries. The ancestors know how hard I had to fight for them! Our glorious host does not believe the rewards of rank have any place on the march."

Stammering his thanks, self-conscious of his pale white feet, Sorweel sat erect on the settee's edge.

The Successor-Prince frowned at his rigid posture, made a waving gesture with the back of his hand. "*Uwal mebal! Uwal!*" he urged, throwing himself back and wriggling into the soft cushions.

"Lean back," Obotegwa translated.

"*Aaaaaaaah!*" the Prince gasped in mock joy.

Smiling, Sorweel did as he was told, felt the cool fabric yield about his shoulders and neck.

"*Aaaaaaaah!*" Zsoronga repeated, his bright eyes laughing.

"*Aaaaaaaaah!*" Sorweel gasped in turn, surprised at the relief that soaked through his body simply for saying it.

"*Aaaaaaaaah!*"

"*Aaaaaaaaah!*"

Wriggling, they both roared with laughter.

After serving them wine, Obotegwa hovered with the thoughtless discretion of a grandparent, effortlessly interpreting back and forth. Zsoronga wore a silk banyan, simple in cut yet lavish with black stencilled motifs: silhouetted birds whose plumage became branches for identical birds. He also wore a gold-fretted wig that made him positively leonine with silk-black hair—as Sorweel would discover, the kinds of wigs Zeümi caste-nobles wore in leisure were strictly governed by rules of rank and accomplishment, to the point of almost forming a language.

Even though their shared laughter had set Sorweel at his ease, they knew so little about each other—and Sorweel knew so little, period—that they quickly ran short of idle pleasantries. The Successor-Prince spoke briefly about their horses, which he thought brutish to the extreme. He tried to gossip about some of their fellow Scions, but gossip required common acquaintances, and whenever he mentioned anyone,

Sorweel could only shrug. So they came quickly to the one thing they did share in common: the reason two young men from such disparate worlds could share bowls of wine in the first place—the Aspect-Emperor.

"I was *there*," Zsoronga said, "when his first emissaries arrived in my father's court." He had the habit of making faces while he spoke, as though telling stories to a child. "I was only eight or nine at the time, I think, and I'm sure my eyes were as wide as oysters!" His eyes bulged as he said this, as if to demonstrate. "For years rumours had circulated . . . Rumours of *him*."

"It was much the same in our court," Sorweel replied.

"So you *know*, then." Pulling his knees up, the Prince nestled back into his cushions, balanced his wine between long fingers. "I grew up hearing tales of the First Holy War. For the longest time I thought the Unification Wars simply *were* the Three Seas! Then Invishi fell to the Zaudunyani and with it all Nilnamesh. That caused everyone to cluck and scratch like chickens, believe you me. Nilnamesh had always been our window on the Three Seas. And then, when news arrived that Auvangshei was being rebuilt—"

"Auvangshei?" Sorweel blurted, resisting the urge to look at the old Obligate, whom he had actually interrupted. He had witnessed enough interpreted exchanges in his father's court to know that the success of informal conversations of this kind required more than a little pretence on the interlocutors' part. A certain artificiality was inescapable.

"*Sau. Rwassa muf molo kumbereti . . .*"

"Yes. A fortress, a legendary fortress that guarded the frontier between Old Zeüm and the Cenìean Empire, centuries and centuries ago . . ."

All Sorweel knew about the Ceniean Empire was that it ruled all the Three Seas for a thousand years and that the Anasûrimbor's New Empire had been raised about its skeleton. As little as that was, it seemed knowledge enough. Just as his earlier laughter had been his first in weeks, he now felt the first true gleam of comprehension. The dimensions of what had upended his life had escaped him—he had floundered in his ignorance. The Great Ordeal. The New Empire. The Second Apocalypse. These were little more than empty signs to him, sounds that had somehow wrought the death of his father and the fall of his city. But here at last, in the talk of other places and other times, was a glimmer—as though understanding were naught but the piling on of empty names.

"Aside from skirmishing with Sranc," the Successor-Prince was saying, "Zeüm has had no external enemies since Near Antiquity . . . the days of the *old* Aspect-Emperors. In our land, we worship events more than gods. I know that must sound strange to you, but it's true. We do not, like you sausages, forget our fathers. At least the Ketyai keep lists! But you Norsirai . . ."

He shook his head and cast his eyes heavenward, a mock gesture meant to tell Sorweel that he simply teased. Expressions, it seemed, all spoke in the same language.

"In Zeüm," the Prince continued, "each of us has a book that is about us alone, a book that is never completed so long as our sons are strong, our *samwassa*, which details the deeds of our ancestors, and what they earned in the afterlife. Mighty events, such as battles, or even campaigns such as this, are what knot the strings of our descent together, what makes us *one people*. Since everything that is present hangs from these great decisions, we revere them more than you can know . . ."

There was wonder here, Sorweel realized, and room for strength. Different lands. Different customs. Different skins. And yet it was all somehow the same.

He was not alone. How could he be so foolish as to think he was alone?

"But then I'm forgetting, aren't I?" Zsoronga said. "They say your city has stood unconquered for almost three thousand years. The same is the case with Zeüm. The only real threats we have ever faced hearken back to the days of the

Ceniean Aspect-Emperors and the armies they sent against us. The Three Axes we call them, Binyangwa, Amarah, and Hutamassa, the battles we regard as our most glorious moments, whose dead we implore to catch us when we at last fall from this life. So as you can imagine, that name, 'Aspect-Emperor,' is engraved in our souls. Engraved!"

The same, of course, had been true in Sakarpus. It seemed beyond belief that *one man* could incite such fear on opposite ends of the world, that he could pluck distant kings and princes like weeds, then replant them together . . .

That one man could be so powerful. One man!

And in a rush, Sorweel realized what it was he had to do—at last! He fairly shouted aloud, it struck with such sudden obviousness. He needed to *understand* the Aspect-Emperor. It wasn't his father's weakness or pride or foolishness that had seen the Lonely City fall . . .

It was his *ignorance*.

The Successor-Prince's eyes had drifted inward with his retelling, his face brightening with each turn and digression as though at some minor yet critical discovery. "So, when news arrived that Auvangshei had been rebuilt . . . Well, you can imagine. Sometimes it seemed the Three Seas and the New Empire was *all* anyone could speak about. Some were eager, tired of living in the shadow of greater fathers, while others were afraid, thinking that doom comes to all things, so why not High Holy Zeüm? I had always counted my father among the former, among the strong. The Aspect-Emperor's emissaries would change all that."

"What happened?" Sorweel asked, feeling an old timbre returning to his voice. Zsoronga was no different than him, he decided. Stronger perhaps, certainly more worldly, but every bit as baffled by the circumstances that had carried him here, to this conversation in this wild and desolate land.

"There were three of them in the embassy, two Ketyai and one sausage like you. One of them looked terrified, and we assumed he had simply been overwhelmed by the dread splendour of our Court. They strode beneath my father, who glared down at them from his throne—he was very good at glaring, my father.

"They said, 'The Aspect-Emperor bears you greetings, Great Satakhan, and asks that you send three emissaries to the Andiamine Heights *to respond in kind*.'"

Zsoronga had leaned forward in the course of reciting this, hooked his arms about his knees. "'In kind?' my father asked . . ."

The Prince held the moment with his breath, the way a bard might. In his soul's eye, Sorweel could see it, the feathered pomp and glory of the Great Satakhan's court, the sun sweating between great pillars, the galleries rapt with black faces.

"With that, the three men produced razors from their tongues and opened their own throats!" He made a tight, feline swiping motion with his left hand. "*They killed themselves* . . . right there before us! My father's surgeons tried to save them, to staunch the blood, but there was nothing to be done. The men died *right there*"—he looked and gestured to a spot several feet away, as though watching their ghosts—"moaning some kind of crazed hymn, to their last breath, *singing* . . ."

He hummed a strange singsong tune for several heartbeats, his eyes lost in memory, then he turned to the young King of Sakarpus with a kind of pained incredulity. "The Aspect-Emperor had sent us three *suicides*! That *was his message to my father*. 'Look! Look what I can do! Now tell me, *Can you do the same?*'"

"Could he?" Sorweel asked numbly.

Zoronga pulled a long hand across his face. "*Ke amabo hetweru go* . . ."

"I'm too hard on my father. I know I am. Only now can I appreciate the deranged bind that gesture put him in. No matter *how* my father responded, he would lose . . . Perhaps he could find three fanatics willing to return the message, but what kind of barbarity would that be? What unrest would that cause the *kjineta*? And what if they lost heart at the penultimate moment? Who would the people call to account for their shame? And if he refused to respond in kind, would that not be an admission of weakness? Tantamount to saying, 'I cannot rule as you rule . . .'"

Sorweel shrugged. "He could have marched to war."

"I think that's what the devil wanted! I think *that* was his trap. The provocation of rebuilding Auvangshei, followed by this mad diplomatic overture. Think of what would have happened, what a disaster it would have been, had we taken the field against his Zaudunyani hosts. *Look at your city*. Your ancient fathers weathered Mog-Pharau, turned aside the No-God! And the Aspect-Emperor broke you in the space of a morning."

These words hung between them like lead pellets on sodden cloth. There was no accusation in them, no implication of fault or weakness, just a statement of what should have been an impossible fact. And Sorweel realized that his question—his discovery—was the same question *everyone* was asking, and had been asking for years. Everyone who was not a believer.

Who was the Aspect-Emperor?

"So what did your father do?"

Zsoronga snorted in derision. "What he always does. Talk, talk, and bargain. My father believes *in words*, Horse-King. He lacks the courage your father showed."

Horse-King. This was the name they used for him, Sorweel realized. Zsoronga would not have spoken with such ease otherwise.

"And so what happened?"

"Deals were struck. Treaties were signed by flatulent old men. Whispers of weakness began circulating through the streets and halls of High Domyot. And here I am, a Successor-Prince, hostage to an outland devil, pretending that I ride to war, when all I really do is moan to sausages like you."

Sorweel nodded in understanding, smiled ruefully. "You would prefer the fate of my people?"

The question seemed to catch the Successor-Prince by surprise. "Sakarpus? No . . . Though sometimes, when my ardour overmatches my wisdom, I do . . . envy . . . the dead among you."

For some reason, the hooks of this reference to his overthrown world caught Sorweel where all the others had skipped past. The raw heart, the thick eyes, the leaden thought—all the staples of his plundered existence—came rushing back and with such violence he could not speak.

Prince Zsoronga watched him with an uncharacteristic absence of expression. "*Ke nulam zo* . . ."

"I suspect you feel the same."

The young King of Sakarpus looked to the red disc of wine in his bowl, realized that he had yet to take a single sip. Not one sip—all his pain seemed condensed in this idiotic fact. Mere weeks ago, simply holding wine would be cause for celebration, another pathetic token of the manhood he had so desperately craved. How he had yearned for his first Elking! But now . . .

It was madness, to move from a world so laughably small to one so tragically bloated . . . Madness.

"More than you could know," he said.

Sorweel found many things in Zsoronga's company, much more than he was willing to admit to himself, let alone anyone else. The friendship he could acknowledge, as this was a Gift prized by men and gods alike, particularly with someone as resolute and honouable as the Zeümi Prince. His relief was something he *had* to admit, though it shamed him. For some perverse reason, all men found heart in learning that others shared not only their purpose, but their grief as well.

What he could not acknowledge was the relief he found

in *simply speaking*. A true Horselord, a hero such as Niehirren Halfhand or Orsuleese the Faster, viewed speech with the high-handed distaste they reserved for bodily functions, as something men did only out of necessity. Sakarpus found its strength in its solitude, in its lack of intercourse with other babbling nations—it was not called the Lonely City for nothing—so its great men affected to do the same.

But Sorweel had found only desolation. Ever since joining the Scions, his voice had been stopped in the jar of his skull. His soul had turned inward, becoming ever more tangled in the hair of unruly thought. He had wandered about in a stupor, as if suffering the circling disease that sometimes afflicted horses, forcing them to walk around and around in senseless spirals until they collapsed. He too had been on the verge of collapse, pressed to the brink of madness by remorse and shame and self-pity—self-pity most of all.

Words had saved him, even if he could only speak around the fact of his pain. His single greatest fear leaving Zsoronga's pavilion that first night was that the Zeümi Prince, despite all his displays and declarations to the contrary, found him as crude and as disagreeable as his name for Norsirai, "sausages," implied.

That he would be returned to the prison of his backward tongue.

As it turned out, Zsoronga invited him to ride with his retinue the following day, where thanks to Obotegwa's tireless voice, Sorweel found himself a part of the sometimes strange and often uproarious banter of Zsoronga's Brace, as the Zeümi called their boonsmen. The day might have been his first good day in weeks, were it not for the sudden appearance of the Scion's commander—a campaign-grizzled Captain named Harnilias, or Old Harni as they called him. The silver-haired man simply rode into their midst, heavy with armour and airs of authority, searching and dismissing faces with a single sweeping glance. He addressed himself to Obotegwa without so much as a glance in Sorweel's direction. Even still, the young King was not at all surprised when the old Obligate turned to him and said, "The General wants to see you . . . Kayûtas himself."

Sorweel had seen the Prince-Imperial many times since his last summons, but only in glimpses through thickets of cavalrymen, his head bare and bright in the prairie sun, his blue cloak shimmering about its kinks and folds. Each time he caught himself craning his neck and peering like some Sagland churl, when he should have done no more than sneer and look away. Sorweel was always skirmishing over small points of dignity, always losing, but this was different. The sight of the General's battle-standard, which was well-nigh perpetual for some legs of the day-long march, drew his gaze like a lodestone. It was like some unnatural compulsion. He would ride and look, ride and look, and when the intervening masses parted . . .

There. A man who should be a man like any other.

Only that *he wasn't*. Anasûrimbor Kayûtas was more than powerful—more even than the son of the man who had killed King Harweel. It was as if Sorweel saw him against a greater frame, a background deeper than the endless emerald sweep of the Istyuli Plains.

As if Kayûtas were more an *expression* than an individual. A particle of fate.

Walking the short distance to the white-tented complex that formed the General's command, Sorweel struggled with a skin-tingling sense of *exposure*. A kind of anxious reluctance balled like a fist in his chest. He could hear the Prince-Imperial's declaration from their last meeting: "*I need only look at your face to see your soul, not so clearly as Father, certainly, but enough to sound the measure of you or anyone else before me. I can see the depth of your pain, Sorweel . . .*"

This was no mean claim, the kind men make when "measuring tongues," as the Sakarpi said, attempting to cow others with boasts and breast-beating. It was—and Sorweel knew this without reservation—a *fact*. Anasûrimbor Kayûtas could see *through* his arrogant posture, his feeble mask of pride—through *him*.

How? How did one war against such men?

A kind of panic welled through his thoughts as he approached the General's Horse-and-Circumfix standard. He did not want to be known . . .

Least of all *now*, and least of all by *him*.

A mixed cohort of soldiers crowded about the austere tent, some wearing the armour and crimson uniform of the General's Kidruhil guard and standing at attention, others garbed in silk-green beneath corselets of the finest chain and milling at ease—Pillarians, Sorweel would later learn, the personal bodyguard of the Imperial Family. A fair-haired Kidruhil officer barked senseless words at him as he approached, then nodded at his obvious incomprehension, as if there could be only one such fool.

Within heartbeats he found himself inside the command tent. As before, the interior was spare, almost devoid of ornament, and the furnishings severe. The setting sun flared across the westward panels, illuminating everything in white-filtered light. The contrast to Prince Zsoronga's pavilion with its gloomy corners and elaborate trappings could not be more complete. "*Our glorious host*," Sorweel remembered the Zeümi Prince saying, "*does not believe the rewards of rank have any place on the march*."

Only what was needed. Only what was necessary.

Kayûtas sat as before at the same sheaf-covered table, only this time he stared at Sorweel with mild expectation instead of reading. A beautiful woman, her flaxen hair braided and bound about her head, sat to his immediate right, dressed in a gold-and-charcoal gown: Kayûtas's sister, Sorweel realized, glimpsing the familial resemblance in her face. Kayûtas's dark-maned brother, Moënghus, hulked several paces away, fairly bristling with weaponry. There was a taut humidity in the air, the kind found in the wake of heated arguments.

The woman stared at him with the amused boldness of an aunt finally laying eyes on a sister's vaunted child. "*Muirs kil tierana jen hûl*," she said. Though her gaze never wavered, the way she tilted her head told Sorweel she had directed her words at Moënghus behind her.

The dark Prince-Imperial said nothing, simply glared with eyes like chips of sky. His brother Kayûtas snorted in laughter.

Sorweel felt the blood rise to his face. They were scarcely older than him, he realized, and yet he was the boy here—unquestionably so. Was it the same with Zsoronga? Did they have this impact on everyone who came before them?

"How is Porsparian treating you?" the General asked in Sakarpic.

"As well as can be expected," Sorweel replied, though the words felt false on his lips. The Shigeki slave had tended to his modest needs with diligence—this much was true. But the old man's religious zealotry unsettled him: Porsparian was forever praying over the small mouths he moulded in the earth, continually feeding warm food to cold dirt, and forever . . . blessing the young King.

At least there had been no more episodes like that first night.

"Good," Kayûtas said nodding, though for the merest sliver of a heartbeat, a shadow crossed his face. "My father has at last chosen your tutor," he continued in a *you-must-be-wondering* tone, "a Mandate Schoolman named Thanteus Eskeles. A good man, I am told. He will accompany you throughout the remainder of the march, teach you Sheyic while you ride . . . I trust you will defer to his wisdom."

"Of course," Sorweel said, quite at a loss as to what to think. Moënghus and the nameless woman continued staring at him, each with their own variety of contempt. Sorweel found himself looking to his feet, fuming. "Is there anything else?" he asked with more heat than he intended.

He was a king! A *king*! What would his father say, seeing him like this?

General Kayûtas laughed aloud, said something in the same language spoken by the woman moments earlier. "I'm afraid so," he continued in effortless Sakarpic. He spared a droll glance at his sister—whose name Sorweel suddenly recalled: Serwa. Anasûrimbor Serwa.

"As you might imagine," the fair-haired General continued, "the line between insolence and sacrilege is a rather hazy one in an endeavour such as this. But there are those who . . . watch such things. Those who keep count."

Something in his tone pried Sorweel's gaze upward. Kayûtas was leaning forward now, his elbows on his knees, so that the white silk of his robe hung in a series of luminous arcs below his throat. Behind him, his brother had turned away in apparent boredom, gnawed at what looked like a section of dried meat. But the woman continued watching as intently as before.

"You *are a king*, Sorweel, and when you return to Sakarpus you will rule as your father had ruled, with all of your privileges intact. But *here*, you are a soldier and a vassal. You will salute others in accordance to rank. In the presence of myself or my brother and sister, you will kneel and lower your face, so that when you look straight ahead, your eyes are focused on a spot one length before you. You may then look at us directly: This is your privilege as a king. When you encounter *my father*, no matter what the circumstance, you are to place your forehead to the ground. And never look at him unless invited. All men are slaves before my father. Do you understand?"

The tone was gentle, the words were nothing if not politic, and yet there could be no mistaking the cutting edge of reprimand. "Yes," Sorweel heard himself say.

"Then show me."

A breeze bellied the eastward canvas panels; ropes creaked and poles groaned. There was a burning tightness to the air, like the tinkle of old coals in an old fire, making breathing not only uncomfortable, but dangerous. It happened without him even willing it to happen: His knees simply bent, folded like stiff leather, then fell to the crude-woven mat that had been rolled across the floor. His chin dropped on the swivel of his neck, as though obeying an irresistible accumulation of weight. He found himself looking at the Prince-Imperial's sandalled feet, at white skin and pearl nails, at the yellow-orange calluses climbing the pads of his toes.

Forgive me . . .

"Excellent." A breathless pause. "I know that was difficult."

His every sinew, it seemed, tensed about his frame, cramped about his father's bones. Never had he been so utterly immobile—so utterly silent. And somehow, this became his accusation.

"Come, Sorweel. Please stand."

He did as he was instructed, though he continued staring at the General's feet. He looked up only when the silence became unbearable. Even in this, they were unconquerable.

"You've made a friend," Kayûtas said, gazing at him with the amiable air of an uncle fishing for some reluctant truth. "Who is it? Zsoronga? Yes. It only stands to reason. That interpreter of his . . . Obotegwa."

The young King's shock was such that he paid no heed to his expression. Spies! Of course they were watching him . . . Porsparian?

"I have no need of spies, Sorweel," the Prince-Imperial said, snatching the thought from his face. He leaned back and with a gentle laugh added, "My father is a god."

CHAPTER ELEVEN

The Osthwai Mountains

Since all men count themselves righteous, and since no righteous man raises his hand against the innocent, a man need only strike another to make him evil.

—NULLA VOGNEAS, *THE CYNICATA*

Where two reason may deliver truth, a thousand lead to certain delusion. The more steps you take, the more likely you will wander astray.

—AJENCIS, *THEOPHYSICS*

Early Spring, 19 New Imperial Year (4132 Year-of-the-Tusk), the Osthwai Mountains

The Scalpoi called the mountain the Ziggurat, apparently because of its flat summit. None among the Skin Eaters knew its true name—perhaps even Cleric had forgotten. But Achamian had dreamt of it many, many times.

Aenaratiol.

When the Nonman had first mentioned the Black Halls, Achamian had thought only of the expedition, of reaching

Sauglish by midsummer. By the time they made camp that evening, the relief had all but evaporated and the implications of what they were about to attempt—for want of a better word—stabbed at him. The world was old, strewn with ancient and forgotten hazards, and short of Golgotterath, few could match the peril that was Cil-Aujas.

The Skin Eaters had their own lore. Given that it flanked the southern approaches of the Ochain Passes, the Ziggurat and the derelict Nonman Mansion that plumbed its foundations had been the subject of countless fireside speculations. What shreds of fact they might have possessed had been burned long ago as fuel for brighter wonderings, and what remained was out-and-out fantastical. Pestilence. Exodus. Invasion. It seemed they had concocted every tale to explain the fate of the Black Halls save the actual one.

Refuge.

When Achamian began telling the true story, he found himself the focus of all attention, to the point where it almost seemed comedic: hard and warlike men hanging on his words like children, asking the same guileless questions, watching with the same timid impatience. Xonghis, in particular, would begin calling out what he thought would happen next, only to catch himself and trail mumbling. Achamian would have laughed, had he not understood what it meant to be stranded as these men were stranded, had he not known the power of words to parent the orphaned present.

The true name of the mountain, he told them, was Aenaratiol.

Smokehorn.

More and more Skin Eaters gathered about their fire as he spoke, including Sarl and Kiampas. Mimara sat with her head resting against Achamian's shoulder, her eyes lifted high and searching each time he glanced at her. The flames tossed and twined in the mountain wind, and he basked in its heated glow. Sinking from the clouds, the sun leaned hot and crimson against the mountains, before slipping behind the uneven teeth of the mountains, trailing a shrinking patina of gold, violet, and blue. The land was tossed to the horizon, slopes and sheer drops, growing ever more black.

He told them about the Nonmen, the Cûnuroi, and the glory of their civilization in the First Age, when Men lived as savages and the Tusk had yet to be written. He told them about Cu'jara Cinmoi, the greatest of the Nonmen Kings, and the wars he fought against the Inchoroi, who had fallen in fire from the void, and how those wars left the survivors mateless and immortal, with no will to resist the Five Tribes of Men. And then he told them of the First Apocalypse.

"If you want to look at the true ruin," he said, nodding to the barren knoll where the Captain sat alone with his inhuman lieutenant, "look no farther than your Cleric. Reduced. Dwindled. They were once to us as we are to Sranc. Indeed, for many among the Nonmen, we were little more."

He described the Meori Empire, the great White Norsirai nation that once had ruled all the lands on the Long Side of the mountains, as the Scalpoi called it, the wilderness that was their hunting grounds. He described its destruction at the hands of the No-God, and how the great hero, Nostol, fled south with the remnants of his people, and found refuge in the lands of Gin'yursis, the Nonman King of Cil-Aujas. He described how the two of them, hero and king, defeated the No-God and his Consult at Kathol Pass, and so purchased a year's respite for the entire world.

"But what does it mean," he asked the faces about the fire, "when angels walk the very ground we trod? What does it mean to be *mortally* overshadowed, to toil in the dazzle of another race's glory? Do you admire? Do you bend knee and acknowledge? Or do you envy and hate?

"Nostol and his Meöri kinsmen *hated*. Dispossessed, they coveted, and coveting, they maligned those they sought to rob. They did what all men do, you, me, throughout the entirety of our lives. They confounded need for justice, want for writ. They turned to the tangled strings of their scriptures and pulled out the threads that spoke to their fell ends."

"Betrayal," Mimara murmured from his side.

"Refuge," Achamian said. He then narrated the three versions of the tale as he knew them. In the first, Nostol instructed his chieftains and thanes to woo the Emwama concubines, the slaves the Nonmen used as substitutes for their long-dead wives. Nostol, he explained, hoped to incite the Nonmen to some act of violence, something he could use as a pretext to rally his people behind his planned atrocities. Apparently the Meöri were zealous in the prosecution of his orders, impregnating no less than sixty-three different concubines.

"Talk about farting in the queen's bedchamber!" Pokwas exclaimed.

"Indeed," Achamian said, adding to the chorus of laughter with the mock gravity of his tone. "And there are no windows in the deeps of Cil-Aujas . . ."

In the second, Nostol himself seduced Weyukat, whom the Nonman King prized above all his other concubines, since she had twice carried his seed to pregnancy, if not to term—among few human women ever to do so. In this version, the Nonmen of Cil-Aujas had rejoiced, thinking that the resulting child, if female, could herald the resurrection of their dying race—only to discover that the infant boy was wholly human. The child, named Swanostol in the legends, was subsequently put to the sword, providing the outrage Nostol required to incite his Meöri kin.

In the third, Nostol commanded his chieftains and thanes to seduce not the Emwama, but the highest among the Nonmen nobility, the Ishroi, knowing that the resulting passions would be certain to create the friction he required. This, Achamian had always thought, was far and away the most likely tale, since most contemporary chroniclers placed the Fall of Cil-Aujas within a year of the Battle of Kathol Pass—scarcely enough time for plots involving seduction, pregnancy, and birth to unfold. And it seemed to accord with the scraps he could remember from Seswatha's Dreams.

Nevertheless, each of the versions had its own poetic virtues, and they all came to the same: war between Men and Nonmen.

He described the glare of riot lighting the deeps. He told them about fury hunting grief, about bared blades raised to low ceilings and naked skin falling to chiselled floors. He spoke of corridors blocked by spears, of underworld houses soaked in flame. He described wild and desperate Men, Chorae bound against their throats, howling through the trackless deeps. He explained the blind stands of the Ishroi, their sorceries cracking through labyrinthine halls. He told them how Nostol, his beard all filth, his hair blood-matted, struck down the Nonman King as he wept and laughed upon his throne. How he murdered Gin'yursis, ancient and renowned.

"With courage and fell cunning," Achamian said, his face hot in the firelight, "Men made themselves masters of Cil-Aujas. Some Nonmen hid, only to be found in the course of time, by hunger or iron, it mattered not. Others escaped through chutes no mortal man has ever known. Perhaps even now they wander like Cleric, derelict, cursed with the only memories that will not fade, doomed to relive the Fall of Cil-Aujas until the end of days."

The mountain shadows had ascended to the arch of heaven, revealing a sky so deep with stars it tugged at the heart simply to glance at them. A chill crept through the old Wizard.

"I've heard this story," Galian ventured as the windy silence grew leaden, his palms held out to the flames. "This is why the Galeoth are cursed with fractiousness, is it not? The fugitives you describe were their forefathers."

Several of the Galeoth scalpers howled in complaint.

Achamian pursed his lips, shook his head in a way that

made him feel campfire wise and mountain sad. "The King of Cil-Aujas was not so discriminate in his dying," he said, staring into the pulsing coals. "According to the legends, all Men bear this curse.

"We are all Sons of Nostol. We all bear the stamp of his frailty."

The following morning revealed cloudless skies, the clarity measured in the concave spine of the mountains fading to purple as they reached into the horizon, the cold measured in the white that capped their ragged heights. Sunlight glared nascent from hanging fields of snow, flashed gold and silver. It sharpened the breath, simply staring.

The company loaded their mules with little or no conversation, then set out toward the Ziggurat. What Lord Kosoter had called the Low Road seemed anything but. Not only was it little more than a track, it climbed far more than otherwise, following the course of various ridges, before dropping into some gullied interval to scale higher courses. But always, however circuitous its route, it stalked the great fissure that hoofed the Ziggurat's knuckled base. No matter what earth-and-rock enormity the Low Road placed before them, the fissure inevitably climbed back into view, larger, darker, more sinister for the concentration of detail.

The mighty oaks and elms of previous days had yielded altogether, giving way to scrawny poplars and twisted screw pine where trees could be found at all. Most of the time the company scuffed and clopped across expanses of bare stone, surrounded by the wind-combed remains of the previous year's bracken. Everything seemed to shiver. Everything that had once lived.

It was long past noon ere they descended into the delta of gorges at the base of the great fissure. The Ziggurat, by this time, occupied the whole of the sky before them, cowing them into consensual silence. They tramped onward in a kind of stupor. The Coffers were forgotten, as was the distraction of Mimara's hips. Perhaps it was the humility of seeing fundamentals upended, the very ground wracked and beaten, hauled into scarps and slopes, heaved to heights that could defeat sun and clouds let alone the aspirations of mere men. Perhaps it was the weight of the inexpressible, the hard bone of the world rearing into horns that hooked the skirts of heaven. The titanic precipices, the pulverizing leaps, the distances ramping into the clouds. The Skin Eaters, each in their own way, seemed to understand that this was the prototype, what tyrants aped with their God-mocking works, mountains into monument, migrations into pageant and parade. This was the most primordial rule—the world itself—too vast, too elemental, to be called sacred or holy.

And it weakened the knees, as all true spectacle should.

The Ziggurat had become as much argument as mountain, posed not in claims or premises, but in immensities, in features that encompassed experience, saying, murmuring, *You are small . . .* So very small.

And they walked, willingly, between the cracks of its hoary fingers.

The sky was pinched into a shining slot. The air became dry and still, like the gap in a dead man's mouth.

The Kianene, Sutadra, was the first to notice they walked the ruins of some ancient road. It almost seemed a trick of the eyes, for once they noticed the telltale signs, it seemed impossible they could have seen otherwise. Something, snowmelts perhaps, had sawed a long winding gully across and over its course, gutting the broad planes of what once must have been a grand processional avenue. There was little enthusiasm in the discovery. It seemed to trouble the Skin Eaters somehow, knowing they walked in the footsteps of gold-clad kings and shining armies, rather than those of wayfarers such as themselves. There was comfort in a simple track, Achamian supposed, an assurance that the world they walked did not laugh at them.

Several hours passed before they rounded the final bend and saw it before them. The fissured wall climbed high, straining the neck with its gouged dimensions. It loomed as only natural works could loom. The random line of fracture and millennial erosion, of rock sculpted in mystery and accident. Black outcroppings with mossed bellies. Long cracks dangling anemic weeds. And set in its heart, like some shrine to intellect and intention, the enormous Obsidian Gate, looming over the ruins of an ancient fortress.

The company gathered on the platform beneath it, loose clots of men drifting to a halt, mouths open. The Skin Eaters had expected many things, daydreams of a storied destination, but they were quite unprepared for what they beheld. Achamian could see it in the way they craned and peered, like emissaries of a backward yet imperious people trying to see past their awe. The entrance was unbarred, an ovoid of impenetrable black set in an immense arched recess, which was panelled with reliefs that formed a skein over yet deeper narratives, so that the scenes depicted possessed a startling depth. Nonmen figures twined across every surface, weathered to the point where you could scarcely distinguish the armoured from the naked, frozen in antique postures of triumph or ceremonial tedium. Shepherds with lambs about their shoulders. Warriors fending lions and jackals. Captives baring necks to the swords of princes. On and on, the lives of the dead in miniature. Four pillars flanked the threshold, the outermost pair soaring tall as netia pine, yet hollow, great cylinders of interlocking figures and faces; the innermost solid, three snakes intercoiling, their heads lost in the vaulted gloom, their rattled tails forming three-pronged bases.

Curses filled the silence, some murmured, others spoken quite out loud. Such was the monumental delicacy, the profusion of figure and detail, that the forms seemed more revealed than rendered, as though the sheeted cliffs were naught but mud rinsed from the stone of ossified souls. Even half-ruined, there was too much, too much beauty, too much detail, and certainly too much toil, a grandeur made wicked by the demands it exacted on simpler souls. It was a place that begged to be challenged, overthrown.

For the first time, Achamian thought he understood the crude bronze of Nostol's betrayal.

"What are we doing?" Mimara whispered from his side.

"Recalling ourselves . . . I think."

"Look," Xonghis said in his deadpan accent. "The other companies . . ." He nodded to the left serpentine pillar: Various symbols had been scratched into the lower coils, childish white slashes across weathered scales. "Their signs."

The Skin Eaters gathered round, careful to heed the invisible line that marked the entrance side of the pillar. Xonghis knelt between two of the rattle tails, which rose like roots, each thicker than a man. He ran his outstretched fingers and palm over each mark, as though testing extinguished fires for heat. Different Skin Eaters called out the names of the companies they recognized as he did so. He lingered over the sign of a weeping eye. "This one," he said, looking back significantly, "was marked the most recently."

"The Bloody Picks," Galian said, frowning. "They left, when?"

"More than a fortnight ago," Pokwas replied.

The following silence persisted longer than it should. There was heartbreak in these furtive marks, a childishness that made the ancient works rising about them seem iron heavy, nigh invincible. Scratches. Caricatures with buffoonish themes. They were so obviously the residue of a lesser race, one whose triumph lay not in the nobility of arms and intellect, but in treachery and the perversities of fortune.

"See," Achamian heard Kiampas mutter to Sarl. "There . . ." He followed the direction of the man's finger, saw what looked like a Galeoth kite-shield chalked long and skinny across the lower coils of the serpents.

"The High Shields, as I said."

"It can't be their sign," Sarl snapped, as though assertion alone could make things true. "Their bones lie on the Long Side." Even as he said this he stooped to fetch a stone from his feet. Everyone watched as he began scratching the mark of the Skin Eaters across one of the serpent's backs: a mandible with gumless teeth.

"What I would like to know," Sarl said, the gravel of his tone rendered thin and abrasive by the soaring works of glass and stone, "is how we could have gone so long without coming here."

His meaning was plain. The Skin Eaters were a legend, as was this place, and all legends were drawn together sooner or later—such was the song that decided all things. Such was the logic.

His face pinched into a cackle. "This *is* the slog of slogs, boys!"

Cleric, meanwhile, had wandered forward, effortlessly crossing the incorporeal boundary that seemed to hold everyone else back, turning in a slow circle as he did so.

"Where are you?" he bellowed—so violently even the hardest of the Skin Eaters started. "The Gate unguarded? And with the world grown so dark? This is an outrage! Outrage!"

Despite his stature, he seemed a mere sliver, frail and warm-blooded, before the great maw of black about him. Only the depth of his sorcerous Mark bespoke his might.

"Cûncari!" he boomed, growing frantic. "Jiss! *Cûncari!*"

The Captain strode to him, clapped a hand on his shoulder. "They're dead, you fool. Ancient dead."

The cowled darkness that was his face turned to the Captain, held him in eyeless scrutiny, then lifted skyward, as though studying the lay of illumination across the hanging slopes. As the gathered company watched, he raised two hands and drew back, for the first time, his leather hood.

The gesture seemed obscene, venal, a flouting of some aboriginal modesty.

He turned to regard his fellow scalpers, smiling as if taking heart in their astonishment. His fused teeth gleamed with spit. His skin was white and utterly hairless, so much so that he looked fungal, like something pulled from forest compost. His features were youthful, drawn with the same fine lines and flawless proportions as all his race.

The face of a Sranc.

"Yes," he said, closing lashless eyelids. His pupils seemed as big as coins when he opened them, black with hooks of reflected silver. "*Yes*," he fairly cried, laughing now.

"They *are* dead."

Night did not so much rise over the great fissure as the day was snatched away.

They had difficulty scrounging for fuel, so the entire company ended up crowding about a single fire, oppressed by the works hanging above them. Small desultory conversations marbled the silence, but no one took the stage and addressed the company as a whole, aside from Sarl of course, who had the habit of pitching his declarations in all directions. Most simply sat, knees hooked in the ring of their arms, and stared up at the thousand lozenge faces and figures above them, black-limned in flickering yellow-white. With the outer reliefs set like grillwork over the inner, the firelight seemed to animate the panels, to imbue them with the illusion of strain and motion. Several Skin Eaters swore that this or that scene *had* changed. Sarl, however, was always quick to make fools of them.

"See that one there, with the little one bending with the water urn before the row of tall ones? See it? Now, look away. Now *look back*. See? See! That big one popped his prick in the little one's arse, I swear it!"

Laughter, honest, yet rationed all the same. Dread encircled them, and Sarl kept careful watch, making sure it did not take hold in his Captain's men.

"Dirty Nonmen buggers, eh, Cleric? Cleric?"

The Nonman merely smiled, as pale as a ghoul in the firelight.

Time and again, Achamian found himself stealing glances in his direction. It was almost impossible not to ponder the connection of the two, the ruined Mansion, harrowed in the First Apocalypse, and the ruined Nonman, as old as languages and peoples. Cil-Aujas and Incariol.

Mimara leaned against him, and in some distracted corner of his soul he noted the difference, the way she leaned rather than clutched at his hand as her mother had. She was talking to Soma, who sat cross-legged next to her, staring at his palms like a shy poet. More out of the absence of alternatives than out of concern, Achamian listened, his gaze drifting from scene to engraved scene.

"You have the look and the manner of a Lady," the Nilnameshi said.

"My mother was a whore."

"Ah, but what is parentage, really? Me? I burned my ancestor lists long ago."

A mock disapproving pause. "Doesn't that frighten you?"

"Frighten?"

"Look around you. I would hazard that all these men, even the most vicious, bear some record of their forebears."

"And why should that frighten me?"

"Because," Mimara said, "it means they're bound to the unbroken line of their fathers, back into the mists of yore. It means when they die, entire hosts will cast nets for their souls." Achamian felt her shoulders hitch in a pity-for-the-doomed shrug. "But *you* . . . you merely wander between oblivions, from the nothingness of your birth to the nothingness of your death."

"Between oblivions?"

"Like flotsam."

"Like flotsam?"

"Yes. Doesn't that frighten you?"

Achamian found himself scowling at the shadowy pageants chiselled above. An improbable number of faces stared out and down from the graven dramas, their eyes gouged into blank pits, their noses worn to points over mouthless chins. The priest to the right of the butchered stag. The child at the knee of the nursing mother. The warrior with the broken shield. Among the thousands of figures that vaulted the blackness above their fire, hundreds watched those who would watch them, as though the moments that framed them could not isolate their attention.

Proof of souls.

Skin prickling, Achamian glanced back toward Cleric, who stared as before into the pit of the entrance. Several heartbeats passed before the immaculate face turned—inevitably, it seemed—to answer his scrutiny. A kind of blank intensity leapt between them, born more of exhaustion than affinity, flattening the dozen or so Skin Eaters who leaned in and out of their line of sight.

They watched each other, Wizard and Nonman, for one heartbeat, two, three . . . Then, without rancour or acknowledgment, they looked away.

"I suppose it does," Achamian heard Soma admit after a long silence. The man invariably erred, Achamian had noticed, when it came to honesty. He was always revealing too much.

"Frighten you?" Mimara replied. "Of course it does."

Soon the talk sputtered out altogether, and the scalpers unrolled their mats and bedding across the pitted stone of the platform. Men kicked stones clicking into the night. The moon hung over the fissure for a time, disclosing the scarps and ravines in a curious light, one that argued stillness, uncompromising, absolute, like mice in the panning eyes of owls.

Few slept well. The black mouth of the Obsidian Gate seemed to inhale endlessly.

The ruins revealed in the morning light were more melancholy than malevolent. Hands eroded into paws. Heads worn into eggs. The layered panels appeared more riddled with fractures, more pocked with gaps. For the first time, it seemed, they noticed the little appendages scattered like gravel across the platform. Nocturnal fears had become sunlit fragments.

Even still, the company ate in comparative silence, punctuated by the low comments and laughs typically reserved for recollections of hard drinking. Forced normalcy as a remedy for uncertain nerves. Their small fire burned through what little fuel remained before Achamian had a chance to boil water for his tea, forcing him to mutter a furtive Cant. This filled him with dread for some reason.

They paused to watch Xonghis confer in low tones with Lord Kosoter. Then they entered the Black Halls of Cil-Aujas with nary a commemorating word, let alone the fanfare Men typically attach to fatal endeavours. They simply assembled, leading their mules, then followed Cleric and their Captain in a file some thirty-five souls long. With Mimara at his side, Achamian glanced skyward one final time before joining the string of vanishing figures. In the slot of a hanging ravine, the Nail of Heaven twinkled alone in the endless blue, a beacon of all things high and open . . .

A final call to those who would dare the nethers of the earth.

CHAPTER TWELVE

The Andiamine Heights

Little snake, what poison in your bite!
Little snake, what fear you should strike!
But they don't know, little snake—oh no!
They can't see the tiny places you go . . .

—ZEÜMI NURSERY SONG

Early Spring, 19 New Imperial Year (4132 Year-of-the-Tusk), Momemn

Kelmomas had known his father had returned almost immediately. He saw it in a host of subtle cues that he didn't even know he could read: an imperceptible contraction in the Guards' posture, an alertness of pose and look in the Apparati, and a long-jog breathlessness in the slaves. Even the air assumed a careful taste, as though the drafts themselves had grown wary. Nevertheless, Kelmomas didn't realize he knew until he overheard one of the choir slaves gossiping about the Yatwerian Matriarch pissing herself beneath the Holy Mantle.

He's come to console Mother, the secret voice said.

Alone in the playroom, Kelmomas continued working on his model of Momemn, carving meticulous little obelisks out of balsa, long after darkness draped the Enclosure. A kind of childish indecision had overcome him, a listless need to continue poking at whatever he happened to be doing, to simply exist for a petulant time, thinking and acting stubbornly counter to fact.

It had always been like this with his father. Not fear, just a kind of canny reluctance, rootless and long-winded.

Eventually he had to relent—that too was part of the game—so he made his way to his mother's private apartments. He could hear his older brother, Inrilatas, ranting about the Gods in his locked room. His brother had broken his voice bludgeoning the walls years ago, yet still he croaked, on and on and on, as though flooding his room in some lunatic search for leaks. He never stopped raving, which was why he was always kept locked in his room. Kelmomas had not seen him for more than three years.

His mother's apartments were located down the hallway. He padded across the rug-strewn floor as silently as he could, his ears keen to the sound of his parents' voices filtering through innumerable wheezing cracks and surfaces. He paused outside the iron door, his breath as thin as a cat's.

"*I know it pains you,*" Father was saying, "*but you must have Theliopa with you in all your dealings.*"

"*You fear skin-spies?*" his mother replied.

Their voices possessed the weary burnish of a long and impassioned conversation. But the roots of his father's exhaustion stopped short of the deeper intonations that warbled in and out of his discourse. A heart-easing hum, and a kind of ursine growl, far too low to be consciously heard by Mother. These spoke from something as unwinded as it was inscrutable, an occluded soul, entirely hidden from lesser ears.

He manages her, the voice said. *He sees through her face the way you do, only with far more clarity, and he shapes his voice accordingly.*

How do you know? Kelmomas asked angrily, stung by the

thought that anyone, even Father, could see further than him. Further into her.

"*The nearer the Great Ordeal comes,*" Father said, "*the more desperate the Consult grows, the more likely they will unleash what agents remain. Keep Theliopa with you at all times. Aside from my brother, she's the only one who can reliably see their true faces.*"

Kelmomas smiled at the thought of the skin-spies. Agents of the Apocalypse. He loved hearing the stories about their wicked depredations during the First Holy War. And he had gurgled with delight watching the black one being flayed—carefully, so that Mother wouldn't see, of course. Somehow, he just knew he would be one of the few who could see past their faces, just as he could see past his father's voice. If he found one, he decided, he would keep it secret, he would simply watch it, spy on it—he so dearly loved *spying*. What a game it would make!

He wondered who was faster . . .

"*You fear they'll attack the Andiamine Heights?*" Real horror shivered through Mother's voice as she said this, the horror of events scarcely survived.

All the more reason to trap it like a bug, Kelmomas decided. He would say things, cryptic things, that would make it wonder. He needed something to tease now that Samarmas was gone.

"*What better way to distract me than by striking at my hearth?*"

"*But nothing distracts you,*" Mother said, her tone so desolate that only silence could follow. Kelmomas found himself leaning toward the door, such was the ache that emanated from the quiet beyond. It seemed he could hear them breathing, each following their own tangled string of thoughts. It seemed he could smell the absence of contact between them. Tears welled in his eyes.

She knows, the voice said. Someone has told her the truth about Father.

"*When must you leave?*" Mother asked.

"Tonight."

Kelmomas made ready to push through the door . . . Mother was hurting! And it was Father—Father! How could he have missed this before?

He'll see you, the voice warned.

Father?

None know how much he sees . . .

This puzzled the young Prince-Imperial. He stood motionless before the cast door, his hand arrested mid-air . . .

But she needs me—Mommy! Think of the warm cuddling, the tickles, the kisses on the cheek!

He's the root, the voice replied, and you're but the branch. Remember, the Strength burns brightest in him.

For reasons Kelmomas was entirely unable to fathom, that dropped his hand like lead.

The Strength.

He turned, ran like a loping athlete—one-two-three-leap!—down the halls past the bemused Pillarian Guards. As a Prince-Imperial, he had the run of the Andiamine Heights, though he was forbidden to leave its halls and gardens without the express permission of the Empress. So run he did, down the tapestried halls, through the slave barracks and into the kitchens. It was here that he palmed a silver skewer. A couple of the more matronly slaves stopped to ruffle his hair and pinch his cheeks. "Poor boy," they said. "You loved your brother dearly, didn't you?" He looked through their faces, made them blush with compliments. He worked his way to the Atrium, but the great doors to the Imperial Audience Hall had long been shut. No matter, the entrance to one of the second-floor galleries remained propped open. He decided to climb the twining stairs upside down, walking on his hands.

He flipped back to his feet when he reached the summit. All was shadows. He could only see the airy hollows of the Hall by looking through the slot between the pillars and the immense tapestries that hung between. For some reason, it seemed both more vast and smaller when seen from this vantage. When he reached the final pillar, it unnerved him to see that he could look down on the Mantle and his mother's seat. It dawned on him that no matter how great, no matter how pure and concentrated one's Strength, it was always possible that someone unseen looked down.

He secured his hands and hooked his feet along the edge of the immediate tapestry, slid like a bronze weight to the polished expanse of the floor. The grand pillars astonished him—or so he pretended in the name of his epic feat. Laughing, he climbed the steps to the Mantle, the great throne of ivory and gold from which his father passed dread judgment upon the Known World.

"*Skuh-skuh-skin spies!*" he whispered to himself. How long would it be before they showed themselves?

He couldn't wait!

He climbed onto the throne's hard seat, sat swinging his feet for several moments, hoping for the onset of absolute power, becoming bored when it failed to arrive. A sparrow caught in the netting above cried *tweet-tweet-tweet* in forlorn tedium. He craned his neck up and back to stare at its shadow. It periodically thrashed, a rustle like a dog's hind leg scratching. The stars beyond twinkled without sound.

He wished he had a stone, but all he had was the skewer.

The world he walked was far different from the world walked by others. He did not need the voice to tell him that. He could hear more, see more, know more—everything more than everybody save his father and maybe his uncle. His sense of smell, in particular . . .

He pressed himself from the throne, from the residual aura of his mother, and trotted down the steps to the Auditory floor. The smell of his uncle, the Shriah, he could recognize readily enough, but the smell of the other, the stranger, was pungent with unfamiliarity. He squatted, bent his face to the smear of evaporated urine—a fuzzy patch of grease in the moonlit gleam.

He breathed deep the Matriarch's rank odour. It transported him, enlightened him in the manner of petty things followed deep.

Then he stood and turned, leapt the stair to the dais in a single, effortless bound. He wandered onto the balcony behind the thrones, stared out across the moon-silvered distances of the Meneanor Sea.

There was something ominous about the Sea at night, the unseen heaving, the black curling beneath the booming surf, the sunless hissing. Only in the dark, it seemed, could the trackless extent of its menace be perceived. Vast. Impenetrable. All-embalming. Every struggle wrapped in a fizzing haze. Every death a dropping into the fathomless unseen . . .

Ever did Men drown in blackness, even in sun-spliced waters.

The young Prince-Imperial leapt over the balustrade.

The sorcerous Wards he need not worry about. He could see them easily enough. And the Pillarian Guards, who endlessly prowled the halls of the Andiamine Heights, he could hear around corners. Even if they were to catch him, something that still happened despite the years he had spent perfecting his game, the consequences of discovery would consist of little more than a lecture from Mother.

The Eöthic Guards, on the other hand, were a different matter. A relic of the old Ikurei Dynasty, they patrolled the grounds beyond the Holy Palace, the Imperial Precincts. Kelmomas imagined they would recognize him close up, his face held to torchlight; the problem lay in the inordinate skill and number of their bowmen. Every summer, Coithus Saubon, one of his father's two Exalt-Generals, sponsored archery contests across the Middle-North, with purses awarded to the runners-up and a tenure as a Guardsman granted to the winners. With the exception of the Galeoth Agmundrmen, they were the most celebrated archers in the Three Seas. And though the *risk* of being stuck like some quail or straw-stuffed target appealed to Kelmomas, the possibility most certainly did not.

It was no easy task, culling risks from possibilities.

Slinking from rooftop to rooftop, the Prince-Imperial climbed down the seaward faces of the Andiamine Heights, careful to always eel his way along interior corners and abutments, wherever fortune and architecture piled the shadows deep. He kept his belly snake-low. He avoided windows tumescent with light.

He warred against the savagery of his grin the entire way.

But how could he not exult? Here and there he passed solitary Guardsmen, creeping on fingers and toes with nary a sound, gliding on a dark benediction, with a grace malevolent and unseen. He watched them, the men he eluded, studied their armoured forms in the moonlight, all the while riven with a duping glee. *Here I am!* he cackled in his thoughts. *Here I am in the dark behind you!*

One sentry almost saw him, a restive Pillarian who paced back and forth and sent routine looks sliding to the shadows. Kelmomas was forced to hang motionlessness no less than five times, to trust utterly the dark line that he followed. It was a curious, bodily faith, an intoxicating rush of terror and certainty, something animal and original, as alive as anything could be. He shook with excitement afterwards, had to bite his lip to keep from howling aloud.

But the rest of the Guardsmen, Pillarian or Eöthic, stared out in utter ignorance of their ignorance, their expressions flattened by a hapless indifference to the oblivion that encircled them. It was as though they guarded a world where Kelmomas didn't exist and so could act with reckless abandon. It was good, the Prince-Imperial decided, that he *tested* them the way he did. What if he were a skin-spy? What then? In a moment of pious fury, he even settled on the lesson they had failed to learn. The darkness, he wanted to tell them, was not empty.

It was never empty.

He spent some time huddled in the crook formed by the chimney on the roof of the Lesser Stables, staring across the Batrial Campus at the monumental facade of the Guest Compound. No shafts had come whistling out of the darkness, no alarums had been raised, and it seemed that this was at once impossible and inevitable, as though he had cracked the world in two with his subterfuge. One capricious, the other to be disposed with as he pleased.

And on this night, only the latter was to be believed.

Immediately below him, in the light of poled torches, several slaves harnessed a horse to a wain loaded with what appeared to be empty casks and bushels. A group of drunken cavalrymen, Kidruhil, heckled them from a table that had been dragged into the cobbled yard. "Do you hear thunder?" one of them called out, raising a storm of laughter from his fellows.

Kelmomas lowered himself over the roof's edge, then dropped as softly as silken rope. He circled behind the ridge of freshly heaped hay that the slaves, according to the soldier's catcalls, were clearing room for in the stables. He burrowed into the loose thatch at the pile's terminus, several paces down from the wain, then waited for the slaves to embark. He breathed deep the smell of chaff and the dust of dried-out life.

Peering through a straw skein, he watched one of the slaves, a balding man with a panicked face, climb the bench and urge the harnessed horse, a sturdy black, forward with a low whistle and flick of the reins. The Kidruhil paused in their laughter, as though struck by this moment of common mastery. Wielding pitchforks, the other slaves were already heaving great manes of hay into the air. The torches coughed and sputtered.

Kelmomas focused on the horse, timed the clopping tempo of his legs, closer, closer, until its bobbing head blotted the image of the driver. Shod hooves falling like hammers. Knuckled legs trotting, bending stiff and tensile like unstrung bows. Closer.

Kelmomas leapt into the thundering clatter, reached—

His hands hooked to the harness's nethers, he pressed himself against the veined belly, willed himself into the animal's torpid heat. The whole world rumbled. The great body floating above him, flexing to and fro. The cobbles rushing beneath, falling into the rapping wheels. The young Prince-Imperial laughed aloud, knowing the racket would swallow his every sound.

They rattled across the Batrial Campus, and as they passed the Guest Compound at a tangent, Kelmomas released and twisted, landing face down on his palms and toes. He was sprinting the instant the wain's box cleared him, a shadow flitting toward the succession of arches along the ground-floor portico.

Then he was in the Guest Compound.

Her scent was clear now, a bitter old woman smear, like the trail a worm might make. He followed it up to the third floor, paused before turning down the hall that led to her suites. He heard yet another guard's heartbeat.

He looked then hid in a single motion, one eye daring the wall's edge. A blink was all he needed. The details he could safely consider in the light of his soul's eye: a lantern-lit corridor ornate with a faux colonnade and marble mouldings. A long length of carpet, trimmed with white vining, the blue so deep that most would think it black. A single sentry, neither Pillarian or Eöthic, standing rigid before the smell of her door.

No noise, save the lanterns and their endless glowing exhalation.

Kelmomas turned the corner and began stomping down the hall, sob-crooked lips, a peevish, mucus-filled moan, tears and a look of ruinous self-pity. The sentry smiled in a manner that confirmed his fatherhood, and so his familiarity with little-boy-tantrums. He leaned in tsk-tsk commiseration, the Golden Sickle of Yatwer emblazoned on his black-leather cuirass.

Kelmomas stepped into the fan of his multiple shadows.

"Come, now, little man—"

The motion was singular, abrupt with elegance. The skewer tip entered the sentry's right tear duct and slipped into the centre of his head. The ease of penetration was almost alarming, like poking a nail into soft garden soil. Using the bone along the inner eye socket for leverage, Kelmomas wrenched the buried point in a precise circle. There was no need, he thought, to mutilate geometry as well.

He stepped to the side, his arm held high while the man toppled. The sentry's face lolled to the left and turned almost upright as his weight yanked his skull clear the gleaming skewer. He twitched opened-eyed on the carpet, his fingers pawing the fabric like a purr-drunk kitten—but only for a heartbeat or two.

Kelmomas tugged the man's knife from its sheaf.

The brass-strapped door was unlocked.

Cloth had been drawn over the windows, so that the light creaking in from the hallway was the room's only illumination. "Hello?" somebody called—one of the body-slaves sleeping on the floor of the antechamber. The others awoke, leaned forward into the bar of light. Four altogether, blinking. At first, they seemed little more than disembodied faces, then, when he stepped among them, levitating howls. He hacked at them, striking along the interstices between flailing shadow-limbs. No game, it seemed, had ever been so thrilling. To not be tagged by skin or soiled by blood. To walk the cracks between heartbeats. To kill as though a wind, without any trace of passing.

The faces fell one by one, gushing like slashed wineskins.

The Matriarch was quite awake by the time the little boy slipped into her bedroom. "*Tweet!*" he trilled. "*Tweet-tweet!*" His giggling was uncontrollable . . .

Almost as much as her shrieking.

Anasûrimbor Esmenet casually dismissed the four Shrial Knights they found standing rigid in the hallway, looked around sourly at the ostentatious decor—anything but the dead Yatwerian sentry slumped across the carpet. In the Ikurei days, guests had been housed within the Andiamine Heights, something that simply wasn't possible given the greater administrative demands of the New Empire. The Guest Compound was one of the Holy Dynasty's first works, raised in the heady days before the fall of Nilnamesh and High Ainon, when Kellhus seemed to hold the world's own reins within his haloed fists. The marble, with its distinctive blue bruising, had been transported all the way from quarries in Ce Tydonn. The towering panels, each depicting heroic scenes from the Unification Wars in relief, had been drafted by Niminian himself and carved by the most renowned Nansur stonemasons.

All to the glory of the Aspect-Emperor.

She had no desire to revisit the carnage beyond the threshold. Esmenet had witnessed her fair share of death, perhaps more than any woman in the Three Seas, but she had no stomach for murdered faces.

"We'll wait here," she told the two men who had taken up positions on either side of her. As always, Phinersa's look seemed to flitter about the outskirts of her form. Captain Imhailas, on the other hand, was a study in contrast. He could stare with decisive constancy—too decisive, Esmenet sometimes thought. The man always seemed to be communicating urges he scarcely knew he possessed. Sometimes an arrogant curiosity would creep into his look, and he would press his manner to the very brink of transgression, standing almost too close, speaking in a way that was almost too familiar, and smiling at thoughts to which only he was privy. And as every prostitute knew, the only thing more threatening than eyes that had too many qualms were eyes that had too few. What had the strength to seize also had the strength to choke.

Moments afterwards, Maithanet appeared in the doorway, stepping carefully to avoid the clotted threads and buttons of blood. He was dressed plainly: no felt-shouldered vestments, no hems swaying with stitched gold, only a tunic possessing the satin gloss of a horse on parade. Ochre-coloured, it etched the contours of his limbs and torso in detail, revealing the kind of chest and shoulders that stirred some feminine instinct to climb. For the first time, it seemed, Esmenet realized how much the intimation of sheer physical strength contributed to his sometimes overawing presence.

The Shriah of the Thousand Temples was a man who could break necks with ease.

Both Phinersa and Imhailas fell to their knees, bowed as low as jnan required of them.

"I came as soon as I heard," he said. To better cultivate the distinction between the political and the spiritual organs of the Empire, Maithanet always resided in the Cmiral temple-complex, never the Imperial Precincts, when he stayed in Momemn.

"I knew you would," Esmenet replied.

"My brother—"

"Gone," she snapped. "Shortly before word of . . . of *this* . . . arrived. I ordered the area sealed as soon as I heard of it. I knew you would want to see for yourself."

His look was long and penetrating. It seemed to concede her worst fears.

"How, Maitha? How could they reach so deep? A *mere Cult*. The Mother of Birth, no less!"

The Shriah scratched his beard, glanced at the two men flanking her. "The Narindar, perhaps. They possess the skills . . . perhaps."

The Narindar. The famed Cultic assassins of yore.

"But you don't believe as much, do you?"

"I don't know what to believe. It was a shrewd move, that

much is certain. Figurehead or not, Sharacinth was our royal road, our means of seizing control of the Yatwerians from within, or at the very least setting them at war from within . . ."

Phinersa nodded appreciatively. "She has become their weapon now."

Esmenet had concluded as much almost the instant she had stepped into the blood-spattered antechamber earlier that night. *She* was going to be blamed for this. First the rumours of the White-Luck Warrior, then the Yatwerian Matriarch herself assassinated while a guest of the Empress. The bumbling preposterousness of it mattered not at all. For the masses, the outrageousness of the act would simply indicate her fear, and her fear would suggest that she believed the rumours, which in turn would mean the Aspect-Emperor *had to be a demon . . .*

This had all the makings of a disaster.

"We must make sure no word of this gets out," she heard herself saying.

Each of the men save the Shriah averted their gaze.

She nodded, tried to press her snort of disgust into a long exhalation. "I suppose that's too late . . ."

"The Imperial Precincts," Phinersa said apologetically, "are simply too large, your Glory."

"Then we must go on the offensive!" Imhailas exclaimed. Until this moment, the handsome Exalt-Captain had done his best to slip between the cracks of her Imperial notice, his eyes wired open by the certainty that he would be held accountable. The security of the Imperial Precincts was his sole responsibility.

"That is true in any event," Maithanet said gravely. "But we have another possibility to consider . . ."

Esmenet found herself studying Sharacinth's ash-grey bodyguard, quite numb to what she was seeing. The smell of corruption was already wafting through the hall, like sediment kicked up in water. How absurd was it for them to have this discussion—this council of war—here in the presence of the very circumstantial debris they hoped to bury? People were dead, whole lives had been extinguished, and yet here they stood, plotting . . .

But then, she realized, the living had to forever look past the dead—on the pain of joining them.

"We must ensure this crime is decried for what it is," she said. "Few will believe us, but still, it's imperative that an Inquiry be called, and that someone renowned for his integrity be made Exalt-Inquisitor."

"One of the Patriarchs of the other Cults," Maithanet said, studying the carpets meditatively. "Perhaps Yagthrûta . . ." He raised his eyes to her own. "The man is every bit as rabid as his Patron God when it comes to matters of ritual legality."

Esmenet found herself nodding in approval. Yagthrûta was the Momian Patriarch, famed not only because he was the first Thunyeri to reach such an exalted rank, but because of his reputed piety and candour. Apparently, he had journeyed across the Meneanor from Tenryer to Sumna in naught but a skiff—a supreme gesture of faith if there ever was one. Best of all, his barbaric origins insulated him against the taint of the Shrial or Imperial Apparati.

"Excellent," she said. "In the meantime, it is absolutely crucial we find this Psatma Nannaferi . . ."

"Indeed, your Glory," Imhailas said, nodding with almost comic grandiloquence. "As the Khirgwi say, the headless snake has no fangs."

Esmenet scowled. The Captain had a habit of spouting inane adages—from some popular scroll of aphorisms, no doubt. Usually she found it charming—she was not above forgiving handsome men their quirks, particularly when *she* was their motive—but not on a matter as grievous as this, and certainly not in the presence of rank carnage.

"I'm afraid I've nothing new to add, your Glory," Phinersa said, his gaze ranging across the scenes of war and triumph along the walls. "We still think she's somewhere in Shigek. Think. But with the Fanim raiding the length of the River Sempis . . ." His eyes circled back only to flinch the instant they met her own.

Esmenet acknowledged the dilemma with a grimace. After spending years simply running, Fanayal ab Kascamandri had suddenly become aggressive, extraordinarily aggressive, effectively cutting the overland routes to Eumarna and Nilnamesh and, according to the latest reports, storming fortified towns on the river itself—using *Cishaurim* no less! All Shigek was in an uproar—precisely the kind of confusion the Mother-Supreme needed.

Weakness, she realized. They smelled weakness, all the enemies of the New Empire, be they heathen or Orthodox.

"Unless you issue warrants for the *arrest* of the High-Priestesses," Phinersa continued, "we simply will not find this Nannaferi."

Of course by "arrest" he meant torture. Esmenet found herself looking to Maithanet. "I need to consider that . . . Perhaps if our Exalt-Inquisitor is disposed to blame Sharacinth's murder on some kind of feud *within* the Cult, it might provide the pretext we need."

The Shriah of the Thousand Temples pursed his lips. "We need to proceed cautiously. Perhaps, Empress, we should consult the Aspect-Emperor."

Esmenet felt her look harden into a glare.

Why? she found herself thinking. *Why doesn't Kellhus trust you?*

"Our immediate priority," she declared, pretending he had not spoken, "is to prepare for the eventuality of riots. Phinersa, you must recruit infiltrators. Imhailas, you must *assure* that the Precincts are secured—I will not have this happen a second time! Tell Ngarau that we are to be provisioned for the possibility of a siege. And contact General Anthirul. Have him recall one of the Arcong Columns."

For a moment all of them stood as motionless as the dead.

"Go! Both of you! Now!"

Startled into action, the two men hastened back the way they had come, the one tall and flashing in his ceremonial armour, the other dark and fluid in his black-silk robes. Esmenet found herself nagged by the certainty that Phinersa had momentarily glanced at Maithanet for confirmation . . .

So many looks. So many qualms. It was always the complexities that overwhelmed us. It was always the maze of others that robbed us of our way.

My *little boy is dead*.

But she squelched her misgivings, stared at the Shriah of the Thousand Temples squarely. "Skin-spies," she said. She suddenly found herself dizzy with exhaustion, like a water-bearer balancing one bowl too many. "You think skin-spies did this."

Anasûrimbor Maithanet replied with uncharacteristic reluctance. "I find this turn . . . incalculable."

A memory struck her then, not so much of an event as of a feeling, the murky sense of being harassed and hemmed in, the tightness of breath that belonged to the besieged. A memory of the First Holy War.

For an instant, she thought she could smell the septic reaches of Caraskand.

"Kellhus told me they would come," Esmenet said.

Chapter Thirteen

Condia

Damnation follows not from the bare utterance of sorcery, for nothing is bare in this world. No act is so wicked, no abomination is so obscene, as to lie beyond the salvation of my Name.

—ANASÛRIMBOR KELLHUS, NOVUM ARCANUM

Spring, 20 New Imperial Year (4132 Year-of-the-Tusk), Condia

In Sakarpus, *leuneraal*, or hunched ones (so-called for their habit of stooping over their scrolls), were so despised that it was customary for Horselords and their Boonsmen to bathe after their dealings with them. The Men of Sakarpus considered weakness a kind of disease, something to be fended with various rules of interaction and ritual cleansings. And no men were so weak as the leuneraal.

But Sorweel's new tutor, Thanteus Eskeles, was more than a hunched man. Far more. Were he merely a scholar, then Sorweel would have had the luxury of these rules. But he was also a *sorcerer*—a Three Seas Schoolman!—and this made things . . . complicated.

Sorweel had never doubted the Tusk, never doubted that sorcerers were the walking damned. But try as he might, he could never square this belief with his fascination. Through all his innumerable daydreams of the Three Seas, nothing had captivated him quite so much as the Schools. What would it be like, he often wondered, to possess a voice that could shout down the World's Holy Song? What kind of man would exchange his soul for that kind of diabolical power?

As a result, Eskeles was both an insult and a kind of illicit opportunity—a contradiction, like all things Three Seas.

The Mandate Schoolman would join him each morning, usually within a watch of the march getting underway, and they would while away the time with drill after laborious language drill. Though Eskeles encouraged him to believe otherwise, Sorweel's tongue balked at the sound and structure of Sheyic. He often went cross-eyed listening to Eskeles drone. At times, he feared he might slump unconscious from his saddle, the lessons were so boring.

Once he enlisted Zsoronga to hide him in the middle of his retinue, he came to dread the sorceror's appearance so. The Successor-Prince promptly betrayed him, but not before having his fill of laughing at the sight of the Schoolman riding on his burrow craning his neck this way and that. Old Obotegwa, he explained, was growing weary speaking for two men.

"Besides," he said, "how can we be sure we're talking to each other at all? Perhaps the old devil makes it all up so he can laugh himself to sleep."

Obotegwa simply winked and grinned mischievously.

Eskeles was a strange man, obese by Sakarpi standards, but not so fat as many Sorweel had seen in the Ordeal. He never seemed to get cold, despite wearing only a red-silk tunic with his leggings, one cut to expose the black fur that crawled from his belly to his heard, which even oiled and plaited never quite seemed under control. He had an affable, even merry face, high cheeks beneath pig-friendly eyes.

This, combined with a lively, even careless manner, made him exceedingly difficult to dislike, despite his sorcerous calling and the brownish tinge of his Ketyai skin.

At first Sorweel could scarcely understand a word he said, his accent was so thick. But he quickly learned how to listen through the often bizarre pronunciations. He discovered that the man had spent several years in Sakarpus as part of a secret Mandate mission posing as Three Seas traders.

"Dreadful, dreadful time for the likes of me," he said.

"I suppose you missed your Southron luxuries," Sorweel jeered.

The fat man laughed. "No-no. *Heavens*, no. If you knew what me and my kind dreamed each night, your Glory, you would understand our profound ability to appreciate the simplest of things. No. It was your *Chorae Hoard* . . . Quite extraordinary really, dwelling in the vicinity of so many Trinkets . . ."

"Trinkets?"

"Yes. That's what we Schoolmen like to call them—Chorae, that is. For much the same reason you Sakarpi calls Sranc—what is it? Oh, yes, *grass-rats*."

Sorweel frowned. "Because that's what they are?"

Despite his good humour, Eskeles had this sly way of appraising him sometimes, as if he were a map fetched from the fire. Something that had to be read around burns.

"No-no. Because that's what you *need them to be*."

Sorweel understood full well what the fat man meant—men often used glib words to shrink great and terrible things—but the *true lesson*, he realized, was quite different. He resolved never to forget *that Eskeles was a spy*. That he was an agent of the Aspect-Emperor.

Learning a language, Sorweel quickly realized, was unlike learning anything else. At first, he thought it would be a matter of simple substitution, of replacing one set of sounds with another. He knew nothing of what Eskeles called *grammar*, the notion that a kind of invisible mechanism bound everything he said into patterns. He scoffed at the sorcerer's insistence that he first *learn his own tongue* before venturing to learn another. But the patterns were undeniable, and no matter how much he wanted to dispute the fat man and his glib *I-told-you-so* smile, he had to admit that he could not speak without using things such as subjects and predicates, nouns and verbs.

Though he affected an attitude of aloof contempt—he was in the presence of a leuneraal, after all—Sorweel found himself more than a little troubled by this. How could he know these things *without knowing them?* And if something as profound as grammar could escape his awareness—to the point where it had simply not existed—what else was lurking in the nethers of his soul?

So he came to realize that learning a language was perhaps the most profound thing a man could do. Not only did it require wrapping different sounds around the very movement of your soul, it involved learning things somehow already known, as though much of what he was somehow existed apart from him. A kind of enlightenment accompanied these first lessons, a deeper understanding of self.

None of which made the lessons any less boring. But thankfully even Eskeles's passion for Sheyic would begin to wane by midafternoon, and his disciplined insistence on the drills would lapse. For a few watches, at least, he would let the young King indulge his curiosity about more sundry things. Sorweel spent much of this time avoiding the topics that really interested him—sorcery because he feared it sinful, and the Aspect-Emperor for reasons he could not fathom—and asking questions about the Three Seas and the Great Ordeal.

So he learned more details about the Middle-North and its peoples: the Galeoth, the Tydonni, and the Thunyeri. The Eastern Ketyai: the Cengemi, the Conriyans, and the

Ainoni. And the Western Ketyai: primarily the Nansur, the Shigeki, the Kianene, and the Nilnameshi. Eskeles, who, Sorweel was beginning to realize, was one of those vain men who never seemed arrogant, discussed all these peoples with the confidence and wicked cynicism of someone who had spent his life travelling. Each nation had its strengths and weaknesses: the Ainoni, for instance, were devious plotters but too womanish in their affect and attire; the Thunyeri were savage in battle but about as sharp as rotten fruit—as Eskeles put it. Sorweel found all of it fascinating, even though the sorcerer was one of those men whose animate enthusiasm actually seemed to deaden rather than liven the subject matter.

Then, one afternoon several days into his instruction, Sorweel summoned enough courage to mention the Aspect-Emperor. He related—in a form abbreviated by embarrassment—the story Zsoronga had told him about the emissaries cutting their own throats before the Zeümi Satakhan. "I know he's your master . . ." he ended awkwardly.

"What about him?" Eskeles replied after a thoughtful pause.

"Well . . . *What is he?*"

The sorcerer nodded in the manner of those confirmed in their worries. "Come," he said cryptically, spurring his mule to a trot.

The Kidruhil typically rode near the forward heart of the Great Ordeal, where they could be sent in any direction given the unlikely event of an attack. But word of Sranc activity to the west had led to their redeployment on the extreme left flank. This meant the sorcerer and his ward need press neither hard nor far to ride clear of the slow roping columns. Looking absurd on his mule—his legs straight rather than bent, his girth almost equal to his mount's—Eskeles pressed along the shoulders of a long low knoll. Sorweel followed, alternately smiling at the sight of the man and frowning at his intentions. Beyond the crest of the knoll, the farther plains sloped up into the horizon, bone-coloured for the most part but shot with whorls of grey and ash black. The green of the more lush lands to the south had become little more than a haze.

Staring off into the distance, the sorcerer reined to a halt at the summit, where Sorweel joined him. The air was crisp and chill.

"So dry," Eskeles said without looking at him.

"It often is. Some years the grasses all die and blow away . . . Or so they say."

"And that," Eskeles continued, pointing toward the north-west. "What is that?"

There was a Kidruhil patrol in the distance, a line of tiny horses, but Sorweel knew that Eskeles pointed beyond them. The sky was a bowl of endless turquoise. Beneath it the land ascended a series of rumps, then spread bluing into a series of flats and folds, like a tent after its poles had been dropped. Reaching in and out of the horizon, an immense band cut across the plain, mottled black and grey near its centre and fading into the natural grain of the surrounding grasslands along its edges.

"The great herds," Sorweel said, having seen such tracks many times. "Elk. Endless numbers of them."

The sorcerer turned in his saddle, nodding back the way they had come. The breeze pulled a comb of hairs from his beard.

"And what would you say *that* is?"

Perplexed, Sorweel wheeled his horse about, followed Eskeles's bemused gaze. Not since Sakarpus had he seen the Great Ordeal from its edge, and he found himself shocked at the difference of watching something that had encompassed him from afar. Where before the world had seemed to roll into the immobile masses, now the masses rolled over an immovable world. Thousands upon thousands of figures, scattered like grain, thrown like threads, knitted into slow heaving carpets, gradually creeping across the back of the earth. Arms twinkled to the horizon.

"The Great Ordeal," he heard himself say.

"No."

Sorweel searched his tutor's smiling eyes.

"This," Eskeles explained, "*this* . . . is the Aspect-Emperor."

Mystified, Sorweel could only turn back to the spectacle. Though he couldn't be sure, he thought he saw the Aspect-Emperor's own banner rising from faraway mobs: a white-silk standard the size of a sail, emblazoned with a simple blood-red Circumfix. Struck by unseen priests, the Interval hummed out across the arch of the sky, deep and resonant, fading as always in increments too fine to detect, so that he was never quite sure when it stopped sounding.

"I don't understand . . ."

"There are many, many ways to carve the world, your Glory. Think of the way we identify different men with their bodies, with the position they occupy in place and time. Since we inherit this way of thinking, we assume that it is *natural*, that it is the only way. But what if we identify a man *with his thoughts*—what then? How would we draw his boundaries? Where would he begin, and where would he end?"

Sorweel simply gazed at the man. Damned leuneraal.

"I still don't understand."

The sorcerer frowned in silence for a time, then with a decisive grunt leaned back in his saddle to root through one of his packs. He huffed and cursed in some exotic tongue as he pawed through his belongings—the effort of twisting back and sideways obviously strained him. Without warning, he dismounted with a heavy "*Oooof!*" then began rifling the opposite pack in the same way. It wasn't until he searched the rump pack—made of weather-beaten leather like the others—that he found what he was looking for: a small vase no bigger than a child's forearm and just as white. With a triumphant expression, he held it shining to the sun: porcelain, another luxury of the Three Seas.

"Come-come," he called to Sorweel, stamping his left boot in the grass to wipe mule shit from his heel.

Securing his pony's reins to the pommel of the mule's saddle, Sorweel hastened after the sorcerer, who walked kicking through winter-flattened grasses—to clean off more dung, the young King supposed, until, that is, Eskeles cried, "Aha!" at the sight of rounded stone rising from the turf.

"This is called a *philauta*," the sorcerer said, raising the slight vase and shaking it. A clipped rattle issued from within. The sunlight revealed dozens of little tusks raised along its length. "It's used for sacramental libations . . ."

He smashed it across the back of the stone. To his chagrin, Sorweel flinched.

"Now look," Eskeles said, squatting over the wreckage so that his belly hung between his knees. A small replica of the vase—what had made the rattling sound, Sorweel realized—lay beneath the sorcerer's bulk, no longer than a thumb. Otherwise, fragments lay scattered across the stone and between the twisted threads of last year's grass, some as small as cat's claws, others the size of teeth, and still others as big as coins. The sorcerer shooed away a spider with stubby fingers, then lifted one of the tinier pieces, little more than a splinter, to the glinting light.

"Souls have *shapes*, Sorweel. Think of how I differ from you"—he raised another splinter to illustrate the contrast—"or how you differ from Zsoronga," he said, raising yet another. "Or"—he plucked a far larger fragment—"think of all the Hundred Gods, and how they differ from one another, Yatwer and Gilgaöl. Or Momas and Ajokli." With each name he raised yet another coin-sized fragment.

"Our God . . . *the* God, is broken into innumerable pieces. And this is what gives us life, what makes you, me, even the lowliest slave, sacred." He cupped several pieces in a meaty palm. "We're not equal, most assuredly not, but we remain *fragments of God* nonetheless."

He gingerly set each of the pieces across the top of the stone, then stared intently at Sorweel. "Do you understand what I'm saying?"

Sorweel did understand, so much that his skin had pimpled listening to the sorcerer speak. He understood more than he *wanted*. The Kiünnatic Priests had only rules and stories—nothing like this. They had no answers that made . . . sense of things.

"But . . ."

The young King trailed, defeated by the weakness of his own voice.

Eskeles nodded and smiled, so openly pleased with himself that he seemed anything but arrogant or haughty. "But what is the Aspect-Emperor?" he asked, completing Sorweel's question.

Using his fingers, he combed the chipped replica of the vase from the grass below his left knee. He held it between thumb and forefinger, where it shone as smooth as glass, identical to the original philauta in every respect save for its size.

"Huh?" The Schoolman laughed. "Eh? Do you see? The soul of the Aspect-Emperor is not only greater than the souls of Men, it possesses the *very shape* of the Ur-Soul."

"You mean . . . your God of Gods."

"*Our* God of Gods?" the sorcerer repeated, shaking his head. "I keep forgetting that you're a heathen! I suppose you think *Inri Sejenus* is some kind of demon as well!"

"I'm trying," Sorweel replied, his face suddenly hot. "I'm trying to understand!"

"I-know-I-know," the Schoolman said, this time smirking at his own stupidity. "We'll discuss the Latter Prophet, er . . . later . . ." He closed his eyes and shook his head. "In the meantime, ponder this . . . If the Aspect-Emperor's soul is cast in the very form of the God, then . . ." He trailed nodding. "Huh? Eh? *If* . . ."

"Then . . . He is the God in small . . ." A kind of supernatural terror accompanied these words.

The sorcerer beamed, his teeth surprisingly white and straight compared to the dark frazzle of his beard. "You wonder how it is so many would march to the ends of the earth for him? You wonder what could move men *to cut their own throats* in his name. Well then, there you have your answer . . ." He leaned forward, his pose rigid in the manner of men who think they possess world-judging truths. "Anasûrimbor Kellhus *is the God of Gods*, Sorweel, come to walk among us."

Somehow Sorweel had fallen from a crouch to his knees. He remained breathless still, staring at Eskeles. To move his hands or even to blink his eyes, it seemed, would be to quake and to spill, to reveal himself a thing of sand.

"Before his coming, me and my kind were damned," the sorcerer continued, though he seemed to be speaking more for his own benefit than Sorweel's. "We Schoolmen traded a lifetime of power for an eternity of torment . . . But now?"

Damnation. Sorweel felt the cold of dead earth soak through his leggings. An ache climbed into his knees. His father had died in sorcerous fire—how many times had Sorweel tormented himself with that thought, imagining the shriek and scream, the thousand blistering knives? But what Eskeles was saying . . .

Did it mean *he burned still?*

The Mandate Schoolman gazed at him, his eyes wide and bright with a kind of uncompromising joy, like a man in the flush of infatuation, or a gambler delivered from slavery by an impossible throw of the number-sticks. When he spoke, more than admiration—or even worship—trilled through his voice.

"Now I am *saved*."

Love. He spoke with love.

Rather than go to Zsoronga's pavilion that evening, Sorweel shared a quiet repast with Porsparian in the white-washed air of his own tent. He sat on the end of his cot, his head bent to his steaming gruel, knowing yet not caring that the Shigeki slave stared at him wordlessly. A kind of incipient confusion filled him, one that had slipped the cup of his soul and spilled through his body, a leaden tingle. The sounds of the Great Ordeal fell through the fabric effortlessly, thrumming and booming from every direction.

Save the sky. The sky was silent.

And the earth.

"*Anasûrimbor Kellhus is the God of Gods incarnate, Sorweel, come to walk among us . . .*"

Men often make decisions in the wake of significant events, if only to pretend they had some control over their own transformations. Sorweel's first decision was to ignore what had happened, to turn his back on what Eskeles had said, as though rudeness could drive his words away. His second decision was to laugh—laughter was ever the great ward against all things foolish. But he could not harness the breath to see it through.

Then he finally decided to think Eskeles's thoughts, if only to pretend they had not already possessed him. What was the harm of thinking?

As a young boy he spent most of his solitary play in the ruined sections of his father's palace, particularly in what was called the Overgrown Garden. Once, while searching for a lost arrow, he noticed a young poplar springing from some far-flung seed beneath a thicket of witch-mulberry. Wondering whether it would live or die, he checked on it from time to time, watched it slowly labour in the shadow.

Several times he even crawled into the mossy interior of the thicket, wriggling in on his back, and bringing his cheek close to the newborn's stem so that he could see it leaning, extending up and out to the promise of light shining through the fretting of witch-mulberry leaves. Over days and weeks it reached, thin with inanimate effort, straining for a band of golden warmth that descended like a hand from the sky. And then finally, it touched . . .

The last time he had looked, mere weeks before the city's fall, the tree stood proud save for the memory of that first crook in its trunk, and the mulberry bush was long dead.

There *was* harm in thinking. He not only knew this—he could *feel* it.

What Eskeles had shown him had the power of . . . of *sense*. What Eskeles had shown him had explained, not only the Aspect-Emperor . . . but himself as well.

"*. . . we remain fragments of the God, nonetheless.*"

Was this why the Kiünnatic Priests had demanded that all Three Seas missionaries be burned? Was this why spittle had flecked their lips when they came to his father with their demands?

Had they been a bush, fearful of the tree in their midst?

"*I keep forgetting that you're a heathen!*"

After darkness fell and Porsparian's breathing dipped into a rasping snore, Sorweel lay awake, riven by thought after cascading thought—there was no thwarting them. When he curled beneath his blankets, it seemed he could see *him* as he was on that day of war and rain and thunder, the Aspect-Emperor, ringlets dripping about a long face, beard cut and plaited in the way of Southron Kings, eyes so blue they seemed a glimpse of another world. A glaring, golden figure, walking in the light of a different time, a brighter sun.

A friendly scowl, followed by a gentle laugh. "*I'm rarely what my enemies expect, I know.*"

And Sorweel told himself, commanded himself, mouthed

about clamped teeth, *I am my father's son! A true son of Sakarpus!*

But what if . . .

Hands lifting him from his knees. "*You are a King, are you not?*"

What if he came to believe?

"*I'm no conqueror . . .*"

He awoke, as had become his habit, several moments before the sounding of the Interval. For some reason, he felt a kind of long-drawn relief instead of the usual clutch of fear. The plains air, the breath of his people, sighed through his tent, made the bindings creak where Porsparian had tied them down. The silence was so complete he could almost believe that he was alone, that all the rolling pasture about his tent was empty to the horizon—abandoned to the Horse-King.

Then the Interval tolled. The first calls to prayer climbed into the skies.

He joined the Company of Scions where their Standard had been planted the previous evening, numbly followed Captain Harnilias's barked instructions. Apparently his pony, which Sorweel called Stubborn, had done some soul searching the previous night as well, because for the first time he responded wonderfully to Sorweel's demands. He'd known the beast was intelligent, perhaps uncommonly so, and only refused to learn his Sakarpic knee-and-spur combinations out of spite. Stubborn had become so agreeable, in fact, that Sorweel breezed through the early on-the-march drills. He even heard several of the Scions call out, "*Ramt-anqual!*"—the word Obotegwa always translated as "Horse-King."

When chance afforded he leaned forward to whisper the Third Prayer to Husyelt into the pony's twitching ear. "One and one are one," he explained to the beast afterward. "You are learning, Stubborn. One horse and one man make *one warrior*."

A bolt of shame passed through him at the thought of "one man," for in fact he was not a man. He never would be, he realized, given that his Elking would likely never happen. A child forever, without the shades of the dead to assist him. This set him to gazing, once again, out over the marching masses that engulfed his surroundings. Shields and swords. Waddling packs. Innumerable souls behind innumerable faces, all toiling toward the dark line of the north.

How could wonder make a heart so small?

When Sorweel finally settled next to Zsoronga and Obotegwa in the column, the Successor-Prince commented on his haggard expression.

Sorweel paid no attention, simply said, "The Ordeal. What do you think of it?"

Zsoronga's expression went from bemusement to concentrated worry as he listened to Obotegwa's frowning translation. "*Ke yusu emeba*—"

"I think it may be the end of us."

"But do you think it's *real*?"

The Prince paused, gazed out across a landscape dizzy with distances. He wore what he called his *kemtush* over his Kidruhil tunic, a white sash dense with black hand-painted characters that listed the "battles of his blood," the wars fought by his ancestors.

"Well, I think *they* believe it's real. I can only imagine what it must seem like to you, Horse-King. You and your stranded city. Me? I come from a great and ancient nation, mightier by far than any of the individual nations gathered beneath the Circumfix. And still, I have never seen the like. To concentrate so much glory, so much power, for a march to the ends of the Eärwa! This is something no Satakhan in history, not even Mbotetulu! could have brought about—let alone my poor father. Whatever this is, and whatever comes of it, you can rest assured that it will be *recalled* . . . Recalled to the end of all time."

They rode in silence for some time, lost in the thoughts.

"And what do you think of *them*?" Sorweel eventually asked.

"Them?"

"Yes. The Anasûrimbor."

The Successor-Prince shrugged, but not without, Sorweel noticed, a quick glance around him. "Everyone ponders them. They are like the mummers the Ketyai are so found of, standing before the amphitheatre of the world."

"What does 'everyone' say?"

"That he is a Prophet, or even a God."

"What do you say?"

"What the lines of my father's treaty say: that he is a Benefactor of High Holy Zeüm, Guardian of the Son of Heaven's Son."

"No . . . What do *you* say?"

For the first time, Sorweel saw anger score the young man's handsome profile. Zsoronga momentarily glared at Obotegwa, as though holding him responsible for Sorweel's relentless questioning, before turning back to the young King with mild and insincere eyes. "What do you think?"

"He's so many things to so many people," Sorweel found himself blurting. "I know not what to think. All I know is that those who spend any time with him, *any time with him whatsoever*, think him some kind of God."

The Successor-Prince once again turned to his Senior Obligate, this time with questioning eyes. Though the drifting pace of their parallel horses meant that Sorweel could only glimpse Obotegwa's face on an angle, he was certain he had seen the old translator nod.

While the two exchanged words in Zeümi, Sorweel struggled with the dismaying realization that Zsoronga had secrets, powerful secrets, and that compared to the intrigues that likely encircled him, his friendship with an outland king, with a sausage, could be little more than diversion. The Son of Nganka'kull was more than a hostage, he was a *spy* as well, a chit in a game greater than Sorweel could imagine. The fate of empires bound him.

When Zsoronga returned his gaze, the pinch of merriment that characterized so much of their discourse had utterly vanished, leaving a curious, questioning intensity in its place. It was almost as if his brown eyes were begging Sorweel, somehow . . .

Begging him to be someone High Holy Zeüm could trust.

"*Petatu surub—*"

"Have you heard the story of Shimeh, of the First Holy War?"

Sorweel shrugged. He felt at once honoured and gratified. A prince of a great nation confided in him. "Not much," he admitted, careful to pitch his voice at the same low tenor as his friend.

"There is this book," Zsoronga said, the squint in his eyes complementing the reluctance in his voice. "This *forbidden* book, written by a sorcerer . . . Drusas Achamian. Have you heard of him?"

"No."

Zsoronga's bottom lip pressed the line of his mouth into an upsidedown crescent. He nodded, not so much in affirmation or approval, but as though to acknowledge his succinct honesty. "*Bpo Mandatu mbal—*"

"He was a Mandate Schoolman, like your own tutor."

Sorweel found himself glancing about, fearing that Eskeles would arrive any moment. Men had a way of hearing their names, even when spoken across the arc of the world. "And?"

"Well, he was present when the Anasûrimbor joined the First Holy War. Apparently he was his first and dearest friend—his *teacher*, both before and after the Circumfixion."

"So?"

"Well, for one, the Empress—you know, the woman on the silver kellics, the mother of our dear, beloved General Kayûtas—Achamian was her *first* husband. Apparently the Anasûrimbor *stole her*. So at the conclusion of the First Holy War, when the Shriah of their Thousand Temples crowns the Anasûrimbor Aspect-Emperor, this Achamian *repudiates him* before all those gathered, claims he is a fraud and deceiver."

Something of the old Zsoronga had returned, as though he were warming to the gossip of the tale.

"Yes . . ." Sorweel said. "I'm sure I've heard this . . . or a version of it, anyway."

"So he leaves the Holy War, goes into exile, becomes, they say, the only Wizard in the Three Seas. Only the love and shame of the Empress prevent his execution."

"Wizard?"

Another grave turn in his ebony expression. "Yes. A sorcerer without a School."

The Company of Scions was but a clot in a far larger column of Kidruhil companies, and a conspicuous one, given that its members had leave to wear native ornamentations over their crimson uniforms. They had followed the column over the crest of a scrub-choked rise, then leaned back against their cantles as they descended into a broad depression. The black track became viscous with water and muck. The susurrus of countless hooves stamping marshy ground rose about them—the wheeze of sinking grounds. What had looked like mist from the sloped heights became clouds of midges.

"And this is where he writes this book?" Sorweel asked, pitching his voice over the tramping clamour. "In exile?"

"Our spies brought my father a copy some six years ago, saying that it had become a kind of scripture for those who still resist the Anasûrimbor in the Three Seas. It's titled *A Compendium of the First Holy War*."

"So it's a history?"

"Only apparently. There are . . . *insinuations*, scattered throughout, and descriptions of the Anasûrimbor as he was, before he gained the Gnosis and became almost all-powerful."

"Are you saying this Mandate Schoolman *knew* . . . that he knew what the Aspect-Emperor was?"

Zsoronga paused before answering, looked at him as though rehearsing previous judgments. Among those who would contest the power of the Aspect-Emperor, Sorweel understood, no matters could be more essential.

"Yes," Zsoronga finally replied.

"So. What does he say?"

"Everything you might expect a cuckold to say. That's the problem . . ."

An ambient *eagerness* bloomed through Sorweel's limbs. The knowledge he needed was *here*—he could sense it. The knowledge that would cleave certainty out of mangled circumstances—that would see his honour redeemed! He squeezed the reins tight enough to whiten his knuckles. "Does he call him a demon?" he asked almost with breath. "*Does* he?"

"No."

A vertiginous, dumbfounded moment, as if he had leaned forward expecting an answer to brace him. "What then? Do not play me on such matters, Zsoronga! I come to you as a friend!"

The Successor-Prince somehow grinned and scowled all at once. "You must *learn*, Horse-King. Too many wolves prowl these columns. I appreciate your honesty, your overture, I truly do, but when you speak like this . . . I . . . I fear for you."

Obotegwa had softened his sovereign's tone, of course. No matter how diligently the Obligate tried to recreate the tenor of his Prince's discourse, his voice always bore the imprint of a long and oft-examined life.

Sorweel found himself looking down at the polished

contours of his pommel, so different from the raw hook of iron on Sakarpi saddles. "What does this-this . . . Achamian say?"

"He says the Anasûrimbor is a *man*, neither diabolic nor divine. A man of unheard-of intellect. He bids us imagine the difference between ourselves and children . . ." The black man trailed into silence, his brows furrowed in concentration. He had this habit of staring down and to the left when pondering, as though judging points buried deep in the ground.

"And?"

"The important thing, he says, isn't so much what the Anasûrimbor is, *as what we are to him*."

Sorweel glared at him in exasperation. "You speak in riddles!"

"*Yusum pyeb—!*"

"Think to your childhood! Think of the hopes and fears. Think of the tales the nursemaids told you. Think of the way your face continually betrayed you. Think of all the ways you were mastered, all the ways you were moulded."

"Yes! So?"

"That is what you are to the Aspect-Emperor. That is what we *all* are."

"Children?"

Zsoronga dropped his reins, waved his arms out in grand gesture of indication. "All of this. This divinity. This apocalypse. This . . . *religion* he has created. They are the kinds of lies we tell children to assure they act in accord with our wishes. To make us love, to incite us to sacrifice . . . This is what Drusas Achamian *seems* to be saying."

These words, spoken through the lense of wise and weary confidence that was Obotegwa, chilled Sorweel to the pith. Demons were so much easier! This . . . this . . .

How does a child war against a father? How does a child not . . . love?

Sorweel could feel the dismay on his face, the bewilderment, but his shame was muted by the realization that Zsoronga felt no different. "So what *are* his wishes, then? The Aspect-Emperor. If all this is . . . is a fraud, then what are his true ends?"

They had climbed out of the shallow marsh and now crested a low knoll. Zsoronga nodded past Sorweel's shoulder, to where, in the congestion of the near distance, the young King could see Eskeles's absurd form fairly bowing the back of his huffing donkey. More lessons . . .

"The Wizard does not say," the Successor-Prince continued when he glanced back. "But I fear that you and I shall know before this madness is done with."

That night he dreamed of Kings arguing across an ancient floor.

"*There is the surrender that leads to slavery*," the Exalt-General said. "*And there is the surrender that sets one free. Soon, very soon, your people shall know that difference.*"

"*So says the slave!*" Harweel cried, standing in a flower of outward-hooking flames.

How bright his father burned. Lines of fire skittering up the veins wrapping his arms. His hair and beard a smoking blaze. His skin blistering like pitch, shining raw, trailing lines of fiery grease . . .

How beautiful was his damnation.

At first he battled the slave, crying out. Porsparian was little more than hands in the darkness, fending, pressing, and then as Sorweel eventually calmed, soothing.

"*Ek birim sefnarati*," the old slave murmured, though it sounded more like a mutter in his broken wood-pipe voice. "*Ek birim sefnarati . . . Shhh . . . Shhh . . .*" Over and over, little more than a shadow kneeling at the side of Sorweel's cot.

Illumination slowly tinted the greater dark beyond the canvas planes of his tent, a slow inhalation of light.

"I saw my father burn," he croaked to the uncomprehending slave.

For some reason, he did not begrudge the gnarled hand that rested on his shoulder. And it seemed a miracle the way the slave's cracked-leather features gained reality in the fading gloom. Sorweel's own grandfather had died on the Pale when he was very young, so he had never known the indulgent warmth of a father's father's adoration. He had never learned the way the years opened the hearts of the old to the miraculousness of the young. But he thought he could see it in Porsparian's strange yellow-smiling eyes, in the rattle of his voice, and he found himself trusting it completely.

"Does that mean he's *damned?*" he asked thickly. A grandfather, it seemed, would know. "Dreams of burning?"

The shadow of a stern memory crossed the old Shigeki's face, and he pressed himself to his feet. Sorweel sat up in his cot, absently scratched his scalp while watching his slave's shadowy labour. Porsparian stooped to pull the mat from the turf floor, then knelt in the manner of an old woman worshiping. As Sorweel had seen him do so many times, he plucked away the turf, then pressed the form of a face into the soil—a face that seemed unmistakably feminine despite the gloom.

Yatwer.

The slave brought dirt to his eyes, then began slowly rocking to a muttered prayer. Back and forth, without any discernible rhythm, like a man struggling against the ropes that bound him. On and on he muttered, while the dawning light pulled more and more details from obscurity: the crude black stitching of his tunic's hem, the tufts of wiry white hair that climbed his forearms, the cross-hatching of kicked and pressed grasses. A kind of violence crept into his movements, enough to draw Sorweel anxiously forward. The Shigeki jerked from side to side, as though yanked by some interior chain. The intervals between the spasms shrank, until it seemed he flinched from a cloud of bee stings. A series of convulsions . . .

Sorweel leapt to his feet, stepped forward, hands held out. "Porsparian!" he cried.

But something, some rule of religious witness perhaps, held him back. He remembered the incident with the tear, when Porsparian had burned his palm, and a hollowing anxiousness seized him. He felt like a thing of paper, creased and rolled and folded into the shape of a man. Any gust, it seemed, could make a kite of him, toss him to the arches of heaven. What new madness was this?

His soiled fingers still to his eyes, the old man writhed and bucked as though kicked and beaten from within. Breath whistled from flaring nostrils. His voice had sputtered into a ragged gurgle . . .

Then, like grass springing back to form in the wake of boots, he was upright and still. Porsparian drew aside his hands, looked to the earth with eyes like red gelatin . . .

Gazed at the earthen face.

Sorweel caught his breath, blinked as though to squint away the madness. Not only had the slave's eyes gone red (a trick, some kind of trick!), somehow the mouth pressed into the soil face had *opened*.

Opened?

Forming a plate with his palms, Porsparian lowered his fingers to the lower lip, received the waters pooling there. Old and bent and smiling, he then turned to his master and stood. His eyes had returned to normal, though the knowingness they possessed seemed anything but. He stepped forward, reached out. Muck trailed like blood from the pads of his fingers. Sorweel shrank backward, nearly toppled over his cot.

Standing across the morning-glowing canvas, Porsparian actually seemed a creature made of shadowy earth, like something moulded from the mud of an ancient river watching with the forever look of yellow eyes. "Spit," the old slave said, stunning him with the clarity of his Sakarpic pronunciation. "To keep . . . face . . . clean."

For several heartbeats Sorweel simply stared, dumbfounded. Where? Where had the water come from?

What kind of Three Seas trickery . . .

"You *hide*," the old slave gasped. "Hide in gaze!"

But a kernel of understanding anchored his panic, and something within him wept, shouted in anguish and relief. The Old Gods had not forgotten! Sorweel closed his eyes, knowing that this was all the permission required. He felt the fingers smear his cheek, press in the firm manner of old men who do all things at the limit of their strength, not for anger, but to overmatch the thoughtless vitality of the young. He felt *her* spit at once soil and cleanse.

A mother wiping the face of her beloved son.

Look at you . . .

Somewhere on the plain, the priests sounded the Interval: a single note tolling pure and deep over landscapes of tented confusion. The sun was rising.

Chapter Fourteen

Cil-Aujas

The world is only as deep as we can see. This is why fools think themselves profound. This is why terror is the passion of revelation.

—AJENCIS, *THE THIRD ANALYTIC OF MEN*

Spring, 20 New Imperial Year (4132 Year-of-the-Tusk), south of Mount Aenaratiol

Age. Age and darkness.

For the peoples of the Three Seas, *The Chronicle of the Tusk* was the ultimate measure of the ages. Nothing was more ancient. Nothing *could be*. Yet the Skin Eaters found themselves walking halls older than even the *language* of the Tusk, let alone the ivory into which it had been cut. No one had to tell them this, though they sometimes glanced at Achamian as if pleading to be told otherwise. They could see it scrawling through the light about them. They could smell it hanging in the dust. They could feel it creeping through meek bones and chastened hearts.

Here was a glory that no human, tribe or nation, could hope to match, and their hearts balked at the admission. Achamian saw it floating in their faces: lips drawn into lines, teeth set in slack jaws, eyes roaming without focus, the vacant look of blowhards confronting their folly. Even these men, so quick to celebrate sin and debauchery, had thought the blood of Gods coursed through their veins.

Cil-Aujas, for all its silence, boomed otherwise.

What Achamian had thought a vast entrance gallery turned out to be a subterranean road. The line of walkers quickly coalesced into two bands, one following Cleric and his hanging point of sorcerous light in the lead, the other crowding Achamian and his Surrillic Cant of Illumination. For a time they seemed to shuffle more than stride, a gawking band staring up and around, painfully aware of their trespass. Everyone cringed at the sound of voices. Fragments of what might have been bone gravelled their steps. Dust fogged their ankles.

Images. Images planked every surface, virginal as exhumed graves, soaked in the gloom of unwitnessed ages. The style mirrored that of the Obsidian Gate: the walls banded with layered pictorial reliefs, the outer set like impossibly elaborate grillwork over the inner, vaulting some forty feet. The sedimentary grain, whorls of charcoal black veined with grey, made it obvious that it had been hewn from living rock. Whole sections shone like brown and black glass. Pinned between their passing points of light, the walls literally seethed with counterfeit motion.

It was the absence of weathering that distinguished the hall from the Gate. The detail baffled the eye, from the mail of the Nonmen warriors to the hair of the human slaves. Scars striping knuckles. Tears lining supplicants' cheeks. Everything had been rendered with maniacal intricacy. The effect was too lifelike, Achamian decided, the concentration too obsessive. The scenes did not so much celebrate or portray, it seemed, as *reveal*, to the point where it hurt to watch the passing sweep of images, parade stacked upon parade, entire hosts carved man for man, victim for victim, warring without breath or clamour.

Pir-Pahal, Achamian realized. The entire hall was dedicated to it, a great and ancient battle fought between the Nonmen and the Inchoroi. He could even recognize the principals: the traitor, Nin'janjin, and his sovereign, Cu'jara Cinmoi, the Nonman Emperor. The mighty hero, Gin'gûrima, with arms like a man's thighs. And the Inchoroi King, Sil, armoured in corpses, flanked by his inhuman kinsmen, winged monstrosities with wicked limbs, pendulous phalli, and skulls grafted into skulls.

Achamian nearly stumbled when he saw the Heron Spear raised high in Sil's articulated arms.

"Those things . . ." Mimara whispered from his side.

"Inchoroi," Achamian muttered. With a kind of wonder, he thought of Kellhus and his Great Ordeal, of their mad march across the wasted North to Golgotterath. The war depicted on these walls, he realized, had never ended, not truly.

Ten thousand years of woe.

"These are their memories," Achamian found himself saying aloud. "The Nonmen cut their past into the walls . . . as a way to make it as immortal as their bodies."

The faces of several scalpers turned toward him, some in expectation, others in annoyance. Speaking seemed a kind of sacrilege, like ill-willed gossip in the light of a funeral pyre.

On and on they walked, deeper into the bowels of the mountain. Miles passed without a terminus or a fork, just warring walls, stamped as deep as outstretched arms. The way before them resolved out of obscurity. Behind, the light of the entrance dwindled into a star, solitary in a field of absolute black.

Then with horrifying suddenness, a second gate welled out of the darkness. Several gasps echoed through the stale air. The company stumbled to a halt.

Two wolves towered before them, standing like men to

either side of an unbarred portal, eyes bulging, tongues lolling. The contrast was dramatic. Gone was the intricacy of the underworld road, replaced by a more ancient, more totemic sensibility. Each wolf was three wolves, or the same wolf at three different times, the graven heads warped into three distinct postures, their stylized expressions ranging from sorrow to savagery, as if the ancient artisans had rendered an entire animal existence in a single moment of stone. Writing ringed the casings of each, densely packed in vertical columns, pictograms like numeric slashes, at once elegant and primitive. Auja-Gilcûnni, Achamian realized, the so-called First Tongue, so old that even the Nonmen had forgotten how to read or speak it—which meant this gate had to be as ancient to Nonmen as the Tusk was to Men. Everything about it spoke of rude souls awakening to the subtleties of artistic wonder . . .

But the fascination wilted as quickly as it had sparked. Achamian found himself swaying on his feet, light-headed, as if he had leapt too quickly from a slumber. Mimara also stumbled, brought both hands to her forehead, held them like a tent over her brows. Several mules spooked, stamped and jerked against their ropes. There was more than the ache of ages in the air. There was . . . something else, a *lack* of some kind, running perpendicular to the geometry of the real, bowing its lines with its cavernous suck. Something that whispered from the blackness between the graven beasts.

Something abyssal.

The gate swam in the Wizard's eyes, not so much a portal as a *hole*.

Without warning, Cleric's light waxed, bleached the heights of stone. Shadows crawled from the great wolf snouts hanging above. The Nonman turned before the entrance, blasted by illumination. Several raised their hands against the glare.

His voice seemed to boom into the surrounding darkness.

"Kneel . . ."

The Skin Eaters stared at him dumbstruck, watched as he slumped to his knees. For a heartbeat his eyes glared without focus, then he looked to the Men standing about him, his expression slowly tightening. Pained lines climbed his scalp.

"*Kneel!*" he shrieked.

Sarl cackled, though the smile that broke his barbed goatee seemed far from amused. "Cleric. Come now . . ."

"This was the war that broke our back!" the Nonman thundered. "This . . . *This!* All the Last Born, sires and sons, gathered beneath the copper banners of Siol and her flint-hearted King. Silverteeth! Our Tyrant-Saviour . . ." He rolled his head back and laughed. Two lines of white marked the tears that scored his cheeks. "This is our . . ." The flash of fused teeth. "Our *triumph*."

He shrunk, seemed to huddle into his cupped palms. Great silent sobs wracked him.

Looks were exchanged, short-lived with embarrassment. There was something eerie about the light, apart from the way it hung sourceless above them, something that rendered each of them in a distinct cast of brilliance. Perhaps it was the black walls, or the curls of white refracted across the polish of innumerable figures, but none of the shadows seemed to match up. It was as if everyone stood in the unique light of some different morning, noon, or twilight. Perhaps it was his race, or maybe it was his pose, but only Cleric seemed to belong.

Lord Kosoter crouched at his side, placed a hand on his broad back, began muttering something inaudible. Kiampas stared at the floor. Sarl looked about, eyes darting, apparently more unnerved by this act of intimacy than by the substance of Cleric's words.

"*Yessss!*" the Nonman hissed, as though grasping something essential and overlooked.

"This is just a fucking place," Sarl growled. "Just another fucking place . . ."

All of them could feel it, Achamian realized, looking from face to stricken face. Some kind of dolour, like the smoke of some hidden, panicked fire, pinching them, drawing their thoughts tight . . . But there was no glamour he could sense. Even the finest sorceries carried some residue of their artifice, the stain of the Mark. But there was nothing here, save the odour of ancient magicks, long dead.

Then, with a bolt of horror, he understood: The tragedy that had ruined these halls stalked them still. Cil-Aujas was a *topos*. A place where hell leaned heavy against the world.

He turned to Mimara, surprised to find himself gripping her hand. "Haunted," he murmured in reply to her wondering eyes. "This place—"

"Listen," Kiampas called, apparently in the grip of some abrupt resolution. "Stow your tongues—all of you! You saw the marks at the gate, all the companies that have vanished into this place. Granted, they didn't have Cleric, they didn't have a guide, but the fact remains *they vanished.* Maybe they lost their way, or maybe the skinnies got them. Either way, this is a *slog*, boys, as deadly as any other. From here on in, we march *at the ready*, you understand?"

"He's right," Xonghis called from the gloom to their rear. He was crouched near the wall, his Jekki pack high on his shoulders, his mailed forearms pressed against his knees. He reached to the ground before him, raised a long bone from the dust, something that could have belonged to a dog. "Dead skinny," he said. He held it to the light, then peered through it like a tube: The knobs at either end had been snapped off. He turned to the rest of the company, shrugged. "Something was hungry."

The scalpers looked around, cursed at the sight of bones scattered everywhere, like the remains of some forgotten flood, sticks beneath silt. Lord Kosoter continued to mutter in Cleric's ear, a grinding discourse, full of hate. The words "miserable wretch" climbed into clarity. Achamian found himself staring into the black portal between the towering wolves, expecting, any moment now, something . . .

When he blinked, he saw yammering figures from his Dreams.

"Sranc?" one of the Galeoth scalpers cried—Hoat. "What *eats* Sranc?" He had to be the youngest of the Skin Eaters, his body still hooked by an adolescent ranginess.

Every one of them, Achamian realized, every company that had dared these halls. All of them had paused before this broken gate and suffered the very same premonition. And still they marched onward, carrying their war, whatever it was, deeper, deeper . . .

Never to be seen again.

"Where are the doors?" Galian blurted. He looked around in the quarrelsome manner that some use to conceal their fright. "What does it mean? Gates without doors?"

But questions always came too late. Events had to be pushed passed the point of denial; only then could the pain of asking begin.

They spent their first night in the grand chamber beyond the Wolf Gate. Achamian hung his sorcerous light high in the air, an abstract point of brilliance that illuminated the ceiling and the finned capitals of the pillars ascending about them. The light seemed to creep down, dim enough to be shut out by closed eyes, expansive enough to provide the illusion of security. Alien images glared from on high, their recesses inked in utter black.

True to his word, Kiampas organized shifts and posted sentries along their perimeter of light. Cleric sat alone on the dust and stone, gazing into the passageway they would take upon waking. Lord Kosoter stretched across his mat and seemed to fall instantly asleep, even though Sarl sat cross-legged at his side, muttering inanity after inanity, pausing only to cackle at the turns of his own wit. The rest of the company formed sullen clots across the floor, tossing on their mats or sitting and talking in low tones. Their crowd of mules stood in the nearby shadows, looking absurd against the surrounding grandeur.

The air remained chill enough to fog deep exhalations.

Achamian sat next to Mimara with his back against one of the columns. For the longest time she seemed transfixed by the light, staring endlessly at its silver flare.

"The script," she said, her voice thick from disuse. "Can you read it?"

"No."

An inaudible snort. "The all-knowing Wizard . . ."

"No one can read it."

"Ah . . . I was worried I had misjudged you."

He looked at her prepared to scowl, but the mischief in her eyes demanded he chuckle. A great weight seemed to fall through him.

"Remember this, Mimara."

"Remember what?"

"This place."

"Why?"

"Because it's old. Older than old."

"Older than him?" she asked, nodding toward the figure of Cleric sitting in the pillared gloom.

His momentary sense of generosity drained away. "Far older."

A moment passed, suffused by the low tingle of repose in perilous circumstances—a dripping sense of doom. Mimara continued her furtive examination of Cleric.

"What's wrong with him?" she eventually whispered.

He did not want to think of the Nonman, Achamian realized, let alone speak of him. Travelling with an Erratic was every bit as perilous as traveling these halls, if not more so. A fact that begged the forbidden question: How much would Achamian risk to see his obsession through? How many souls would he doom?

His mood blackened.

"Hush," he said, frowning in habitual irritation. What was she doing here? Why did she plague *him*? Everything! Twenty years of toil! Perhaps even the world! She risked it all for a hunger she could never sate. "They can hear far better than we can."

"Tell me in a tongue he can't understand then," she replied, speaking flawless Ainoni.

A long look, too sour to be surprised. "Ainon," he said. "Is that where they took you?"

The curiosity faded from her eyes. She slouched onto her mat and turned without a word—as he knew she would. Silence spread deep and mountainous through the graven hollows. He sat rigid.

When he glanced up he was certain he saw Cleric's face turn away from them . . .

Back to the impenetrable black of Cil-Aujas.

The Library of Sauglish burned beneath him in his Dream, its towers squat and monumental within garlands of flame. Dragons banked about mighty plumes of smoke. The glitter of sorcery sparked across the heights—the blinding calligraphy of the Gnosis.

Its wings threshing the air, Skafra bared corroded teeth, shrieked out to the horizon, to the whirlwind roping black across the distant plains. A rumble deeper than a final heartbeat.

And Achamian hung unseen, an insubstantial witness . . . Alone.

Where? Where was Seswatha?

They found the mummified corpse of a boy no more than a hundred paces down the passageway Cleric had chosen for them. He was curled as though about a kitten, his back to the wall. He had been at most thirteen or fourteen summers old, Xonghis estimated. The Imperial Tracker had no idea how long he had lain there, but he pointed to the propitiatory coins that had been set on his hip and thigh: three full coppers, two grey with dust, one still bright. gifts for the Ur-Mother—not the coins, but the acts of surrendering them. Apparently others had passed this way as well. With the rest of the company clustered about him, Soma fell to one knee and added a fourth, whispering a prayer in his native tongue. His eyes sought out Mimara afterwards, as though seeking confirmation of his gallantry.

"You need to watch that one," Achamian murmured to her as they continued down the corridor. They had not spoken since waking, and he found himself regretting the way he had cut short their conversation the previous night. It seemed absurd, offering words like coins in the bowels of a mountain, but the small things never went away, no matter how tremendous the circumstance. Not for him, anyway.

"Not really," she said with a weariness Achamian found vaguely alarming. Their was peril in feminine exhaustion—men understood this instinctively. "It's usually the quiet ones you need to watch. The ones waiting for the door to clap behind them . . ."

The sound of other voices welled into her silence. A debate had broken out regarding the fate and provenance of the dead child. Strangely enough, the boy and the mystery of his end had inspired a return to normalcy of sorts.

"Ainon taught me that," she added with reassuring bitterness. "You know . . . where they took me."

The expedition marched on, a collection of pale faces in the long murk. The conversation, quite inexplicably, turned to which trades were the hardest on the hands. Galian insisted that fishermen had the worst of it, what with all the knots and nets. Xonghis described the cane fields of High Ainon, endless miles of them along the upper Secharib Plains, and how the field slaves always had bleeding fingers. Everyone agreed that if you included feet, fullers were the sorriest lot.

"Imagine marching in piss day in and day out—and without moving a cubit!"

Then they started on beggars, trading tales of this or that wretch. Soma's claim to have seen a beggar without arms or legs was met with general derision. Soma was always claiming things. "So how did he pick up his coins?" one of the younger wits asked. "With his pecker?" In the spirit of mockery, Galian went one better, saying he saw a *headless* beggar when he was in the Imperial Army. "For the longest time we thought he was a sack of ripe turnips, until he began begging, that is . . ."

"And what did he beg for?" Oxwora asked. The giant's voice always seemed to boom, no matter how low he pitched it.

"To be turned right side up, what else?"

Laughter crashed through the abandoned halls. Only Soma remained unimpressed.

"How could he speak without a head?"

"You seem to manage well enough!"

A cackling swell. The crew always enjoyed a good joke at Soma's expense.

"In Zeüm—" Pokwas began.

"The beggars give *you* money," Galian interrupted. "We know."

"Not at all." The Sword-Dancer laughed. "They trek into the Wilds to skin skinnies . . ."

A general cry of outrage and laughter.

"Which explains all the silver you owe me," Oxwora exclaimed.

And on it went.

Judging by her expressions, Mimara found the banter

terribly amusing, a fact not lost on the scalpers—Somandutta in particular. Achamian, however, found it difficult to concede more than a smile here and there, usually at turns that escaped the others. He could not stop pondering the blackness about them, about how garish and exposed they must sound to those listening in the deeps. A gaggle of children.

Someone listened. Of that much he was certain.

Someone or something.

With Lord Kosoter at his side, Cleric led them through a veritable labyrinth. Corridors. Halls. Galleries. Some struck as straight as a rule, others wound in the random pose of worms suspended in water, or like the writing of weevils beneath the bark of dead trees. All of them hummed with the enormity of the mountain they plumbed: the walls seemed to bow, the floors buckle, the ceilings tingled with crushing weight. At some point, their entombment had become palpable. Cil-Aujas became a world of wedged things, of great collapses, immense torsions, all held in check by stone and ancient cunning. More than once, Achamian found himself gasping, as though breathing against some irresistible grip. The air tasted of tombs—stone joists and age-long motionlessness—but it was plentiful enough. Even still, something animal within him cried suffocation.

It was the lack of sky, he decided. He tried not to think of his earlier premonitions.

The banter dwindled into silence, leaving the arrhythmic percussion of footfalls and the sonorous complaints of this or that mule in its wake.

The sound of water rose so gradually out of the silence that it seemed sudden when they finally noticed it. The walls and ceiling of the passage they followed flared outward, like the mouth of an intricately carved horn, becoming ever more dim in the twin points of sorcerous light. After several steps, the walls fell away altogether, and they stepped into booming space. Through membranes of mist, the lights reached out, paling, revealing hanging scarps and cavernous spaces—a great chasm of some kind. The floor became a kind of stone catwalk, slicked with rust-coloured moulds. Water tumbled beneath, a rush of diamonds, broken only by the shadow of the catwalk, leaping and wheeling into void. Achamian found himself looking away, dizzied by how its sheeting plunge made his footing drift. He heard the mules kick and scream in the train immediately behind him. Near the head of their long file, he could see Cleric's light gather against the cavern's far heights, then fold into the tubular hollows of another corridor.

Except that it wasn't another corridor, but the entrance to some kind of shrine. The room was neither large nor small—about the size of a temple prayer floor—with a low circular ceiling spoked like a wheel. Friezes panelled the walls—were-animals with multiple heads and limbs—but not to the convoluted depths found elsewhere. The scalpers, Achamian could tell, thought them representations of devils: More than a few whispered homespun charms. But he knew better, recognizing in the figures a sensibility kindred to that of the Wolf Gate. It wasn't monsters that glared from the walls, he knew, but rather the many poses of natural beasts compressed into one image. Before they began forgetting, the Nonmen had been obsessed with the mysteries of time, particularly with the way the present seemed to bear the past and the future within it.

Long-lived, they had worshipped Becoming . . . the bane of Men.

While the company milled beneath the low ceilings, Sarl and Kiampas organized the replenishment of their water supply. The leather buckets they normally used to scoop water from gorges were unpacked. A relay was set up, and soon armed men were squatting all across the chamber filling skins. Achamian paced the walls in the meantime, studying the graven images with Mimara in tow. He showed her where innumerable ancient penitents had worn indentations into the walls—with their foreheads, he explained.

When she asked him whom they prayed to, he cast about looking for Cleric, once again loath to say anything the Erratic might overhear. He found him standing at the far end of the chamber, his bald head bowed and gleaming. A great statue loomed before him, a magisterial Nonman hewn from the walls, at once hanging with arms and legs outstretched—a pose curiously reminiscent of the Circumfix—and sitting rigid upon a throne, his knees pressed together beneath flattened hands. Mould had stained the stone black and crimson, but otherwise the figure seemed untouched, blank eyes staring out. Rather than answer Mimara's query, Achamian simply motioned for her to follow, pressing past the crowded scalpers toward Cleric.

"*Tir hoila ishrahoi,*" the Erratic was saying, his eyes and forehead covered by a long-fingered hand—the Nonman gesture of homage. There could be no doubt he spoke *to* the statue, rather than prayed to something beyond.

"*Coi ri pirith mutoi' on . . .*"

Achamian paused and, for reasons he did not understand, started translating, speaking in a low murmur. Compared to the harmonic resonances of Cleric, his voice sounded as coarse as yarn.

"'You, soul of splendour, whose arm hath slain thousands . . .'"

"*Tir miyil oitossi, kun ri mursal arilil hi . . . Tir . . .*"

"You, eye of wrath, whose words hath cracked mountains . . . You . . ."

"*Tirsa hir' gingall vo'is?*"

"Where is your judgment now?"

The Nonman began laughing in his mad, chin-to-breast way. He looked to Achamian, smiled his inscrutable white-lipped smile. He leaned his head as though against some swinging weight. "Where is it, eh, Wizard?" he said in the mocking way he often replied to Sarl's jokes. His features gleamed like hand-worn soapstone.

"Where does all the judgment go?"

Then without warning, Cleric turned to forge alone into the black, drawing his spectral light like a wall-brushing gown. Achamian gazed after him, more astounded than mystified. For the first time, it seemed, he had seen Cleric for what he was . . . Not simply a survivor of this ruin, but of a piece with it.

A second labyrinth.

Mimara stepped into the Nonman's place, apparently to better peer at the statue. Their water-skins filled, the scalpers had begun filing past them, their looks unreadable. Mimara seemed so small and beautiful in the shadow of their warlike statue that Achamian found himself standing as though to shield her.

"Who is it?" she asked.

The underworld cataract thundered up through the surrounding stone.

"The greatest of the Nonman Kings," Achamian replied, reaching out two fingers to touch the cold stone face. It was strange, the heedless way that statues stared and stared, their eyes bound to the panoply of dead ages. "Cu'jara Cinmoi . . . the Lord of Siöl, who led the Nine Mansions against the Inchoroi."

"How can you tell?" she asked, cocking her head the same as her mother. "They all look the same . . . *Exactly* the same."

"Not to each other . . ." He sketched a line through the mould across the Nonman King's polished cheek.

"But how can *you* tell?"

"Because it's written, carved into the rim of the throne . . ." He drew back his fingers, pinched the silken residue between them.

"Come," the Wizard said, deliberately cutting off her next question. When she persisted, he snapped, "Leave an old man to think!"

They had palmed their lives, as the Conriyans were fond of saying.

They had palmed them and given them to a Nonman—to an *Erratic* . . . To someone who was not only insane, but literally addicted to trauma and suffering. Incariol . . . Who was he? And more importantly, *what would he do* to remember?

Kuss voti lura gaial, the High Norsirai would say of their Nonmen allies during the First Apocalypse. "Trust only the thieves among them." The more honourable the Nonman, the more likely he was to betray—such was the perversity of their curse. Achamian had read accounts of Nonmen murdering their brothers, their sons, not out of spite, but because their love was so great. In a world of smoke, where the years tumbled into oblivion, acts of betrayal were like anchors; only anguish could return their life to them.

The present, the now that Men understood, the one firmly fixed at the fore of what was remembered, no longer existed for the Nonmen. They could find its semblance only in the blood and screams of loved ones.

Beyond the Cujaran Shrine they descended into a maze of desolate habitations. The darkness became liquid, it seemed so deep, and their light became the only air. Walls reared into visibility as though squeezed of ink. Doorway after doorway gaped to either side of them, revealing lanes of interior floor, featureless for the dust, swinging in counterpoise to their sorcerous lights. Stairwells climbed into rubble. Stone faces watched with callous immobility.

Eventually they came to a subterranean thoroughfare, one of several that wound along natural occlusions in Aenaratiol's heart. Seswatha had walked these, two thousand years previous, and Achamian found himself mourning the wrack and ruin. This was where the Ishroi had stacked their palaces, street upon street, climbing the sides of each fissure. Enormous pitch lanterns had burned in the open spaces, suspended in webs of chain. Gold and silver foils had skinned the fluted walls. Fountains had flowed, their waters like ropes of refracted fire.

Now all was dust and dark. For the first time, it seemed to Achamian, the company grasped the dread scale of their undertaking. It was one thing to crowd halls hunched against the mountain above them, it was quite another to file through hollows as vast as this, a thread of light and furtive movement. Where before the dark had enclosed them, now it exposed . . . Anything, it seemed, might descend upon them.

They made camp next to the wreckage of a collapsed lantern wheel. Bronze bars curved like ribs, reaching as high as small trees. A massive three-faced head had crashed from some unseen perch above, forming a barricade of sorts not so far away. The more daring scalpers explored the doorways and passages along the short section of street between, but only as far as the white light would take them. The rest broke into tired clots, making seats of the debris or simply sitting upon the powdered floor. Some could do no more than ponder their shadows.

Achamian found himself with Galian and Pokwas. All the Skin Eaters were sleeping in their armour by this point. Galian wore a hauberk of crude-ringed Galeoth mail, like many others, only belted and cinched in the Imperial fashion. Pokwas wore a shirt of fine Zeümi steel, which had been patched on his right arm and left abdomen with sections of cruder Galeoth links. Over this, across his collar and shoulders, he wore the traditional Sword-Dancer halter, but the plates were too waxy to reflect much more than lines of white and dark. The silvering had been scrubbed away long ago.

From the rehearsed character of their questions, Achamian could tell they had decided to corner him sometime earlier. They wanted to know about dragons, particularly the possibility that one might reside in the vast galleries beneath their feet.

The old Wizard wasn't surprised: Ever since Kiampas's outburst at the Obsidian Gate, he had overheard the word "dragon" or its Galeoth cognate, "huörka," at least a dozen times.

"Men have little to fear from dragons," he explained. "Without the will of the No-God, they are lazy, selfish creatures. We Men are too much trouble for them. Kill one of us today, and tomorrow you have a thousand hounding you."

"So there *are* dragons out there?" Galian asked. The former Imperial Columnary was the nimble sort, like Sarl, perhaps, only tempered with Nansur sensibility. Where the sergeant perpetually squinted, Galian's eyes were clear, even if they promised to frost at the slightest provocation. Pokwas, on the other hand, possessed that warm-hearted confidence that seemed to belong exclusively to men with quick wits and big hands. Unlike Galian, he was someone you only had to befriend once.

"Certainly," Achamian replied. "Many Wracu survived the First Apocalypse, and they're as immortal as the Nonmen . . . But like I said, they avoid Men."

"And if," Galian pressed, "we were to wander into one's lair . . ."

The Wizard shrugged. "It would simply wait for us to leave, if it sensed any strength in us at all."

"Even if—?"

"He's saying they're not like wild animals," Pokwas interrupted. "Bears or wolves would attack because they don't know better. But dragons *know* . . . Isn't that right?"

"Yes. Dragons know."

Achamian found himself speaking against a queer reluctance, one that he confused with shyness at first. Some time passed before he realized that it was in fact *shame*. He didn't want to be like these unruly men, much less respect them. Even more, he didn't want their trust or their admiration, things that both men had obviously granted him days ago, given the way they had risked their lives for his lie.

"Tell me," Pokwas said, staring with an interest that seemed almost threatening for its intensity. "What happened to the Nonmen?" Whether it was the way he steered his voice or the wariness in his eyes, Achamian knew that the Sword-Dancer was every bit as worried about Cleric as he.

"I thought I already told that story."

"He means what happened to their *race*," Galian said. "Why have they dwindled so?"

A momentary flash of cruelty passed through the old Wizard, not for them as men, but for their beliefs. "You can look to your Tusk for that account," he said, taking peevish relish in the word "your." "They're the *False Men*, remember? Cursed of the Gods. Our ancient fathers destroyed many a Mansion as great as this." In his soul's eye he could see them, the Prophets of the Tusk, as stern and as spare as the words they would carve into ivory, leading hide-clad savages through deep halls of glory, calling out in guttural tongues, murdering those who had been their slavers.

"But I thought their back had already been broken," Pokwas said. "That the Five Tribes came upon them in their twilight."

"True."

"So what happened?"

"The Inchoroi came . . ."

"You mean the Consult?" Galian asked.

Achamian stared at the man, not quite stunned, but speechless all the same. That a mere scalper could mention the Consult with the same familiarity as he might mention any great and obvious nation seemed beyond belief. It was a sign, he realized, of just how profoundly the world had changed during his exile. Before, when he still wore the robes of a Mandate Schoolman, all the Three Seas had laughed at him and his dire warnings of the Second Apocalypse. Golgotterath. The Consult. The Inchoroi. These had been the names of his disgrace, utterances that assured the mockery and condescension of any who might listen. But now . . .

Now they were *religion* . . . The holy gospel of the Aspect-Emperor.

Kellhus.

"No," he said, feeling that peculiar wariness when one crossed uncertain lines of knowing. "This was before the Consult . . ."

And so he told them of the millennial wars between the Nonmen and the Inchoroi. The two scalpers listened with honest fascination, their eyes lost in the middle ground between the telling and the glorious riot of the told. The first Wracu descending. The first naked hordes of Sranc. The Nonmen Ishroi whipping their chariots into screaming horizons . . .

Even Achamian found himself curiously overawed. To speak of distant grounds and faraway peoples was one thing, but to sit here, in the derelict halls of Cil-Aujas, speaking of the ancient Nonmen . . .

Voices could stir more than the living from slumber.

So instead of lingering in his explanations as he might have otherwise, Achamian struck through the heart of the matter, relating only what was essential: the treachery of Nin'janjin, the Womb-Plague and the death of Hanalinqû, the doom slumbering in the bones of the survivors' immortality. The two scalpers, it turned out, already knew many of the details: Apparently Galian had studied for the Ministrate before, as he put it, drink, hash, and whores had saved his soul.

Achamian laughed hard at that.

Every so often he glanced at Mimara to make sure all was well. She sat like a cross-legged vase with Somandutta, indulging the young castenoble's vanity with questions about Nilnamesh. He liked the man well enough, Achamian supposed. Somandutta seemed to be one of those peculiar caste-nobles who managed to carry their sheltered upbringing into adulthood: sociable to a fault, almost absurdly confident that others meant him well. Were this Momemn,

Invishi, or any other great city, Achamian had no doubt he would be one of those dog-eager courtiers, one everyone would dismiss with smiles rather than sneers.

"*Do you know*," the caste-noble was saying, "*what my people say about women like you?*"

Even still, the old Wizard remained wary. He knew enough about scalpers to know they weren't easily known. Their lives demanded too much from them.

"Tell me," Achamian asked Galian directly. "Why do you do this? Hunting Sranc. It can't be for the bounty, can it? I mean, as far as I can tell you all leave places like Marrow as poor as you arrive rich . . ."

The former Columnary paused in reflection. "For some, it is the money. Xonghis, for instance, leaves most of his share with the Custom House—"

"He'll never spend it," Pokwas interrupted.

"Why would you sa—?" Achamian pressed.

But Galian was shaking his head. "Your question, sorcerer, is not so wise. Scalpers scalp. Whores whore. We never ask one another why. Never."

"We even have a saying," Pokwas added in his resonant, accented voice. "'Leave it to the slog.'"

Achamian smiled. "It all comes back to the slog, does it?"

"Even kings," Galian replied with a wink, "shod their feet."

The conversation turned to more mundane fare after this. For a time, Achamian listened to the scalpers argue over who was the true inheritor of the Ancient North's greatness, the Three Seas or Zeüm. It was an old game, men taking pride over meaningless things, passing time in good-natured rivalry. He thought of how strange it must be for long-dead Cil-Aujas to hear the glory of small and petty words after so many entombed ages, let alone to feel the polishing touch of light. Perhaps that was why the entire company seemed to fall mute sooner than their weariness merited. There was a greater effort in speaking overheard words, an effort that, though infinitesimal, quickly accumulated. And this dark place, whether from the drowsing edge of dreams or with ears pricked in malice, did listen.

The disappointment on Somandutta's face was almost maudlin when Mimara abandoned him to rejoin her "father."

They had slept side by side since she had joined the company, but somehow, this night, they ended up laying face to face as well—a position that Achamian thought uncomfortably intimate but didn't seem to trouble Mimara at all. It reminded him of her mother, Esmenet, how the habits of prostitution had coloured so much of what she said and did. Wearing her nakedness the thoughtless way a smith might wear a leather apron. Talking cocks and congress the way masons might discuss trowels and arches.

So many calluses where he had only tender skin.

"Everything . . ." she said in a wistful tone. Her eyes seemed to track the passage of ghosts.

"Everything what?"

"The walls . . . The ceilings. *Everywhere*, limbs and people cut out of stone—images atop images . . . Think of the toil!"

"It wasn't always such. The Wolf Gate is an example of how they once adorned their cities. It was only when they began forgetting that they turned to this . . . this . . . excess. These are their annals, the accounting of their deeds—great and small."

"Then why not simply paint murals the way we do?"

Achamian found himself approving of this question—another long-dead habit, tingling back to life. "Nonmen can't see paintings," he said with an old man's shrug.

A frowning smile. Despite the anger that always seemed to roll about the nethers of her expression, her skeptical looks always managed to promise a fair accounting.

"It's true," Achamian said. "Paintings are naught but gibberish to their eyes. The Nonmen may resemble us,

Mimara, but they are far more different than you can imagine."

"You make them sound frightening."

An old warmth touched him then, one that he had almost forgotten: the feeling of carrying another, not with arms or love or even hope, but with *knowledge*. Knowledge that made wise and kept safe.

"At last," he said, closing eyes that smiled. "She listens."

He felt her fingers press his shoulder, as though to poke in friendly rebuke but really just to confirm. Something swelled through him then, something that demanded he keep his eyes shut in the pretence of sleep.

He had been lonely, he realized. Lonely.

These past twenty years . . .

"A place where my line can outlive me," the High-King said.

Seswatha frowned in good-natured dismissal. "You have no need to fear . . ." Achamian leaned back in his chair, forced his thoughts from the conundrum facing him on the benjuka plate between them. Most of the private rooms in the King-Temple Annexes were little more than slots between walls of cyclopean brick, and Celmomas's study was no exception. The towering scroll-racks only added to the cloistered air. "Our foe has no hope against the Ordeal you have assembled. Think. Nimeric . . . Even Nil'giccas marches."

The names seemed to relax his old friend.

"Ishuäl," Celmomas said, smiling at his own wit—or lack of it. He reached for his chalice of apple mead. "That's what I call it."

Seswatha shook his head. "Is it stocked with beer or with concubines?"

"Seeds," Celmomas replied, his eyes smiling over the rim of his cup. The golden wolf's head braided into the centre of his beard seemed to glower from beneath his wrist.

"Seeds?"

The High-King's demeanour faltered. There was always such an aura of care about him, at least when it came to the little things, like making sure he replaced his cup on the same ring of condensation.

He could be so reckless otherwise.

"For the longest time," he said, "I refused to believe you. And now that I believe . . ."

"Yes?"

Celmomas had a long face, one that suited the dynastic glory of his name. Solemn. Nimble yet strong-jawed. But it was too given to expressions of melancholy, especially in rooms where the gloom lay heavy. He laughed as much as the next man, Seswatha supposed, but the looks that inevitably followed—eyes slack with quiet sorrow, lips drawn into a pent line—always seemed more primitive somehow, closer to the native tenor of his heart.

"Nothing . . ." the High-King said with a release of old and weary air. "Just premonitions."

Seswatha studied him with new concern. "The premonitions of kings are never to be taken lightly. You know that much, old friend."

"Which is why I have built a ref—"

The creak of bronze hinges. They both yanked their gazes to the shadows that concealed the entrance. The fires pulled and twirled in the tripods set to either side of the game-table. Achamian heard the scuff of little feet, then suddenly Nau-Cayûti hurtled into his father's arms and lap.

"Whoopa!" Celmomas cried. "What warrior leaps blindly into the arms of his foe?"

The boy chortled in the grinding way of children fending fingers that tickle. "You're not my *foe*, Da!"

"Wait till you get older!"

Nau-Cayûti grinned with clenched teeth, struggled against his father's ringed hand, growling as much as laughing. The boy surprised him by jerking and twisting like a summer pike, clutched his white-woollen robe in an effort to brace his feet on his father's thighs. Celmomas pulled back, nearly toppled in his chair.

Achamian roared with laughter. "A *wolf*, my King! The boy's a wolf! You better hope he's never your enemy!"

"Cayû-Cayû!" the High-King cried, holding his hands out in surrender.

"What's this?" the young Prince asked, fumbling in the interior pockets of his father's robe. With a little grunt, he pulled a golden tube into the wobbling light. A scroll-case, cast in the likeness of twining vines.

"For me?" he gasped at his grinning father.

"Nay," Celmomas replied with mock gravity. "It's a great and powerful secret." The High-King's look found Seswatha past the boy's flaxen curls. Nau-Cayûti turned as well, so that both faces—the one innocent, the other careworn—hung motionless in the pale light.

"It's for your uncle Seswa," the High-King said.

Nau-Cayûti clutched the golden tube to his breast, more in a delighted than a covetous way. "Can I give it to him, Da?" he cried. "*Please?*"

Celmomas nodded in chuckling assent, but a gleam of seriousness lingered in his gaze. The Prince bounced from his father's lap, made both men start in alarm when he almost bowled into one of the tripods, then he was leaning against Seswatha's knee, beaming with pride. He held out the scroll-case in hands too small not to be clumsy, saying, "Tell me, Uncle Seswa. Tell-me-tell-me! Who's *Mimara?*"

Achamian bolted from his blanket with a gasp . . .

. . . only to find Incariol kneeling over him in the deep shadow. A line of light rimmed his scalp and the curve of his cheek and temple; his face was impenetrable otherwise.

The Wizard made to scramble backward, but the Nonman clasped his shoulder with a powerful hand. The bald head lowered in apology, but the face remained utterly obscured in shadow. "You were laughing," he whispered before turning away.

Achamian could only squint, slack-mouthed.

As dark as it was, he was certain that Cleric had sobbed as he drew away.

Achamian awoke far older, it seemed, than when he'd fallen asleep. His ears and teeth ached, as did every joint he had words to describe. While the Skin Eaters busied themselves preparing to depart, he sat cross-legged on his crude mat, forearms heavy against his knees, glaring more than watching. The twin lights hung above them as before, the differences in their cast as subtle and as profound as the differences in their casters. His eyes traced the verge of their illumination, from the hanging bronze of the fallen lantern wheel, along the slot-windowed walls, to the great fragments of face leaning in the debris of the ruined head. Part of him was horrified, even affronted, to discover that the previous day had not been a dream—that Cil-Aujas *was real.* He breathed deep the indescribable must hanging in the air, fought the urge to spit. It seemed he could feel the black miles hanging above them.

When Mimara asked for a third time what was the matter, he decided that he hated the young. Smooth faces and lithe strong limbs. Not to mention the certainty of ignorance. In his soul's eye he saw them doing jigs down blasted halls, while all he could do was hobble after them. Pompous wretches, he thought, with their dark hair and hundred-word vocabularies. Pissants.

"*Huppa!*" Somandutta called to him at one point, shouting the word they used to goad their mules. "Huppa-huppa! No bones are so heavy!"

"And no fools are quite so dense!" he snapped in return. He didn't so much regret the words as the general laughter that greeted them. He stared down Mimara's look of reproach, felt the petty satisfaction of winning petty contests of the will. A stab of fear accompanied the thought that he might be taking ill.

With the others watching, he had no choice but to quickly gather his things. He reminded himself that foul humours were the most slothful humours of all, and that, just as the old Ceneian slave-scholars insisted, one need only walk to escape them. He cursed himself for groaning aloud as he hoisted his pack.

Sure enough, his mood mellowed as his limbs warmed to the company's motivated pace. For a time, he did his best to recollect what Seswatha had known of Cil-Aujas, to build a map of sorts in his soul's eye. But the best he could conjure was a hazy sense of myriad levels, with the nimil mines tangling the mountain's roots and the commons and habitations reaching Aenaratiol's gouged peak. It seemed he could feel the Mansion's hollows reach like roots through the buried distances: all the enclosed spaces you might find in a great mannish city, from granaries to barracks to temples to lowly hearths, stacked one upon another, hanging in the compressed heart of a mountain. But he could pull nothing definite from these imaginings, certainly nothing that would be of any use to their journey. Even in Seswatha's day Cil-Aujas had been largely abandoned, and few were the Nonmen who could find their way through the Mansion's outer reaches. The most the old Wizard could say was that Cleric *seemed* to lead them true. So long as they continued following the thoroughfares that traversed these great fissures, he knew they drew nearer the Mansion's northern gates. There was comfort enough in that . . .

For now.

Not a watch passed, however, when the last fissure came to an end, closing above them like clutched palms. After passing through yet another hallway with historical friezes set like grillwork over deeper friezes, they came to a chamber so vast that the walls opened above and beyond the reach of either his or Cleric's light, so that it seemed they crossed a ground suspended in the void. Shrinking from the abyssal dark, the scalpers pressed close, to the point where they continually ran afoul of one another. Even Mimara walked with her cheek pressed against Achamian's arm. Not a moment passed without someone softly cursing this mule or that man. Few words were traded otherwise. Those who did call out were silenced by the sound of their own echoes, which returned so transformed as to seem another voice.

Though unnerved by the blackness, Achamian actually felt more relieved than otherwise. For the first time since passing the Wolf Gate, he thought he knew where they stood in Aenaratiol's mazed bowels. This, he was certain, was the Repositorium, where the Nonmen had shelved their dead like scrolls. And it meant not only that they had travelled almost half the way, but more importantly, that Cleric actually did remember the path through the ruined Mansion.

For the longest time nothing loomed out of the encircling darkness. With the dust chalking the air about their ankles and knees, it almost seemed they crossed a desert on some sunless world. Once Cleric called them to a clanking halt, and the entire company spent several dozen heartbeats simply standing, ears pricked, listening to the iron-hard silence . . . The sound of their entombment.

The appearance of bones at their feet caused more curiosity than alarm—at first. The skulls were so ancient they crumpled like beehives beneath their soles, and the bones flattened like paper. Clots of them emerged here and there, like flotsam dropped by eddies in long-dried waters, but after a while the floor became thick with them. The dull sound of the Skin Eaters' trudging became the whisk and thump of men kicking through sandy leaves. A battle had been fought here long, long ago, and the toll had been high. Soon the murmur of prayers could be heard among the men, and wide eyes sought confirmation of their fear. Sarl laughed as he always did when he sensed apprehension getting the best of his "boys," but the echoes that fell back out of the blackness sounded so sinister that he went as rigid and as pale as any of them.

Then, out of nowhere, a great slope of debris reared before them, forcing a general halt. The company milled in blank-faced confusion while Lord Kosoter and Cleric consulted. Because of the dark, it was impossible to determine the scale of the obstruction. One of the young Galeoth, Asward, began babbling in a panicked voice, something about fingers reaching up from the dust. Both Galian and Xonghis tried to talk some sense into the young man, casting wary glances at their Captain while doing so. Sarl watched with an expression of repellant satisfaction, as though eager to exercise some bloodthirsty Rule of the Slog.

Tired and annoyed, Achamian simply walked into the blackness, leaving his sorcerous light hanging behind him. When Mimara called out, he simply waved a vague hand. The residue of death stirred no horror in him—it was the living he feared. The blackness enveloped him, and when he turned, he was struck by an almost gleeful sense of impunity. The Skin Eaters clung to their little shoal of light, peered like orphans into the oceans of dark. Where they had seemed so cocksure and dangerous on the trail, now they looked forlorn and defenceless, a clutch of refugees desperate to escape the calamities that pursued them.

This, Achamian thought to himself, *is how Kellhus sees us . . .*

He knew the sound of his arcane voice would startle them, that they would point and cry out at the sight of his mouth and eyes burning in the blackness. But they needed to be reminded—all of them—of who he was . . .

He spoke the Bar of Heaven.

A line appeared between his outstretched arms, shimmering white, bright enough for the blood to glow through his hands. Then it sundered the shrouded heights, brilliant and instantaneous as lightning. In a blink, the Repositorium lay revealed unto its farthest corners . . .

The ruined cemetery of Cil-Aujas.

Great ribs and sockets of living stone ravined the ceiling. Hanging from its contours, hundreds of ancient chains cluttered the open reaches, some broken midway to the floor, others still bearing the bronze lantern wheels that had once served as illumination. The floors beneath stretched for what seemed a mile, white with illumination and dust, puckered and furrowed by the long wandering lines of ancient dead. In the distances behind and to either side of the company, walls had been hewn from the scarped confusion, gaining heights easily as great as any of Carythusal's famed towers. Tombs pocked them, row upon row of black holes framed with graven script and images, lending them a wasp-nest malignancy. Immediately before the company, however, the enormous sheaves of debris continued climbing and climbing, sloping up to the very ceiling . . . Some kind of catastrophic collapse.

The implication was as obvious as it was immediate: The way was barred.

Everyone—save Lord Kosoter and Cleric—gawked and blinked at the spectacle. Achamian could feel the Captain's bone-hollowing gaze as he walked toward the others. The Bar faded like a furnace coal, allowing the darkness to reclaim its dominion. Within heartbeats, the company was every bit as stranded as before.

Kiampas, answering to some unseen signal, suddenly declared the day's march over, though no one had any way of knowing whether a day had in fact passed. As awed as they were dismayed, the Skin Eaters began stumbling about, preparing camp. Mimara clutched Achamian's arm, her eyes alight with a kind of enthralled greed . . .

"Can you teach me that!" she cried under her breath.

He knew her well enough to see she was bursting with questions, that she would likely plague him for hours if she could. And to his surprise, he found himself disarmed by her interest, which for the first time seemed *honest* instead of fraught with anger and calculation as before. To be a student required a peculiar kind of capitulation, a willingness not simply to do as one was told, but to surrender the movements of one's soul to the unknown complexities of another's. A willingness, not simply to be moved, but to be *remade*.

How could he not respond? Despite all his violent resolutions to the contrary, his was a teacher's soul.

But the time wasn't right. "Yes-yes," he said, speaking with gentle impatience. He grasped her shoulder to forestall her protest, sought Cleric through the commotion. He needed to know just how much the Nonman remembered. Their passage through the Repositorium was blocked, thanks to the ancient calamity heaped before them. If Cleric knew of no other way through the peril that was Cil-Aujas, they would be forced to backtrack, to begin the long trek back to the Obsidian Gate. If he pretended or remembered falsely, they could very well be dead.

He was about to explain as much to Mimara when Lord Kosoter suddenly appeared next to them, reeking in his hoary old Ainoni armour and dress. Steel grey hairs manged his plaited beard. Beneath his mailed breast, his Chorae hummed with unseen menace.

"No more," he said, his voice as flat as frozen water. "No more"—his tongue tested the edge of his teeth— "antics."

It was impossible not to be affected by the man's dead gaze, but Achamian found himself returning his stare with enough self-possession to wonder at the man's anger. Was it simple jealously? Or did the famed Captain fear that awe of another might undermine his authority?

"What?" Mimara said angrily. "We should have stumbled on through the dark?"

Achamian watched the eyes slouch toward her, glimpsed the mayhem behind their frigid calm. For all her ferocious pride, his gaze bled her white.

"As you wish," Achamian said quickly, like a man trying to call the attention of wolves. "Captain. *As you wish.*"

Lord Kosoter continued staring at Mimara for several heartbeats. When he looked back at Achamian, his eyes seemed to carry some mortal piece of her. He nodded, not so much at Achamian's concession, it seemed, as at the fear that stuttered through the Wizard's heart.

Your sins, the dead eyes whispered. *Her damnation.*

They sat about a fire of bones. Without the merest wind, the smoke spewed directly upward, a column of black floating into black. The reek of it was strange, like something sodden and already burned.

The Skin Eaters had congregated at the edges of the rubble, where streams of ruin had created a bowl with boulders large enough for men to sit and lean forward. Lord Kosoter sat between his two sergeants, Sarl and Kiampas, absorbed in the shining length of his Ainoni sword. Again and again, he drew his whetstone along its length, then raised it, as if to study the way the edge cut the play of reflected flames. Everything about his manner spoke of indifference, utter and absolute, as though he sat with a relative's hated children. Achamian had taken a seat nearly opposite him, with Mimara at his side. Galian, Oxwora, and the other Bitten formed the first tier, those close enough to actually feel the fire's acrid heat. The others sat scattered through the shadows. Cleric squatted apart from them all, high on the back of a monolithic stone. The shadow of his perch rode high on his chest, so that only his right arm and head fell in the firelight. Whenever Achamian looked away from him, he seemed to lose substance, to become a kind of dismembered reality . . . A headless face and a palmless hand, come to speak and to seize.

For the longest time the chatter was small, with words traded only between those seated side by side, or nearly such. Many simply gnawed on their salted rations, staring into the firelight. When men laughed they did so quietly, with the between-you-and-I circumspection of temple services and funeral pyres. No one dared mention the precariousness of their situation, at least no one that Achamian heard. Fear of fear was ever the greatest censor.

Eventually the talk petered out, and a gazing silence fell over the company. Ash glowed ruby and orange through blackened eye sockets. Fused Nonmen teeth gleamed like wet jewels.

Then without warning, Cleric addressed them from on high.

"I remember," he began. "Yes . . ."

Achamian looked up in exasperated relief, thinking the Nonman meant he remembered another way through Cil-Aujas. But something in the regard of the others told the Wizard otherwise. He glanced around at those nearest the fire, noticed Sarl staring at him, not the Nonman, with manic intensity. *See!* his expression seemed to shout. *Now you shall understand us!*

"You ask yourselves," Cleric continued, his shoulders slumped, his great pupils boring into the flames. "You ask, 'What is this that I do? Why have I followed unknown men, merciless men, into the deeps?' You do not ask yourself *what it means*. But you *feel* the question—ah, yes! Your breath grows short, your skin clammy. Your eyes burn for peering into the black, for looking to the very limit of your feeble vision . . ."

His voice was cavernous, greased with inhuman resonances. He spoke like one grown weary of his own wisdom.

"*Fear*. This is how you ask the question. For you are Men, and fear is ever the way your race questions great things."

He lowered his face to the shadows, continued speaking to his palms and their millennial calluses.

"I *remember* . . . I remember asking a wise man, once . . . though whether it was last year or a thousand years ago I cannot tell. I asked him, 'Why do Men fear the dark?' I could tell he thought the question wise, though I felt no wisdom in asking it. 'Because darkness,' he told me, 'is ignorance made visible.' 'And do Men despise ignorance?' I asked. 'No,' he said, 'they prize it above all things—all things!—but only so long as it remains invisible.'"

The words implied accusation, but the Nonman's tone was reassuring, as though he ministered to the wretched and the lost. He spoke true to his slog-name, Achamian realized, as the inhuman priest of scar-hearted men.

Cleric.

"We Nonmen . . ." he continued telling his hands, "we think the dark *holy*, or at least we did before time and treachery leached all the ancient concerns from our souls . . ."

"The dark?" Galian said, and his voice warm and human—and as such, so very frail. "Holy?"

The Nonman lifted his flawless white face to the light, smiled at the Nansur scalper's questioning gaze.

"Of course . . . Think on it, my mortal friend. The dark is oblivion made *manifest*. And oblivion encircles us always. It is the ocean, and we are naught but silvery bubbles. It leans all about us. You see it every time you glimpse the horizon—though you know it not. In the light, *our eyes* are what blinds us. But in the dark—in the *dark!*—the line of the horizon opens . . . opens like a mouth . . . and oblivion gapes."

Though the Nonman's expression seemed bemused and

ironic, Achamian, with his second, more ancient soul, recognized it as distinctively Cûnuroi—what they called *noi'ra*, bliss in pain.

"You must understand," Cleric said. "For my kind, holiness begins where comprehension ends. Ignorance stakes us out, marks our limits, draws the line between us and what *transcends*. For us, the true God is the unknown God, the God that outruns our febrile words, our flattering thoughts . . ."

These words trailed into the wheezing murmur of their fire. Few of the scalpers, Achamian noted, dared look the Nonman in the eye as he spoke, but rather watched the flames boil into noxious smoke.

"Do you see now why this trek is holy?" the deep voice resumed. "Do you see the prayer in our descent?"

No one dared breath, let alone reply. The hanging face turned to survey each of them.

"Have any of you ever *knelt so deep*?"

Five heartbeats passed.

"This God of yours . . ." Pokwas said unexpectedly. "How can you pray to something you cannot comprehend? How can you worship?"

"Pray?" A snort of breath that might have indicated amusement in a man. "There is no prayer, Sword-Dancer. But there is *worship*. We worship that which transcends us by making idols of our finitude, our frailty . . ." He rolled his face as if working an ancient kink, then repeated, "We . . . we . . ."

He slumped into himself, his head bowed like a galley slave chained about the neck. The fire of bones gleamed across the white of his bare scalp.

Achamian battled the scowl from his face. To embrace mystery was one thing, to render it divine was quite another. What the Nonman said sounded too like *Kellhus*, and too little like what Achamian knew of Nonmen mystery cults. Again he found himself contemplating the blasted complexion of the Erratic's Mark: Whomever he was, he was as powerful as he was old . . . With scarce thousands of Nonmen remaining, how could have Achamian not heard of him?

Incariol.

"If the dark truly is the God," Sarl muttered through gravel. He squinted out at the black spaces with the leather of his face. "I'd say we're in *His* almighty belly right about now . . ."

Throughout the entirety of Cleric's sermon, Lord Kosoter had continued sharpening his sword, as though he were the reaper who would harvest the Nonman's final meaning. At long last, he paused, stood to sheath his fish-silver blade. The fire lent him an infernal aspect, soaking his tattered battledress in crimson, gleaming across the plaits of his square beard and filling his eyes as surely as it filled the skulls at his feet.

A sparking air of expectancy—the Captain spoke so rarely it always seemed you heard his voice for the first vicious time.

But another sound spoke in his stead. Thin, as if carried on a thread, exhausted by echoes . . .

The shell of a human sound. A man wailing, where no man should be.

Blinking in the bright light of another Bar of Heaven, the company fanned out over the vast expanse of the Repositorium, their shadows stretched as long as walking trees across the ashen floor before them.

The cry had trailed into nothingness almost as soon as it had appeared, leaving the company scrambling for their weapons and their feet. Everyone instinctively turned to Cleric seated upon his high stone dolmen. The Nonman had simply pointed into the blackness, perpendicular to the way they had originally come.

The seven youngest of the Skin Eaters remained with the

mules, while the twenty-odd others struck out in the direction indicated by Cleric, swords drawn, shields raised. As unnerved as any of them, Achamian and Mimara took their place in the wide-walking line, their backs bathed in light, their faces in shadow. Galian and Pokwas moved to the right of them, while Sarl and the Captain advanced to their left. No one uttered a word, but walked, like Achamian, with ears so keen the silence seemed to roar. Drawn like tendons before them, their shadows were so black that their boots vanished into them with every step.

For almost an entire watch, they traversed an either-or world of light and dark, with a crevassed landscape for a ceiling and black-mouthed tombs for walls. The ancient lantern chains, though evenly spaced and sparely positioned, flayed the open spaces, forming curtains across the grim distances. And Achamian could not but think that here was an image of the Apocalypse that threatened them all.

Despite the brilliance of the light behind them, the darkness grew ever more bold. Soon they seemed a peculiar line of half-men, backs without bodies, moving as thin as branches waving in the wind. The dust that fogged their strides formed ethereal shadows across the lanes of light between them, like steam in low morning sun. Still no one spoke. Everyone held shield and sword at the ready.

And the mighty Repositorium gaped on and on.

When they found the man, he was kneeling in a desert plain of dust, his face raised to the glittering vision that was the now distant Bar of Heaven. The Skin Eaters formed a thin and wary circle about him, peering against the tricks of the gloom. Though his eyes were clearly open, he did not seem to see any of them. He was another scalper—the necklaces of teeth he wore atop his hauberk made that much plain. His skin was Ketyai dark, and his beard had been crudely plaited in the Conriyan fashion, though none of his gear seemed to hail from that nation. At first he seemed greased in pitch, so pale was the distant light. None of the Skin Eaters saw the crimson sheen until they were but several paces away.

"Blood." Xonghis was the first to mutter. "This man has battled . . ."

"Perimeter positions!" Sarl yelled to the astonished company. "Move-move!"

The Skin Eaters scattered, their gear clanking as they raced to form a thin rank in the murk beyond the stranger. Achamian approached with the Captain and the others, holding Mimara a pace behind him with an outstretched arm. They gathered to either side of the man, standing so as not to obscure the light. Answering to some look or gesture from Lord Kosoter, Xonghis tossed his shield to the floor and knelt before the unknown scalper. Achamian stepped over the shield, glimpsing the three shrunken Sranc heads, joined at the chins, that adorned its centre. Where before he had pressed Mimara back, now he could feel her tugging on the back of his hide cloak, silently urging him to keep his distance. When he glanced back at her, she nodded toward the stranger, directing his gaze to the man's lap.

The scalper held on to a hand, its fingers cupped like dearly won gold between his palms . . .

A woman's severed hand.

"I've seen him before," Kiampas said. "He's one of the Picks. The Bloody Picks."

The smeared face flinched at those words. For the first time, the dark eyes wandered from the Bar of Heaven, which rose incandescent on the ingrown horizon. He seemed to search the gaps between their leaning faces.

"*Light . . .*" the Pick whispered. He brought the severed hand to his cheek, closed his eyes, and swayed like a child. *"Didn't I promise you light?"*

He shrunk from the fingers Xonghis placed on his shoulder. "What happened?" the Imperial Tracker asked, the sternness of his tone somehow softened by the cadences of his Jekki accent. "Where's your company?"

The man looked at him as though he were some kind of tragic intrusion. "My company . . ." he repeated.

"Yes," the Tracker said. "The Bloody Picks. What happened to them? What happened to . . ."

Xonghis looked up to Kiampas, but it was Lord Kosoter who said, "Captain Mittades."

"Captain Mittades," the Tracker repeated. "What happened to *him*?"

The man began shaking. "M-my-my-my . . ." he began, blinking his eyes with each stutter. "M-m-m-my c-c-company?" The severed hand had sunk back to his lap.

"Yes. What happened?"

A look of incredulity stretched about rigid terror.

"My c-company? It was too-too-too-too dark—too dark to see the blood . . . You could only *hear* it!" His expression clenched at this, his lips pulled inward, as though he were suddenly toothless. "He-he-hear it sucking at their feet as they ran, slapping the walls like little boy hands. Draining like piss . . . *It was too daaaark!*"

"Whose feet?" Sarl's saw-toothed voice broke in. "Whose hands?"

"There's no light inside," the man sobbed. "Our skin. Our skin is too *thick*. It wraps—like a shroud—it keeps the blackness in. And my heart—*my heart!*—it looks and looks and it can't see!" A shower of spittle. "*There's nothing to see!*"

Something wild and violent jerked through the man, as if he were a sack filled with rabid vermin. And in the light, it all seemed too stark, too obvious to the naked eye, the twitch and fracture of a man's breaking. His eyes rolling beneath a stationary film of reflected white. His face caped in black, the lines of his anguish bleeding ink this way and that. Even Xonghis leaned backward.

The stranger began rocking side to side. A kind of pained

tooth-to-tooth grin broke his beard. "In the dark there is always *touch* . . . you see?" He waved the severed hand in a bawling, loose-wristed manner. A thread of blood pattered across Mimara's tunic. "I held on. I-I didn't l-l-let go! I held on. I held on. I held on. I h-he-held on!" His eyes ceased seeing anything illuminated, became so crazed as to seem painted. "Gamarrah! Gamarrah! I got you! Don't let go. No-no, don't! *Don't!* Don't let go!"

Lord Kosoter stepped forward, stood so that his shadow blotted the Pick entirely. He pressed Xonghis to the side with his left hand.

"*I held on!*" the Pick shrieked.

As though breaking hard ground with a spade, the Captain plunged his sword down through the man's corselet, snapping one of the Sranc-teeth necklaces. He drove the point deep, from the man's clavicle to his belly. The Pick jerked and spasmed, shook like sodden cloth on a slave's drying-stick. The Captain wrenched his sword clear; the body fell backward, arms unrolling, its feet pinned beneath it. The severed hand rolled soundlessly through the dust. Of its own volition, the man's hand seemed to twitch and grope. Senseless fingertip touched senseless fingertip.

Lord Kosoter spat. In a hiss that was almost a whisper, he said, "*Sobber.*"

Sarl's face crunched into a wheezing laugh. "No sobbers!" he cried, bending his voice to the others. "That's the Rule. No sobbers on the slog!"

Achamian glanced from Xonghis to Kiampas, saw the same expressionless mask he hoped to fake. The Nonman, Cleric, stood with his mouth open, as though trying to catch some taste of what they all smelled. Achamian blinked, let go a shuddering breath. Everything had happened so quickly, too quickly for his heart to feel, let alone for his soul to comprehend. All he knew was that something was wrong . . .

Something in the man's gibberish had carried the deep bruise of truth.

It looks and looks and it can't see!

"Cut him open," he heard himself say to Xonghis, who by now was standing at his side.

"What?"

"Cut him open . . . I need to see his heart."

Our skin is too thick . . .

The Imperial Tracker glanced from his Captain to Sarl, who said, "Do as he says," pinched through a scarcely restrained cackle. For all the world, the bandy-legged sergeant seemed like a man who had gambled everything on the mad turns of this encounter—nothing could spoil his run. Xonghis knelt in their midst, pulling a Jekki saw-knife from his boot as he did so. The dead Pick lay in his own inert shadow, his blood making black wool of the surrounding dust. His chest thudded like a broken drum when Xonghis cracked his ribcage. The Tracker worked with the thoughtless concentration of a long-time hunter: deer, wolf, or man, it was all the same to him, it seemed.

He pulled the heart from the overflowing cup that was the Pick's breast, held the gory mass up for Achamian to inspect. The shadow of his arm fell long across the floor beyond.

"Rinse it."

With a kind of bemused scowl, the Imperial Tracker shrugged and reached back with his free hand. He raised his waterskin to his teeth to unstop, grinning as though it were whisky. His fingernails shone fresh and pink as he gingerly rinsed the blood from the lobes. The water drained rose from the back of his knuckles. He kneaded the heart, turning the clear meat to his palm. The tubular cluster at the top was soaked white.

Suddenly he stopped. Everyone leaned forward, breathless, struck by the sight of a scar or suture along one of the heart's fat-sheathed chambers. With his thumb Xonghis pressed open the upper lid . . .

A human eye stared at them.

"*Sweet Seju!*" Sarl hissed, stumbling back bandy-limbed.

The Imperial Tracker laid the heart on the Pick's gore-soaked stomach, but carefully, as though fearful of waking something asleep.

"What does it mean?" Kiampas cried.

But Achamian was staring directly at Cleric. "Do you know the way forward?" he asked. "Do you *remember?*"

The ageless face regarded him for an inscrutable moment. "Yes."

"What does it mean?" Kiampas fairly shouted, demanding the Wizard's attention. "How did you know?"

Achamian looked to him. "This place is cursed."

"It's not time to follow the donkey shit home yet," the Captain growled.

"Cursed?" Kiampas pressed. "What do you mean? Haunted?"

Achamian matched the sergeant's gaze, silently thanked the Hundred for his sober eyes. The two of them had much to discuss.

"What happened here—"

"Means *nothing*," Lord Kosoter grated, his voice and manner as menacing as the dead eye watching. "There's nothing here *but skinnies*. And they're coming to shim our skulls."

The Captain's word signalled the end of the matter. Nothing was said to the others, but they all knew that something had happened. On the long walk back, Sarl harangued them with the Captain's story. The skinnies had got the best of the Bloody Picks, true, but then they were the *Picks*, and not the Skin Eaters. They didn't have their Captain, nor did they have *two* "light-spitters," as scalpers were wont to call sorcerers.

"This is the slog of all slogs, boys!" he cried with a peculiar, red-faced savagery that was all his own. "We run for the Coffers, and nothing—*nothing!*—will stop us!"

Certainly not skinnies.

Those who had seen the eye in the Pick's heart could only trade worried glances. The grandeur of the underworld Mansion had become hoary with threat. The long ache of emptiness and uncertainty had been replaced with the pang of teeming things. Mimara even clutched Achamian's hand, but every time he glanced at her, she was staring at the cavernous hollows opening above them, peering through the chains, as though following the stages of brightening light. She seemed younger, somehow, more fragile with beauty. The curve of her cheeks, like the outer edge of an opened oyster shell. Her compact lips. Her wide eyes, lashed with quill strokes. For the first time, it seemed, he noticed how much lighter her skin was than his or her mother's. For the first time he wondered about her real father, about the twist of caprice that had seen her born, rather than aborted by Esmenet's whore-shell.

They would survive this, he told himself. They had to survive this.

The great sheaf of debris that had originally halted them rose white in the light of the blinding Bar, so that it resembled the decayed outskirts of a glacier. Those left behind to guard the mules and supplies came running toward them like farm dogs: Obviously they had spent the entire time stewing in their terror. Sarl and Kiampas immediately began shouting, instructing everyone to stow their gear and ready the mules—despite the obvious exhaustion of all.

There would be no more sleep in the Black Halls of Cil-Aujas.

The Outside was leaking in. Hell.

The Bar of Heaven had burned for quite some time; Achamian could feel the picking toll of maintaining its meaning in the nethers of his soul—like holding a sum in thought for a span of hours. Even still, he hesitated before dispelling it, struck by the image of the Skin Eaters bending and bustling in its soaring glare. Sarl watching, more priest than slaver, with a scrutiny that could only be called ravenous. Kiampas wandering among the company's more recent recruits, or the Herd as the originals called them, slapping shoulders and tightening straps, offering what small wisdoms and assurances he could. Galian working closer to Xonghis than was necessary, shooting pressing looks at the almond-eyed Tracker whenever opportunity afforded. The former Columnary was too savvy not to know something was amiss. Achamian imagined it was only a matter of time before they all knew that Sarl was "coughing up their cracks"—as they liked to put it. Pokwas berating a harried Somandutta, who because of his refusal to relinquish his Nilnameshi garb was perpetually delaying the others. Every so often the tall black man glanced at the others, flashed them the broad smile hidden behind his outraged expression. Glum Sutadra, the Kianene everyone insisted was a Fanim heretic, packing his kit with the slow-handed intensity of a mortal ritual. Monstrous Oxwora towering head and shoulders above the rest, laughing at something thought or heard, pinch-faced Sranc heads swinging in his wild Thunyeri mane. One of the younger Galeoth boys, Rainon, scratching the veined cheek of his favourite mule, whispering encouragements he obviously didn't believe . . .

And Cleric standing over the Captain as he tightened the lacing on his Ainoni boots, staring with bland fixity at Achamian, his eyes so much older than the ceramic face that held them—like holes.

"What is it?" Mimara asked from his periphery.

"Nothing," Achamian said, looking away from the

Nonman, letting go the cramped meaning that was the Bar of Heaven. The line dimmed, as if it were a seam in a slowly closing door, then was clipped into nothingness. There was a moment of jeering cries and blackness, so utter it seemed to possess its own sound, followed by a sorcerous murmur and the reappearance of the twin points of light, like the eyes of two different races opening in the same invisible face.

The Skin Eaters resumed their work, though now many cast anxious looks into the darkness that leaned heavy about them.

The plan, Sarl announced after conferring with Lord Kosoter, was simply to continue with all possible haste. Odds were, he told them, they would encounter nothing at all, given the vast extent of Cil-Aujas. Odds were, whatever destroyed the Bloody Picks had withdrawn to the depths to lick their wounds and to count their spoils. Nevertheless, they were to march "on the sharp," as he put it, which meant without undue noise and with eyes and hearts and weapons held ready. "From here on in," he ground out, "we'll be the only ghosts in these halls."

These words, Achamian was quite certain, had been directed at him.

They resumed their march, skirting the flanks of the enormous collapse, walking for the most part beyond the tailings thrown by the catastrophe. The twin lights soundlessly mapped the tangle of debris, painting this or that clutch of monolithic stone, throwing double shadows that here and there resembled wings. The ancient slaughter, or whatever it was that had scattered so many dead across these reaches, continued to choke the floor, but the bones were so reed-brittle that the scalpers kicked through them the way they might humps of grass. With every step, Achamian saw knobs and shards of mouldered bone thrown free of the dust. He found himself wondering if this was the place . . .

The place where grief had burned through the rind of worldly things.

"How?" Mimara whispered in Ainoni from below his shoulder, her tone such that he immediately knew she referred to the dead scalper. "I saw no sorcery, and neither did you—I could see it in your face. So how could a heart *have an eye in it?*"

He found himself glancing to either side, counting those who might overhear. "Has anyone told you what happened when the First Holy War camped on the Plains of Mengedda?"

"Of course. The Battleplain. The earth began vomiting the dead within it. Mother told me that bones choked the grasses."

He swallowed rather than immediately reply. There was much he had intended to say, but a chorus of unwanted memories knelled through him, of how he and her mother had fled the Plains of Mengedda for the mountains, of how they had loved between sunlit trees . . .

And declared themselves man and wife.

"This is like that."

He could almost taste the sourness of her pause. "I feel enlightened already."

She had a Gift for smacking the generosity from him, he would grant her that much.

"Look," he said. "The boundaries between the World and Outside are like those between waking and sleep, reason and madness. Wherever the World slumbers or goes mad, the boundaries break down, and the Outside leaks *through* . . ." He glanced about to make sure no one was listening. "This place is a topos, like I already said. We literally walk the verge of Hell."

When she failed to immediately reply, Achamian congratulated himself on having silenced her.

"You mean the Dialectic," she said after several thoughtful steps. "The Dialectic of Substance and Desire . . ."

Though Achamian knew the phrase—knew it very well—it struck him as incomprehensible.

"You've read Ajencis," he said with more sarcasm than he intended. The Dialectic of Substance and Desire was the cornerstone of the great Kyranean philosopher's metaphysics, the notion that the differences between the World and the Outside were more a matter of degree than kind. Where substance in the World denied desire—save where the latter took the form of sorcery—it became ever more pliant as one passed through the spheres of the Outside, where the dead-hoarding realities conformed to the wills of the Gods and Demons.

Mimara was staring at her booted feet plowing through the dust. "Kellhus," she said. "You know, the man you hope to kill? He encouraged me to explore his library . . ." She stared at him, her expression mussed with conflicting passions. "I once thought I could be like my father."

The accusation in her voice called for pity, and yet he found himself with nothing but bitter words to answer. "Father? And who might that be?"

They walked without speaking for what seemed a long while. It was odd the way anger could shrink the great frame of silence into a thing, nasty and small, shared between two people. Achamian could feel it, palpable, binding them pursed lip to pursed lip, the need to punish the infidelities of the tongue.

Why did he let her get the best of him?

The Skin Eaters laboured in the circumscribed lights, leaning beneath the bulk of their packs like caste-menials beneath firewood. The younger ones led the mules in short trains of two or three, while the others walked the wary margins of the group, swords or spears drawn against the blackness. Though the memory of the Repositorium burned bright in his soul's eye, Achamian could not shake the sense that they marched into the void. If Cil-Aujas indeed plumbed the World to its very limit, as he had told Mimara, might they not simply wander into the precincts of Hell?

He occupied himself with this thought for a time, pondering his various readings of those who had allegedly passed alive into the Afterlife. The legend of Mimomitta from ancient Kyranean lore. The parable of Juraleal from *The Chronicle of the Tusk.* And of course the rumours his slave, Geraus, had told him about Kellhus . . .

Mimara walked beside him as before, but her damp presence had hardened into something prickling sharp. *Is it true,* he wanted to ask, *that Kellhus wears the severed heads of demons about his girdle?* These words, he was certain, would heal their momentary feud. As loath to encourage her as he had been, he had made a habit of avoiding her opinions.

The simple act of asking would say much.

Instead, he rubbed his face, muttering curses. What kind of rank foolishness was this? Pining over harsh words to a cracked and warped woman!

"I watched you," Mimara abruptly said, staring at the procession of chains through the upper reaches of his light. For a moment he assumed this was just more hounding, then she said, "You don't trust the Nonman. I could see it in your eyes."

Achamian scanned the distance to be sure Cleric was far enough away not to hear, then looked at her with the mixture of annoyance and mystification that was fast becoming his "Mimara-face," even as part of him recognized that this was *her* peace offering.

"Now is not the time, girl," he said brusquely. That she could worry about such a thing given what they had just heard—not to mention what they might find—was beyond Achamian. If anything made her seem crazed, he told himself, it wasn't so much her intellect as the disorder of her cares.

"Is it his Mark?" she persisted, again speaking in Ainoni. "Is that why you fear him?"

As though to match her absurdity with his own, Achamian

began mumbling the song his slave's children had sung and sung until he had cried aloud for them to stop. It seemed he could even hear them, piping about the edges of his husky baritone, voices that had floated with innocence and chanting delight. Voices he dearly missed.

"Stinky feet, hide my sweet, walk the river cool . . ."

"Sometimes," Mimara persisted, "when I glimpse him in the corner of my eye . . ."

"Stinky bum, sniff your thumb, swim the water pool . . ."

". . . he seems like something monstrous, a shambling wreck, black and rotted and . . . and . . ."

Suddenly the song and the peevishness that had provoked it were forgotten. Achamian found himself listening with arched attentiveness—a horror-spurred concentration.

She worked her mouth for a moment, lips pert about some lozenge of inexplicability, then looked to him helplessly.

"And it's like you can *taste* his evil," he heard himself say. "Not so much on your tongue as in your gums. Your teeth ache for it."

A peculiar vulnerability afflicted her look, as though she had admitted something beyond her courage. "Not always," she said.

"And it's more than just the Nonman, isn't it?" Something peculiar fizzed through his voice, something like a pang, but too fraught with fear. "Sometimes . . . Sometimes *I look this way* as well, don't I?"

"So you see the same?" she blurted.

He shook his head in a way he hoped seemed lackadaisical. "No. What I see is what you see typically, the shadow of ruin and decay, the ugliness of the deficient and incomplete. You're describing something different. Something *moral* as opposed to merely aesthetic . . ." He paused to catch his breath. What new madness was this? "What antique Mandate scholars called the Judging Eye."

He had watched her carefully as he spoke, hoping to see

the glint of thrill in her eyes. But there was naught but concern. This had been gnawing at her for quite some time, he realized.

"The Judging Eye," she repeated in flawless Ainoni. "And what is that?"

His heart crawled into his throat. He coughed it loose, then swallowed it back into his chest. "It means that you don't simply apprehend the Mark of sorcery, *you see the sin as well . . .*" He trailed, then laughed, despite the horror that flexed through him.

"And that's *funny*?" she asked, her voice warbling with indignation.

"No, girl . . . It's just that . . ."

"That *what*?"

"Your stepfather . . . Kellhus."

He had improvised this, not willing to stray too far into the truth. But once spoken it seemed every bit as true and far more terrible with significance. Such was the perversity of things that Men often recognized their own arguments only after they had spoken them. "Kellhus . . ." he repeated numbly.

"What about him?"

"He says the Old Law has been revoked, that Men are at long last ready for the New . . ." The words the Mandate Catechism came back to him unbidden, and with the heat of truths drawn intact from the crucible of deception. *Though you lose your soul, you shall gain the world . . .*

"Think," he continued. "If sorcery is no longer abomination, then . . ." Let her think it was this, he told himself. Perhaps it would even serve to . . . discourage her. "Then why would you see it as such?"

He was surprised to discover he had stopped walking, that he stood riven, staring at the woman whose parentage had stirred so many echoes of heartbreak and whose unscrupulous obstinacy threatened everything. The last of the Skin Eaters had passed them, casting dubious backward glances as they marched with the mule-train beyond the limits of his light. Within heartbeats it was just the two of them, flanked by knolls of heaped basalt, plains of dust, and bones bleached as light as charcoal by the ages. Cleric's light had tapered to a point, and the company had dwindled to a floating procession of shining helms and trudging shadows.

Silence sealed them as utterly as the blackness.

"I always knew something was . . . wrong," she said softly. "I mean, I read and I read, everything I could find about sorcery and the Mark. And nowhere, not once, was there any mention of what I see. I thought it was because it was so . . . unpredictable, you know, just when I would see the . . . the good of the evil. But when I see it, it burns so . . . so . . . I mean, it strikes me so much deeper than at any other time. It was too profound to go without saying, to be left out of the records . . . I just knew that something had to be different. That something had to be wrong!"

First her arrival, and now this. She had the Judging Eye—she could see not just sorcery, but the *damnation* it betokened . . . To think he had convinced himself the Whore of Fate would leave him be!

"And now you're saying," she began hesitantly, "that I'm a kind of . . . proof?" She blinked in the stammering manner of people finding their way through unsought revelations. "Proof of my stepfather's . . . *falsity*?"

She was right . . . and yet what more proof did he, Drusas Achamian, need? That night twenty years ago, on the eve of the First Holy War's final triumph, the Scylvendi Chieftain had told him everything, given him all the proof he would ever need, enough to fuel decades of bitter hate—enough to deliver these scalpers to their doom. Anasûrimbor Kellhus was Dûnyain, and the Dûnyain cared for naught but domination. Of course he was false.

It was for *her* sake that the Wizard trembled. She possessed the Judging Eye!

He thought of their coupling, and the sordid passions that had driven it. A cold sweat compressed the skin and wool beneath his pack. He could feel the pity hanging like wet string in his expression, the way his look saw past what she was now—the pale image of her mother standing small in white light—into the torment that awaited her.

"We have more immediate concerns at the moment," he said in a rallying voice.

"You mean Cleric," she replied, her little hands balled into slack fists. She was looking at him with the kind of wilful focus that spoke of contravening interests. Soon, he knew, she would come at him with questions, relentless questions, and he needed to consider carefully the kinds of answers he could and could not give.

"Yes," he said, drawing her by the elbow after the others. "Incariol." He thought of how men always did this, managed the thoughts of others, and wondered why it should exact such a toll from him. "His Mark means he's old . . . older than you could imagine. And that means he's not only a Quya Mage, but Ishroi, a Nonman noble . . ."

He could feel the note of falsity, like a cold coin in the slick palm of his voice. He cursed himself for a fool, even as he sought her gaze, hoping that a sincere look might carry what his words could not. The Erratic and his ability to lead them through this deserted warren was their immediate concern. The fact that Achamian used them to another purpose . . . Weren't all words simply tools in the end?

"So he's Ishroi, then . . ." Mimara said. The lilt in her tone told him that she knew something was amiss. When had he ever urged her into the murk of his ruminations?

"Such figures don't easily slip through the cracks of history, Mimara. And what history I haven't lived through Seswatha, I've *read* many times. Moithural, Hosûtil, Shimbor—all the mannish translators and chroniclers of the Nonmen. I assure you, there's no mention of any Incariol, nowhere, not even in their own *Pit of Years* . . ." Despite himself, his voice was striking more, not fewer, tin notes of insincerity.

Her gaze was bolt-forward now, apparently following Cleric's light and the small mob of men and pack animals labouring beneath it. From their vantage, the Skin Eaters seemed to pick their way across the vast back of nothingness. Here and there small clearings of floor opened between them, bloomed colourless and flat in the illumination, only to be obscured by kicked dust and the drift of shadowy legs.

They had travelled past the point of sturdy grounds.

"This Judging Eye," she said with cool resignation. "It's a *curse*, isn't it? An affliction . . ."

Many years had passed since last he had suffered this feeling, not simply of too much happening too quickly, but of some dread intent in motion, as though all these things, the Nonman, the Captain, the dead scalper out there, and now Mimara, were like the suckered arms of the octopuses he and his father had sometimes pulled from the Meneanor Sea—limbs webbed in the sinew of a singular Fate.

Circumstances always encompassed, but sometimes they encircled as well, as many-chambered as this mountain and every bit as dark. His heart seemed to beat against sagging bandages.

"Just legends," he said. "Nothing more."

"But you've read them all," she said in a high, scathing voice.

He raised a knobbed hand to silence her, nodded to the interval of darkness separating them from the company. A figure had surfaced from the advancing perimeter of their light, became what looked like, for a mad moment, a wizened ape armoured in human rags . . .

It was Sarl. He waited for them, alone in the darkness, smiling, his lips stretched longer than the arc of his gums and teeth. "Well-well-well," he called in the tones of a cracked flute. Even in the dark the man squinted.

"We'll speak of this later," Achamian said to Mimara,

halting her with a gentle hand on her elbow. She frowned and in a careless moment looked to the sergeant with naked fury. Though the man remained some several paces distant, there was no way he could have failed to see her anger.

"You take the light," Achamian said quickly.

"Me?"

"You have the Gift of the Few. You can grasp it with your soul, even without any real sorcerous training . . . If you think on it, you should actually be able to *feel* the possibility."

For the bulk of his life, Achamian had shared his calling's contempt of witches. There was no reason for this hatred, he knew, outside the capricious customs of the Three Seas. Kellhus had taught him as much, one of many truths he had used to better deceive. Men condemned others to better celebrate themselves. And what could be easier to condemn than women?

But as he watched her eyes probe inward, he was struck by the practicality of her wonder, the way her expression made this novelty look more like a recollection. It was almost as if women possessed a kind of sanity that men could only find on the far side of tribulation. Witches, he found himself thinking, were not only a good thing, they could very well be a necessity. Especially the witch-to-be before him.

"Yes," she said. "I *can* feel it. It's like . . . It's . . ." She trailed in smiling indecision.

"It's a small Cant," he said, grateful that Sarl, for whatever reason, had granted them this moment together. With a finger, he redirected the light so that it rested several feet above her head. "Something called the Surillic Point . . ."

"Surillic Point," she repeated, her voice hot with breath.

"So," he continued, "picture yourself in your soul's eye." He paused a heartbeat. "Now picture the light, not as you see it, but as you *see its Mark.*"

She nodded, staring at him with forked concentration. The light stretched the outline of her face across her breast and shoulder.

"Now picture you and the Point *walking together*. Hold fast that image. It'll be trying at first, but with practice it'll become thoughtless, like any other reflex."

Her gaze fell blank to his wool-covered chest. Without prompting, she took two steps, her eyes climbing in upward astonishment to watch the glaring light track her move for move. She looked back about to laugh, only to stub her toe against some dust-furred detritus. She grinned as she snatched back her balance. Her shadow bloomed and compressed beneath her.

"Hurry," he said. "Catch the others."

She made no secret of her disgust as she strode past the sergeant, walking like a slave with an amphora poised atop her head. Then she began trotting down the path the others had sloughed through the dust.

And she glowed, the old Wizard thought, not only against the stalking black, but against so many memories of harm.

Achamian followed her as far as Sarl. The man stood slightly humped beneath the weight of his pack, the straps of which had bunched folds of mail across the front of his hauberk. Standing so close to him reminded Achamian of the dead Pick, the heart, and the knowledge that they were not alone in these black-bowel deeps. Mimara's light was fast receding, and he saw Sarl's eyes flit toward the encroaching darkness. Without a word, they both began following the woman.

"What do you want, Sergeant?" The company's passage had left an aura of dust in the air, and Achamian could feel it fur the insides of his mouth. His chest wanted to cough the words.

"The Captain asked me to speak to you." Sarl looked even more wrinkled in the gloom. His face was grey and grimace-marked, like a corpse exhumed from black peat. The Wizard breathed against the bristle of bodily alarm, fought the urge to ball his hands into fists. He almost always felt this whenever Sarl strayed too near, ever since the man had smashed his wine-bowl in the Cocked Leg.

"Did he now."

"Yes," Sarl said in a breathy rasp, smiling like an uncle fishing for a nephew's love. That was the thing about the man's ceaseless posturing: Even when the passions were appropriate, the underlying intensities were all wrong. "You see, he thinks you're . . . too *honest*, let us say."

"Honest."

"And arrogant."

"Arrogant," Achamian repeated. There was something deadening about the discourse of fools. It was as if his patience were a pool that was only so deep, and Sarl's every word were a rock . . .

"Look," Sarl said. "We are learned men, you and I—"

"I assure you, Sergeant, there's *very* little that you and I share."

"Oho! The grief old Sarl gets for his diplomacy!"

"Diplomacy."

"Yes, *diplomacy*!" he cried in sudden savagery. "Fine fucking words spoken to fine fucking fools!"

Mimara had drawn far ahead of them by now, so that they walked in the least glimmer of light, more the rims of men than possessing human substance, stepping by memory of grounds glimpsed ahead. Sarl was a threat, both to him and his quest—if Achamian had suspected as much before, he knew now. All he need do was speak to the madman in his *true voice*, right here, right now, and that threat would vanish, become more ash to powder this dead Mansion's floor.

"What?" the fool continued. "Did you not think the Captain *knew* we walked through a vast tomb? Did you not think he would have commanded Cleric to illuminate it? And what do you do? You decide to show the bones to all! To let simple men know they walked beneath inhuman tombs. Darkness shields as much as it threatens, Schoolman! And you must remember the first rule!"

There was reason in what he was saying. But then that was the problem with reason: It was as much a whore as Fate. Like rope, you could use it to truss or snare any atrocity . . .

Another lesson learned at Kellhus's knee.

"Another Rule of the Slog, is it?"

"Oh yes . . . The rules that have made this company a legend in the Wilds. Do you hear me? A *legend*!"

"So what is the first rule, Sergeant?"

"The Captain *always knows*. Do you hear me? The Captain always knows!"

All at once, the hand-waving, wire-grinning complexity of the sergeant seemed to focus into one simple truth: Sarl did not just revere his Captain, *he worshipped him*. Achamian nearly spit, so sour was the disgust that welled through him. To think that after all these years, he marched in the company of fanatics once again!

"You think you can cow me?" he heard himself shout. "A Holy Veteran, like your Captain? What my eyes have seen, Sergeant. I have spat at the feet of the Aspect-Emperor himself! I possess a strength, a might, that can scar mountains, rout entire hosts, turn your bones into boiling oil! And you presume—presume!—*to threaten me?*"

Sarl laughed, but with a breath clipped by wariness. "You've stepped outside the circle of your skill, Schoolman. This is the *slog*, not the Holy War, and certainly not some infernal School. Here, our lives depend upon the resolve of our brothers. The knee that cracks pulls ten men down. Recall that. *There will be no second warning*."

Achamian knew he should be politic, conciliatory, but he was too weary, and too much had happened. Wrath had flooded all the blind chambers of his heart.

"I am not one of you! I am not a Schoolman, and I am

certainly not a Skin Eater! And this, my friend, is not your—"

His anger sputtered, blew away and outward like smoke. Horror plunged in.

Sarl actually continued several more steps before realizing he was alone. "What?" he called uneasily from the almost total dark. The lights ahead of them seemed to hang in absolute blackness, a vision of little men toiling into the void.

Over the course of his long life, Achamian had been asked many times what it was like to see the world with the arcane senses of the Few. He would usually answer that it was just as manifold and multifarious as the world revealed by mundane senses—and every bit as difficult to describe. Sometimes he would say it was like a different kind of hearing.

Sarl forgotten, he found himself looking down, even though he could see neither the ground nor his feet. It seemed he could hear calling: the Skin Eaters shouting out their names.

There were galleries immediately below them, stretching many miles into the entombed fundament. Before, he had known this as an abstraction, as something drawn from the uncertain palette of memory. But now he could *feel* those wending spaces, not directly, but through the constellation of absences, the pits in the stitch of existence, that moved through them.

Chorae . . .

Tears of God, at least a dozen of them, borne by something that prowled the halls beneath their feet.

The riot of thought and passion that so often heralded disaster. The apprehension of meaning to be had where no sense could be found, not because he was too simple, but because he was too small and the conspiracies were too great.

Sarl was little more than a direction in the viscous black. "Run!" the Wizard cried. "*Run!*"

CHAPTER FIFTEEN

Condia

If the immutable appears recast, then you yourself have been transformed.

—MEMGOWA, *CELESTIAL APHORISMS*

Spring, 20 New Imperial Year (4132 Year-of-the-Tusk), Condia

The Interval tolled long and low over the landscape of tents.

Blowing into his hands against the morning chill, Sorweel sat outside the entrance to his tent blearily watching Porsparian prepare their morning fire. The old man crouched like a beggar before a small, smoking pyramid of bound scrub and grasses, his feet bare despite the cold. He seemed more ancient somehow, more wise and penetrating for his leathery brown skin.

The Shigeki slave had been an embarrassment at first. But the man quickly had become an enigma, every bit as deep and as frightening as the Anasûrimbor. Something froze within Sorweel whenever the pink-and-yellow eyes fixed him. And though he smiled at his friendly frowns, his quizzical grins, the young King recoiled as well, as if expecting a blow from unseen quarters. Porsparian was neither meek nor innocent nor powerless. Shadows hung from him—terrifying shadows.

The old slave clucked in satisfaction as the first flames soaked his grasses. Sorweel pretended to grin. An involuntary hand drifted to his cheek, touched the memory of the soil the man had smeared across his face days earlier.

Somehow, simply thinking her name, *Yatwer*, had become a kind of premonition. And it shamed him. She was the Goddess of the weak, the enslaved, and now she was his.

Eskeles was the first to arrive, of course. The rotund Schoolman groaned and huffed as he lowered his bulk next to Sorweel on the mat. "The Library of Sauglish," he muttered as he tried to wrestle comfort from his posture. "Yet *again*." The sorcerer was forever complaining about his Dreams, enough for Sorweel to start losing interest in them.

Zsoronga arrived shortly afterwards, stiff in his *basahlet*, the traditional dress of the Zeümi caste-nobility. His battle-sash seemed all the more crisp and white now that the Kidruhil tents surrounding them had become grey and mottled for travel.

With Obotegwa absent, Eskeles was forced to translate their conversation, something Sorweel found more and more irksome. Over the previous weeks, Obotegwa's mellow and throaty tones had simply *become* his friend's voice. Hearing the Successor-Prince speak through Eskeles only reminded Sorweel of the chasm of tongues between them. For his part, Zsoronga quite obviously distrusted the Mandate Schoolman, and so kept his remarks to a formal minimum. And Eskeles, of course, simply could not refrain from adding his own commentary, so that Sorweel was never quite certain where Zsoronga began and the sorcerer ended. It reminded him of when he had first joined the Great Ordeal, the dark days when all he could understand were the recriminations of his own voice.

After drinking the tea prepared by Porsparian, the three of them strolled down the avenues and the byways of the encampment, making their way to the Umbilicus, the palatial pavilion belonging to the Aspect-Emperor. The air of carnival permeated the Great Ordeal even during the most sober times. But today, when Sorweel had expected all to be riot and celebration, they found only camp after subdued camp. Some Men of the Circumfix clustered here and there sharing muted talk around smoking breakfast fires, while others simply laid in the sunlight snoozing.

"They have nothing to do," Zsoronga remarked.

Sorweel found himself staring at a young Galeoth warrior laying between guy-ropes with his eyes closed, his head propped on the tear-shaped shield he had lain against his pack. He was stripped to his waist, and his skin shone as white as a child's teeth. A pang of envy struck the young King as deep as a stabbing. After weeks of fear and indecision, he now knew that he, Varalt Sorweel III, was simply an ordinary fool, no wiser, no stronger, than the next man. He had been born with the gifts of the mediocre, and yet here he was, stranded in the role of a captive king. He was cursed, cursed with the toil of pretending, endlessly pretending to be more.

Cursed to war, not across plains as heroes do, but within the wells of his soul—to war as cowards do.

Today was but one more example.

For reasons unknown, the Aspect-Emperor had declared a day of rest and consultation. Sorweel and Zsoronga, alone out of the Company of Scions, had been summoned to the Council of Potentates, a gathering of the Great Ordeal's senior planners and most powerful participants. Since Sorweel had yet to master the rudiments of Sheyic, Eskeles had been assigned his interpreter.

Something in his heart leapt at the thought of seeing *him* once more, even as the greater part of him quailed. It all seemed a gaggle of voices, nagging, warning, accusing, a chorus of contradictions. Porsparian and the Goddess. Zsoronga and his blasphemous book. His father. Kayûtas and his preternatural scrutiny. Eskeles and his fanatic enthusiasm.

In the hearts of heroes, words cancelled out words, so that only truth and certainty remained. Not for him. In his heart, words simply accumulated, piled one on top of the other. He went through his daily motions well enough, discharged his paltry duties, but it all seemed an accident, like walking paths in the dead of night.

And he was about to face the Aspect-Emperor—Anasûrimbor Kellhus!

He was about to be discovered.

The Umbilicus loomed over the near horizon of tents, black, yet brocaded with patterns like the scales on a lizard's hide. With its many posts, it seemed a miniature mountain range, with curved conical faces warming in the pink morning sun. The Interval tolled again as they walked clear the last of the obscuring tents, near enough for its full resonance to press against their ears and chests, yet still somewhere unseen. The outer panels of the Umbilicus had been stitched with elaborate representations of the Circumfixion embroidered in gold across the great skirts of black: a nude man hanging upside down, his wrists and ankles bound to an iron ring. For the first time, Sorweel realized how innocuous and commonplace the symbol now seemed. It had fairly hummed with wickedness and revulsion before Sakarpus's fall . . .

Hundreds of shining figures populated the intervening pasture, crowds of them, threaded with slow-moving files that converged on an entrance in the southern quarter of the Umbilicus: the senior caste-nobility of the New Empire, filling the air with the sound of low laughter and concentrated discussion. Sorweel's instinct was to hesitate, to ponder and enumerate the strangers about to encompass them, but Eskeles forged ahead without a second glance. Within a dozen paces it seemed Sorweel had walked the Three Seas end to end. Glimpses became nations. A painted Nilnameshi Satrap comparing blades with a long-bearded Tydonni Earl. A doddering mage leaning hard on the shoulder of a boyslave.

Green-and-gold-clad Guardsof the Hundred Pillars standing shoulder to shoulder in triangular threes. Two long-limbed Thunyeri staring off in the distance as they talked. A Conriyan Palatine in full martial regalia.

Sorweel found himself running nervous palms over the padded fabric of his royal parm, fearing that he looked as backward and as outlandish as he felt. He envied Zsoronga and the thoughtless confidence of his stride. The Successor-Prince walked as a man should, as though what set him apart also set him *above*. But it was more than his bearing: The glory of his Zeümi heritage shouted from his garb and accoutrements, down to the jaguar-skin kilt he wore over his leggings. Sorweel's road-stained parm communicated far more humiliating facts: ignorance, poverty, crude manners, and foolish conceits.

The crowds bullied Sorweel with their shuffling proximity. He was accustomed to the company of physically powerful men: His father's Boonsmen had raised him as much as his father. But the strangeness of faraway lands and customs soaked the Lords of the Ordeal in menace. He saw knife strokes in the oddities of their affected manner, condemnation in the gold-threaded complexity of their dress. He heard insult and affront in their incomprehensible tongues.

He tried, as men so often do, to rally his pride with a kind of defensive contempt. Why, he told himself, should he fear these men when they could not even *speak*? They were no better than animals, the Galeoth barking like dogs, the Nansur thrumming like swallows, and the Nilnameshi cackling like geese.

But he knew these thoughts for what they were: the shallow posturings of a boy. He could feel it in the way his eyes flinched from the glare of others, in the empty bubbles that crept through his bones.

Stone-faced Pillarian Guards flanked the entrance, freighted with splinted mail and various arms. In the press,

Sorweel almost stumbled into one of them. Powerful hands clamped his shoulders, a dark face sneered a thumb's length from his own, and a memory of Narsheidel dragging him through Sakarpas on the day of its fall shuddered through him. A jostling moment passed, and he found himself in the shadowy confines of the Umbilicus.

For a moment he simply stood gaping, his shoulders yanked this way and that as the Men of the Circumfix shoved past him. He heard several muttered curses, the Sheyic phrase for Shit-herder among them.

He was a plainsman, accustomed to camps on the Pale, and yet never had he stood in a tent so colossal. It was bigger than Vogga Hall, and far more luxurious, despite being a temporary structure of wood, hemp, and leather. The interior was cool, and the rumble of voices possessed an outdoor air. Shining silk banners ribboned the open spaces, swaying in unseen drafts, each incorporating the Tusk, the Circumfix, and the devices of innumerable nations and factions. A wooden amphitheatre had been raised about the outer walls, a horseshoe of rising tiers that were already teaming with various Lords of the Ordeal. A long table formed of many small camp tables occupied the broad space between, packed with obviously important personages, some with their chairs pulled close, others with their chairs pushed back or turned to follow some conversation. Two massive carpets covered the intervening expanses to either side, each with brocaded panels depicting various events: desert marches, walls assailed and defended, burning city heights. It was only when he saw the naked man bound to a Circumfix amid masses of starved warriors did Sorweel realize that the panels told the story of the First Holy War, the great Three Seas bloodletting that had made the New Empire and the Great Ordeal possible. Eskeles had already backtracked to fetch him by this time, so the young King was forced to scan the rest of the pictorial narrative while in the Schoolman's tow.

Rumbling commotion surrounded them as Sorweel took his seat between Zsoronga and Eskeles. "I have always wanted this," the rotund sorcerer said. "We see such sights in our Dreams, things you could scarce imagine. But to witness such glory with *living eyes*, my King! I hope the day comes when you can fathom your fortune. Despite all the pain, all the wrenching loss, there is no greater glory than a complicated life."

Sorweel feigned distraction, once again troubled by the way parts of his soul always rose in seditious agreement with the sorcerer's words—the leuneraal's words. He glanced at Zsoronga, searching for encouragement in his imperturbable pride, but the Zeümi Prince simply gazed out, his expression as empty and as guarded as Sorweel's own. The look of a boy striving to pass unnoticed in the company of men.

Zsoronga could feel it as well, Sorweel realized. There was something in the air . . . something beyond the visible signs of warlike nobility, something that hung like a nimbus about outward observances. A kind of *knowledge*.

Sorweel twitched for the force of the realization when it came to him, as if some inner tendon had been plucked. Despite the differences in garb and armament, despite the differences in tongue, custom, and skin, something singular and implacable encompassed these men, defined them to their unguessed core.

Belief.

Here was belief, rendered sensuous for its intensity, made palpable in lilting voices and shining eyes.

Sorweel had known he marched in the company of fanatics, but until now he had never . . . touched it. The fever of jubilation. The lunacy of eyes that witnessed without seeing. The smell of commitment, absolute and encompassing. The Men of the Circumfix were capable of *anything*, he realized. They would weary, but they would not pause. They would fear, but they would not flee. Any atrocity, any sacrifice—nothing lay outside the compass of their possibility. They could burn cities, drown sons, slaughter innocents; they could even, as Zsoronga's story about the suicides proved, *cut their own throats*. Through their faith they had outrun their every scruple, animal or otherwise, and they gloried in the stink of it—in the numbing smell of losing oneself in the mastery of another.

The Aspect-Emperor.

But how? How could any one man command such mad extremes in men? Zsoronga had said that it was a matter of intellect, that Men were little more than children in the presence of the Anasûrimbor—this was what Drusas Achamian, the Wizard-Exile, had claimed.

But who could be such a fool? And short of heaven how could such an intellect be? Eskeles had claimed that his soul was the God's soul in small, that divinity was the cipher. If a man were to think *the thoughts of a god*, would not Men be as children before him?

What if the world really was about to end?

Through the course of his ruminations, Sorweel's gaze had waded across the pavilion's chaotic interior, insensible to the sights they chanced upon. He found himself staring at the grand black-and-gold tapestry that dominated the far wall, reaching to the pavilion's highest recesses. At first his eyes rebelled—something about the brocaded patterns defeated his ability to focus. Absent scrutiny, it had seemed to consist of abstract geometric designs, not so different from the Kianene rugs his father had hung in their chambers. But now, each shape he glimpsed, or thought he glimpsed, found itself undone by the natural play of eyes discerning figures. At every turn, the lines, be they ruler straight or twined into curlicues, betrayed the representations they seemed to constitute. Everything was yanked short of sense, held in a kind of puzzling in-between. And when he averted his gaze, looked through the sideways lense of his periphery, the almost-figures appeared to resolve into patterned strings, as though they were unreadable sigils of some kind . . .

Sorcerous, he realized with a shudder of dread. The tapestry was sorcerous.

Raised on a low dais, the Great Ordeal's twin Exalt-Generals sat to either side of the towering arras, their seats turned so they faced both the long table and the rising crowd of caste-nobles. Of the two, King Proyas seemed the more refined, not for any nicety of his garb or ornament, but because of the austerity of his demeanour. Where he looked out over the bustling tiers with stern curiosity, nodding and smiling at those who caught his gaze, the King of Eumarna fairly glared. There was piety and confidence in King Saubon's look, to be sure, but their was a miserly, embittered air as well, as if he had won his stature at too great a cost and so continually found himself returning to the scales, seeking to weigh what he had lost.

Several Schoolmen sat at the table below them: an old bearded man wearing robes similar to Eskeles, only trimmed in gold; a Nilnameshi with ringed nostrils and tattooed cheeks; a stately silver-haired man dressed in voluminous black; and an ancient blind man, whose skin seemed as translucent as sausage rind. "The Grandmasters of the Major Schools," Eskeles explained, obviously watching his wandering gaze. Sorweel had guessed as much; what surprised him was the sight of Anasûrimbor Serwa in their midst, wearing a plain white gown that seemed all the more alluring for its high-necked modesty. Young—implausibly so. Flaxen hair drawn back in a braid that began in the small of her back. The incongruity of her presence would have looked absurd had she not so obviously carried the otherworldly stamp of her father's blood.

"Striking, no?" the Mandate Schoolman continued in a lowered voice. "The Aspect-Emperor's daughter, and Grand-mistress of the Swayal Compact. Serwa, the Ladywitch herself."

"A witch . . ." Sorweel murmured. In Sakarpic, the word for witch was synonymous with many things, all of them wicked. That it could be applied to someone so exquisite in form and feature struck him as yet another Three Seas obscenity. Nevertheless, he found his gaze lingering for the wrong reasons. The word seemed to pry her open somehow, make her image wanton with tugging promise.

"Ware her, my King," Eskeles said with a soft laugh. "She walks with the Gods."

This was an old saying from the legend of Suberd, the legendary King who tried to seduce Aelswë, the mortal daughter of Gilgaöl, and so doomed his line forever. The fact that the Schoolman could quote the ancient Sakarpi tale simply reminded Sorweel that he had been a spy—and remained one still.

Serwa's older brothers, Kayûtas and Moënghus, sat on the opposite side of the long table, with a dozen other Southron generals that Sorweel did not recognize. As before he was struck by the difference between the two brothers, the one slender and fair, the other broad and dark. Zsoronga had told him the rumour: that Moënghus was not a true Anasûrimbor at all, but rather the child of the Aspect-Emperor's first wife—Serwa's namesake, the one who had been hung with the Anasûrimbor on the Circumfix—and a Scylvendi wayfarer.

At first this struck Sorweel as almost laughably obvious. When the seed was strong, women were but vessels; they bore only what men planted in them. If a boy-child was born white-skinned, then his or her father was white-skinned, and so on, down to all the particularities of form and pigment. The Anasûrimbor simply couldn't be Moënghus's true father, and that was that. It had been a revelation of sorts to realize the Men of the Circumfix, without exception, overlooked this plain fact. Eskeles even referred to Moënghus as a "True Son of the Anasûrimbor" forcefully, as though the wilful application of a word could undo what the world had wrought.

But another glimpse of the madness that had seized these men.

The Interval tolled, its resonant sound eerie because of the way it passed through the pavilion. The last of the stragglers filed in, three long-haired Galeoth, a lone Conriyan, and a contingent of goateed Khirgwi or Kianene—Sorweel still had difficulty telling them apart. Dozens of men still shuffled along the various tiers searching for gaps or friends, including two Nansur who shimmed past their knees with fierce yet apologetic smiles. The pavilion took on the open roar of men attempting to press in final comments and observations, a stacking of voices that was progressively doused into murmurs.

It would have reminded Sorweel of Temple—were it not for the skidding sense of doom.

"Tell me, your Glory," Eskeles muttered close in his ear. His breath smelled of sour milk. "When you look into these faces, what do you see?"

Sorweel thought the question so strange that he glared at the sorcerer, suspecting some kind of joke at his expense. But the fat man's friendly expression shouted otherwise. He was genuinely curious. The young King found this alarming in a vague way, like a spontaneous and inexplicable pain. "Gulls," he heard himself blurt. "Gulls and fools!"

The Mandate Schoolman chuckled, shook his head like someone too familiar with the ways of conceit not to be amused.

The Interval's second sounding hung prickling in the avid air, soaking all other noise. Sorweel saw faces turn in curiosity across the tiers, at first to one another, then, as though bent to some singular will, to the pavilion floor . . .

He failed to see the prick of light at first, perhaps because his gaze shied from the eye-twisting planes of the arras. Some twenty Shrial Knights, resplendent in white and silver and gold, had taken up positions across the front of the dais, accompanied by three of the surviving Nascenti, the first of the Aspect-Emperor's disciples, clad entirely in silken black. It was the shadows thrown from the shoulders of these newcomers that drew his eyes to the glittering point behind them.

It twinkled at first, like a star watched with tired eyes. But it *resolved*, became more dense with blank incandescence. The Interval tolled again, deeper this time, like the boom of faraway thunder drawn into a string. The braziers wheezed into strings of smoke. Skirts of gloom fell from the tented heights.

A sloped landscape of faces—bearded, painted, clean-shaven—watched.

Seven heartbeats of soundless thunder.

Blinking brilliance . . . and *there he was.*

He sat cross-legged, but not upon any surface Sorweel could see, his forehead bowed to the spear-point of his hands, which had been pressed, elbows out, together in prayer. A halo shone about his crownless head, like a golden, ethereal plate, laying at an angle behind his scalp. The image of him seemed to scald unblinking eyes.

A murmuring wave passed through the Lords of the Ordeal: furtive exclamations of joy and wonder. Sorweel cursed himself for clasping his chest, for quick breaths drawn through a throat like a burning reed.

Demon! he cried to himself, trying to summon his father's face in his soul's eye. *Ciphrang!*

But the Aspect-Emperor was speaking, his voice so broad, so simple and obvious, that *gratitude* welled through the young King of Sakarpas. It was a beloved voice, almost but not quite forgotten, here at last to soothe the anxious watches, to heal the sundered heart. Sorweel understood none of the words, and Eskeles sat slack and dumbstruck, apparently too overawed to translate. But the voice—the *voice!* Somehow spoken to many, and yet intended only for one, for him, for Sorweel alone, out of all the hundreds, the thousands! *You,* it whispered. *Only you . . .* A mother's scolding cracked into laughter by love. A father's coaxing crimped into tears by pride.

And then, just when this music had wholly captured him, the assembled Lords of the Ordeal crashed into it with a booming chorus. And Sorweel found himself *understanding* the words, for they belonged to the first thing Eskeles had taught him in Sheyic, the Temple Prayer . . .

> *Sweet God of Gods,*
> *Who walk among us,*
> *Hallowed are your many names . . .*

And somehow, through the entirety of the recitation, the Anasûrimbor's voice remained distinct, like a thread of milk in slow-curling waters. Sorweel pinched his lips into a line, steeled himself against the pitch of collective voices—against the tidal urge to *pray with*. At that moment, he understood what it meant to look out while others bowed their faces in worship. The groping of unanswered expectations, clammy and intangible. The fouled sense of defiance, like the sin of creeping awake through a house of sleepers. He exchanged a look with Zsoronga and saw in his eyes a more caustic version of his own bewildered dissent.

They were the fools here, not because they dared stand in the company of kneelers, but because being a fool consisted of no more than being thought so by others.

The chorus trailed into ringing silence.

His head bowed beneath a nimbus of gold, the Aspect-Emperor hung in a honey glow.

"*Ishma tha serara!*" one of the Nascenti, little more than a black silhouette before the image of his master, hollered to the darkest pockets of canvas. "*Ishma tha*—"

"Raise your faces," Eskeles hissed almost inaudibly, apparently recalling his interpretive duties. "Raise your faces to the gaze of our Holy Aspect-Emperor."

"What does he me—?" Sorweel began asking the sorcerer, but the flash of warning in the man's eyes silenced him.

Scowling, Eskeles nodded toward the Aspect-Emperor. *There* . . . his expression said.

Look only there.

A breathless intensity slipped about the neck of the proceedings, a mingling of hope and anxiousness that Sorweel felt only as fear. Without exception, the assembly turned to the Anasûrimbor, so that all eyes reflected the white points of his otherworldly light. Only the twin demon heads, bound by their hair to the Anasûrimbor's girdle, stared off in contrary directions.

The Aspect-Emperor floated out over the Table of Potentates, his legs still crossed, his simple white cassock the one thing gleaming to a fixed light. He moved so slowly that at first Sorweel blinked at the unreality of it. The Lords of the Ordeal followed his passage, angling their faces with near perfection, so that no shadows marred their features. Soft light combed through their beards and moustaches, shimmered across their finery. Something, a sub-audible rumbling, accompanied his movement, a noise like slow-sailing thunderheads.

Sorweel almost coughed with relief when the impossible figure veered to the opposite side of the pavilion. Soon the Anasûrimbor hung luminous before the shadowy Men, no more than two lengths away, scrutinizing them as he followed the tier's line at a beetle's crawl. Sorweel saw faces squint as though expecting a sudden blow. But most stared back with lunatic poise—some rejoicing, others proclaiming, and still others *confessing*—confessing above all.

Tear-scored cheeks shimmered in the passing light. Grown men, warlike men, wept in the wake of their sovereign's divine passage . . .

The Aspect-Emperor paused.

The man beneath his gaze was an Ainoni, or so Sorweel guessed from the styling of his square-cut beard, ringlets about flattened braids. He sat on one of the lower tiers, and rather than descend, the Aspect-Emperor simply tilted in his floating posture to study him. The rings of light about his head and hands gilded the man's face and shoulders with a patina of gold. The caste-noble's dark eyes glittered with tears.

"*Ezsiru*," the Aspect-Emperor began in a voice that seemed to coil about Sorweel's ears, "*ghusari histum mar*—"

Leaning until his beard brushed Sorweel's shoulder, Eskeles whispered, "Ezsiru, since your father, Chinjosa, kissed my knee during the First Holy War, ever has House Musammu been a bastion of the Zaudunyani. But the feud between you and your father has festered too long. You are too harsh. You do not understand the difference between the infirmities of youth and the infirmities of age. So you play father to your father, punish his weaknesses the way he once punished yours . . ."

One of the demon heads began opening and closing its white mouth like a fish. Horrified, Sorweel saw the glimmer of needle-teeth.

"Ezsiru, tell me, is it right that the father take the rod to the child?"

A throaty answer. "Yes."

"Is it right that the child take the rod to the father?"

A pause that tugged a pang from the back of Sorweel's throat. "No," Ezsiru said, his voice pitched high through phlegm and sobbing.

"Love him, Ezsiru. Honour him. And always remember that old age is rod enough."

Onward the Aspect-Emperor moved, floating no more than a length before pausing before another Lord of the Ordeal, this one Nilnameshi. "*Avarartu . . . hetu kah turum pah*—"

On and on it continued, each exchange at once momentary and interminable, as though the timelessness of the consequences had somehow soaked backward into the act. And in each case, nothing more than some human *truth* was summoned forth, as though the Anasûrimbor need only look into the face of one who stumbled to set every man in attendance upon sure footing. How the loss of a wife exempted you from the laws of manliness. How shame at being thought a fool made fools of us all in the end. How cruel natures corrupted piety into excuses to indulge their evil.

Truth. Nothing more than truth.

And the sheer clarity of it bewildered Sorweel, shook him as deeply as anything since the death of his father and the humiliation of his people. Truth! The Anasûrimbor spoke only truth. How? How could a *demon* do such a thing? What demon would?

And how? How could such a thing be . . .

Be miraculous?

Sorweel's heart began pacing the Aspect-Emperor's arcane transit once he reached the apex of the horseshoe and began moving toward them. Dread cinching his chest, he watched the expressions of those who believed, upturned and rapt, brightening as he soundlessly passed, then falling into shadow. The floating figure drew closer and closer, as inexorable as an equation, as bright as a prison window, until Sorweel's heart seemed to be beating *against* him. Finally, the Aspect-Emperor slowed, came to a hissing stop no more than two lengths away. He tilted back on an invisible axis to regard someone on the highest tier.

"*Impalpotas, habaru—*"

"Impalpotas," Eskeles said with a quaver, "tell me, how long has it been since you were dead?"

A collective intake of breath. The man called Impalpotas sat four people abreast of Sorweel—three of Eskeles—and two rows higher. The young King of Sakarpus found himself peering against the shining proximity of the Anasûrimbor: The Inrithi had the clean-shaven look of a Nansur but seemed different in dress and hair. A Shigeki, Sorweel guessed. Like Porsparian.

"*Impalpotas . . .*" the Aspect-Emperor repeated.

The man smiled like a rake caught wooing a friend's daughter—an expression so at odds with the circumstances that Sorweel's stomach reeled as if pitched from a cliff.

Impalpotas leapt—no, *exploded*—from the tiers, sword out and flashing in divine light. A crack of voice greeted him in the interval, a word shouted beneath the skins of all present. Bald and searing light flooded the pavilion to the seams. Sorweel blinked against the glare, saw the Shigeki hanging before the Anasûrimbor, pinned to nothing, encased in a calligraphy of blinding lines. Impalpotas's sword had dropped from nerveless fingers and now lay upright between the feet of a Conriyan on the bottom tier, its point buried into carpet and turf the depth of a palm.

The assembly broke out in roaring commotion. Like fire across desert scree, outrage leapt from face to face, a wrath too feral to be called manly. Beards opened about howls. Swords were brandished across the rows, like shaking teeth.

The Anasûrimbor's voice did not so much cut through the din as *harvest* it—the uproar collapsed like wheat about the scythe of his declaration. "*Irishi hum makar*," he said, continuing to scrutinize those seated before him. Save for his tongue and lips, he had not moved.

Eskele's stunned and stammering voice was several heartbeats in translating. "Be-behold our foe."

The Shigeki assassin had sailed out around the Aspect-Emperor and now floated behind his haloed head, a brighter beacon. The light that tattooed his skin and clothes flared, and his limbs were drawn out and away from his body. He hung, a different kind of proof, revolving like a coin in open space. He panted like an animal wrapped in wire, but his eyes betrayed no panic, nothing save glaring hate and laughter. Sorweel glimpsed the curve of his erect phallus through his silk breeches, looked away to his sigil-wrapped face, only to be more appalled . . .

For it flexed about invisible faults, then opened, drawn apart like interlocking fingers. Articulations were pried back and out, revealing eyes that neither laughed nor hated, that simply *looked*, above shining slopes of boneless meat.

"*Rishra mei . . .*" the Aspect-Emperor said in a voice that sounded like silk wrapped about a thunderclap. "I see . . ." Eskele's murmured in reedy tones, "I see mothers raise still-born infants to blinded Gods. The *death of birth*—I see this! with eyes both ancient and foretold. I see the high towers burn, the innocents broken, the Sranc descend innumerable—innumerable! I see a world *shut against Heaven!*"

The assembly cried out, a cacophony of voices and hand-wringing gestures, piteous for the terror, frightening for the fury. With wild glances Sorweel saw them, the Men of the Ordeal, standing or clutching their knees, their faces cramped as though they listened to news of recent catastrophe. Wives dead. Clans scattered. *No!* their expressions shouted. *No!*

"*Rishra mei*—"

"I see kings with one eye gouged, naked save for the collars from which their severed hands swing. I see the holy Tusk sundered, fragments cast to the flames! Momemn, Meigeiri, Carythusal and Invishi, I see their streets gravelled in bones, their gutters black with old blood. I see the temples overgrown, the broken walls rot over empty, savage ages.

"I see the Whirlwind walk—Mog-Pharau! Tsurumah! I see the *No-God* . . ."

Spoken like a groan, like air struck from dead lungs.

"***Behold!***" the Aspect-Emperor bellowed in tones that ripped nerves from skin, yanked them to the farthest tingling corners. "***See!***"

The thing—the faceless thing—hung skinned in arcane light. One rotation passed in breathless witness. Another. Then, like smoke inhaled, the brilliant lattice imploded, against the beast, *into* the beast. The sound of scissions, multiple and immediate, whisked through the air. The sorcerous light winked out. What remained simply dropped, a curtain of slop raining to the ground.

Breathless silence. A return to the holy gloom. It had happened, and it had not happened.

"*Rishra mei,*" the impossible visage said, sweeping his gaze across the astonished tiers. And the silence roared about him. Sorweel could only stare at the severed Ciphrang heads hanging like sacks from his hip, their white mouths laughing or howling.

His haloed palms spread wide, the Aspect-Emperor continued following the same unseen geometric curve. He was so close that Sorweel could see the winding Tusks embroidered white upon white into the hem of his cassock, the three pink lines wrinkling the outside corners of his eyes, the scuff of soil that marked the toe of his left white-felt slipper. He was so close that the image of him burned the surrounding spaces to black, so that the curving tier of forms and faces sunk into void.

The Anasûrimbor.

A scent preceded him, a draft that seemed to brush away the cloying perfumes worn by the more effete attendants. The smell of damp earth and cool rain. Weary truth.

The demons' puckered sockets seemed to watch him—recognize him.

Please! Sorweel found himself thinking, begging. *Please let it be Zsoronga!*

But the luminous form came to a stop directly before him, too vivid to possess depth, to be framed—to be truly seen. Sorweel's heart stomped against his breast. It seemed that animals thronged within him, that each of his fears had become gibbering terrors, creatures with their own limbs and volitions. What would he see?

How would he punish?

"Sorweel," a voice more melodious than music said in the

tongue of his fathers. "Sad child. Proud King. There is nothing more deserving of compassion than an apologetic heart."

"Yes." A noise more kicked out of his lungs than spoken.

Never!

Though he had not moved, though he sat mild and meditative, the Aspect-Emperor somehow towered over every region of sight and sound. Summer-blue eyes, not seeing so much as sacking. Plaited golden beard. Lips shaped about a pit without bottom. The intensity of his presence boiled against the limits of the senses, seeped into the faults, steamed into the unseen recesses . . .

"Do you repent your father's folly?"

"Yes!" Sorweel lied, his voice cracking for fury.

Demon! Ciphrang! The Goddess names you! Names you!

An old friend's wry smile, as plain and as guileless as a joke about a girl, as sudden as a mother's slap.

"Welcome, young Sorweel. Welcome to the glory that is the God's Salvation. Welcome to the company of Believer-Kings."

Then the godlike figure was gone, floating to his left, searching for the face of another penitent, another troubled soul. Blinking, Sorweel saw the Lords of the Ordeal watching and smiling. The pavilion's embroidered interior seemed to become sky wide with sweet, breathable air.

"Gulls," he heard Eskeles murmur with sarcastic good-nature beside him. "Fools . . ."

The day wore on with speech, prayer, and debate. Afterwards, the fat Schoolman would cough back tears and hold him, hug him as a mother or a father might hug their son.

Against a desolate backdrop, Zsoronga simply watched, speaking not a word.

Sorweel insisted on walking back to his tent alone.

For a time he made his way in numb peace, simply enjoyed

the sense of free calm that often follows tumultuous events. Sometimes the bare fact of time passing is enough to seal us from painful experience. Stripped of worry, warmed by the crimson sun and the wind that had raised so much consternation in the Council of Potentates, he found himself staring at the endless succession of makeshift camps with earnest curiosity. A bowl of tea steaming unaccompanied on the trampled grass. A lone Tydonni repairing a braid in his hair. A forgotten game of benjuka. Shields bracing shields in pairs and trios. Two Nansur muttering and smiling as they oiled the straps of their cuirass.

The awe was not long in coming. There were simply too many warriors from too many nations not to be astonished in some small way. And the field of wind-lashed banners was simply too great. Some of the Inrithi returned his gaze with hostility, some with indifference, others with open cheer, and it struck Sorweel that they were *simply Men*. They grunted upon their wives, fretted for their children, prayed against rumours of a hungry season. It was what they *shared* that made them seem remarkable, even inhuman: the omnipresent stamp of the Circumfix, be it in gold or black or crimson. A single purpose.

The Aspect-Emperor.

It was at once glorious and an abomination. That so many could be folded into the intent of a *single* man.

The calm slipped from his heart and limbs, and the mad rondo of questions began batting through his soul. What had happened at the Council? Did he see? Did he not see? Did he see and merely pretend not to see?

How could he, Sorweel, the broken son of a broken people, shout hate beneath the all-seeing eyes of the Aspect-Emperor, and not be . . . not be . . .

Corrected.

He quickened his pace, and the details of his surroundings retreated into half-glimpsed generalities. His left hand strayed to his cheek, to the warm memory of the muck Porsparian had smeared there. To the earthen spit of the Goddess . . .

Yatwer.

He found Porsparian busy preparing his evening repast. Their small camp bore all the signs of a laborious day. The sum of Sorweel's meagre wardrobe hung across the tent's guy-ropes. The contents of his saddle packs lay across a mat to the left of the tent entrance. The tent, which stood emptied of all its contents, had been washed, its sun-orange panels drying in the failing light. The old Shigeki had even set his small camp stool next to the swirling of their humble fire.

Sorweel paused at the invisible perimeter.

The High Court of the Sakarpic King.

Seeing him, Porsparian scurried to kneel at his feet, a bundle of old brown limbs.

"What did you do?" Sorweel heard himself bark.

The slave glanced up at him, his wrinkled look as resentful as alarmed. Sorweel had never addressed him as a servant, let alone as a slave.

He grabbed the old man's arm, yanked him to his feet with an ease that he found shocking. "What?" he cried. He paused, screwed his face in an expression of frustration and regret, tried to remember the Sheyic words Eskeles had taught him. Surely he could ask this—something as simple as this!

"What you do?" he cried.

A wild look of incomprehension.

Sorweel thrust him back, then maintaining his glare, made a pantomime of taking soil and rubbing it across his cheeks. "What? What you do?"

Like a flutter of wings, Porsparian's confusion flickered into a kind or perverse glee. He grinned, began nodding like a madman confirmed in his delusions. "*Yemarte . . . Yemarte'sus!*"

And Sorweel understood. For the first time, it seemed, he actually *heard* his slave's voice.

"Blessed . . . Blessed you."

Chapter Sixteen

Cil-Aujas

A soul too far wandered from the sun,
walking deeper ways,
into regions beneath map and nation,
breathing air drawn for the dead,
talking of lamentation.

—PROTATHIS, *THE GOAT'S HEART*

Spring, 20 New Imperial Year (4132 Year-of-the-Tusk), Mount Aenaratiol

She is terrified and alive.

Mimara runs over mouldered bones, a pinch of sun-brilliance carried high in the air above her. In her soul she thinks circles, while with her eyes she sees the light swing and seesaw, and she ponders the impossibility of it, how the light shed is the same light as any other, baring the surfaces of things, and yet at the same time *not quite whole*, as though strained through a filter—robbed of some essential sediment.

Sorcerous light, stretched over the ruin like moulted skin. *Her* light!

Fear crowds the moment, to be sure. She knows why the Wizard has given her this Gift, perhaps better than he. Part of her, she realizes, will not survive this underworld labyrinth . . .

Great Cil-Aujas.

She is inclined to see history as degeneration. Years ago, not long after her mother had brought her to the Andiamine Heights, an earthquake struck Momemn, not severe, but violent enough to crack walls and to set arms and ornaments toppling. There had been one mural in particular, the *Osto-Didian*, the eunuchs called it, depicting the First Holy War battling about Shimeh, with all the combatants cramped shield to shield, sword to sword, like dolls bound into sheaves. Where the other murals had been webbed with fractures, this one seemed to have been pounded by hammers. Whole sections had sloughed away, exposing darker, deeper images: naked men across the backs of bulls. In shallow sockets here and there even this layer had given out, especially near the centre, where her stepfather had once hung out of proportion in the sky. There, after dabbing away the white powder with her fingertips, she saw a young man's mosaic face, black hair high in the wind, child-wide eyes fixed upon some obscured foe.

That, she understood, was history: the piling on of ages like plaster and paint, each image a shroud across the others, the light of presence retreating, from the Nonmen to the Five Tribes to the New Empire, coming at last to a little girl in the embrace of hard-handed men . . .

To the daughter who dined with her Empress mother, listening to the tick of enamel tapping gold, watching the older woman's eyes wander lines of sorrow, remorse thick enough to spit.

To the woman who raged beneath a wizard's tower.

To now.

She is inclined to see history as degeneration, and what greater proof did she need, now that they walked beneath the mural of mannish strife, now that they touched the glass of first things?

Cil-Aujas. Great and dead, a mosaic exposed. What was human paint compared to this?

Everything everywhere has the smell of age, of air so leached of odour and event that the dust they scoop into the air with their boots actually makes it seem young, ushers it into a more human scale. Ageless air, she thinks. Dead air, the kind that lingers in the chests of corpses.

And everything everywhere has the look of weight and suffocation. It makes her think of her furies, those times when she wants to pull all roofs down, so that her perishing could be her vengeance. What would it be like, she wonders, to be slapped between mountain palms? Every ceiling plummeting, so that it seems the floor bucks up. The light snuffed. The thunder of sound crushed to nothing. Everything captured, even the dust. Limbs little more than blades of grass. Life seeping through fault and fracture.

The darkness that dwells inside stones.

She bears the light of presence—a Surillic Point, he had called it—and she runs across floors older than the most ancient nations of Men. She stands beneath all empire and ambition, and she *illuminates*. So simple, she knows—so paltry as to be pathetic. But this is how all greatness begins.

She carries a sphere of sight about her, bloated and invisible save where its touch frosts the floor and ruin white. She *is a witch* . . . at last! How can she not clamp tooth to tooth in dark glee? How many times had she dreamed, her limbs pinned to pillows, of speaking light and fire?

The company has ceased marching, receives her with wonder and consternation. She tells them that Sarl and Achamian follow close behind. She sees the tilt in their looks, the way they take a step back in their eyes, as though to regain some lost perspective. The light tingles. A strut haunts her limbs, and she thinks of her slave-sisters back in Carythusal, the way they posed like rare and precious things when wearing something new. She too had cried over dresses.

The Skin Eaters turn to the dark behind them, searching the flat blackness. When their eyes fail them, they turn their scrutiny to her. They seem a wall, even though they stand scattered among their mules. Her light gilds the texture of their armour. It shines along the rims of their shields, bares the dents of metal hammered over wooden edges. It warms old leather, forks and branches along gut-stitched seams. It bares their anxious faces, bobs silver up and down the hone of their restless swords. It paints white circles in their beasts' black gaze.

Fierce men, with the wild pride of the dispossessed. They would eat her skin, were it not for the Wizard. They would glory in the stink of her. They would wear her the way they wear shrivelled bits of Sranc, as a charm, a trophy, and a totem. As a seal and a sign.

It seems she has always known that men were more animal than women were animal. She was sold before her mother could tell her this, but still she knew. The animal continually leans forward in the souls of men, forever gnaws the leash. Even here, in the Black Halls of Cil-Aujas, this truth is no less ancient.

Even here, so tragically out of their depth, they lean to the promise of her vulnerability.

"Where's the Wizard?" someone asks.

She retreats a step, and her shadow falls behind her. She has lost her light to the space between her and the Skin Eaters—a space she has never owned. She can sense the Captain standing to the right of her, turns to risk his dominating gaze but finds herself staring at the pocked dust instead. She has been tricked, it seems, into a posture of submission.

"Mimara," a voice calls. "What's the matter, girl?" It's

Somandutta, the one man here that she trusts, and only then because he is no man.

"You have no call to fear us . . ."

A chorus of shouts greets the abrupt arrival of Sarl and Achamian. In a heartbeat she is forgotten by all save Somandutta, who comes to her side, saying, "The *light* . . . How did you do that?"

She bites her lower lip, curses down the urge to lean her head against the armour scaling his chest. Of Achamian she can see nothing but the congregated backs of the scalpers with their packs and their slung shields. But she hears his voice between the figures, speaking to the Captain with quarrelsome urgency, something about Chorae moving through the halls immediately below them. Someone, Kiampas, immediately suggests the Bloody Picks, but the Wizard is dubious, asking why anyone wealthy enough to own a Chorae would be fool enough to hunt Sranc for money. Mimara wonders if their Chorae-bearing Captain will take offence.

Then Cleric says, "He's right." The inhuman voice doesn't so much reach farther as it reaches *deeper*, carried through the stone of the floor into her bones. "I sense them too."

The Skin Eaters open, back away, each staring at the company of prone shadows splayed across the dust scuffed about their feet. She knows they think they can feel the Chorae too . . .

Then suddenly *she feels them*. Her limbs jolt, and she sways, for her body had thought the ground solid, and now she senses open space, breaths and plummets between leagues of stone. Chorae, bottomless punctures in being, traverse them, a necklace of little voids carried by something that runs in a lumbering file . . . something.

"They travel in the direction I lead us," Cleric says, "toward the Fifth Anterograde Gate . . ."

"You think they mean to cut us off?" Kiampas asks.

No one speaks.

She sees Sarl, gazing with his pond-scum eyes, his manic face rutted and pale. But when she looks at the other old man, Achamian, she finds that her *Judging Eye has opened . . .* She has read her stepfather's writing on sorcery, his *Novum Arcanum*. She knows that the God peers through all eyes, and that the Few—sorcerer or witch, it did not matter—were simply those whose sight recollected something of His all-seeing gaze and so could speak with the dread timbre of His all-creating voice.

She sees Achamian as others do, stooped in his mad hermit robes, his beard stiff against his breast, his complexion the dark of long-used skins. She sees the Mark, soiling his colours, blasting his edges.

And though her eyes blink and roll against it, she sees the Judgment . . .

He is carrion. He is horror. His skin is burned to paste.

Drusas Achamian is damned.

Her breath catches. Almost without thinking, she clutches Somandutta's free hand—the slick cool of iron rings and the grease of leather shocks her skin. She squeezes hard, as though her fingers need confirmation of their warm-blooded counterparts. The Chorae and their inscrutable bearers move beneath her feet, each a point of absolute chill.

Part of her, she realizes, will not survive this underworld labyrinth.

She prays that it is the lesser part.

"Fucking mules! How can you run with fucking mules!" the Zeümi Sword-Dancer cries after Sarl has once again screamed at them to make haste. The haunches of the beasts are already shagged with blood from the prick and slap of the scalpers' weapons. The clopping of their hooves makes a curious clatter across the dust and stone, like wood without the hollow, an avalanche of axes chopping. Their packs wobble drunkenly—one has already lost its entire burden. Stepping about the debris, tents and cooking utensils, adds material to Mimara's sense of panic.

Achamian has said nothing since leaving the airy blackness of the Repositorium. He labours beside her; the slight tick in his leg has swollen into a hobble. His breath comes hard and greedy, as though he needs to feed all the years baled within him. When he coughs, his chest sounds damp and torn, more rotted wool than flesh.

The vaulted hallways scroll above and about them, the basalt seemingly shocked by the sudden onset of their lights. The images rise and arch and fall away, as quick as life. There is no time to ponder the dead eyes that had once dreamed them. The company runs to survive.

Hope and urgency have become a single jarring note.

She can no longer feel the Chorae beneath them—their pursuers have outrun them using deeper halls, and now no one knows where and when they will strike. The Skin Eaters wrap their horror about their trust in their Captain, say nothing save to joke or to gripe. Questions have become perverse, an indulgence fit only for the obese.

Cleric leads them through a gallery of branching corridors, some so narrow the company is stretched into a single file longer than their sorcerous illumination. Those scalpers trapped in the rear cry out against the rising darkness. When Mimara glances back, it's as though she looks down a throat or a well—walls narrowing until blackness smothers them. She can scarce see the sheen roll across the laggards' helms.

A pain climbs into her chest, and she imagines an eye squinting from her heart.

There is no doubt they move through the deeps now. Only when the walls are tight and the ceilings low can you feel their constricting aura—or so it seems. Only the threat of closure makes the boggling enormity plain. They are sealed from *all things*, not simply sun and sky. The very world walls them in.

She looks up and around in an effort to throw off the oppressive sense of cringing. The stone reliefs seem to burn, so near are they to the encased light, so stark and immediate. Hunters wrestling lions, shepherds balancing lambs upon shields, on and on, all struck speechless in the stone of ages. The illumination crosses a lip; the ancient vignettes fall away, as though over inverted cliffs. They have come to another great chamber, not as vast as the Repositorium, but great enough. The air seems cold and graceful.

They rope from the narrow hall, gather in milling clots, gawking at this latest wonder. Their mules bray and tremble for exhaustion. One collapses amid echoing curses.

The columns are square, panelled in more animal manifolds, and even though she can see only the lower and outer limits of them, she knows they form great aisles across the darkness, that the company stands in some underworld forum or agora. Achamian is leaning against his knees next to her, staring into his shadow, mustering the spit to swallow. His teeth bared in exhaustion, he bends his head back, looks to the looming gallery.

"The High Halls," he gasps. "The High Halls of Mû—"

*Haroo**oooooooooooom!***

Men twist and whirl about. The dust shivers. The sound seems to filter, to rise, as though they can only hear what mounts the surface of their ears. Sranc horns.

They feel it in their teeth—not so much an ache as a taste.

Never before has she heard them, and now she understands their antique power, the madness that saw mothers strangle their own children in besieged cities of yore. Their depth is tidal in its compass, yet riddled with thin and piercing notes, like a shriek unbraided into wincing threads, each towed wide across the unnameable. A portent hangs within them, a promise of what is other and impenetrable, of things that would glory in her lament. They remind her of her humanity the way burnt edges speak of fire.

Temple silence rises in their wake. There is a distant sound—like leaves skidding over marble flagstones. It seems to tighten her skin to the prick of moments passing.

Cleric calls, and they follow. They leave the fallen mule where it lays grunting.

They run, but the slow succession of pillars seems to diminish their pace. Their arcane lights throw shadows that swing and sweep out with monumental elegance. The greater blackness hangs from them, shrouding the hollows beyond the adjacent aisles.

The horns have a swelling nearness to them now, a cracking blare. Only the stone forest of columns divides them from their pursuers—she knows this with a herd animal's certainty. For the first time a part of her dares believe that she's about to die. Her bowels loosen to the jolt of her steps. Her stomach tightens to a burn. She throws her gaze wildly about, desperate to find something that she *doesn't recognize*. For it seems to her that she has known this place all along, that her soul, like an old knot undone, bears the kink and imprint of her future . . . The pillars braced against cataclysmic burdens. The bestial totems, their many limbs flattened into the dark. The stink of her exertions. The sense of loss and mortal misdirection. The gnashing of teeth and iron in the arching maze of black behind her . . .

They are coming. Out of the pit they are coming. The flutter of rever-berations in her chest seems to confirm it. This is where she dies.

The outer reaches of their lights flatten against a wall, roll back the vertical murk with twin rings of illumination, the one wider and brighter because of Cleric's position out in front of Achamian. Mimara stumps to a stop with the others. The dust rolls forward, makes skirts about their waists. She cranes her neck, absently rubbing a stitch in her side—despite her terror she is relieved to simply breathe. Narrative reliefs band the wall, stacking high into the darkness, but the graven figures are not carved nearly so deep or so realistically as so the others. A heartbeat passes before she sees the hair and beards and chains that mark the forms as Men.

All at once, her earlier sense of recognition drains away. Only the premonition remains.

She has read enough to know these are not just any Men. They are the original Men of Eärwa, the Emwama, the slaves exterminated by her ancestors in the earliest days of the Tusk. She can even see a woman bound to a train of naked captives—a woman that could be her. And for some reason, this point of *connection* strikes a nauseating note through the whole of Cil-Aujas, renders it alien to the point of revulsion, as though all of it had been smeared with reek and contagion . . .

They are coming. And she is just a child—a child! Everything everywhere chatters with dread and threat. Angles become knives. Inaction becomes blood. A mad part of her kicks and bucks and screams. Her shriek bunches like a fist at the base of her throat. She must get out. She *has to* . . .

Out-out-*out!*

But the old Wizard is holding her by the shoulders, telling her not to fear, not to fret, but to trust in his heart and his power. "You want me to teach?" he cries. "I will give you such a lesson!" His laugh is almost genuine.

No sobbers, his eyes warn her. *Remember!*

Her breathing becomes both easier and more difficult after that, and she finds herself wary of the Captain. The mere thought of him has scared the panic from her—this, she realizes, is his warlike Gift. All about her the Skin Eaters assemble, shield to shield, shoulder to shoulder, forming a single rank around her and the mules. They look motley with their different heights and scavenged armour . . . Motley and fierce.

"Toe to the line!" Sarl cries across the horn's thundering back. "Come now, boys, *toe to the line!*"

Suddenly all the reasons she feared these barbaric men become reasons to prize them. Those hoary trophies. Those deep-chested bodies, girt with chain, leather, stink, and soiled cloth. That bullying saunter. Those wideswinging arms, with hands that could break her wrists. And for some strange reason, their fingernails, each as broad as two of her own, rimmed in black crescents. Everything she had scoffed at or despised she now sees with thin-lipped understanding. The glib cruelty. The vulgar posturing. Even the glares that nicked her when she was careless with the cast of her eyes.

These are Skin Eaters, and their slogs are the stuff of legend. They would eat her if they could—but only because they walk so near the world's teeth.

She hears Achamian arguing with Kiampas on the far side of two stamping mules. "We should have stayed in the Repositorium . . ."

"But here we can choke them in the aisles."

"And those with the Chorae?"

The Nansur's grin is haphazard, as though hooked by a hard-to-see scar. His jaw, normally clean-shaven, is spackled grey. "Trifles, Wizard. Believe you me, we know how to stack skinnies . . ."

The man trails, cocks his head to the sudden quiet.

The horns have stopped.

The silence, she knows, is the silence they have marched through since entering the Obsidian Gate, the silence of their shutting in, the silence of corpses in their tombs. The ageless roar of Cil-Aujas.

Her limbs seem buoyant for the thickness of it.

All this time she has simply stood witless amid the mules.

Now Kiampas is before her, issuing instructions—stay with the animals, keep the torches, staunch wounds by pressing like *this*—and asking questions—Do you know how to bind a tourniquet? Can you use that pretty sword? He peers into her eyes with calming seriousness, speaks only to the point. He is a handsome father. She answers him as honestly as she can. In her periphery she sees Achamian conferring with Cleric and the Captain. Sarl continues barking at his line, his gravelly voice recalling slogs gone by. "Oh, yes, boys, this is going to be a *chopper*. A classic chopper!"

She unpacks the torches and wedges five of them at intervals along the wall using chiselled hollows in the friezes. She strikes a sixth and it flares with curious transparency—violet wrapping into yellow—in the arcane light, but burns and smokes all the same. She lights all five, and the engraved Emwama seem to glow with the colours of their long-lost life. She walks among the restless mules, running her hands across the bristle of their necks, scratching their jaws and ears, and it seems that she mourns them.

Their small army falls motionless. The twin Surillic Points lean white against the engraved planes of the nearest columns, dwindle in grey stages the farther they reach down the lanes. Though soundless, the light seems to hiss with suspense.

The Skin Eaters have formed a bristling shell some thirty men strong, reaching from the wall, about their beasts of burden, back to the wall. Lord Kosoter stands just behind the apex, rigid with solitary concentration. With his plaited beard and tattered finery he almost looks as ancient as Cil-Aujas. His round shield, which she has seen many times hanging from a mule pack, is dented and scored. Barely legible across its centre are the enamel remains of an Ainoni pictogram: the word "umra," which in Ainoni means both duty and discipline. He holds his sword pointed down to his side. She sees he has drawn a quarter arc through the dust across the stone. Because he wears his Chorae over his heart, she cannot shake the sense that he's not quite alive.

Achamian stands with Kiampas at his side several paces to the Captain's left. Cleric stands likewise with Sarl to his right. Their Marks remind her of their power, and their company's hope.

Still holding the torch, she draws her sword: a Gift from her mother, forged of the finest Seleukaran steel. The disparate lights slip like liquid across its sheen. Squirrel, she calls it, because of the way it always seemed to tremble in her hand. It trembles now. She tries to remember all the years she spent training with her half-brothers, but the glow of the Andiamine Heights cannot penetrate this deep place . . . Nothing can.

"*They come*," the Nonman says, his black eyes as inscrutable as the darkness they plumb.

Mimara expects to feel the Chorae weaving out in the black. Instead she hears something, a nail-against-stone scratching that spreads like flood-water across the unseen spaces, reaching wider and higher until it seems the company stands in the piped centre of a gnawed bone . . .

Louder. Louder. A reek steams into the air, like the rot of inhuman mouths.

Her hand burns for squeezing her sword's pommel.

"Just as the Captain said," Sarl rasps. "*Skinnies*." He shoots a pointed look at Kiampas, every wrinkle grinning with his greasy lips.

"Remind me how much I hate this," Galian says to no one in particular.

"Like a knife up the bung?" Xonghis asks.

"No. Worse."

"I thought it was the knife too," Soma says.

"No," Pokwas replies. "It was beating your scrotum with, ah . . . *thistles*, right?"

"Exactly," Galian says, nodding sagely. "Like beating my pouch with thistles. My poor pretty pouch."

"Yes-yes," Xonghis snorts. He bangs his helm with the flat of his sword.

"Just think of all the gold," Somandutta replies—always the lackwit. Poor Soma.

"Pfah!" Pokwas cries, scowling. "Hard to spend it when the whores are busy laughing at his flayed hard-boileds, now isn't it?"

She feels a tick of sweat every time they utter that word. *Whore*.

Galian nods once again, this time as if at some tragic human truth. "The sluts laugh enough as it is."

They speak more to their terror than to one another, she realizes. Ever do men play the mummer, strutting on the stage of themselves to avoid the parts the world has assigned them. Women would speak of their fear.

"My ass itches," the giant Oxwora suddenly announces. "Does anyone have an itchy ass?"

"Just aim it the other way," Galian calls back. "I'm sure the skinnies will oblige you."

A wave of snorts and guffaws passes through the line.

"Aye. But then my ass would *stink!*"

An almost crazed outburst of laughter, one that catches fear as fuel, blotting the sounds of the scabrous onrush . . .

"Soma!" the giant cries. "You pare your nails! Lend me your pretty finger, would you?"

And the laughter is doubled.

Old Sarl calls through it in a gravelly voice. "May I remind you boys that our lives are in mortal danger!" His grin, however, belies his approval.

Lord Kosoter stands motionless.

Distracted, Mimara doesn't see Achamian stepping to the fore of the line. When she glimpses him, her heart opens into something that clutches, that claws. She opens her mouth to call him back, but her breath has fallen through the bottom of her. She fears she might swoon, so frail he looks beneath the towering blackness, so exposed!

But he's already speaking, and in a voice that slaps the remaining laughter from the scalpers' mouths. Even the nearing roar seems to falter. A Ward cups the spaces immediately before him, a lens of bluish light. A cerulean glare limns his white hair and wolf-skin cloak; he suddenly looks the Gnostic Wizard he is.

One of the Surillic Points goes dark, and an increment of grimness shadows everything. Kiampas cries for a torch. Numb to the fingertips, she wades through the mules, hands him the one she carries, then returns to fetch another, which she lights by touching to the centre-most torch on the wall. She turns in time to see the sergeant heave the torch down the aisle in front of the Wizard. It pockets the dark with a ring of stark gold . . .

She glimpses something crouch in and out of the blackness, something white and snarling and shiny-thin. She wraps her sword arm around the nearest mule's neck, hugs the beast tight. "Bastion," she calls him, without knowing the why or the where of the name. "Bastion . . ." She cares not who thinks her a fool!

The darkness itself seems to rasp and chip and clank and wheeze. Inhuman barks ring across the unseen ceilings.

She sees Cleric stride through the line to Achamian's right. His cloak cast away, he stands planked in silvery armour, plates skirted in impossibly fine chain, his greatsword swinging from his left hip. *Ishroi*, she thinks, recalling Achamian's word from earlier. The Nonman joins the smaller Wizard in his arcane chanting. Deep words well up out of the root of things, so indecipherable they seem to yank at her eyes.

Above her, the remaining Point fades like an errant thought, and the company is reduced to the roiling glitter of torchlight. The eternal dark of Cil-Aujas closes about them.

The glow of sorcery paints all their faces.

Mimara is already running to Kiampas when he calls her, the remaining torches hugged tight to her breast. One by one she lights them, tries to purse the tremor from her lips while he heaves them with athletic violence into the dark. They arc high enough to brush the vaults with fluttering visibility. Some fall and spark across vacant floor. Two roll to the brink of the shrouded horde, providing the merest of glimpses: swords of notched iron held dowsing low, wet eyes glittering, white limbs folding into the black. The last chips a graven visage, then twirls blue down into the hunched midst of them. She glimpses a clutch of white faces, Nonmen faces, only pinched into grotesque parodies of expression.

Canine shadows stamp the torch into oblivion.

She stumbles back to Bastion, pulls his head to her breast. The dull immovability of the beast heartens her for some reason, soothes the quaking from her limbs. She whispers in his ear, congratulates him for his idiot bravery. Before her stands Lord Kosoter, unmoved, unmoving, the knots of his caste-noble braid gleaming down the cleft of his splint-armoured back. The line of his Skin Eaters reaches out to either side, and over their shields, she glimpses fragments of Cleric and Achamian, little more than silhouettes against the curved planes of their Wards.

She feels the Chorae . . . pinpricks of nothingness fanning across the far dark.

The horns caw through the black. The underworld horde surges forward, overruns the torches and their pools of fallow light. She glimpses a tide of howling faces and septic swords and dog-ribbed torsos—

Living light glitters out to meet them.

The two magi shout into the gibbering thunder, the one

high and human, the other low and booming. Blinding lines spoke the air, their precision too beautiful to be true. The aisles beneath the columns are writ with theorems and axioms, Quyan and Gnostic, and the frenzied onslaught breaks beneath them, collapses into slops and severings. Basalt planes burst. Blood gouts. Flame dazzles.

The two magi shout into the shrieking thunder . . . The nearest column crumbles at the ankle, at once implodes and topples, and the scalpers cry out in terror. Gravel and debris rain smoke across the Wards. The sorcerous lines hiss through rolling plumes of dust. They parse and measure the open expanses, dissect the heaving mass, Sranc packed as tight as worms, their Nonman faces screeching back, waving like festival palms, thrashing like dogs in the jaws of lions.

Another column collapses, and Mimara thinks she hears Achamian screaming, "*Nooooo!*" through the mountainous clacking. Cleric's maniacal laugh rides the clamour.

A stench rains across them. Sranc blood, she realizes. Burning.

She sees only fractions through and over the scalpers, lightning glimpses. Baying mobs. Brilliant geometries sawing. Heaped tangles of dead. She feels the first Chorae bearer before she sees it, the forward plummet of absence and anathema . . . Several in the line cry out.

"Not one knee cracks!" Sarl screams in blood-raw tones. "Do you hear me? *Not one knee!*"

The old Wizard scrambles back through the line, blunders into Kiampas. He's crying new Cants and Wards before he's even recovered his balance . . . ***"yioh mihiljoi cuhewa aijiru . . ."***

"*Bashrag!*" a scalper cries. "*Seju! Sweet Seju!*"

Even as the word registers, she sees it, a shadow stamping through the smoking dead, towering over the seething rush, as high at the waist as men are at the shoulder.

"Not! One! Knee!"

The eyes have rules. They are bred to the order of things and mutiny when exposed to violations. At first she can only blink. Even though she has read innumerable descriptions of the obscenity, the meant of it overwhelms her faculties. Elephantine proportions. Cabbage skin. Amalgam limbs, three arms welded into one arm, three legs into one leg. Moles like cancers, ulcerous with hair. A back bent in a fetal hunch. Hands that flower with fingers.

The Bashrag charges the scalpers, its swiftness contradicting the trampling shamble that is its gait. The Men raise shouts and arms. A spear snaps against the hauberk of crude iron scales draping its midsection. Its axe falls with the force of siege-engines, cleaving shield and arm and chest before the momentum of the iron becomes the momentum of the man and the two slap into the floor. It bats aside the scalper to the right. It throws the dead man high in raising its axe, like soaked cloth from a hammer, leaps roaring toward the old Wizard. Achamian shrinks behind his useless Wards.

Mimara is already charging. Squirrel is out, a glittering arc that catches the abomination below the elbow. The steel cuts true. Bone cracks. Severed muscle snaps into knots beneath the hide. But only one of the limb's three spokes is undone.

The Bashrag wags its great head in a mucus-plucking roar. The vestigal faces across its cheeks grimace with their own musculature. The skulls bound to its hair make a wooden clatter. It turns to her, the lower lids of each eye drawn to the pink by the weeping sockets below. It bares its misbegotten teeth. There is a moment of animal recognition. The truth of predator and prey hangs like possibility in the air between them. It raises its axe to the popping of ill-joined bones, and it seems that here, in the moment of her death, all justice stands revealed . . .

Smoke blown from the bonfires of domination.

She cries out . . . Something more plea than prayer.

But Oxwora has barrelled out of nowhere, crashing shoulder against shield into the creature's gut, bearing it back and down. The Thunyeri grunts in human savagery, sets to with his axe, hacking and hewing. But a Sranc leaps upon his back, drives its blade into his neck. The giant scalper cries out and arches, lets slip the haft of his axe. He catches the thing in his free hand, lifts it squealing and choking—

Only to drop it, speared in the gut by another Sranc. He staggers to his knees, then miraculously heaves back to his feet. Blood spills from his lips like wine from a bowl, mats his flaxen beard. His eyes cloud, but his face still snarls in rage. He seizes the spear holder in a back-breaking embrace, topples upon it as though hugging a child.

The choked one has turned to Mimara. It grimaces at her trembling blade, its face bunched into a crazed sneer, as though its skin were merely wrapped about, not anchored to, the slick bone beneath. Its loincloth has twisted into a rope, and its phallus arches against its corselet, quivering. Rape floats through its glittering black eyes.

Her body becomes thick with the blood it aches to spill.

Then it's gone, swatted into the gloom as if struck by some immense and invisible club. Over the Bashrag's humped corpse, she glimpses Achamian on his knees, his mouth and eyes incandescent.

She looks wildly about, sensing the onrush of more Chorae. All is screaming panic among the mules and shouting disorder among the scalpers. She sees Pokwas dancing with his great tulwar, cutting against a cat-shrieking tide of Sranc: Lord Kosoter braced, stabbing around his shield, puncturing necks and faces and armpits. She glimpses Cleric riding the shoulders of another Bashrag down, his greatsword buried in the monstrosity's eye.

And she thinks, *Ishroi . . .*

"Hold to!" Kiampas cries. "Hold to!" The javelin that

takes him in the mouth doesn't seem to move so much as *appear*, a black skewer through his head. He falls backward, nailed to the other wet shadows in the periphery of her panicked attention.

One of the mules has caught fire . . . Gold light washes across what was wicked and dark.

"Mimara!"

Achamian has her by the arm. He jerks her back, unguessed iron in his old man grip. She sees one of the young Galeoth crouched, teeth gritted as he tries to wrench a javelin from his thigh. She sees another Bashrag stomping into the scalpers, hammering them aside like effigies of straw. It begins hacking into the mules, whips of blood arcing. The beasts fly apart in scrambling disorder, as though scattering from the plunge of something on high. She sees Bastion, his haunches rent, hoof-skidding beneath the lurching monstrosity. The axe catches the hump of his neck. She sees his head fold back on a glistening flank, vanish beneath the body as he crumples forward.

"We've lost this battle!" the old Wizard is crying. Blood flecks his beard, little rubies caught between coarse strands. Only now does she notice the Ward about them, an unearthly curvature.

"Toe to the line!" Sarl is screaming. Does any line remain?

Sranc throw themselves against the spectral screens, thrashing, shields smoking, skin blistering, blades scraping sparks. She clutches the old Wizard, stares in something too numb to be fear or terror. Starved and hairless. Draped in flayed skins laced with iron rings. They are hunger. They are horror. They are the quick that renders hatred vicious in Men.

She hears the Wizard's sorcerous call through his chest—the birth of his words. Incandescent lines flare from his palms, strike along the Emwama Wall, begin scissoring to his gesticulations.

White light carves the darkness deep. The Sranc jerk and scream and burn.

Then one of them simply steps through the Ward, swinging a sword of rotted iron. For mere heartbeats the Chorae have floated out there, little abyssal holes, long enough for her to have forgotten. She raises Squirrel in time, though her arm numbs at the concussion. The rabid creature howls, punches Achamian with its free hand, the one cramped about the Trinket . . .

The Wizard falls backward, rolling along her slack arm. The Sranc swings its blade up and about . . .

Her sword and her lunge are a single being. The point catches the obscenity in the windpipe. It gags, throws clawed fingers to its throat. The Chorae drops to the floor.

She does not see the Sranc fall kicking through the fading Ward.

Chorae. Tear of God. Trinket . . .

It wrenches the eyes even to glance at it, to see both the plain iron ball tacked in Sranc blood and the pit that scries into oblivion. She clutches it, she who is not yet cursed, presses it against her breast and bodice. Nausea wrings her like a wineskin. The vomit surprises her mouth, her teeth.

Something strikes her and she blinks, suddenly on her hands and knees, coughing, retching. Darkness swirls, as though it were a liquid chasing cracks in the light. And she understands with graven finality . . . No one recognizes their own death. It comes inevitable and absolute.

It comes as a stranger.

Achamian grimaced, blinked at the sting that was the only thing he could feel. Tears or blood or sweat, it did not matter. He knew he was sprawled across the floor, the back of his head caught in a crook in the engravings across the Emwama Wall. He knew his life was over. He knew these things, but in the manner of whims or idle reveries. What was hard had become detached, ghostly. The world had lost its needling grit, and all substance had fled to abstractions.

He could see the regions about him greased in dingy torchlight: his legs as immovable as the mountain, the slump of the girl, the verges of the inhuman killing floor. But beyond . . .

His eyes climbed into blackness.

"Seju! Kellah! Fuck!"

Eyes wincing at blood. Head rolling. Her heart fluttering against the bourne of oblivion. Glances of a nightmare existence.

"Did you see Cleric? Did you see him?"

"Sweet Kellah, would you just fucking grab her?"

"Come, boys. Quickly. Quickly."

"What's wrong with his face?"

"Just salt. From the Tears of Go—"

"Enough with the fucking questions! Move-move!"

Shadows consult. Pain presses the first of its many pins into her skull. Arms hoist her like a basket against a scale-armoured chest. Tears and torchlight make gold and water of her bearer's face. But she recognizes the smell: myrrh through the reek of entrails . . .

Soma.

He is a landmark, and the lay of her circumstances comes crashing back to her. "Akka!" she croaks. They are running with wounded haste, a meagre party of nine or ten or maybe more. Soma tells her to clutch his neck, raises her chin to his shoulder. Between ragged breaths, he tells her the Wizard lives but that they know no more. She can feel the Chorase between their two hearts. He explains how she's lucky to be alive, how a Sranc javelin had capped her. He begins naming the fallen.

But she's no longer listening. A lick of hair has dropped past her brow, threading the blood from her eyes to her cheek and lips. They are running along the Emwama Wall, and she can see their lost position in the light of a single remaining torch, the wreckage of Men and Sranc and mules. She sees one of their number limp-running, becoming slower and more precarious with every step. She sees him wobble, skid to his knees. She sees the Captain farther back, sprinting alone, a shimmering silhouette against the torchlight. She sees him raise his sword to strike the laggard down.

And beyond, in the distance, as though peering into a well without walls, she *sees Cleric shining*, afire in sorcerous light. Javelins explode like birds against the curve of his Wards. Sranc throng and heave before him, cut and rent by the glittering fury of his song. Three Bashrag close with him, stump-haired obscenities that lurch untouched through weaving geometries of incandescence, each bearing echoes of the absence that pockets her left breast. The Nonman leaps out of their monstrous reach, sails into the midst of more Sranc, his sword falling in an oblique arc. Sorcerous lines mirror his every stroke, and smoke spits from everything they trace. The very air seems to shriek. White light etches the pillared hollows of the gallery, the graven vaults, the panelled surfaces, revealing a floor clotted with hosts of Sranc, aisle after aisle, packed as thick as wind-tossed wheat . . .

And Cleric laughs and sings and exacts his dread toll, the last heir to Cil-Aujas.

The Emwama Wall comes to an end. Soma turns with the fugitive party into the dark. Stonework draws across the mad scene, blotting the horror and the glory with the desperate practicalities of flight.

And she thinks, *Incariol* . . .

Flee.

She has heard and read the word many times; she has even pretended to have lived it. Did she not flee her mother? Did she not flee the ingrown strife of the Andiamine Heights?

No.

Fleeing is when terror digs across you like a million ticks. Fleeing is when you run so hard the very air begins to strangle. Fleeing is when the howls of your pursuers cut the nerves from your skin. Fleeing is when you listen to the others balk at carrying the Wizard, and a slow heartbeat of doubt passes where you wonder whether the old man might stall your hunters, like silver kelics thrown to a mob of beggars.

Fleeing is when all the world's directions crash into one . . .

Away.

The mazed depths of Cil-Aujas humour them. No gates bar their way. No collapses pinch their path into a fatal cul-de-sac. Like a miracle, every black threshold opens onto yet another hallway.

Away! Away!

They have two torches between them. One quickly sputters into black. When the corridors tighten, she is so short that all she sees of their light is its stark tumble across the ceilings. All else is glint and innuendo. Blood-slicked shoulders. Notched blades. Soaked tourniquets. Now and again she glimpses profiles: Sarl chewing his lips, a kind of shock-senility blearing his eyes. Achamian lolling unconscious, his cheek and temple caked in a tree-cancer white. Pokwas swatting tears, his looks pinned to his periphery . . .

Only Lord Kosoter has carried his inscrutability away intact. He and Soma, who has not let go her hand since she began running on her own. Time and again her glances find him: She had not thought him the equal of this enormity. There is a wrath in his look, grim and unconquerable. His eyes have become beacons of his caste-nobility.

They run so fast with so little light that they see only the kick of the dust and nothing of the hanging haze. But they know the trail they leave is mortally obvious. They see nothing of their pursuers—they can scarce see themselves—but they can hear them baying through the halls: an infernal chorus of shrieks and shrill yapping, frothing up behind them, outrunning their panicked gait, filtering through the dark halls about and before them, so that every other moment echoes trick them into turning or spiralling down ancient stairs.

Once again the horns swell through the deeps, a yawing menace. The rumble fills them, thins them with terror, until they become rags blown on a dread wind. The halls and the vaults and the graven panels flash into sight and fall into oblivion. Men moan and cry.

They are all sobbers now. Doom creeps like lead into their limbs, so that they lurch against their own bulk. Doom ignites the air, so that they hack with furnace lungs. Doom shreds their thoughts, so that they become flying fragments, souls that break and crumble with every jerk and turn.

They don't even pause when the bronze door leaps into the torchlight, but throw themselves against it, wailing and cursing. It slaps them back. Pokwas drives a spear into the aperture, begins prying. Mimara stares without breath or thought at the shackled nudes stamped across it—more Emwama slaves. Galian, Xonghis, and the others turn to the curtains of blackness behind them, to the concentrating clamour. Lord Kosoter seizes her by the back of the neck, throws her at the unconscious Wizard. She needs no explanation. She clutches Achamian's cheeks, sobs at the rasp of salt against her right palm. "Akka!" she cries. "Akka! Akka! *We need you!*"

His eyes flutter.

The haft of the spear snaps. Pokwas shouts something in his native tongue, begins punching blood from his fists. The dust of their exertions clouds the torchlight, chalks their mouths.

"Akka! Akka, please!"

The roar is palpable, a pang shivering out from the graven walls. The Chorae leans like an ache against her heart.

"*Here they come!*" Galian cries.

"Akka! *Akka!* Wake up! Seju damn you! *Wake up!*"

Then, like a vision, a figure trots out of the blackness . . .

Cleric.

The scalpers stumble back, bewildered and horrified. Awash in Sranc blood, his skin and armour are filmed in soaked dust. Basalt dark, he looks like an apparition. Cil-Aujas made animate.

He laughs at the astounded Men, waves Pokwas from the door. His sorcerous murmur makes a deep-water pop in Mimara's ears. His eyes and mouth flare white, and something, a flickering wave of force, shimmers through the air. There is a deafening crack; the bronze doors fly ajar.

"Time to run," the Nonman says, his voice miraculously audible through the screeching roar.

With awe too brittle to be hope, the survivors scramble into the blackness beyond the bronze rim.

Down. Down. Down to more guttural stone.

Gone are the image-pitted walls, level floors, and barrelled ceilings. They race through rough-hewn tunnels, so deep, so near the mountain's root, even the air seems compressed. The chapped rock becomes hot to the touch, like stone just drawn from a fire's perimeter. And the air *moves*, always hot, always against them, as though they chase the source of some endless exhalation. A sulphurous tincture bitters their tongues.

They have entered the *mines*, she realizes, the toil of a thousand human generations, slaves begetting slaves, dredging holy nimil for their Nonman masters. And the Sranc host pours after them, lunging down straights, bursting from bottlenecks, somehow seeing by bark and scream. They are closing, so much the scalpers can hear the whisk of their claws, the clap and scrape of their weapons, the sputum boiling through their cries. The company is a skiff twirling and slipping on the edge of a breaking wave. And yet the sheer fury and numbers of their pursuers seem to slow them, to draw them out in wild ropes. Several times Cleric stops to face them, leaving the scalpers with the rush-ragged gloom of their only torch. They hear his laughter booming behind them, the whisper of his sorcery whirring through their bones, the clack and rumble of unimaginable weights. But the fear is that the Sranc will range out ahead through the worming of parallel tunnels. So the Captain veers left and down at every fork, hoping to scatter them in the mazed deeps.

And the world piles higher and higher above them.

Her throat leathers for gasping. The heat drugs her exhaustion, makes her fall as much as run, chasing stride after drunken stride with her boots. She has fallen behind herself. A sensation soaks through her, so warm, so consoling it seems sacred, a kind of revelatory horror, bodiless and floating and so heartbreakingly clear. She has thrown herself to the ends of terror and will, and nothing remains but to pirouette and plummet . . .

She has run to the very edge of Away.

Forgive me . . .

The hard things have become water; only the ground can break her. She falls, more sack than human. She even lacks the strength to raise her hands. Grit pummels her face. Dust burns her gums.

The Sranc will have her, and she will die, speared by their brutalities.

Forgive me, Mother.

She hears shouts, rage wrung into weeping. She smells myrrh . . .

She is thrown across a broad chest, hung like dripping cloth from arms.

"*You will not perish for me!*" She hears his voice rasp. "*I'll carry you across the doors of hell! Do you hear me? Mimara! Do you hear me?*"

She reaches for his cheek, but her hand is a stone swinging from a string.

She lets her head carry her eyes where it will. It jolts and rolls to the rhythm of his exertions—only the mailed crook of his arm, it seems, prevents it from spinning free. The fissures across the walls and ceiling scrawl and arc and cross and explode into pits and crags. The scalpers sprint and toil, their figures bent by tears and angles, paced by a gliding palm of light. The Wizard slumps between two of them, his toes scratching furrows through the sand, kicking up against butts of stone.

The passage dips and twists in a dog-tail bend, ending, miraculously, in a maw of pumpkin orange, waxing as bright as a horizon-scorching sun. The sight of it stiffens her neck, and for a time she simply stares, watching the shadows of the company wander across its luminous expanse.

"*Light*," she murmurs. "Wh-what?"

"Light," Soma croaks in affirmation. "We don't know."

"Cleric?"

"Lost. Behind us."

Suddenly she feels the heat felting the air, making ash out of emptiness. It seems she has always sensed it, only as a shadow through the slick-skin chill of unconsciousness.

The world sets its hooks deep, ever drawing souls tight across its infinite contours. Circumstances are reborn, and hearts are renewed. A spark throbs through her gutted muscles, returns slack extremities to her will. She glances at the man bearing her—Soma, stripped of his earnest foolery—and it seems she is a child in a swing.

She knows that he loves her.

Light, luxuriant and smoking. The tunnel opens like the mouth of a battered horn. A hiss that had escaped their hearing crashes into a gasping roar. An all-burning stench lies in the air like a sting in the skin. They stumble down slopes of fiery gravel—the bowl of a ruined amphitheatre, she realizes—staring agog at the ravines that hang in the distances above them, cliffs piled upon cliffs, their bellies braised in smouldering crimson. Below them, at the base of the amphitheatre's ruined tiers, a hemisphere of pillars, roofless cripples, enclose a terrace covered in wrack. Light rims the brink, blackens heaped foundations. Sulphur crabs the backs of their throats. The air undulates with heat.

No one speaks as they stagger toward the edge. In the open, the fact of their losses seem to condemn them. Wounded, culled of friends and shorn of provisions, the Skin Eaters are little more than a remnant of what they were.

They squint. They purse their lips against grins of exhaustion. The heat pricks their teeth. Many fall to their knees between the pillars, stare across the vista in dismay and horror. A lake of fire, sparking like iron beneath the smith's hammer. A vast sheet, as mottled as an old crone's skin, only with skittering fire and belligerent light.

Soma sets Mimara down and falls onto all fours, staring into the grit, his back heaving. She crawls to where Pokwas has dumped Achamian in unceremonious exhaustion. He breathes. He seems intact. She rolls him onto his back, draws his slack head onto her lap. Her shoulders yank to her breathing, and she wonders whether she weeps.

"*Mimara*," the Wizard whispers. She bites her lower lip in joy, blinks tears.

But he thrusts her back, weakly kicks a heel through the debris. "Chorae," he rasps, his head pulled back in anguish.

Somehow she has forgotten it, though it pulls like a fatal fall against her breast. As if attention makes real, the sudden nothingness of it sucks the voice from her throat.

"Hell!" Pokwas cries in shrill panic, like a man deciding he is in fact awake. On one knee, he leans against his tulwar. He lowers his forehead to its pommel. "We've fled too far—*too deep!*"

Sarl raises his fists to either side of his skull, claws at his grease-grey hair. There is an infant in his face, bawling out through skin so wrinkled it seems made of cord and twine. He cackles through gum-rimmed teeth, weeps.

"It's true!" Xonghis shouts, eyes round and darting. Only he and Lord Kosoter remain standing. The wavering air flushes the substance from their figures, makes them wicker thin. They are writ with filth and Sranc blood.

"This isn't Hell," the Captain says.

"*But it is!*" Sarl cackles and screams, rocking like a widow beneath her husband's pyre. "Look! *Look!*" He raises crooked fingers to the spectacle before them.

Somehow the Captain's sword has leapt shining from its sheath. Its point tongues the pubis hollow beneath the sergeant's chin, probes wiry hair. For a moment, Sarl continues rocking, drawing the shining blade to and fro with his throat. Then he falls very still.

"This," the Captain grates, "isn't Hell."

"How do you know?" Galian cries.

"Because," the Holy Veteran says, his voice so cold it seems the sound should fog or frost. "I would *remember*."

With a reptilian twitch, he scores his sergeant's rutted cheek, then turns from his company. He picks his way across the ruin to the far corner of the terrace, begins descending a stair cut into the soaring crevasse walls.

For several heartbeats the scalpers stare after their

Captain. No one speaks or moves. Then a bark peals through the ambient roar, and all eyes jerk to the tunnel above.

Screeching and howling, the Sranc come, like lice spilling from a dead man's ear. Cleric has fallen, she realizes with plummeting horror.

Cil-Aujas has slain her last remaining son.

Mimara finds herself racing on legs woven out of terror, following close behind Galian and Soma, who hold the semiconscious Wizard between them. They run like the lost, like those whose hearts rail more against fate than foes. Their peril is fatal and immediate, yet she stumbles and gasps, stricken with a reeling vertigo. The fall wheels out to her left, beckoning, staggering . . .

The lake of fire shimmers across the distances, a brilliant plate across the bottom of a vast cavern, rutted like the hollow of a long-dead tree. Soaring basalt faces steep in the heat, black rimmed in ox-blood crimson. Where the stone leans close to the glowering surface, across the grottos that hive the farther reaches, fire falls in curtains and streams. Burning gases blow in skirts across the wavering expanses. Eruptions spew radiance the height of Momemn's greatest towers.

They *have* fled too far, too deep. They have passed beyond the rind of the World into the outer precincts of Hell. There can be no other explanation . . .

Not lost. *Damned.*

Lord Kosoter awaits them on the first landing, his sword still drawn. She follows his gaze to the bend of the stair above them. Masses of Sranc stream across the terrace they had occupied mere moments before, literally hacking at one another to funnel onto the steps. Around the looming abdomens of stone, she can see hundreds more pouring from the tunnel's horn-mouth entrance, their white faces pinked by the hellish glow. The first of the Bashrag wade through them. The cavern roar seems to meld with their shrieks, to add thunder to their cacophony.

Their Captain's pose says it all. Away is lost to them. Only death and bitter vengeance remain.

Here the Skin Eaters stand.

"We all knew it would come to this!" Sarl cries and cackles. The cut on his cheek bleeds and grins. "Hell and skinnies, boys! Hell and *Sranc!*"

Achamian is dumped across the steps immediately below the landing. Those who haven't cast away their shields form a new line, five abreast, from the cavern wall to the landing's rotted edge. The Sranc plunge head-long toward them, their faces twisted in fury and licentious hunger. She sees several tumble off the stairs edge, kick screaming into the sheets of fire below.

Lord Kosoter seizes her shoulder with his free hand. "Rouse him, girl!" he shouts, his eyes fixed on the wild-limbed deluge about to descend upon them. He need not utter the sum of his intent: *Rouse the Wizard or we're dead.*

She squats next to Achamian. A scab of salt has fallen away, and blood wells across his flayed cheek, but he has slumped back into unconsciousness. The heat buffets her, and for a dizzied moment she almost topples, would have slipped were it not for *Achamian's* sudden grip.

She stares at him. A clutched joy sparks through her, only to be pinched into oblivion by his crazed look.

His lips work in palsied twitches. "*Esmi?*" he cries.

"Akka! Sranc come . . . Only you can save us!"

"Don't you see, woman? He's *Dûnyain*! He awakens us to drive us deeper into sleep! *He makes us love!*"

"Akka! Please!"

"Origins! Origins are the truth of us!" A fury screws his face, so poisonous she feels the shame of it even through her panic. "*I will show you!*" he snarls.

A numbness sops through her, a recognition . . .

"Akka."

Inhuman baying. Her body whips her face around of its own accord.

"*Move!*" Pokwas booms, pressing between his brothers to stand at the fore of the line. The rising stair has become a rope of wagging blades and caterwauling faces. The creatures scramble down the steps like famished apes. Those at the fore literally launch themselves from several steps up, come hacking down on the black-skinned scalper. The great tulwar swoops around and out and the grim dance begins, body and sword swinging in flawless counterpoise. Pitted blades shatter. Crude shields are cloven. Limbs are struck spinning. The Sword-Dancer does not so much kill as harvest, keening in his strange Zeümi tongue. Blood slaps the chapped walls, greases the stair, sails in rags and strings over the plummet.

Mimara stands above the Wizard, one foot planted on the landing, the other two steps down. She yanks Squirrel from its sheath, holds the Seleukaran steel high, so that it seems to boil with the hellish light.

She is Anasûrimbor Mimara, child-whore and Princess-Imperial. She will die spitting and brawling, be it at Cil-Aujas or the Gates of Hell.

"My dreams show me the way!" the unhinged Wizard bellows from her feet. He fumbles trying to press himself from the stone. "I will *track* him, Esmi! Pursue him to the very womb!"

For eleven miraculous heartbeats Pokwas stems the descending tide. The foremost Sranc begin panicking, try to claw back in terror, but the mobs above drive them skidding down the gored steps, into the arc of the Zeümi blade. The corpses heap before the Sword-Dancer, sluice outward like piled fish.

Then the black javelins begin falling . . .

One of the surviving Galeoth scalpers is killed outright,

caught above the clavicle and punched backward. He trips over the Wizard and topples downward, spinning across a dozen steps before scudding over the stair's edge. Mimara merely stands dumbfounded as two javelins lance the open spaces to either side of her, ripping the air like gauze. Pokwas literally bats one with his sword, sends it darting over the edge. But a second rings off his battle cap. He crashes in a tangle at the feet of his fellow Skin Eaters.

The Sranc fall upon them.

Roaring, the scalpers lean into their shields and hack and hammer. They exact a cleaving, puncturing toll. Somehow, Pokwas is pulled clear. Lord Kosoter skewers the frenzied skinny drawn with him, kicks its face to slush. Her boots skidding, Mimara throws her shoulder to the press, even manages to spear two by poking Squirrel through the thicket of straining limbs and locked weapons. But looking up, she sees the savage multitudes that bear down upon them. The crush pitches one Sranc after another over the stair's outer brink. Some even crawl across the bristling surface of their brethren. The first of the Bashrag lumber near, one with a Chorae gouging hollow its grotesque breast. And the crazed column piles higher and higher, winding along the contour of the cavern wall, to the peak of the stair, to the terrace . . .

She sees *Cleric*, stepping out *over* the ruined amphitheatre, hanging, shimmed in white light against the black-and-ruby ramparts. The Nonman turns toward them, striding across empty air. His sorcerous song somehow rises through all noise and clamour, like blood squeezed from the world's own marrow. Brilliant parabolas hook across the open spaces, fall at intervals along the teeming stair. And arcs beget arcs, jumping from Sranc to shrieking Sranc, multiplying to the force and tenor of Cleric's arcane call. He comes to a halt, hangs motionless over the burning lake, his eyes and mouth glittering like stars, his hands outstretched. Incandescent scissions. Looms of light. The Skin Eaters cease their backward skid, begin hewing their way forward. Above them, their foes are thrashing and burning, caught in blinding webs, dazzling geometries.

Their inhuman screams sink needles into their ears.

And she thinks, *Ishroi* . . .

Lord Kosoter is bellowing, commanding them to run, but Mimara finds herself stumbling to a pause on the second landing. Above, the stairs are pulped with smoking Sranc corpses. But two Bashrag remain untouched—Chorae-bearers. She watches them heave blistered corpses across the long fall between them and Cleric. Three fall short, revolving like thrown axes as they arc into the cauldron below. A fourth slaps across the Nonman's Quyan Ward, which had been all but invisible for the glare. The carcass smokes, drawing a burning smear as it slides down and away, into the incinerating brilliance below.

Laughing, Cleric calls out yet another Cant, and lines like the glimmer along a razor parse the intervening air. They slice into the base of the precarious stair, and the steps falls away, immolated in streamers of black dust. The lower Bashrag slides on malformed heels and plummets, shrieking with elephantine lungs. The other flees back up the stair, stamping through the glistening dead.

But Soma has her by the arm, pulls her running after the others. For the first time she catches the whiff of cooler air twining through the blanketing convections. The force of it grows and grows, until it numbs her face and dandles her hair, slides aching fingers across her sweat-lathered scalp. Lobes of black stone submerge the base of the stair, ridged and wrinkled like skin. She and Soma run across them with ginger strides, hastening to catch the others. She sees them vanish into the mouth of a partially buried corridor—the source of the frigid blast.

Hair and clothing whip out behind them. A vacant howl

overpowers all other sound. She leans against the gust, which seems to pull her onto her toes. Her jerkin flattens against her, as chill as dead skin. She glances back to the lake of fire and the wrecked amphitheatre, but her eyes are too pinched with cold to see much more than pitch blots and hairy explosions of crimson and gold.

The corridor descends at a shallow gradient, so that the petrified flow presses them tighter beneath the ceiling vaults. Soon they are crouching. Soma shouts something to her, but his words are blown away like fluff. The wind is so cold it scalds their flushed skin, drives nails down to the bone. The ceiling angles lower and lower, and it seems all Aenaratiol's mountainous weight closes about them. They are on their hands and knees, literally climbing against a tempest gale. Sting and blackness blind them.

The wind abates. They tip forward, as though thrown clear of white-water currents. Hands clutch them from the dark.

Mouths screeching into light. Shadows flitting across devious angles.

Run! something cried within him. *Sweet-sweet Sejenus! You must run!*

And yet Achamian sat at his ease, his alarm more coloured by curiosity than by panic. He wore the fine cloth of a courtier, and the tang of incense mellowed the air. Jasmine. Cinnamon-musk.

The low ceilings of the Annexes hung about him, the groaning post-and-lintel architecture of an age before arches. He smiled at the image of his High-King across the benjuka plate, then looked down to the little boy leaning into his lap, Nau-Cayûti bearing a gilded scroll-case too heavy for his tender arms. Father and son laughed as he hefted the golden tube.

The shouts of the dying scraped across stone . . . but in some other place.

"What is it, Da?" the young Prince called to his father.

"A *map*, Cayû. To a strong place. A hidden place."

"Ishuäl," Seswatha said, mussing the child's hair with his free hand.

"I *love* maps, Da! Can I see it? Please? What's Ishuäl?"

"Come . . ." Celmomas said, his smile at once dark and indulgent—the smile of a father bent on hardening his son to a vicious world. The boy obediently darted back to his father's side. Achamian studied the golden vines twining along the case's length, the Umeri script stamped into concentric rings at either end. It seemed implausibly heavy—enough to make wrists wobble.

"A king," Celmomas was saying, "stands before his people in all things, Cayû. A king rides at the fore. This is why he must always make ready, always prepare. For his foe is ever the future. Condic marauders on our eastern frontier. Assassins in an embassy of Shir. Sranc. Pestilence . . . Calamity *awaits us all*, even you, my son.

"Some petition astrologers, soothsayers, false prophets in all their guises. Low men, mean men, who exchange words of comfort for gold. Me, I put my faith in stone, in iron, in blood, and in secrecy—secrecy above all!—for these things serve in all times. All times! The day words conquer the future is the day the dead begin to speak."

He turned to Seswatha. The wolf's head braided into his beard flashed in the glowering light.

"This, my friend—this is why I built Ishuäl. For Kûniüri. For House Anasûrimbor. It is our final bulwark against catastrophe . . . Against the darkest future."

Achamian placed the scroll-case on the table before him, so that it seemed the prize of the pieces arrayed on the benjuka plate beyond it. He looked up to meet his chieftain's pensive gaze, found himself pondering the archaic script. "*Doom*," it read, "*should you find me broken*."

"The inscription . . . What does it mean?"

"Keep it, old friend. Make it your deepest secret."

"These dreams you have been having . . . You must tell me more!"

The ages seemed to lie like a mountain above them, centuries compressed into stone, hope suffocated beneath the heaping of generations. Strangers warred and screamed . . . Somewhere, in the catacombs with them.

Toe! Toe to the line!

"Keep it," Anasûrimbor Celmomas said. "Bury it in the Coffers."

There is music in the wind. A whistling smeared into a discordant call, a song played to the rhythms of blowing rags and floating dead.

Even after her eyes adjust, she can scarce credit what has happened. She simply lies, her back and limbs pressed against the heat radiating from the clumped stone, her skin shrinking from the chill that courses over her. She breathes. Her clothing grips like moss. Cramps gnaw at the vast numbness that floats through her. She is rooted, immovable, barely alive.

The entrance is little more than a horizontal slot, the petrified stone runs so high. It glows a baleful orange, their only source of light.

The company lies scattered about her in the gloom. Galian has collapsed on his shield, breathing in spasms. Pokwas is on his stomach where he was dropped, his cheek pressed into a black-glistening pool of blood. His back rises and falls to the rhythm of slow life. Achamian lies unconscious as well, or near-unconscious. His head periodically jerks to the pluck of some unseen tendon. Soma sits in the posture of a mystic, his head lolling against the wall. Sarl is curled on his side, heaving spittle. The others, Xonghis, Sutadra, Conger, and three whose names she cannot remember, are likewise sprawled across the stone.

The last of the Skin Eaters.

Only Lord Kosoter stands. His head hangs like a stone from his shoulders. His helm lost, his grey-and-black hair ropes down, twines outward in the wind, obscuring his face and terrible gaze. Somehow his shadow, thrown from the pale entrance light, seems to fall across them all.

They lie in a chamber of some kind, the dimensions of which escape the feeble light, gathered in a corner where the cycling gusts are broken by the confluence of walls. The air is too fleet and too cold to possess smell. She first notices the graffiti while watching Soma. Strings of white-scratched characters score the wall all about him, the lines so dense where the hardened flow meets the wall as to almost seem like decoration, but thinning out into lone scribbles about his shoulders and neck—according, she realizes, to the original floor and the limited reach of its ancient authors.

The wind flutes in the dark, eerie and disharmonious.

She ponders the scratches with the clarity of concentration that comes only with absolute exhaustion. Her soul, which so often seemed to be petalled like a flower, a thing of frail confusion, has become as simple as a stone, a lamp that can shine upon one thing and one thing only. The signs themselves mean nothing to her, nor, she imagines, to anyone living. But the character of their scratching almost shouts too loud. These are human signs, she realizes, scraped in the throes of human anguish. Names. Curses. Pleas.

And somehow she just knows: This was once a place of great suffering.

A shadow blots the entrance glow, and alarm beats hot blood into the clay of her body. She sits up, as do several others. She sees a silhouette crawl through the slender orange maw, then stand.

Cleric steps into their midst, the gore on his face and nimil armour blown into crazed patterns by the wind. She sees the same white chapping across his forehead and scalp as Achamian, though not nearly so severe: Skin salted from Choric near misses, she realizes. Unwinded, he stares with spent curiosity at the spent Men, trades a long look with the Captain before turning to scan the shrouded spaces. There is a clarity and a command in his dark eyes that she has never seen before—one that both heartens and frightens her. He seems to ponder something only his eyes can descry.

"We're safe," he eventually says to Lord Kosoter. "For a time."

Finally able to move, she crawls across the uneven stone—tongues laid across tongues—to Achamian. The panic receding, she at last has room to worry, perhaps even to mourn.

"The wind," Xonghis croaks. "It's *cold*. High mountain cold . . ."

The Nonman lowers his chin in assent. "The Great Medial Screw runs near here . . . An immense stair that runs the entire height of the Aenaratiol."

"Can we use it to escape?" Galian blurts. He hugs his knees, slowly rocking. She glimpses a tremor fluttering through one of his hanging thumbs.

"I think so . . . If it is still as I . . . remember."

The relief is soundless and palpable. This entire time, the scalpers have had breath enough—heart enough—only for what was essential. Safety. Escape. The possibility of these secured, their souls once more slacken, their thoughts fork down paths less urgent. They look about them and wonder.

"What is this place?" Xonghis asks.

Cleric's black eyes hold Mimara for an appraising instant. "A kind of barracks . . . I think. For ancient captives."

"A slave pit," Mimara croaks, so softly that several of the others turn to her frowning. But she knows the Nonman has heard.

A serpentine blink. His grin reveals the arc of his fused

teeth—the same as the Sranc, only not fanged and serrated. He speaks, and for a heartbeat, his face becomes a mask before the sun . . .

A Surillic Point sparks to life in the air above him; white light blows out and across the darkness.

The chamber is massive. Terraces climb about their lonely corner. How high or how far none can tell, since the height and breadth quickly outrun the light. But they can clearly see the chap-bronze cages that pack each of the terrace walls—cruel confinements no larger than a single man—enough for hundreds, even thousands, standing hollow save for shadows, their wretched prisoners having rotted free long, long ago.

Even though Mimara can imagine how the room once looked, the tiers of piteous faces and clutching hands, it is the graffiti, scratched out along the lowermost wall as far as the light can reach, that most afflicts her heart. The Emwama, and their proof of misery, she realizes. She can almost see their shades, massed in hopeless clots, looks averted from the horrors hanging above, ears aching . . .

A shudder passes through her, so deep her eyes and limbs seem to rattle in their sockets.

And she thinks, *Cil-Aujas . . .*

Some moments pass before she realizes that no one, not even Soma, shares any inkling of her dread. Instead, they are all staring into the gloom toward the corner opposite. Even Lord Kosoter.

"Sweet Sejenus!" Galian hisses, slowly coming to his feet. The wind bats his leather skirts, toggles the loose ends of the tourniquet bound about his left calf. Xonghis is already walking toward the point of their converging gazes. Gusts paw him from his stride.

"Could it be?" Xonghis calls out, his voice warbling in the wind's howl.

Several heartbeats pass before her eyes discern it, jutting

from the surface of the laval ground. There, a cage of a different kind, large enough to shell a seafaring galley. Great ribs rise from the stone like a portcullis grill, curve up to meet their counterparts in a kiss of bowed spears. She sees a jawed carapace yards away, as though carried on a different current, submerged and tilted, yet standing as tall as a man, an empty eye socket just clearing the petrified stone.

"I pity you," Cleric says. "To carry such sights for so short a span."

Sarl trips to his knees, his hair drawn into a crazed rag halo. "I called him a fool!" he cries to his fellows, grinning out of some maniacal reflex. "A *fool!*"

The Skin Eaters gather, beaten by gust and fate alike, gazing in awe at the iron bones of a dragon.

Wracu.

The source of the wind's cold hymn.

With light comes reason.

The Skin Eaters waste few words on the dragon, though all idle gazes seem inevitably drawn toward the rust-pitted bones. They do not speak of their fallen friends. They are scalpers, after all, violent men leading the most violent of all lives. They are long accustomed to the gaps between them—Kiampas, Oxwora, and many others. The pyre is their only constant friend.

Instead they prepare and make plans.

Somehow Galian and Xonghis have become the guiding personalities. Bleak necessity has rewritten the ranks between them, as is so often the case in the aftermath of catastrophe. Sitting on a hump of stone, the Captain simply watches and listens, grants assent with curt nods. Sarl mopes against a graffiti-etched wall, says nothing, and does little save probe the cut on his cheek with his fingers.

The mark of a sobber.

Mimara tends to Achamian while Cleric ministers to Pokwas and the others with his haphazard healing lore. The Nonman gives them all a tiny pinch of black powder, medicinal spores, which he produces from his leather satchel. "Qirri," he calls it. He claims that it will rejuvenate them, as well as help them cope with the lack of food or water. He even tells them to sprinkle some in the mouths of the two unconscious men.

It tastes of dirt and honey.

A peculiar shyness leans against her eyes whenever she looks at the Nonman. His recent exercise of power clings to him like an aura, an intimation of some dread disproportion. He seems heavier, harder by far than the Men surrounding him. It reminds her of watching Kellhus on the Andiamine Heights: the sense of gazing at a presence that somehow eclipses sight, that reaches out, arching beyond the limits of your vision, to link hands behind you . . .

Beneath you.

She finds herself rehearsing Achamian's earlier worries. What would he make of what she had seen? There can be no doubt, she decides. Like the Aspect-Emperor, this Incariol, or whatever his name, is one of the world's powers. An Ishroi of old.

She can still see him, leaping alone into howling masses of Sranc, hanging bright above smouldering lakes of fire. These memories, combined with the glories of the Upper Halls and the atrocities soaked into the stone of this room, seem to confirm her suspicion that Men are little more than animals to Nonmen, a variety of Sranc, a corruption of their own angelic form.

Using what spit she can muster, she begins carefully cleaning around the scabs of salt along the side of the Wizard's face. The white swatches do not coat the skin, they *are* the skin, down to individual moles and pores, only raised and puckered by the inflamed flesh beneath. The damage is literally skin deep and certainly not life-threatening. After the incident on the stair, his wits are what concern her the most, even though Cleric assures her he will quickly recover, especially once the qirri soaks into his veins.

"But you should not lean so close," he says, nodding to the Chorae still stuffed beneath her jerkin.

Assured that Achamian is as comfortable as possible, she sits some distance from him, and at last draws the Chorae from the sweaty pocket it has pressed into her breast. Though she has grown accustomed to its inverted presence, there is a surreality to the act of taking it into her hand, a sense that it is not the Trinket that moves so much as it is the whole of creation about it. She has no clue why it should compel her. Everything about it shrieks anathema. It is the bane of her heart's sole desire, the thing she must fear above all once she begins uttering sorcery. What almost killed Achamian.

The light of the Surillic Point does not touch it, so that even its worldly aspect seems an insult to her eyes. It is a ball of shadow in her palm, its iron curve, its skein of ancient writing, illuminated only by the low crimson glow that leaks through the entrance. It seems to brood and to seethe. The abyssal dimensions of its Mark are a greater insult still. She can scarce focus when she looks with the eyes of the Few. It is as if it rolls from her sight and thought each time she centres her attention upon it.

And yet she stares and stares, like a boy gazing at some remarkable bug. Low voices flutter through the portals of the wind. She can hear some of the scalpers hammering at the dragon's teeth—even in disaster, their mercenary instincts have not abandoned them. The Wizard lies prone in her periphery.

Shivers scuttle like spiders from her palm to her heart

and throat, pimpling her entire skin. She glares at it, concentrates her breath and being upon its weightless horror, as if using it to mortify her soul the way shakers use whips and nails to mortify their flesh. She floats in the prickle of her own sweat.

The suffering begins. The pain . . .

It's like thumbing a deep bruise at first, and she almost revels its odd, almost honey sweetness. But the sensation unravels, opens into an ache that swells about wincing serrations, as if teeth were chewing their own mouth through sealed muscle and skin. The violence spreads. The clubs begin falling, and her body rebels down to its rooted bowel, gagging at memories of salt. *Emptiness itself* . . . Lying cupped in her palm, a sheering void, throwing hooks about her, a million lacerating stings.

She grunts spit between clenched teeth, grins like a dying ape. Anguish wracks her, as deep as deep, but the smallest nub of her remains, an untouched sip, still conscious of the Wizard lying in her periphery, and it sees that he is the same yet transfigured, an old ailing man, and a corpse boiled in the fires of damnation . . .

The Judging Eye has opened.

She feels it leaning through her worldly eyes, pressing forward, throwing off the agony like rotted clothes, snuffing fact from sight, drawing out the sanctity and the sin. With terrible fixation it stares into the oblivion spilling from her palm . . .

And somehow, impossibly, *passes through*.

She blinks on the far side of contradiction, her face and shoulders pulled back in a warm wind, a breath, a premonition of summer rain. And she sees it, a point of luminous white, a *certainty*, shining out from the pit that blackens her grasp. A voice rises, a voice without word or tone, drowsy with compassion, and the light grows and grows, shrinking the abyss to a rind, to the false foil that it is, burning to dust, and the glory, the magnificence, shines forth, radiant, blinding . . .

And she holds *all* . . . In her hand she holds it!

A Tear of God.

Through the cold of the wind's preternatural singing, she hears, "*Mimara?*"

She sits hunched over her prize, utterly bewildered.

"*Are you okay?*"

She holds a light in her hand, a different light, one that shines but does not illumine, a star that glitters as bright as the Nail of Heaven.

"Where did you get that?" Soma asks. He is crouching before her, nodding to the Chorae in her palm—or to what used to be a Chorae . . .

"You see it?" she asks, coughing at the waver in her voice.

He shrugs. "A Tear of God," he says with matter-of-fact exhaustion. "Here we are, trying to hammer loose dragon teeth, and you've already found your fortune."

"I did not come for riches." She studies his dark, handsome face through the threads of shining white radiating from her palm. "So you don't see the light?"

He glances up at the Surillic Point, frowning. "I see it plainly enough . . ." He looks back to her, eyebrows raised. "It's *you* I'm having difficulty seeing, with that thing pressed against your skin. You look like a . . . breathing shadow . . ."

"I mean *this*," she says, raising her palm. "What do you see when you look at this?"

He makes the face he always makes when he suspects the others are joking at his expense: a mingling of hurt, resentment, and an eagerness to please. "A ball of shadow," he says slowly.

She pulls her empty coin purse from beneath her belt, hastily drops the Chorae in it. She vaguely hears Soma say,

"Ah, much better," but pays him no attention. She cranes around looking for Lord Kosoter. She can sense his Chorae the way she can sense her own, but it also feels different, like an outward shining instead of a pinprick of inhaling black. She sees him dozing against the wall with several others, his square beard crushed against the blood-painted splint of his hauberk. But since his Chorae is pocketed, she has no way of knowing whether it also shines in her natural sight.

Fear flushes through her, seems to pull the ancient slave chamber into a slow roll about the axis of her heart. *Something is happening to me . . .*

This is when she notices the stranger.

There, in the very *midst* of them. She initially thinks that it's Cleric—his face is all but identical—but Cleric sits several paces beyond, his legs crossed, his head bowed in prayer or exhaustion.

Another Nonman?

He sits the way the others sit, back hunched against the wind, eyes closed, as though taking inventory of inner pains. An archaic headdress falls to his back and shoulders, a crown of silvered thorns chased by a skirt of tiny black rods. His garb is violet and voluminous but wrapped in a manner that reveals segments of his corselet, a kind of mail wrought from innumerable golden figurines. White skin is visible beneath, as smooth as ivory.

For a moment she can neither breathe nor speak. Then at last she says, "So-soma?"

"Mim-Mimara?" he replies, trying to sound mocking. He is always trying to rally her.

"Who," she asks without looking at the Nilnameshi caste-noble, "is *that?*" For a moment, she is frightened that he won't see this as well . . .

That she has gone mad.

The following pause both reassures and terrifies. "What the—?"

She hears him draw his sword, a sound that, even through scarcely audible in the wind, instantly rouses the others.

Everyone is up and shouting, raising battered shields and notched swords. Soma steps before Mimara, falls into stance, his scimitar raised above his head. On the figure's far side, Cleric lifts his eyes, blinks with feline curiosity.

Turning his head on a slow swivel, the stranger looks about, but never quite at any of them. He then lowers his face to his sandalled feet once again. Mimara notices that the wind does not touch the lavish cloth about his shoulders, though it whips and pins the clothing of everyone standing about him.

"Sweet Seju!" Galian hisses. "He . . . he *has no shadow*!"

"Quiet," Lord Kosoter grates, invoking an instinct Mimara feels all too keenly. A sense of mortal peril seems to ride the wind, a tingling certainty that the Nonman before them is less flesh or blood than a dread gate, a catastrophic threshold.

He is perfectly motionless. He possesses a predator's vigilance for sound and motion.

Even still, Cleric warily approaches the figure, his nimil armour shining through the webbing of blood. His expression is astonished, so stunned that he almost seems human. He kneels below the figure and, looking up, gently calls, "Cousin?"

The face rises. The small bars on his headdress swing about his jawline. They shine like obsidian.

No sound comes from the opening lips. Instead, the entire company starts when they hear Pokwas and Achamian rasp, "***You****-you* . . ." in ragged unison.

Sarl cackles like a drunk who has scared tears from his grandchildren.

"Yes, Cousin . . . I have returned."

Again the lips move, and the voices of the two unconscious men rise into the void of sound, the one reeded by age, the other deep and melodious.

"**They**-*they* **called**-*called* **us**-*us* **false**-*false*."

"They are children who can never grow," Cleric replies. "They could do no different."

"**I**-*I* **loved**-*loved* **them**-*them*. **I**-*I* **loved**-*loved* **them**-*them* **so**-*so* **much**-*much*."

"So did we all, at one time."

"**They**-*they* **betrayed**-*trayed*."

"They were our punishment. Our pride was too great."

"**They**-*they* **betrayed**-*trayed*. **You**-*you* **betrayed**-*trayed* . . ."

"You have dwelt here too long, Cousin."

"**I**-*I* **am**-*am* **lost**-*lost*. **All**-*all* **the**-*the* **doors**-*doors* **are**-*are* **different**-*rent*, **and**-*and* **the**-*the* **thresholds**-*holds* . . . **they**-*they* **are**-*are* **holy**-*lee* **no**-*no* **more**-*more*."

"Yes. Our age has passed. Cil-Aujas is fallen. Fallen into darkness."

"**No**-*no*. **Not**-*not* **darkness**-*ness* . . ."

With a flourish, the Nonman King comes to his feet, his hands thrust out and back so that his spine arches, and Mimara can see that his robe is in fact no robe but a dark bolt of silken material wrapped about his armpits and across his shoulders. The shimmering tails of it fall to the ground. His corselet is sleeveless, yet hangs to his sandalled feet, revealing as much of his graven nudity as it conceals. His phallus hangs like a snake in the shadow of his thighs.

"**Hell**-*hell*."

Still kneeling, Cleric gazes up at the impossible figure, anguish and indecision warring across his expression.

"**Damnation**-*shun*, **Cousin**-*sin*. **How**-*How*? **How**-*How* **could**-*could* **we**-*we* **forget**-*get*?"

A sorrow flattens the glittering black eyes. "Not I. I have never forgotten . . ."

The points of their swords sinking, the Skin Eaters gape at the two Nonmen, the living and the dead, for they understand that the one bearing the crown draws no breath. Mimara wants to flee. It seems she can feel the whole of her skin, from the cuts about her knuckles to the folds of her sex, alive to some plummet she cannot see or fathom. But she remains as motionless as the others.

Cleric knows him.

The wind prods her in contrary directions, thumbs without substance. The jutting bones of iron hum and howl, a dirge to dragon hollows. The cage-ringed walls rise into black. Across the rising tiers, the ancient bronze begins to creak, to rattle . . .

The lips of the apparition move without sound.

Mimara whirls, sees Pokwas groan and curse beneath the astonished eyes of his fellows. And Achamian too! The old Wizard has rolled to his hands and knees. She flies to him, clutches his shoulders. He blinks at the wrinkled stone beneath his fingers, frowns as though it were a language he should be able to read. He spits—at the taste of qirri, she realizes.

"Mimara?" He coughs at the ground.

She swallows a sob of relief. "Goddess be praised!" she hisses. "Oh, sweet, *sweet* Yatwer!"

"Wh-where are we?" He chokes on his own throat. "What's happening?"

She finds herself almost whispering in his ear. "Akka. Listen to me carefully. You remember what you said? About this place . . . blurring . . . into the Outside?"

"Yes. The treachery . . . The betrayal that led to its fall . . ."

"No. That's not it. It's *this* place. This very room! It's what *they did*—the Nonmen of Cil-Aujas . . . It's what they did to their human slaves!"

Generations bred for the sunless mines. Used up. Cast

away like moaning rubbish. Ten thousand years of sightless torment.

She knows this . . . But how?

"What? What do you mean?" He grimaces in pain and irritation.

Rather than speak, she turns aside so that he can see Cleric still kneeling, listening to the soundless lips of the Nonman King . . . "No!" Cleric calls. "Cousin, please!"

The milk in the Wizard's eyes clears. "What?" He fairly uses her body as a ladder, stumbles swaying to his feet. For several heartbeats he simply gapes at the underworld apparition.

"*Run!*" he cries to the others. "Follow the wind! Courage will be your death here!"

"*Stand your ground!*" the Captain roars.

The Surillic Point hangs immune to the wind, bathing the chapped walls and uneven floor in pale white. Despite their dread Captain's cry, the scalpers back away from the two Nonmen. Black has begun bleeding from the bolt of fabric wrapped about the spectre's back and shoulders, rolling up and out like dark wine in water, as impervious to the blowing as the light above.

Lord Kosoter stands rigid, the point of his sword held to the ground beside him, his hair flailing in steel-grey ribbons. "He has this," he grates, his eyes fixed on Cleric where he kneels beneath the mad apparition.

"Captain," Achamian says, fingers locked so that he hangs from Mimara's shoulder. He's already pressing her backward with staggering steps. "Listen . . ."

The Holy Veteran turns his bearded profile to them, nothing more. "He *has* this!"

But Cleric has lowered his head. Lines of reflected white hook across the contours of his skull. Trailing tendrils of smoke-darkness, the Nonman King steps around him, strides with sandals that do not quite touch ground, then turns so that he stands above Cleric's armoured back.

"*Captain*," the Wizard cries. Now it is Mimara who is drawing him backward, toward the hymn of the dragon bones. Soma grabs the ailing Wizard's other arm.

Where Cleric holds his head bowed, the spectre raises his dead face to the ceiling, as though seeing sky rather the crushing miles of earth. The mouth works in unheard benediction. The rigid arms lift and rotate forward. The elbows fold. The hands, with fingers and thumbs held tight as though in some ritual pose, close about Cleric's shoulders. The scalpers watch their companion raised, a silvery figure framed by a corona of black . . .

Even the Captain is stumbling backward now.

Holding Pokwas between them, Xonghis and Galian retreat with Mimara and the Wizard. Sarl laughs like a child at a puppet show, his yellow teeth gleaming. Conger pulls him in jerking steps.

The Nonman King holds Cleric like a doll before him, like a cup he can spill. He steps forward—into . . .

A violent spasm, like drawing first breath. Limbs fling outward, snap rigid, like ropes weighted with lead. Cleric's whole body arches backward, as if bound across the curves of drawn bows. And both Nonmen can be seen, as though each were solid and the other were glass, naked limbs within armour, nimil plates beneath a gown of chained gold. The Nonman King's face pulls forward, twists in bewildered delirium. Wrath.

For an instant, the company glimpses a floating seal, a savage emblem of hell . . .

The Surillic Point flickers out.

"***I dream***," Cleric's voice booms through the wind howling black, "***that I am a God***."

The Skin Eaters are shouting. Mimara hears herself sob.

Achamian mutters in arcane panic. The light shed from his eyes and mouth paints Soma's blank face against the greater dark.

A new light. It flickers like a star for long hanging heartbeat, then flares with eye-averting brilliance. A *new chamber*. The tiered walls rise into shadow about them, the bronze-barred cages lined like pupae across them—as before. But each encases a mad thrashing, arms reaching, hands clutching, mouths shrieking, a thousand moments of anguish, a thousand souls, condensed into a mad, smoking blur. Eyes stacked upon eyes, drawn across eyes. The arcs of teeth, a shining multitude. Swatches of welted skin.

The Emwama scream, thousands upon thousands of them, forever buried, forever sealed from their native sun. An age of torment compressed into a single wail . . .

Mimara screams with them.

Cleric drifts toward the abject scalpers, floating in a vertical pool of black, like tar spilled across unseen waters, his face submerged, his limbs drowned, beneath the hoary aspect of the Nonman King.

But a hunger, a voice groans through the mountain's foundations. ***A hunger runs through me . . . splits me like rotted stone***.

Achamian is hollering so hard that spittle flecks his matted beard. Even though Mimara stands next to him, she can hear nothing save the million-throated wail.

Despite his weakened state, the Wizard is yanking her backward, away from the looming visage.

How, the voice creaks through the roots of the world, ***could a God hunger?***

Plumes of molten stone erupt from the ground about them, spitting jets of orange, gold, and baleful crimson. One of the scalpers simply vanishes. A limb falls next to Mimara, an unblistered hand attached to a forearm burnt to a charcoal nub. Lord Kosoter, who had stood his ground before the hellish approach, at last turns to run.

The whole company, or what remains of it, is running.

Nonman laughter. She has heard it enough to recognize its peculiarities by now, the deep warbling at its pith, the way its intonations hook into cruelties beyond the range of human comprehension.

Nonman laughter, booming with the lungs of a mountain.

They run, through the bones of the dragon, into the concentrating wind, and it seems a miracle they can battle through it, that they aren't blown skidding like rags into the horror rising behind them.

They scramble crawling into the opposite corridor, and the cold shoots through them, aches bones from end to end. They climb against the wind, whose howl they cannot hear.

The damned call out to them, wailing with the hunger that knots and strangles and sustains all misery . . .

Yearning to see itself visited upon others.

It has entered the corridor behind them. He has entered . . .

The Wight-in-the-Mountain. The Nonman King.

She is an earthen jug, and her innards slosh like curdled milk. A single crack and she will clatter open, spill across the floor. She is failing. She feels it in her flagging attempts to haul the Wizard with her. The others have climbed ahead, almost beyond the light of the Surillic Point.

Even Soma.

Her soul gropes for strength, a kind of inward prayer, Mimara begging Mimara, and suddenly, she feels it, the qirri that Cleric had given them, like stones beneath paddling feet.

"*Come! On!*" she cries at the Wizard.

But the wind whips the words like autumn leaves from her mouth.

The hellish wail stamps them into ash.

They cross the bourne, from the lobed rock, the drowning ground of the slave chamber, the overflown foundations, onto the hewn floor. But it does not matter. The wind has all but defeated Achamian. She is fairly dragging him. And she can see *it*, boiling up through the blackness toward them, the infernal pit.

The old man is shouting. She cannot hear him, but she knows what he cries . . .

Leave me.

Leave me. Daughter, please . . .

But she refuses. This old stranger . . . What is it?

Why should she dare hell?

She heaves, bawling at his arm. Achamian is on his back now, and she scratches him forward, heave after heave after heave, knowing that it does not matter.

She doesn't hear the sorcerous cry until after, only the thunderous crack, the concussion that slaps back the wind, knocks her forward to her knees. She hears it through the all-encompassing clap and rumble . . .

A collapse. Earth hammering ground. A mountain shrugging in and down.

The wind is gone.

A light hangs in a fog.

A ringing like blood in the ears. A sound surfacing . . .

Coughing. An old man coughing. She sees his silhouette resolving through the dust, a tattered old shadow.

"We need to keep moving," a hack-pinched voice says. "I'm not sure this will stop him."

Her eyes burn and blink. Her voice fails her.

"We need to keep moving," the Wizard continues, his tone rueful and encouraging. "If anything he can follow the mile-long streak of shit I dragged across the floor."

Somehow she was holding him, laughing, sobbing "*Akka . . . Akka!*"

"So far so good," he says gently. A hand strokes her hair, and instantly, she is a child clinging. "Mimara . . ."

"I thuh-thought . . . I thought . . . y-you . . ."

"Shush. We need to keep moving."

Arm in arm, they pass through a ruined network of corridors, following the trail kicked by the others across the dust-limned floor. After so many terrors, further fear seems ludicrous, and yet Mimara finds herself breathing against yet another clammy premonition. "How?" she finally asks. "We had the light . . . How could they run so far without us?"

"Because they saw *that*," Achamian replies, nodding at the darkness before her.

She sees it: the outline of an arched entranceway washed in the palest of blue. Even from this distance, a deep sense of recognition suffuses her, a wave of depleted exultation. She knows this light, in ways that run deeper than her waking soul. It was the light her sires were born to, all the way back to the beginning . . .

The light of sky.

Slim shadows move across the entrance. She hears a voice calling her name—Soma. A sudden fury burns against her exhaustion, in the way of wood soaked in mud.

As though reading her thoughts, the Wizard says, "All men are traitors in a place such as this . . ." When she glances at him, he adds, "Now isn't the time for judgment."

His face is beyond haggard in the arcane glare. Its network of ruts and wrinkles are inked black with dust, as are his cheek and temple—across all the flesh rawed by the salting. Even still, intellect and resolution glitter in his eyes, with the merest hint of gallows humour. The old Achamian is back, she realizes, even if he's propped up by the qirri like her. Returned from the paths of the dead.

The surviving Skin Eaters are animated as well, so much so that for an absurd moment Mimara has the sense that she stands with a troupe of players dressed and painted to play a shattered company of scalpers. But it is as much the turn in their fortunes as it is Cleric's nostrums that has heartened them.

They have found their way out of Cil-Aujas.

"I know this place," the Wizard rasps. "Even among the Nonmen, it was a wonder."

"Cleric called it the Screw," Galian says hoarsely, staring up like all the others. He looks different with days of growth across his jaw and chin, less like the cynical wit and more like his brothers. "The Great Medial Screw."

The must of soaked masonry. The ring of voices across stone and water. They stand on a terrace set in curved walls that wrap out through the vagaries of Achamian's light to form a perfect cylinder, one that soars as far as any of them can see, terminating in a point of shining white. Elongated glyphs band the surface, some as tall as a man, others engraved in panels no larger than a hand. A stair ascends from the terrace, as broad as a Galeoth wain, winding in helical loops into the obscurity above. Glittering water threads the open air, falling from unguessed heights into the pool that forms a mirror-black plate three or four lengths below the terrace. For a vertiginous moment, Mimara has the impression of staring up from the bottom of an inconceivable well, as though she were no more than a mite, waiting for gods to draw water. It seems impossible that this shaft runs the entire height of the mountain, that a single work can link the heavens to the hell at their feet.

"It'll take days," she murmurs.

"At least we have water," Pokwas says. He leans out, still precarious on his feet, so that Xonghis and Soma reach out to catch hold his steel-plated girdle. Eyes closed, the Sword-Dancer lists into the nearest of the silver threads and wincing, begins pawing the grime and the blood from his face. He takes a long drink before retreating from the unrailed edge. He warns the others to be wary the water's bite—"It falls fast enough to crack teeth!"—but he swears that it is clean and good. Godsent.

They begin taking turns, the man behind holding the belt or hauberk of the man before.

Agitated, Achamian continually stares into the black depths of the hallway they had just fled from. "We don't have time for this," he warns Lord Kosoter.

A wordless stare is his only reply, and Mimara finds herself relieved.

Suddenly water is the only thing she can think about.

How long has it been since their last drink? Never in her life, not even on the slave ship that still haunts her nightmares, has she suffered such deprivations. The qirri is there, a kind of inner hand holding her upright, assisting cramped limbs, but the body it braces teeters on the brink of collapse. When the qirri wears away . . .

She *must* have water.

Perhaps seeing the thirst in her eyes, Soma surrenders his place in the small crowd. She thanks him grudgingly, unable to forgive the image of his fleeing back as she hauled Achamian alone through the corridor mere moments before. What was it about such circumstances, hidden so far from the sun, that they could incite courage one moment and plunder it the next? Was she so different from Somandutta?

He holds her belt and she leans out over the edge, raises her face to the silver stream. It hurts, just as Pokwas has warned, a bite so cold it numbs. She rinses it across her face, a kind exquisite cruelty, feels it slip like daggers across her scalp. Then she opens her lips to the crystalline plummet, and chill life sluices into her. Her teeth ache unto cracking, but the *taste* is clean as a child's love. She drinks. There is milk in water, when the body is in dire need. Through teary eyes she glimpses the blue star high above, and her heart leaps with the certainty of sky—*sky!* They have passed through Cil-Aujas, survived its underworld teeth. They have walked the outskirts of Hell. Now they stand on the long threshold of freedom . . . Sky!

Sky and water.

She pulls away, her face numbed to a mask, watches the rivulets fall from her, add their concentric ripples to those warring soundless across the black pool below. She glimpses her own reflection, a light-rimmed shadow.

She hears Achamian arguing behind her, explaining that sorcerers cannot fly, they can only walk the echoes of the ground in the sky. "If there is a pit in the ground below," he croaks, "there is a pit in the sky as well!"

Then she *feels* it . . . Feels it?

Soma has pulled her back to the safety of the terrace, but she lingers at the edge, still gazing at the black waters below.

She feels it rising.

She sees a flicker in the deeps, like lightning through dark and distant clouds. "Akka?" she murmurs, but it is too late. She realizes that it is too late. In her soul's eye she sees Xonghis on one knee before the Obsidian Gate, a lifetime ago it seems, scratching the sign of the Skin Eaters next to the signs of all the other lost companies.

It was always too late. No one leaves the Black Halls.

Through dark water, *Hell rises* in the guise of a great graven seal, like a shield stamped with packed skulls and living faces, winding in fractal rings about the long-dead Nonman King. It pauses beneath the surface, its limbs languorous and submerged. Veins of blackness pulse up across the walls. It stares across the bourne, pondering the unspeakable, then raises its lips to kiss the inverted surface, and exhales the shriek and torment that is its air.

The others hear it only as horror, inborn and sourceless, as buried within them as they are buried in Cil-Aujas. Mimara turns to their sudden silence. In a moment of madness it seems that she can see their hearts through their caged breasts, that she can see the eyes open . . .

Achamian falls to his knees, clutching his chest. He looks to her in pleading horror. Lord Kosoter stumbles backward into the corridor. Some clutch their faces; others begin to shriek and scream. Soma stands riven. Sarl cackles and bawls, his eyes pinched into lines between red wrinkles.

"I can't *seeeeee*!" the crease-faced sergeant gibbers. "I-look-I-look-I-look . . ."

The Unholy Seal rears glistening from the water, weeping strings of fire. It towers over them in leaning accusation. It roars, the sound so near, so ingrown that it seems they stand in the throat of a Demon-God. A voice claps through their souls, so loud it draws blood through the pores of their skin.

The Gates are no longer guarded.

Mimara is also on her knees, also shrieking, yet her fingers somehow find her purse, begin fumbling, pinching the Chorae that nearly killed the Wizard. She cringes beneath the looming aspect, a child beneath a collapsing city wall. She hugs her limbs against the piercing pleas of little mouths, the moaning masses of the damned . . .

And somehow lifts her Tear of God.

She knows not what she does. She knows only what she glimpsed in the slave chamber, that single slow heartbeat of light and revelation. She knows what she saw with the Judging Eye.

The Chorae burns as a sun in her fingers, making red wine of her hand and forearm, revealing the shadow of her bones, and yet drawing the eye instead of rebuking it, a light that does not blind.

"*I guard them!*" she weeps, standing frail beneath the white-bleached Seal. "*I hold the Gates!*"

Of all their ordeals, none would be so great as climbing the Great Medial Screw. Where the Sranc had taken their toll in blood and lives, and the Wight-in-the-Mountain, or whatever it was they had encountered in the closeted deeps, had taken its toll in terror and spirit, the endless stairs of the Screw took everything that remained: courage, strength, and endurance—endurance above all. Climbing. Climbing. Climbing. Clinging to seams as they picked their way over collapsed sections. Hurrying past the hundreds of gaping black portals. Bending back their faces to remind themselves of the sky they sought, to wonder at the way it waxed and grew.

The first time the high blue point they climbed toward began darkening they had despaired, fearing they had been shut in, until they realized that it was simply night. They had been buried so long they had forgotten the cycle of the days.

Sometimes, with the inscrutable ideograms struck into the curvature of the endlessly rising walls, it seemed they crawled through the curled inside of a scroll. Sometimes, given the way the Screw crossed the course of some natural shaft, here bricked, here hewn, Achamian was reminded of the canals of Momemn, where cut waterways linked natural estuaries. But always he was struck by the *ambition*, the marriage of patience and hubris that had made such a work possible. A stair as tall as a mountain. There was a kind of madness in the fact of the Screw, one that dwarfed even the famed Ziggurats of Shigek.

Mimara had said nothing in two days. When he tried coaxing words from her, she would simply gaze at him. Her lips would twitch, sometimes they would even part, but no words would come, and a kind of helpless remorse would dim her eyes. He spent quite some time trying to puzzle through what had happened, to make sense of the crazed image of her, holding nothing but a Chorae, the same existential pit she carried beneath her belt now, quailing beneath a horror that should have devoured her whole, from the flesh of her fingertips to the final spark of her soul.

He knew something of demons, Ciphrang, knew that when summoned, a Chorae could destroy their corporeal form. But what faced them had risen on a tide of unreality. Hell had come with him, the shade of Gin'yursis, the last Nonman King of Cil-Aujas, and he should have taken them all, Chorae or no Chorae.

But something had happened. *She* had happened.

Anasûrimbor Mimara, cursed with the Judging Eye.

Despite the pity that filled him, there was a reprieve in her misfortune. It could be no coincidence that she had come to him when she had. The wiles of the Whore were at work here, the treachery of Fate. The more he pondered it, the more it seemed she had been given. It was his doom to hunt down the origins of the Aspect-Emperor, to shed light on the darkness that came before him. Cil-Aujas had resolved that question.

There was a bad period when the last of the qirri drained from them, where the most they could do was lay gasping. Somehow they slept, and somehow they found themselves unharmed when they awoke. After that, the climb was sheer misery. Dizziness and nausea. Cramped limbs. Several fainted for the effort and were only saved by the wits of their fellows. Achamian paused several times to vomit spittle.

The downward wind grew as they climbed, so chill that Achamian added an air warming Huiritic Ring to the Surillic Point they needed to be sure of their footing—yet one more burden for his overtaxed soul. What had been a vast well above them became an endless pit below. Soon they could spy the source of the perpetual water that threaded the open spaces beyond the brink: ice and snow. It clotted the final tracts of the Screw, rising in shining humps against the cloudless plate of the sky.

After clambering across the first ice-sheathed steps and staring up across the angular slopes heaped across the stair, they realized their limbs could take them no farther. There was a look of grim confirmation in the dismay that deadened their eyes, as if they had known all along that Cil-Aujas would never relinquish them. Without explanation, Achamian bid them withdraw behind him. From behind glimmering Wards, he showed them what a Gnostic Wizard could do in the light of day. Ice and snow cracked and crashed, sloughed away in mountainous sheets, thundered so hard against his Wards that the stone of the stair even fractured beneath his feet. But he continued singing Abstractions, pure dispensations of force and light, and the geometries danced and twirled, striking and burning. And when he was done, bars of sunlight could be seen lancing through the mist, warming the bare black stone of Aenaratiol.

This was a kind of final knell for the Skin Eaters, a tipping point of comprehension. At last they understood the abyssal gap that had always existed between them, scalpers and Wizard. Achamian could see it in their sidelong glances. With the exception of their Captain, they began looking at him with an awe and reverence they had once reserved for Cleric.

And he felt an itch, something small and sharp against the buzz of his utter exhaustion . . . Some time passed before he recognized it: the creeping return of his guilt. These men, these strangers he would kill, now seemed his brothers.

It was no small thing to crawl out of the abyss, to rise from Hell to the very roof of the World. Though their eyes had long adjusted, they still stood blinking, scattered atop the snow-encrusted debris that ringed the opening to the Great Screw. It made Achamian, who stood arm in arm with Mimara, think of the first Men, savages of the plains, rubbing their eyes at what they could only comprehend as a blessing.

With light comes life. With sky comes freedom.

The Halls of Cil-Aujas, the dread Black Halls, had at last relinquished them.

Achamian looked to the remnants of their company, knowing they had reached a moment of decision. Aside from Lord Kosoter, only Soma, blessed with the luck of the daft, seemed unscathed. Sarl appeared intact in body but continued to betray a disordered soul—even now he grinned and rocked from heel to heel. Pokwas had gained strength on the climb, despite continuously bleeding from his scalp. The other veteran Skin Eaters, Xonghis, Sutadra, and Galian, wore septic bandages on their arms and thighs but seemed able enough. Of those the Bitten had called the Herd, all three survivors were Galeoth—Conger, Wonard, and Hameron—men Achamian had not known until the arduous climb up the Screw. Wonard was already showing signs of infection, and Conger seemed to hop more than walk. Hameron wept whenever Lord Kosoter's distraction afforded.

Their hair whipping in the wind, bereft of everything save their hauberks and their swords, the company stood, blank before the vista extending about them. Their trials had stained and stamped them: the purplish smear of Sranc blood, the rusty blots of their own, innumerable little cuts across their shins and knuckles, the mottling of sweat-and-dust-soaked skin. Though their stares were dead for fatigue, there was a madness in the quick twitches with which they cast them across the panorama.

They stood in the heart of Aenaratiol's extinct crater, on an island heaped with broken columns and gutted walls. A frozen lake surrounded them, gleaming black where not covered with dunes of snow. More ruins climbed the crater walls, a veritable city of them, walls stacked upon walls. Vacant windows gazed out from them, as black as the labyrinth below, melancholy. Above, beyond the crater rim, taller peaks rose bright and white against the blue, trailing chalk streamers of snow.

The sun gleamed cold and white.

Xonghis raised a blood-dirtied hand against the glare. "That way . . ." he said without emotion. He pointed over the bottomless plummet of the Screw to the crater wall behind them, to where the line of the rim rose like a shark or Sranc tooth. "I recognize that from when we first approached the mountain . . . That way is *home*." He turned back to the direction they had faced when they first ascended. "That is the Long Side."

Achamian caught his breath.

He had not forgotten his dream in the bowel of the mountain, the dream he had sought in vain for so many years. But he had not remembered it either. Circumstances can blot the significance of our revelations as easily as otherwise. What did it matter, the realization of ardent desires, when all was death and damnation?

"*Keep it, old friend. Make it your deepest secret . . .*"

But circumstances had changed. They had escaped Cil-Aujas, and the revelatory memories now glowed through the fog of his privations. He had dreamed it! On the very threshold of hell he had dreamed his long-sought answer. A map, two thousand years old, slumbering beneath ruin and wilderness. A map to Ishuäl, and to the truth of the Aspect-Emperor.

"*Bury it*," the ancient High-King had said. "*Bury it in the Coffers . . .*"

In Marrow, Achamian had mentioned the Coffers the way a trapper baits his snare, as a crude goad meant to drive crude men. But now . . .

His lie. Fate was making his lie true.

The surviving Skin Eaters glanced at Xonghis, then surveyed the competing distances. But this moment, Achamian knew, had already been decided: There were no forks in the road before them. The Whore was driving them like slaves beaten toward a captor's capital.

"Yes . . ." Sarl coughed and laughed. "*Yesss!* The Coffers, boys! The Coffers-yes!"

And there it was. Somehow they were content to let a madman sound and settle the issue. Gazing through shanks of steel-grey hair, Lord Kosoter took the first downward step.

Mobbed beneath the heat radiating from the crimson glow of the Huiritic Ring, the company followed him, trundled down a slope of snow-packed ruin, onto the flat expanse of the frozen lake. A thin carpet of snow covered its nearer reaches, so they didn't see the ancient dead frozen beneath its surface until they had travelled a good portion of its length. Some were little more than shadows, either because the ice was clouded or they lay so deep. Others hung mere inches below the surface, strangely chapped and withered, like dead wasps in cocoons. The eyes looked like the pads of severed fingers. The mouths were all pried open, as though still, after all these ages, trying to draw air from the sky.

The limbs were frozen in innumerable poses of falling. All of them were women and children.

No one spoke as they limped and tramped across them. Whatever curiosity they possessed had been beaten from them, and dread had become a constant companion.

They climbed what stairs they could find, up through the remnants of ancient pleasure-palaces. They saw all the same motifs and architectural flourishes, the same crazed density of image, that had so awed them in the galleries below. But for some reason it seemed tragic, pathetic even, exposed as it was by cracked walls and vanished ceilings. The work of a race that had gone insane for staring inward.

When they reached the summit of the crater rim, the inversion was so utter, the contrast to the buried depths so severe, that several of them fell to clinging whatever the ice or stone afforded. The dishevelled enormity of the Osthwai Mountains unfolded before them, glaring in the crisp high-sky light, great snow-sheathed horns receding across the horizon. The giddy sweep and plunge of endless open spaces encircled them, fluttered in their bellies. For a time at least, it was too much for newly born men.

But there was no question of stopping long. No matter how hard they sucked they could not draw enough air. Despite the heat shed by the Huiritic Ring, their skin purpled and their lips turned blue.

And they were starving.

But as they were about to descened, one of them called out, Soma, pointing back the way they came, at the ruins heaped about the rim of the Great Medial Screw. Achamian crowded with the others, peering to look, but his old eyes could make out nothing more than a speck crossing the snow-swept iron of the frozen lake. A lone figure trudging in their wake . . .

And at long last Mimara broke her silence.

"Cleric," she said.

Interlude: Momemn

The sound of discord carried on the breeze. A riot in faraway streets.

Kelmomas stood with his chin on the balcony rail, staring out over the Enclousure at the stately passage of clouds crossing the light of a moon too low on the horizon to be seen. Woollen blue wisped across the starred firmament, condensing into bellies of black.

The Nail of Heaven flared white from a sailing summit. A distant chorus of shrieks and bellows signalled another brutal torch-lit incursion.

He had no name for his rapture. Calm and slow breathing. Stationary. Stationary amid the clash of all things. The repose of a soul peering out from the world's shrouded centre. The unmoved mover.

The ruler unseen.

Across the sky he heard a many-throated song of defiance crumbling into cries of outrage, shouts of fear and dismay. The heave of hundreds breaking. The clash of arms.

You, the voice murmured. *You made this*.

"What are you doing out there?" his mother called out from the dark entrance to his room. She pulled aside the sheers to see him better.

"I'm scared, Mommy."

Her smile was too fraught to be reassuring.

"Shush. You're safe. They're not that many."

She held out an arm and he fell into it, hugging her about the waist. It was one of the innumerable habits linking little boys to their mothers. They walked to his bed together, into the light cast by a solitary hanging lamp. His new nurse, Emansi, had snuffed all the others.

The lantern's flame was a point that blistered to look at, that could not be touched, that threw all the shadows outward, away from the burnished ring of illuminated things. The crimson embroidery—ducks with interlocking wings—gleamed along the folds of his half-drawn covers. The mosaic of dancing bears stretched in a floriated arc into the darkness of the ceiling.

She pulled aside the covers and guided him into the folds with a gentle hand—yet one more thing he cherished with the ferocity of tears. Then she crawled in after him, cupped his small body in the warm palm of hers. She told herself, he knew, that she came here for his sake, that the loss of a brother was trauma enough, let alone the loss of a twin. Think of how intense their bond had been in infancy!

This was what she told herself, he knew.

He closed his eyes, followed the inner drift to the hazy outskirts of sleep. Her love seemed to encase him, to hold him hot and dry and safe. There was a nothingness in her arms, an oblivion indistinguishable from bliss. All cares fell away and with them, the cold-pocketed world that was their foundation. There was only here. There was only now. Another point of lantern-light, though no longer blistering, because he was the illumination.

Let others burn their fingers. Let them turn aside their eyes.

He rolled and snuggle-wriggled so that he could face her on the pillow. They stared into each other's eyes, mother and son, for several long moments. The immediacy of her was so vivid, so close, that nothing else could ever be as real. She was the only thing.

He ran a fingertip along the embroidered lip of the top

blanket, a small proof of texture. He bent his face into the semblance of petulant concentration.

"I miss Sammi . . ." he lied.

She swallowed and blinked. "Me too, sweetling. Me too."

A part of him, the snake-sneaky part, laughed. Poor Samarmas. Poor-poor Samarmas.

"I didn't get to see Father."

Her eyes hardened beneath a film of tears.

"I'm sorry, Kel. We're at war. Your father, he . . . he has to make sacrifices. We all have to make sacrifices. Even darling little boys like you . . ."

She fell silent and remote, but he could see her thoughts clear enough. *He does not mourn him*. My *husband does not mourn our son*.

"Uncle Maithanet," the little Prince began, "he . . ."

A kind of wariness crept into her expression. Her eyes blinked away the fog of self-pity and suddenly became alert. "What about your uncle?"

"Nothing."

"Kel. What about your uncle?"

"He . . . watches you funny."

"What do you mean *watches*? How?"

"Is he angry at you, Mommy?"

"No. He's your uncle."

An inward look of cycling thoughts and worries.

"Which means he's my brother," she added, but more for her own benefit, he knew, than for his. She reached out to cup his cheek in her left hand, the one bruised by what she called her "ancient tattoo."

The Prince-Imperial fluttered his lids as though overpowered by warmth and weariness. "But he has more power . . ." he whispered, pretending to fall asleep. He would open his eyes later, when her breathing slipped into the long trough of dreams.

Unseen rulers never slumbered, not truly.

Character And Faction Glossary

House Anasûrimbor

Kellhus, the Aspect-Emperor.

Maithanet, Shriah of the Thousand Temples, half-brother to Kellhus.

Esmenet, Empress of the Three Seas.

Mimara, Esmenet's estranged daughter from her days as a prostitute.

Moënghus, son of Kellhus and his first wife, Serwë, eldest of the Prince-Imperials.

Kayûtas, eldest son of Kellhus and Esmenet, General of the Kidruhil.

Theliopa, eldest daughter of Kellhus and Esmenet.

Serwa, second daughter of Kellhus and Esmenet, Grandmistress of the Swayal Sisterhood.

Inrilatas, second son of Kellhus and Esmenet, insane and imprisoned on the Andiamine Heights.

Kelmomas, third son of Kellhus and Esmenet, twin of Samarmas.

Samarmas, fourth son of Kellhus and Esmenet, the idiot twin of Kelmomas.

The Cult of Yatwer

The traditional Cult of the slave and menial castes, taking as its primary scriptures *The Chronicle of the Tusk*, the *Higarata*, and the *Sinyatwa*. Yatwer is the Goddess of the earth and fertility.

Psatma Nannaferi, Mother-Supreme of the Cult, a position long outlawed by the Thousand Temples.

Hanamem Sharacinth, Matriarch of the Cult.

Sharhild, High-Priestess of the Cult.

Vethenestra, Chalfantic Oracle.

Eleva, High-Priestess of the Cult.

Maharta, High-Priestess of the Cult.

Phoracia, High-Priestess of the Cult.

Aethiola, High-Priestess of the Cult.

The Imperial Precincts

Biaxi Sankas, Patridomos of House Biaxi and an important member of the New Congregate.

Imhailas, Exalt-Captain of the Eöthic Guard.

Ngarau, eunuch Grand Seneschal from the days of the Ikurei Dynasty.

Phinersa, Holy Master of Spies.

Porsi, caste-slave nursemaid to Kelmomas and Samarmas.

Thopsis, eunuch Master of Imperial Protocol.

Vem-Mithriti, Grandmaster of the Imperial Saik and Vizier-in-Proxy.

Werjau, Prime-Nascenti and Judge-Absolute of the Ministrate.

The Great Ordeal

Varalt Sorweel, only son of Harweel.

Varalt Harweel, King of Sakarpus.

Captain Harnilias, commanding officer of the Scions.

Zsoronga ut Nganka'kull, Successor-Prince of Zeüm and hostage of the Aspect-Emperor.

Obetegwa, Senior Obligate of Zsoronga.

Porsparian, Shigeki slave given to Sorweel.

Thanteus Eskeles, Mandate Schoolman and tutor to Varalt Sorweel.

Nersei Proyas, King of Conriya and Exalt-General of the Great Ordeal.

Coithus Saubon, King of Caraskand and Exalt-General of the Great Ordeal.

The Scalpoi

Drusus Achamian, former Mandate Schoolman, lover of the Empress, teacher of the Aspect-Emperor, now the only Wizard in the Three Seas.

Idrusus Geraus, Achamian's Galeoth slave.

Lord Kosoter, Captain of the Skin Eaters, Ainoni caste-noble, Veteran of the First Holy War.

Incariol, mysterious Nonman Erratic.

Sarl, Sergeant of the Skin Eaters, longtime companion of Lord Kosoter.

Kiampas, Sergeant of the Skin Eaters, former Nansur officer.

Galian, Skin Eater, former Nansur Columnary.

Pokwas (Pox), Skin Eater, disgraced Zeümi Sword-Dancer.

Oxwora (Ox), Skin Eater, Thunyeri son of Yalgrota.

Somandutta (Soma), Skin Eater, Nilnameshi caste-noble adventurer.

Moraubon, Skin Eater, former Shrial Priest.

Sutadra (Soot), Skin Eater, rumoured to be a Fanim heretic.

Xonghis, Skin Eater, former Imperial Tracker.

Ancient Kûniüri

Anasûrimbor Celmomas II (2089–2146), High-King of Kûniüri and tragic principal of the First Apocalypse.

Anasûrimbor Nau-Cayûti (2119–2140), youngest son of Celmomas and tragic hero of the First Apocalypse.

Seswatha (2089–2168), Grandmaster of the Sohonc, lifelong friend of Celmomas, founder of the Mandate, and determined foe of the No-God.

The Dûnyain

A monastic sect whose members have repudiated history and animal appetite in the hope of finding absolute enlightenment through the control of all desire and circumstance. For two thousand years they have hidden in the ancient fortress of Ishuäl, breeding their members for motor reflexes and intellectual acuity.

The Consult

The cabal of magi and generals that survived the death of the No-God in 2155 and has laboured ever since to bring about his return in the so-called Second Apocalypse.

The Thousand Temples

The institution that provides the ecclesiastical framework of Zaudunyani Inrithism.

The Ministrate

The institution that oversees the Judges, the New Imperium's religious secret police.

The Schools

The collective name given to the various academies of sorcerers. The first Schools, both in the Ancient North and the Three Seas, arose as a response to the Tusk's condemnation of sorcery. The so-called Major Schools are: the Swayal Compact, the Scarlet Spires, the Mysunsai, the Imperial Saik, the Vokalati, and the Mandate (see below).

The Mandate

Gnostic School founded by Seswatha in 2156 to continue the war against the Consult and to protect the Three Seas from the return of the No-God, Mog-Pharau. Incorporated into the New Imperium in 4112. All Mandate Schoolmen relive Seswatha's experience of the First Apocalypse in their dreams.

What Has Come Before . . .

Wars, as a rule, fall within the compass of history. They mark the pitch of competing powers, the end of some and the ascendency of others, the ebb and flow of dominance across the ages. But there is a war that Men have waged for so long they have forgotten the languages they first used to describe it. A war that makes mere skirmishes out of the destruction of tribes and nations.

There is no name for this war; Men cannot reference what transcends the short interval of their comprehension. It began when they were little more than savages roaming the wilds, in an age before script or bronze. An Ark, vast and golden, toppled from the void, scorching the horizon, throwing up a ring of mountains with the violence of its descent. And from it crawled the dread and monstrous Inchoroi, a race who had come to seal the World against the Heavens, and so save the obscenities they called their souls.

The Nonmen held sway in those ancient days, a long-lived people that surpassed Men not only in beauty and intellect, but in wrath and jealousy as well. With their Ishroi heroes and Quya mages, they fought titanic battles and stood vigilant during epochal truces. They endured the Inchoroi weapons of light. They survived the treachery of the Aporetics, who provided their foe with thousands of sorcery-killing Chorae. They overcame the horrors their enemy crafted to people his legions: the Sranc, the Bashrag, and, most fearsome of all, the Wracu. But their avarice at last betrayed them. After centuries of intermittent war, they made peace with the invaders in return for the Gift of ageless immortality—a Gift that was in fact a fell weapon, the Plague of Wombs.

In the end, the Nonmen hunted the Inchoroi to the brink of annihilation. Exhausted, culled of their strength, they retired to their underworld Mansions to mourn the loss of their wives and daughters, and the inevitable extinction of their glorious race. Their surviving mages sealed the Ark, which they had come to call Min-Uroikas, and hid it from the world with devious glamours. And from the eastern mountains, the first tribes of Men began claiming the lands they had abandoned—Men who had never known the yoke of slavery. Of the surviving Ishroi Kings, some fought, only to be dragged under by the tide of numbers, while others simply left their great gates unguarded, bared their necks to the licentious fury of a lesser race.

And so human history was born, and perhaps the Nameless War would have ended with the fading of its principals. But the golden Ark still existed, and the lust for knowledge has ever been a cancer in the hearts of Men.

Centuries passed, and the mantle of human civilization crept along the great river basins of Eärwa and outward, bringing bronze where there had been flint, cloth where there had been skins, and writing where there had been recital. Great cities rose to teeming life. The wilds gave way to cultivated horizons.

Nowhere were Men more bold in their works, or more overweening in their pride, than in the North, where commerce with the Nonmen allowed them to outstrip their more swarthy cousins to the South. In the legendary city of Sauglish, those who could discern the joints of existence founded the first sorcerous Schools. As their learning and power waxed, a reckless few turned to the rumours they had heard whispered by their Nonman teachers—rumours of the great golden Ark. The wise were quick to see the peril, and the Schoolmen of Mangaecca, who coveted secrets above all others, were censured, and finally outlawed.

But it was too late. Min-Uroikas was found—occupied.

The fools discovered and awakened the last two surviving Inchoroi, Aurax and Aurang, who had concealed themselves in the labyrinthine recesses of the Ark. And at their hoary knees the outlaw Schoolmen learned that damnation, the burden all sorcerers bore, need not be inevitable. They learned that the world could be shut against the judgment of Heaven. So they forged a common purpose with the twin abominations, a Consult, and bent their cunning to the aborted designs of the Inchoroi.

They relearned the principles of the material, the Tekne. They mastered the manipulations of the flesh. And after generations of study and searching, after filling the pits of Min-Uroikas with innumerable corpses, they realized the most catastrophic of the Inchoroi's untold depravities: Mog-Pharau, the No-God.

They made themselves slaves to better destroy the world.

And so the Nameless War raged anew. What has come to be called the First Apocalypse destroyed the great Norsirai nations of the North, laying ruin to the greatest glories of Men. But for Seswatha, the Grandmaster of the Gnostic School of Sohonc, the entire world would have been lost. At his urging, Anasûrimbor Celmomas, the High-King of the North's mightiest nation, Kûniüri, called on his tributaries and allies to join him in a holy war against Min-Uroikas, which Men now called Golgotterath. But his Ordeal foundered, and the might of the Norsirai perished. Seswatha fled south to the Ketyai nations of the Three Seas, bearing the greatest of the legendary Inchoroi weapons, the

Heron Spear. With Anaxophus, the High-King of Kyraneas, he met the No-God on the Plains of Mengedda, and by dint of valour and providence, overcame the dread Whirlwind.

The No-God was dead, but his slaves and his stronghold remained. Golgotterath had not fallen, and the Consult, blasted by ages of unnatural life, continued to plot their salvation.

The years passed, and the Men of the Three Seas forgot, as Men inevitably do, the horrors endured by their fathers. Empires rose and empires fell. The Latter Prophet, Inri Sejenus, reinterpreted the Tusk, the First Scripture, and within a few centuries, the faith of Inrithism, organized and administered by the Thousand Temples and its spiritual leader, the Shriah, came to dominate the entire Three Seas. The great Anagogic Schools arose in response to the Inrithi persecution of sorcery. Using Chorae, the Inrithi warred against them, attempting to purify the Three Seas.

Then Fane, the self-proclaimed Prophet of the so-called Solitary God, united the Kianene, the desert peoples of the Great Carathay, and declared war against the Tusk and the Thousand Temples. After centuries and several jihads, the Fanim and their eyeless sorcerer-priests, the Cishaurim, conquered nearly all the western Three Seas, including the holy city of Shimeh, the birthplace of Inri Sejenus. Only the moribund remnants of the Nansur Empire continued to resist them.

War and strife ruled the South. The two great faiths of Inrithism and Fanimry skirmished, though trade and pilgrimage were tolerated when commercially convenient. The great families and nations vied for military and mercantile dominance. The minor and major Schools squabbled and plotted. And the Thousand Temples pursued earthly ambitions under the leadership of corrupt and ineffectual Shriahs.

The First Apocalypse had become little more than legend. The Consult and the No-God had dwindled into myth, something old wives tell small children. After two thousand years, only the Schoolmen of the Mandate, who relived the Apocalypse each night through the eyes of Seswatha, could recall the horror of Mog-Pharau. Though the mighty and the learned considered them fools, their possession of the Gnosis, the sorcery of the Ancient North, commanded respect and mortal envy. Driven by nightmares, they wandered the labyrinths of power, scouring the Three Seas for signs of their ancient and implacable foe—for the Consult.

And as always, they found nothing.

Some argued that the Consult, which had survived the armed might of empires, had finally succumbed to the toll of ages. Others that they had turned inward, seeking less arduous means to forestall their damnation. But since the Sranc had multiplied across the northern wilds, no expedition could be sent to Golgotterath to settle the matter. The Mandate alone knew of the Nameless War. They alone stood guard, but beneath a pall of ignorance.

The Thousand Temples elected a new, enigmatic Shriah, a man called Maithanet, who demanded the Inrithi recapture the holy city of the Latter Prophet, Shimeh, from the Fanim. Word of his call spread across the Three Seas and beyond, and faithful from all the great Inrithi nations—Galeoth, Thunyerus, Ce Tydonn, Conriya, High Ainon and their tributaries—travelled to the city of Momemn, the capital of the Nansurium, to swear their swords and their lives to Inri Sejenus. To become Men of the Tusk.

And so was born the First Holy War. Internal feuds plagued the campaign from the very beginning, for there was no shortage of those who would bend the holy war to their selfish ends. Not until the Second Seige of Caraskand and the Circumfixion of one of their own would this fractiousness be overcome. Not until the Men of the Tusk found a *living* prophet to follow—a man who could see into the hearts of Men. A man like a god.

Anasûrimbor Kellhus.

Far to the north, in the very penumbra of Golgotterath, a group of ascetics called the Dûnyain had concealed themselves in Ishuäl, the secret redoubt of the Kûniüric High-Kings. For two thousand year they had pursued their sacred study, breeding for reflex and intellect, training in the ways of limb, thought, and face—all for the sake of reason, the Logos. In the effort to transform themselves into the perfect expression of the Logos, the Dûnyain had dedicated their entire existence to mastering the irrationalities of history, custom, and passion—all those things that determine human thought. In this way, they believed, they would eventually grasp what they called the Absolute, and so become true self-moving souls.

But their glorious isolation had been interrupted. After thirty years of exile, one of their number, Anasûrimbor Moënghus, reappeared in their dreams, demanding they send to him his son, Kellhus. Knowing only that Moënghus dwelt in a distant city called Shimeh, the Dûnyain dispatched Kellhus on an arduous journey through lands long abandoned by Men—sent him to kill his father.

But Moënghus knew the world in ways his cloistered brethren could not. He knew well the revelations that awaited his son, for they had been his revelations thirty years previous. He knew that Kellhus would discover sorcery, whose existence the forefathers of the Dûnyain had suppressed. He knew that given his abilities, Men would be little more than children to him, that Kellhus would see their thoughts in the nuances of their expression, and that with mere words he would be able to exact any devotion, any sacrifice. He knew, moreover, that Kellhus would encounter the Consult, who hid behind faces that only Dûnyain eyes could see—that he would come to see what Men with their blinkered souls could not: the Nameless War.

For centuries the Consult had evaded their old foe, the School of Mandate, by creating doppelgangers, spies who could take on any face, any voice, without resorting to sorcery and its telltale Mark. By capturing and torturing these abominations, Moënghus learned that the Consult had not abandoned their ancient plot to shut the world against Heaven, that within a score of years they would be able to resurrect the No-God and bring about a second Apocalypse. For years he walked the innumerable paths of the Probability Trance, plotting future after future, searching for the thread of act and consequence that would save the world. For years he crafted his Thousandfold Thought.

Moënghus knew, and so prepared the way for Kellhus. He sent out his world-born son, Maithanet, to seize the Thousand Temples from within, so that he might craft the First Holy War, the weapon Kellhus would need to seize absolute power and so unite the Three Seas against the doom that was their future. What he did not know, could not know, was that Kellhus would see *further* than him, that he would think beyond his Thousandfold Thought . . .

And go mad.

Little more than an impoverished wayfarer when he first joined the Holy War, Kellhus used his bearing, intellect, and insight to convince ever more Men of the Tusk that he was the Warrior-Prophet, come to save mankind from the Second Apocalypse. He understood that Men, who embrace baseless beliefs the way drunkards imbibe wine, would render anything to him, so long as they believed he could save their souls. He also befriended the Schoolman the Mandate had dispatched to watch the Holy War, Drusas Achamian, knowing that the Gnosis, the sorcery of the Ancient North, would provide him with inestimable power. And he seduced Achamian's lover, Esmenet, knowing that her intellect made her the ideal vessel for his seed—for sons strong enough to bear the onerous burden of Dûnyain blood.

By the time the battle-hardened remnants of the campaign at last invested Holy Shimeh, he possessed the host body and soul. The Men of the Tusk had become his Zaudunyani, his Tribe of Truth. While the Holy War assailed the city's walls, he confronted his father, Moënghus, mortally wounding him, explaining that only with his death could the Thousandfold Thought be realized. Days later Anasûrimbor Kellhus was acclaimed Aspect-Emperor, the first in a millennium, by none other than the Shriah of the Thousand Temples, his half-brother, Maithanet. Even the School of Mandate, who saw his coming as the fulfillment of their most hallowed prophecies, knelt and kissed his knee.

But he had made one mistake. He had allowed Cnaiür urs Skiötha, a Scylvendi chieftain who had accompanied him on his trek to the Three Seas, to learn too much of his true nature. Before his death, the barbarian revealed these truths to Drusas Achamian, who had harboured heartbreaking suspicions of his own.

Before the eyes of the entire Holy War, Achamian repudiated Kellhus, whom he had worshipped; Esmenet, whom he had loved; and the Mandate masters he had served. Then he fled into the wilderness, becoming the world's only sorcerer without a school. A Wizard.

Now, after twenty years of conversion and bloodshed, Anasûrimbor Kellhus plots the conclusion of his father's Thousandfold Thought. His New Empire spans the entirety of the Three Seas, from the legendary fortress of Auvangshei on the frontiers of Zeüm to the shrouded head-waters of the River Sayut, from the sweltering coasts of Kutnarmu to the wild rim of the Osthwai Mountains—all the lands that had once been Fanim or Inrithi. It was easily the equal of the old Ceneian Empire in terms of geographical extent, and likely far greater when it came to population. A hundred great cities, and almost as many languages. A dozen proud nations. Thousands of years of mangled history.

The Nameless War is nameless no longer. Men call it the Great Ordeal

Acknowledgements

Some books aim your questions wide and thin, while others, I've discovered, aim them narrow and deep. First and foremost, I need to thank my lovely wife, Sharron, who has become my conscience in all things. Need I list the other usual suspects?

Of course I do.

My brother, Bryan Bakker; my agent, Chris Lotts; my English language editors, Barbara Berson, Laura Shin, David Shoemaker, and Darren Nash; and my dear friends Roger Eichorn and Gary Wassner. With so many judging eyes, both shrewd and gifted, no writer could go wrong.

The Kellian Empire in 4132 Year-of-the-Tusk

Anasûrimbor Kellhus was proclaimed Aspect-Emperor after the defeat of Fanayal ab Kascamandri at Shimeh in 4112. Both the Kianene and the Nansur empires collapsed shortly thereafter, leaving him the undisputed master of the Western Three Seas. Thirteen years of internecine and expansionist war followed. Many factors were instrumental to his success, including his martial brilliance and the fanaticism of his Zaudunyani Inrithi. But it would be his control of the Thousand Temples (which allowed him to so quickly consolidate his gains) and his alliance with the School of Mandate (which gave him the sorcerous advantage on every field of battle) that would prove decisive. The so-called Unification Wars ended with the final capitulation of Nilnamesh in 4126, rendering Anasûrimbor Kellhus the greatest conqueror since Far Antiquity. Not even the legendary Triamis the Great (2456–2577) achieved so much in so short a time.

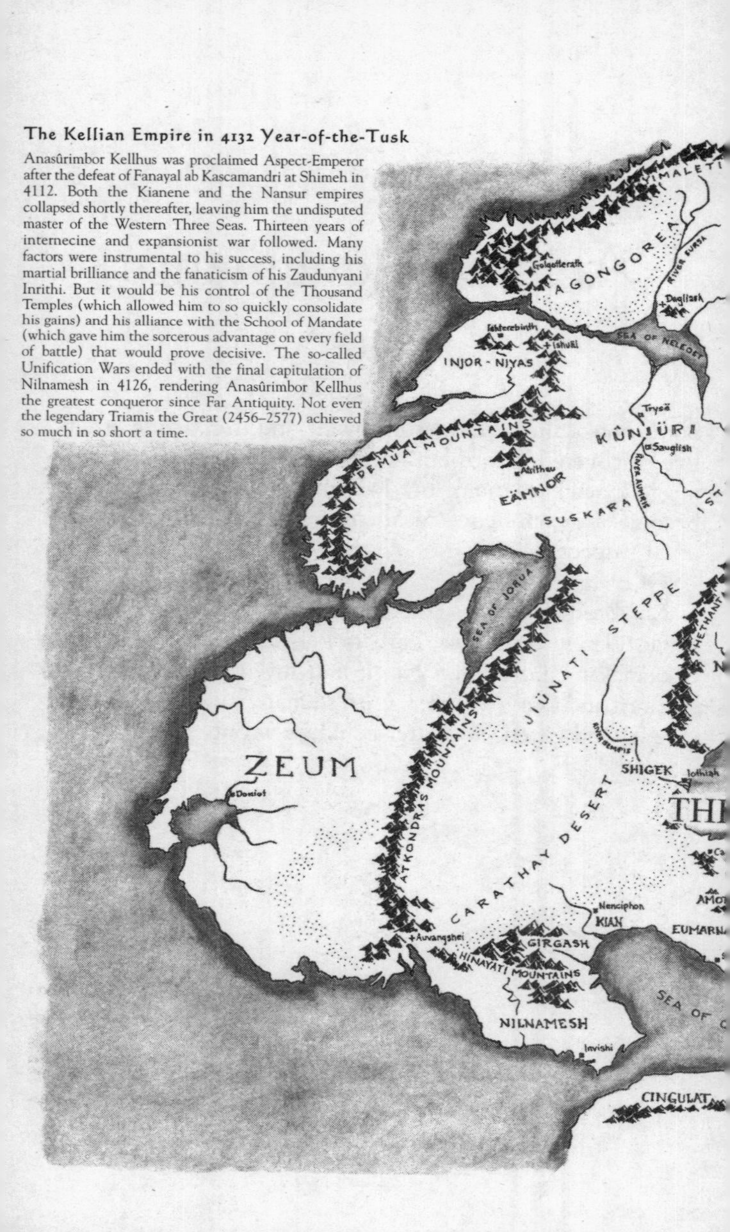

EÄNNA
GREAT KAYARSUS
AKKSERSIA
Myclai
SEA OF CERISH
MEORN WILDERNESS
OSTHWAI MOUNTAINS
THE LONG SIDE
GALEOTH
Oswenta
Marrow
Cil-Aujas
THUNYERUS
ARAXES MOUNTAINS
Meigeiri
CE TYDONN
CENGEMIŚ
JEKHIA
FAMIRI
EMPIRE
AINON
Aöknyssus
Carythusal
CONRIYA
SANSOR
Atyersus
SEA OF NYRANISAS
CIRONJ
GREAT KAYARSUS
KUTNARMU
R.Scott Bakker 2008

extras

www.orbitbooks.net

about the author

R. Scott Bakker is a student of literature, history, philosophy and ancient languages. He divides his time between writing philosophy and fantasy, though he often has difficulty distinguishing between them. He lives in London, Ontario.

Find out more about R. Scott Bakker and other Orbit authors by registering for the free monthly newsletter at www.orbitbooks.net

If you enjoyed
THE JUDGING EYE

look out for

SHADOW AND BETRAYAL

book one of The Long Price

by

Daniel Abraham

Prologue

Otah took the blow on the ear, the flesh opening under the rod. Tahi-kvo, Tahi the teacher, pulled the thin lacquered wood through the air with a fluttering sound like bird wings. Otah's discipline held. He did not shift or cry out. Tears welled in his eyes, but his hands remained in a pose of greeting.

"Again," Tahi-kvo barked. "And correctly!"

"We are honored by your presence, most high Dai-kvo." Otah said sweetly, as if it were the first time he had attempted the ritual phrase. The old man sitting before the fire considered him closely, then adopted a pose of acceptance. Tahi-kvo made a sound of satisfaction in the depths of his throat.

Otah bowed, holding still for three breaths and hoping that Tahi-kvo wouldn't strike him for trembling. The moment stretched, and Otah nearly let his eyes stray to his teacher. It was the old man with his ruined whisper who at last spoke the words that ended the ritual and released him.

"Go, disowned child, and attend to your studies."

Otah turned and walked humbly out of the room. Once he had pulled the thick wooden door closed behind him and walked down the chill hallway toward the common rooms, he gave himself permission to touch his new wound.

The other boys were quiet as he passed through the stone halls of the school, but several times their gazes held him and his new shame. Only the older boys in the black robes of Milah-kvo's disciples laughed at him. Otah took himself to the quarters where all the boys in his cohort slept. He removed the ceremonial gown, careful not to touch it with blood, and washed the wound in cold water. The stinging cream for cuts and scrapes was in an earthenware jar beside the water basin. He took two fingers and slathered the vinegar-smelling ointment onto the open flesh of his ear. Then, not for the first time since he had come to the school, he sat on his spare, hard bunk and wept.

"This boy," the Dai-kvo said as he took up the porcelain bowl of tea. Its heat was almost uncomfortable. "He holds some promise?"

"Some," Tahi allowed as he leaned the lacquered rod against the wall and took the seat beside his master.

"He seems familiar."

"Otah Machi. Sixth son of the Khai Machi."

"I recall his brothers. Also boys of some promise. What became of them?"

"They spent their years, took the brand, and were turned out. Most are. We have three hundred in the school now and forty in the black under Milah-kvo's care. Sons of the Khaiem or the ambitious families of the urkhaiem."

"So many? I see so few."

Tahi took a pose of agreement, the cant of his wrists giving it a nuance that might have been sorrow or apology.

"Not many are both strong enough and wise. And the stakes are high."

The Dai-kvo sipped his tea and considered the fire.

"I wonder," the old man said, "how many realize we are teaching them nothing."

"We teach them all. Letters, numbers. Any of them could take a trade after they leave the school."

"But nothing of use. Nothing of poetry. Nothing of the andat."

"If they realize that, most high, they're halfway to your door. And for the ones we turn away . . . It's better, most high."

"Is it?"

Tahi shrugged and looked into the fire. He looked older, the Dai-kvo thought, especially about the eyes. But he had met Tahi as a rude youth many years before. The age he saw there now, and the cruelty, were seeds he himself had cultivated.

"When they have failed, they take the brand and make their own fates," Tahi said.

"We take away their only hope of rejoining their families, of taking a place at the courts of the Khaiem. They have no family. They cannot control the andat," the Dai-kvo said. "We throw these boys away much as their fathers have. What becomes of them, I wonder?"

"Much the same as becomes of anyone, I imagine. The ones from low families of the urkhaiem are hardly worse off than when they came. The sons of the Khaiem . . . once they take the brand, they cannot inherit, and it saves them from being killed for their blood rights. That alone is a gift in its way."

It was true. Every generation saw the blood of the Khaiem spilled. It was the way of the Empire. And in times when all three of a Khai's acknowledged sons slaughtered one another, the high families of the urkhaiem unsheathed their knives, and cities were caught for a time in fits of violence from which the poets held themselves apart like priests at a dog fight. These boys in the school's care were exempt from those wars at only the price of everything they had known in their short lives. And yet . . .

"Disgrace is a thin gift," the Dai-kvo said.

Tahi, his old student who had once been a boy like these, sighed.

"It's what we can offer."

* * *

The Dai-kvo left in the morning just after dawn, stepping through the great bronze doors that opened only for him. Otah stood in the ranks of his cohort, still holding a pose of farewell. Behind him, someone took the chance of scratching—Otah could hear the shifting sound of fingers against cloth. He didn't look back. Two of the oldest of Milahkvo's black robes pulled the great doors closed.

In the dim winter light that filtered through high-set, narrow windows, Otah could see the bustle of the black robes taking charge of the cohorts. The day's tasks varied. The morning might be spent working in the school—repairing walls or washing laundry or scraping ice from the garden walkways that no one seemed to travel besides the boys set to tend them. The evening would be spent in study. Numbers, letters, religion, history of the Old Empire, the Second Empire, the War, the cities of the Khaiem. And more often these last weeks, one of the two teachers would stand at the back of the room while one of the black robes lectured and questioned. Milah-kvo would sometimes interrupt and tell jokes or take the lecture himself, discussing things the black robes never spoke of. Tahi-kvo would only observe and punish. All of Otah's cohort bore the marks of the lacquered stick.

Riit-kvo, one of the oldest of the black robes, led Otah and his cohort to the cellars. For hours as the sun rose unseen, Otah swept dust from stones that seemed still cold from the last winter and then washed them with water and rags until his knuckles were raw. Then Riit-kvo called them to order, considered them, slapped one boy whose stance was not to his standards, and marched them to the dining hall. Otah looked neither forward nor back, but focused on the shoulders of the boy ahead of him.

The midday meal was cold meat, yesterday's bread, and a thin barley soup that Otah treasured because it was warm. Too soon, Riit called them to wash their bowls and knives and follow him. Otah found himself at the front of the line—an unenviable place—and so was the first to step into the cold listening room with its stone benches and narrow windows that had never known glass. Tahi-kvo was waiting there for them.

None of them knew why the round-faced, scowling teacher had taken an interest in the cohort, though speculations were whispered in the dark of their barracks. The Dai-kvo had chosen one of them to go and study the secrets of the andat, to become one of the poets, gain power even higher than the Khaiem, and skip over the black robes of Milah-kvo entirely. Or one of their families had repented sending their child, however minor in the line of succession, to the school and was in negotiation to forgo the branding and take their disowned son back into the fold.

Otah had listened, but believed none of the stories. They were the fantasies of the frightened and the weak, and he knew that if he clung to one, it would shatter him. Dwelling in the misery of the school and hoping for nothing beyond survival was the only way to keep his soul from flying apart. He would endure his term and be turned out into the world. This was his third year at the school. He was twelve now, and near the halfway point of his time. And today was another evil to be borne as the day before and the day ahead. To think too far in the past or the future was dangerous. Only when he let his dreams loose did he think of learning the secrets of the andat, and that happened so rarely as to call itself never.

Riit-kvo, his eyes on the teacher at the back as much as on the students, began to declaim the parable of the Twin Dragons of Chaos. It was a story Otah knew, and he found his mind wandering. Through the stone arch of the window, Otah could see a crow hunched on a high branch. It reminded him of something he could not quite recall.

"Which of the gods tames the spirits of water?" Riit-kvo

snapped. Otah pulled himself back to awareness and straightened his spine.

Riit-kvo pointed to a thick-set boy across the room.

"Oladac the Wanderer!" the boy said, taking a pose of gratitude to one's teacher.

"And why were the spirits who stood by and neither fought with the gods nor against them consigned to a lower hell than the servants of chaos?"

Again Riit-kvo pointed.

"Because they should have fought alongside the gods!" the boy shouted.

It was a wrong answer. Because they were cowards, Otah thought, and knew he was correct. Tahi's lacquered rod whirred and struck the boy hard on the shoulder. Riit-kvo smirked and returned to his story.

After the class, there was another brief work detail for which Tahi-kvo did not join them. Then the evening meal, and then the end of another day. Otah was grateful to crawl into his bunk and pull the thin blanket up to his neck. In the winter, many of the boys slept in their robes against the cold, and Otah was among that number. Despite all this, he preferred the winter. During the warmer times, he would still wake some mornings having forgotten where he was, expecting to see the walls of his father's home, hear the voices of his older brothers—Biitrah, Danat, and Kaiin. Perhaps see his mother's smile. The rush of memory was worse than any blow of Tahi-kvo's rod, and he bent his will toward erasing the memories he had of his family. He was not loved or wanted in his home, and he understood that thinking too much about this truth would kill him.

As he drifted toward sleep, Riit-kvo's harsh voice murmuring the lesson of the spirits who refused to fight spun through his mind. They were cowards, consigned to the deepest and coldest hell.

When the question came, his eyes flew open. He sat up.

The other boys were all in their cots. One, not far from him, was crying in his sleep. It was not an unusual sound. The words still burned in Otah's mind. The coward spirits, consigned to hell.

And what keeps them there? his quiet inner voice asked him. *Why do they remain in hell?*

He lay awake for hours, his mind racing.

The teachers' quarters opened on a common room. Shelves lined the walls, filled with books and scrolls. A fire pit glowed with coals prepared for them by the most honored of Milah-kvo's black-robed boys. The wide gap of a window—glazed double to hold out the cold of winter, the heat of the summer—looked out over the roadway leading south to the high road. Tahi sat now, warming his feet at the fire and staring out into the cold plain beyond. Milah opened the door behind him and strode in.

"I expected you earlier," Tahi said.

Milah briefly took a pose of apology.

"Annat Ryota was complaining about the kitchen flue smoking again," he said.

Tahi grunted.

"Sit. The fire's warm."

"Fires often are," Milah agreed, his tone dry and mocking. Tahi managed a thin smile as his companion took a seat.

"What did he make of your boys?" Tahi asked.

"Much the same as last year. They have seen through the veil and now lead their brothers toward knowledge," Milah said, but his hands were in a pose of gentle mockery. "They are petty tyrants to a man. Any andat strong enough to be worth holding would eat them before their hearts beat twice."

"Pity."

"Hardly a surprise. And yours?"

Tahi chewed for a moment at his lower lip and leaned forward. He could feel Milah's gaze on him.

"Otah Machi disgraced himself," Tahi said. "But he accepted the punishment well. The Dai-kvo thinks he may have promise."

Milah shifted. When Tahi looked over, the teacher had taken a pose of query. Tahi considered the implicit question, then nodded.

"There have been some other signs," Tahi said. "I think you should put a watch over him. I hate to lose him to you, in a way."

"You like him."

Tahi took a pose of acknowledgment that held the nuance of a confession of failure.

"I may be cruel, old friend," Tahi said, dropping into the familiar, "but you're heartless."

The fair-haired teacher laughed, and Tahi couldn't help but join him. They sat silent then for a while, each in his own thoughts. Milah rose, shrugged off his thick woolen top robe. Beneath it he still wore the formal silks from his audience yesterday with the Dai-kvo. Tahi poured them both bowls of rice wine.

"It was good to see him again," Milah said sometime later. There was a melancholy note in his voice. Tahi took a pose of agreement, then sipped his wine.

"He looked so *old*," Tahi said.

Otah's plan, such as it was, took little preparation, and yet nearly three weeks passed between the moment he understood the parable of the spirits who stood aside and the night when he took action. That night, he waited until the others were asleep before he pushed off the thin blankets, put on every robe and legging he had, gathered his few things, and left his cohort for the last time.

The stone hallways *were* unlit, but he knew his way well enough that he had no need for light. He made his way to the kitchen. The pantry was unlocked—no one would steal food for fear of being found out and beaten. Otah scooped double handfuls of hard rolls and dried fruit into his satchel. There was no need for water. Snow still covered the ground, and Tahi-kvo had shown them how to melt snow with the heat of their own bodies walking without the cold penetrating to their hearts.

Once he was provisioned, his path led him to the great hall—moonlight from the high windows showing ghost-dim the great aisle where he had held a pose of obeisance every morning for the last three years. The doors, of course, were barred, and while he was strong enough to open them, the sounds might have woken someone. He took a pair of wide, netted snowshoes from the closet beside the great doors and went up the stairs to the listening room. There, the narrow windows looked our on a world locked in winter. Otah's breath plumed already in the chill.

He threw the snowshoes and satchel out the window to the snow-cushioned ground below, then squeezed through and lowered himself from the outer stone still until he hung by his fingertips. The fall was not so far.

He dusted the snow from his leggings, tied the snowshoes to his feet by their thick leather thongs, took up the bulging satchel and started off, walking south toward the high road.

The moon, near the top of its nightly arc, had moved the width of two thick-gloved hands toward the western horizon before Otah knew he was not alone. The footsteps that had kept perfect time with his own fell out of their pattern—as international a provocation as clearing a throat. Otah froze, then turned.

"Good evening, Otah Machi," Milah-kvo said, his tone casual. "A good night for a walk, eh? Cold though."

Otah did not speak, and Milah-kvo strode forward, his hand on his own satchel, his footsteps nearly silent. His breath was thick and white as a goose feather.

"Yes," the teacher said. "Cold, and far from your bed."

Otah took a pose of acknowledgment appropriate for a student to a teacher. It had no nuance of apology, and Otah hoped that Milah-kvo would not see his trembling, or if he did would ascribe it to the cold.

"Leaving before your term is complete, boy. You disgrace yourself."

Otah switched to a pose of thanks appropriate to the end of a lesson, but Milah-kvo waved the formality aside and sat in the snow, considering him with an interest that Otah found unnerving.

"Why do it?" Milah-kvo asked. "There's still hope of redeeming yourself. You might still be found worthy. So why run away? Are you so much a coward?"

Otah found his voice.

"It would be cowardice that kept me, Milah-kvo."

"How so?" The teacher's voice held nothing of judgment or testing. It was like a friend asking a question because he truly did not know the answer.

"There are no locks on hell." Otah said. It was the first time he had tried to express this to someone else, and it proved harder than he had expected. "If there aren't locks, then what can hold anyone there besides fear that leaving might be worse?"

"And you think the school is a kind of hell."

It was not a question, so Otah did not answer.

"If you keep to this path, you'll be the lowest of the low," Milah said. "A disgraced child without friend or ally. And without the brand to protect you, your older brothers may well track you down and kill you."

"Yes."

"Do you have someplace to go?"

"The high road leads to Pathai and Nantani."

"Where you know no one."

Otah took a pose of agreement.

"This doesn't frighten you?" the teacher asked.

"It is the decision I've made." He could see the amusement in Milah-kvo's face at his answer.

"Fair enough, but I think there's an alternative you haven't considered."

The teacher reached into his satchel and pulled our a small cloth bundle. He hefted it for a moment, considering, and dropped it on the snow between them. It was a black robe.

Otah took a pose of intellectual inquiry. It was a failure of vocabulary, but Milah-kvo took his meaning.

"Andat are powerful, Otah. Like small gods. And they don't love being held to a single form. They fight it, and since the forms they have are a reflection of the poets who bind them . . . The world is full of willing victims—people who embrace the cruelty meted out against them. An andat formed from a mind like that would destroy the poet who bound it and escape. That you have chosen action is what the black robes mean."

"Then . . . the others . . . they all left the school too?"

Milah laughed. Even in the cold, it was a warm sound.

"No. No, you've all taken different paths. Ansha tried to wrestle Tahi-kvo's stick away from him. Ranit Kiru asked forbidden questions, took the punishment for them, and asked again until Tahi beat him asleep. He was too sore to wear any robe at all for weeks, but his bruises were black enough. But you've each *done* something. If you choose to take up the robe, that is. Leave it, and really, this is just a conversation. Interesting maybe, but trivial."

"And if I take it?"

"You will never be turned out of the school so long as you wear the black. You will help to teach the normal boys the lesson you've learned—to stand by your own strength."

Otah blinked, and something—some emotion he couldn't put a name to—bloomed in his breast. His flight from the school took on a new meaning. It was a badge of his strength, the proof of his courage.

"And the andat?"

"And the andat," Milah-kvo said. "You'll begin to learn of them in earnest. The Dai-kvo has never taken a student who wasn't first a black robe at the school."

Otah stooped, his fingers numb with cold, and picked up the robe. He met Milah-kvo's amused eyes and couldn't keep from grinning. Milah-kvo laughed, stood and put an arm around Otah's shoulder. It was the first kind act Otah could remember since he had come to the school.

"Come on, then. If we start now, we may get back to the school by breakfast."

Otah took a pose of enthusiastic agreement.

"And, while this once I think we can forgive it, don't make a habit of stealing from the kitchen. It upsets the cooks."

The letter came some weeks later, and Milah was the first to read it. Sitting in an upper room, his students abandoned for the moment, he read the careful script again and felt his face grow tight. When he had gone over it enough to know he could not have misunderstood, he tucked the folded paper into the sleeve of his robe and looked out the window. Winter was ending, and somehow the eternal renewal that was spring felt like an irony.

He heard Tahi enter, recognizing his old friend's footsteps.

"There was a courier," Tahi said. "Ansha said there was a courier from the Dai-kvo . . ."

Milah looked over his shoulder. His own feelings were echoed in Tahi's round face.

"From his attendant, actually."

"The Dai-kvo. Is he . . ."

"No," Milah said, fishing out the letter. "Not dead. Only dying."

Tahi took the proffered pages, but didn't look at them. "Of what?"

"Time."

Tahi read the written words silently, then leaned against the wall with a sharp sigh.

"It . . . it isn't so bad as it could be," Tahi said.

"No. Not yet. He will see the school again. Twice, perhaps."

"He shouldn't come," Tahi snapped. "The visits are a formality. We know well enough which boys are ready. We can send them. He doesn't have to—"

Milah turned, interrupting him with a subtle pose that was a request for clarification and a mourning both. Tahi laughed bitterly and looked down.

"You're right," he said. "Still. I'd like the world better if we could carry a little of his weight for him. Even if it was only a short way."

Milah started to take a pose, but hesitated, stopped, only nodded.

"Otah Machi?" Tahi asked.

"Maybe. We might have to call him for Otah. Not yet, though. The robes have hardly been on him. The others are still learning to accept him as an equal. Once he's used to the power, then we'll see. I won't call the Dai-kvo until we're certain."

"He'll come next winter whether there's a boy ready or not."

"Perhaps. Or perhaps he'll die tonight. Or we will. No god made the world certain."

Tahi raised his hands in a pose of resignation.